Gustave Flaubert

was born in Rouen in 1821, the son of a prominent physician. A solitary child, he was attracted to literature at an early age, and after his recovery from a nervous breakdown suffered while a law student, he turned his total energies to writing. Aside from journeys to the Near East, Greece, Italy, and North Africa, and a stormy liaison with the poetess Louise Colet, his life was dedicated to the practice of his art. The form of his work was marked by intense esthetic scrupulousness and passionate pursuit of *le mot juste;* its content alternately reflected scorn for French bourgeois society and a romantic taste for exotic historical subject matter. The success of *Madame Bovary* (1857) was ensured by government prosecution for "immorality"; *Salammbô* (1862) and *The Sentimental Education* (1869) received a cool public reception; not until the publication of *Three Tales* (1877) was his genius popularly acknowledged. Among fellow writers, however, his reputation was supreme. His circle of friends included Turgenev and the Goncourt brothers, while the young Guy de Maupassant underwent an arduous literary apprenticeship under his direction. Increasing personal isolation and financial insecurity troubled his last years. His final bitterness and disillusion were vividly evidenced in the savagely satiric *Bouvard and Pécuchet,* left unfinished at his death in 1880.

GUSTAVE FLAUBERT

THE SENTIMENTAL EDUCATION

Newly Translated by
Perdita Burlingame

With an Afterword by
F. W. Dupee

C

A SIGNET CLASSIC from
NEW AMERICAN LIBRARY
TIMES MIRROR
New York and Scarborough, Ontario

SIGNET CLASSIC TRADEMARK REG. U.S. PAT. OFF. AND FOREIGN COUNTRIES
REGISTERED TRADEMARK—MARCA REGISTRADA
HECHO EN WINNIPEG, CANADA

SIGNET, SIGNET CLASSICS, MENTOR, PLUME, MERIDIAN and NAL
Books are published *in the United States* by
The New American Library, Inc.,
1633 Broadway, New York, New York 10019,
in Canada by The New American Library of Canada Limited,
81 Mack Avenue, Scarborough, Ontario M1L 1M8,
in the United Kingdom by The New English Library Limited,
Barnard's Inn, Holborn, London, EC1N 2JR, England.

FIRST PRINTING, MARCH, 1972

2 3 4 5 6 7 8 9 10

PRINTED IN CANADA

THE
SENTIMENTAL
EDUCATION

PART ONE

Chapter One

It was just before six the morning of September 15, 1840, and the *Ville-de-Montereau* lay at the Quai Saint-Bernard ready to cast off and spouting great clouds of steam.

People were arriving in breathless haste; casks, cables, laundry baskets blocked the way; the sailors brushed questions aside; passengers caromed into each other; the stack of luggage between the two paddle-boxes rose ever higher; and the uproar was dominated by the hiss of steam escaping through the iron plates, and wrapping everything in a white cloud, while the forward bell jangled incessantly.

At last the boat pulled out and the banks, covered with shops, work-yards, and factories, slid past like two broad ribbons unfurling.

A long-haired young man of eighteen stood motionless near the rudder, a sketchbook beneath his arm. He gazed through the fog at the belfreys and buildings he could not identify; then with a final glance he took in the Île Saint-Louis, the Cité, and Nôtre-Dame, and soon, as Paris disappeared, he heaved a heavy sigh.

M. Frédéric Moreau, recently admitted to the University, was on his way back to Nogent-sur-Seine, to languish for two months before leaving to study law.

His mother had sent him to Le Havre, with the irreducible minimum for expenses, to visit his uncle who she hoped might name Frédéric his heir; he had left there only the night before and was making up for not being able to stay on in Paris by taking the longest route back to his province.

The tumult grew calmer; everyone had settled down. Some stood and warmed themselves around the engine, whose stack spurted out its plume of black smoke with a slow and rhythmical rattle. Drops of dew ran down the pipe, a slight vibration made the deck tremble, and the paddle wheels turned rapidly, threshing the water.

The river ran between sandy banks. They encountered masses of logs set rocking by their wash, then a man sitting fishing in a rowboat. The drifting mists melted away, the sun appeared, and the hill which paralleled the Seine on the right slowly dropped lower, and another, nearer one rose on the opposite bank.

This one was crowned with trees growing among small houses with Italian-style roofs. They had sloping gardens divided by newly built walls, iron gates, lawns, hothouses, and pots of geraniums spaced along their terraces which had balustrades to lean on. Seeing these engaging and supremely peaceful homes, several of the passengers longed to own one, to live there till the end of their days, with a good billiard table, or a launch, or a wife, or some other dream. The unaccustomed pleasure of a trip on the water induced an expansive mood. Already some wags were up to their tricks. There was singing and gaiety, drinks were being poured.

Frédéric thought about his room at home, about the plot for a play, about subjects for paintings, about loves to come. He reflected that the happiness his nobility of soul warranted was a little slow in coming. He recited melancholy verse to himself. He walked briskly along the deck, right up to the bow, near the bell—and there, ringed by passengers and sailors, he noticed a gentleman exchanging flirtatious remarks with a peasant girl as he toyed with the gold cross she wore on her bosom. He was a fellow of forty or so with frizzy hair. A black velvet coat covered his robust frame, two emeralds glistened in his fine cambric shirt, and his wide white trousers fell over curious red boots of Russian leather patterned in blue.

He was not the least disturbed by Frédéric's presence. Several times he turned toward him with a comradely wink; then he distributed cigars all around. But, probably bored with his company, he moved on. Frédéric followed him.

At first their conversation touched on different kinds of

tobacco; then, quite naturally, it turned to women. The gentleman in the red boots gave advice to the young man, expounded theories, told stories, cited himself as an example, delivering all this in a paternal tone with an amusing kind of artless corruption.

He was a republican, a traveled man with inside knowledge of theaters, restaurants, newspapers, and all the famous show people, to whom he referred familiarly by their first names; soon Frédéric was confiding his own plans to his companion, who encouraged them.

But the man broke off what he was saying to gaze at the funnel; then he muttered a long calculation to work out "how much power each stroke of the piston, at so many times per minute, must represent," and so on. And, having found the answer, he gave an enthusiastic discourse on the scenery. He said he was happy to have gotten away from his business.

Frédéric felt a certain admiration for him, and could not resist asking his name. In a single breath the stranger answered: "Jacques Arnoux, owner of 'L'Art Industriel,' Boulevard Montmartre."

A servant with gold braid on his cap came up and said to him: "Would Monsieur kindly come below? Mademoiselle is crying." He disappeared.

"L'Art Industriel" was a hybrid establishment, combining an art journal and a gallery. Frédéric had seen the title several times in the window of the Nogent bookshop, on enormous posters featuring Jacques Arnoux's name.

The sun beat straight down, glittering on the iron bands round the masts, on the hammock fixtures, and the water's surface, which the prow cut into two furrows that rolled out to the meadows' edge. Each bend of the river disclosed the same curtain of pale poplars. The countryside was completely deserted. Small, white, motionless clouds speckled the sky, and a vague, pervasive tedium seemed to slow the movement of the boat and render the passengers still more insignificant.

Apart from a few bourgeois traveling first class, the passengers were laborers, or shopkeepers with their wives and children. In those days it was the custom to dress shabbily for a journey, so nearly all of them wore old skullcaps or faded hats, cheap black suits rubbed threadbare against desks, or frock-coats with their buttons splitting open from heavy use at the store; here a shawl-collared waistcoat framed a coffee-stained calico shirt, there a gilt pin caught back a ragged cravat; list slippers were held on by darned straps; two or three rascals carrying bamboo canes with leather cords darted furtive glances around them, and family men gaped and asked questions. Some chatted together, standing or squatting on their luggage, others slept in corners, several ate. The deck was littered with nutshells, cigar butts, pear peelings, and scraps of cold meat which had been brought along in paper wrappings; three cabinet-makers in smocks stood in front of the bar; a shabby harp player rested, leaning his elbow on his instrument; at intervals one could hear the noise of the coal in the furnace, a burst of voices, a laugh—and on the bridge the captain strode incessantly from one paddle-box to the other. To make his way back to his seat, Frédéric pushed open the gate into first class, and disturbed two hunters with their dogs.

It was like a vision:

She sat in the middle of a bench, quite alone—at least, dazzled by the light from her eyes, he perceived no one else. She raised her head as he passed and, involuntarily, he bowed; when he had gone a little farther along the same side of the boat, he stopped and looked back.

She wore a large straw hat, whose pink ribbons fluttered behind her in the breeze. Bands of smooth black hair curved around the ends of her dark eyebrows and then came down very low, as if to press lovingly around the oval of her face. Her light dotted muslin dress spread its many folds around her. She was doing some embroidery, and her straight nose, her chin, her entire figure were silhouetted against the blue sky.

As she kept the same position, he moved several times to right and to left, so as to disguise his purpose; then he took a place by her parasol, which was leaning against the bench, and pretended to watch a launch on the river.

He had never seen anything like the splendor of her dark skin, the seductiveness of her figure, or the delicacy of her translucent fingers. He gazed in wonder at her workbox, as if it were something extraordinary. What was her name, her home, her life, her past? He longed to know how her room was furnished, all the dresses she had worn, the people she saw; even the lust for physical possession vanished before a deeper yearning, a boundless, painful curiosity.

A Negro woman with a silk kerchief around her head appeared, holding the hand of a little girl. The child had just awakened and her eyes were brimming with tears. The lady took her onto her knees and chided her: "Mademoiselle was not behaving like a good girl, even though she would soon be seven; her mother would not love her any more; they indulged her moods far too much." And Frédéric was overjoyed to hear all this, as if he had made a discovery, an acquisition.

He thought she must come from Andalusia, or perhaps she was a Creole; she might have brought the Negro woman over from the islands with her.

A long shawl with violet stripes was draped over the brass rail behind her. On damp evenings in mid-ocean she must often have wrapped herself in it, used it to cover her feet, slept in it! But its heavy fringes were weighing it down; it was gradually slipping and was about to fall into the water. Frédéric leaped forward and caught it.

"Thank you, Monsieur," she said.

Their eyes met.

"Well, my dear, are you ready?" cried Arnoux, appearing in the entrance to the stairway.

Mademoiselle Marthe ran to him and, clinging to his neck, she tugged at his moustache. The notes of a harp rang out; she wanted to see the musician and soon the harpist was following the Negro woman into first class. Arnoux recognized him as a former model and spoke to him familiarly, to the surprise of his audience. Eventually the musician threw back his long hair, stretched his arms forward, and started to play.

It was an Oriental romance dealing with daggers, flowers, and stars. The ragged man sang it in a harsh voice; the throbbing of the engine broke the rhythm of the tune; he plucked harder; the strings quivered; and their metallic sound seemed to breathe sobs, and the lament of a proud and defeated love. On both banks of the river the woods overhung the water; a cool breeze blew; Madame Arnoux gazed abstractedly into the distance. When the music stopped her eyelids fluttered several times, as if she were emerging from a dream.

The harpist approached them humbly. While Arnoux was searching for some change, Frédéric held out his closed hand toward the cap and, opening it, discreetly dropped in a golden louis. It was not vanity that impelled him to make this offering in front of her but a feeling of benediction he connected with her, an almost religious impulse.

Arnoux, leading the way below, had cordially urged him to come with them, but Frédéric said that he had just had

lunch; actually, he was dying of hunger and there was not
a centime left in his purse.

Afterward it occurred to him that he had a perfect
right to go down to the cabin like anyone else.

Some of the more prosperous passengers were eating at
round tables while a waiter moved about serving them.
Monsieur and Madame Arnoux were at the far end of the
room, on the right. He sat down on a long, velvet-covered
banquette, first picking up a newspaper that lay on it.

At Montereau they were going to take the stagecoach to
Châlons. They would travel in Switzerland for a month.
Madame Arnoux reproached her husband for spoiling his
daughter. He whispered into her ear, probably some compliment, for she smiled. Then he stood up to draw the
curtain across the window behind her neck.

The low ceiling, painted an unrelieved white, reflected
the light harshly. Frédéric, from his seat, could see the
shadow of her eyelashes. She moistened her lips in her
glass, crumbled a little bread in her fingers; the lapis
lazuli medallion, which hung from her wrist on a gold
chain, rang against her plate from time to time. The
others in the room, however, seemed not to notice her.

Occasionally, through the portholes, the side of a
launch could be seen as it drew alongside to pick up or
deposit passengers. The people sitting at the tables leaned
through the openings and named off the villages along the
river.

Arnoux complained about the food; he made a great
fuss over the check and had it reduced. Then he took the
young man forward to drink grog. But Frédéric soon
came back beneath the awning, where Madame Arnoux
had returned. She was reading a thin book with a gray
cover. Occasionally, the corners of her mouth curled up
and her face lit with pleasure. He was jealous of the
writer whose work seemed to absorb her. The more he
looked at her the more conscious he became of the abyss
between them. He reflected that he must part from her
soon, irrevocably, without having extracted a single word,
leaving behind him not even a memory! A plain stretched
off to the right, and on the left grassy slopes rose gently to
a hill covered with vineyards and walnut trees; there was
a windmill among the greenery and, farther off, little
roads zigzagged across the white rock that reached to the
edge of the sky. What bliss to climb there, side by side,
his arm around her waist, while her dress swept the
yellow leaves, and he listened to her voice and basked in

the sunshine of her glance! The boat could stop, they had only to get off, and yet to accomplish this simple thing was no easier than shifting the sun in its course!

A little farther on, the pointed roof and square turrets of a château came into view. In front of it lay a flower garden, and there were avenues tunneling like black vaults beneath the tall lime trees. He pictured her walking among the groves. At that moment a girl and a young man appeared on the terrace between the tubs of orange trees. Then the whole scene vanished.

The little girl was playing near him. Frédéric tried to give her a kiss. She hid behind her nurse and her mother scolded her for not being nice to the gentleman who had rescued the shawl. Was this an indirect overture?

"Is she finally going to speak to me?" he wondered.

Time was running short. How could he manage an invitation to visit the Arnoux's? He could think of nothing better than to point out the autumn colors to the husband, adding:

"Soon it will be winter, the season of dances and dinner parties!" But Arnoux was completely preoccupied with his luggage. The Surville waterfront came into view, the two bridges drew closer, they passed a lumberyard, then a row of small houses; there were cauldrons of tar and chips of wood underneath them, and small boys were running along the sand turning cartwheels. Frédéric spotted a man in a waistcoat and shirtsleeves and shouted "Hurry up!" to him.

They arrived. With some difficulty he found Arnoux among the crowd of passengers, and the latter, shaking his hand, replied:

"Till we meet again, sir!"

When he reached the pier Frédéric turned around. She was standing near the stern. He gave her a look into which he tried to put his whole soul; she remained motionless, as if he had done nothing. Then, ignoring his servant's greetings, he snapped:

"Why didn't you bring the carriage right to the pier?"

The man apologized.

"What a bungler! Give me some money!"

And he went to eat at an inn.

A quarter of an hour later he felt an impulse to stroll, as if by chance, through the courtyard where the stage-coaches loaded. Perhaps he would see her again?

"What's the use?" he said to himself.

And he drove off in the phaeton. His mother did not

own both the horses; she had borrowed one from Monsieur Chambrion, the tax collector, to make up the pair. Isidore, who had left home the previous day, had rested at Bray till the evening and had slept at Montereau, so the animals were fresh and trotted out briskly.

The stubble fields seemed to go on forever. The road was bordered with two lines of trees, and they passed one pile of gravel after another. Little by little, Villeneuve-Saint-Georges, Ablon, Châtillon, Corbeil, and all the rest, his whole journey, came back to him so clearly that he now remembered new details, more intimate touches; her foot, in a thin brown silk boot, showed beneath the bottom flounce of her dress; over her head the canvas awning spread a broad canopy, and the little red tassels of its border trembled in the perpetual breeze.

She was like a woman in a romantic novel. There was nothing he would have added, nothing to delete. Suddenly the universe had grown larger. She was the glowing point upon which everything converged and, lulled by the rocking of the carriage, gazing into the clouds through half-shut eyelids, he surrendered himself to an infinite, dreamy joy.

At Bray he did not wait for the horses to be fed but set off down the road alone. Arnoux had called her "Marie." He shouted "Marie!" as loudly as he could. His voice was lost in the air.

A broad streak of purple flamed in the sky to the west. Great ricks of wheat standing in the midst of the stubble fields cast gigantic shadows. A dog started to bark in a distant farmyard. He shivered, touched by an inexplicable disquiet.

When Isidore overtook him, Frédéric climbed onto the box so that he could drive. His moment of discouragement had passed. Somehow, he resolved, he would win his way into the Arnoux's circle and become a friend. It should be an interesting household, and he did like Arnoux, after all; then, who knows? At the thought his face flushed; there was a throbbing in his temples, he cracked his whip, shook the reins, and drove at such a pace that the old coachman kept repeating:

"Easy! Easy! You'll ruin their wind if you go on like that!"

Gradually Frédéric grew calmer and listened to his servant's chatter.

They were all waiting for Monsieur with great impatience. Mademoiselle Louise had cried to be taken along in the carriage.

"Who's that, Mademoiselle Louise?"

"You know—Monsieur Roque's little girl."

"Oh, I'd forgotten," replied Frédéric carelessly.

By now the horses were exhausted. Both of them were limping and the Saint-Laurent church clock was striking nine by the time he reached the Place d'Armes in front of his mother's house. This large mansion, with its garden which ran down to the fields, enhanced Madame Moreau's prestige; she was the most respected person in the neighborhood.

She came from a long line of gentlemen but her family was now extinct. Her husband, a plebeian whom her parents had forced her to marry, had died of a sword wound during her pregnancy, leaving her an inheritance laden with debt. She received visitors three times a week, and from time to time gave a grand dinner party. But the number of candles was calculated in advance, and she waited impatiently for the rent from her farms. This poverty, concealed like a vice, gave her a certain gravity. But her behavior was without bitterness, without any display of prudery. Her least offerings had the air of great benefactions. People asked her advice on the selection of servants, the education of girls, the art of jam-making; and the bishop stayed with her on his episcopal tours.

Madame Moreau had high ambitions for her son. A sort of anticipatory prudence made her dislike listening to criticism of the government. To begin with, he would need patrons; then, thanks to his own talent, he would become a councillor of state, an ambassador, a minister. His triumphs at the school at Sens had justified this pride; he had carried off the top prize.

As Frédéric came into the room everyone got up and there was a great commotion and embracing; the chairs were rearranged to form a large semicircle round the fire. Monsieur Gamblin immediately asked him his opinion of Madame Lafarge. The mention of this celebrated poisoning case, the most controversial of the day, predictably set off a violent discussion. Madame Moreau put a stop to it, to the regret of Monsieur Gamblin who thought it useful for the young man in his role of future lawyer; and he left the drawing room in a huff.

Nothing should come as a surprise from a friend of Old Roque's! By way of Old Roque they passed to Monsieur Dambreuse, who had just bought the Fortelle estate. But the tax collector had drawn Frédéric to one side to ask what he thought of Monsieur Guizot's* latest book. Everyone wanted to hear about Frédéric's prospects, and Madame Benoit neatly broached the subject by inquiring after his uncle. How was his worthy relative? They never heard from him nowadays. Hadn't he a distant cousin in America?

The cook announced that Monsieur's soup was ready and they all tactfully took their leave. As soon as they were alone in the room his mother, in a low voice, said:

"Well?"

The old man had welcomed him very cordially but had not committed himself.

Madame Moreau sighed.

"Where is she now?" he wondered. The coach was rumbling along and, probably wrapped in the shawl, she must be leaning her beautiful, sleeping head against the lining of the carriage.

They were on their way to bed when the boy from the Swan and Cross arrived with a note.

"What is it?"

"It's Deslauriers. He wants to see me."

"Oh! Your friend!" remarked Madame Moreau with a sneer. "Really, what a time to choose!"

Frédéric hesitated, but friendship proved the stronger. He picked up his hat.

"At any rate, don't be too long."

*Guizot was Louis-Philippe's chief minister and foreign secretary from 1840 on. This mention of his name is the first indication of the political theme which forms so large a part of the book.

Chapter Two

Charles Deslauriers' father, a former infantry captain who resigned his commission in 1818, had returned to Nogent to marry; with his wife's dowry he bought a position as an official of the law courts, which brought him barely enough to live on. Embittered by endless injustices, suffering from his old wounds, and always regretting the passing of the Empire, he vented his suffocating anger on those around him. Few children were beaten more often than his son. The boy did not submit, despite the blows. When his mother tried to come between them, she was abused as well. Finally the captain shut the boy in his office, where he kept him bent over the desk copying documents all day long, with the result that his right shoulder was noticeably stronger than his left.

In 1833, at the request of the president of the court, the captain sold his practice. His wife died of cancer. He went to live in Dijon; later he moved to Troyes and went into the business of providing substitutes for those anxious to evade the draft. He managed to get Charles a half-scholarship and sent him to the college at Sens, where Frédéric recognized his former neighbor. But one was twelve years old, the other fifteen, and, furthermore, they were separated by a thousand differences of background and character.

Frédéric had in his bureau all sorts of provisions, and elegant things; a toilet case, for instance. He liked to sleep late in the morning, to watch the swallows, to read plays, and, missing the comforts of home, he found college life harsh.

It seemed good to the captain's son. He worked so well that, at the end of the second year, he moved up a class.

17

Still, either because of his poverty or his quarrelsome
disposition, a muted hostility surrounded him. But one day
when a servant called him a beggar's child right in the
Middle School courtyard, he sprang at his throat and
would have killed him but for the intervention of three
junior masters. Frédéric, overcome by admiration, threw
his arms about him. From that day on their intimacy was
complete. The friendship of a senior must have flattered
the vanity of the younger boy, and Deslauriers happily
accepted the devotion he offered.

His father left him at the college during the holidays.
Opening a translation of Plato by chance, his enthusiasm
was aroused. He took up the study of metaphysics and
made rapid progress, for he came to it with youthful
energies and in the pride of a newly liberated intelligence.
Jouffroy, Cousin, Laromiguière, Malebranche, the Scots,
he read everything in the library. He had to steal the key
in order to get at more books.

Frédéric's pastimes were less serious. He drew a copy of
the genealogy of Christ carved on a doorpost in the Rue
des Trois-Rois, then the portal of the cathedral. After the
plays of the Middle Ages he started on the memoirs:
Froissart, Commines, Pierre de l'Estoile, Brantôme.

He was so powerfully obsessed with the images these
books instilled in his mind that he felt compelled to re-
produce them. His ambition was to become the French
Walter Scott. Deslauriers dreamed of a vast philosophical
system which would have the most far-reaching applica-
tions.

They talked about all this during recreation hours in the
courtyard, opposite the moral inscription painted under
the clock; they whispered about it in the chapel, under
Saint-Louis' nose; they dreamed of it in the dormitory,
which had a view of a cemetery. On the days when they
went out for walks, they fell behind the others and talked
interminably.

They talked of what they would do later, when they had
left school. First they would travel widely, with money
Frédéric would draw against the legacy due him when
he came of age. Then they would return to Paris, they
would work together, they would never separate—and, as
a distraction from their labors, they would have love-
affairs with princesses in satin boudoirs or dazzling orgies
with famous courtesans. Doubts followed hard on these
flights of hope. After verbose fits of gaiety they would
fall into deep silences.

On summer evenings, when they had walked for a long time along the stony roads beside the vineyards or on the main road through the countryside, when the wheat rippled in the sunlight and the air was scented with angelica, they would feel a sort of suffocation and would stretch out on their backs, elated and stupefied. The others played prisoner's base in their shirtsleeves or flew kites. The under-master called them back. They returned past gardens crossed by little brooks, then along boulevards shaded by ancient walls; their steps rang in the deserted streets; the gate opened, they climbed the steps again; and they were as melancholy as if they came from a night of wild debauchery. The dean claimed that they overexcited one another. But, if Frédéric did good work in class it was because of his friend's exhortations. He took him home to meet his mother during the 1837 holidays.

Madame Moreau disliked the young man. He ate enormously, refused to go to church on Sunday, and advanced republican views; and, moreover, she believed he had taken her son to houses of ill repute. Their friendship was kept under close watch. This only strengthened their affection, and when Deslauriers left school the following year to study law in Paris, their parting was a painful one.

Frédéric fully intended to join him there. They had not seen each other for two years now and, when they had embraced, they walked out onto the bridges so that they could talk more freely.

The captain, who was now the proprietor of a billiard parlor at Villenauxe, had flown into a rage when his son asked for an accounting of his trusteeship, and had gone so far as to cut off his income completely. As he hoped to compete later for a professorial chair at the law school and had no money, Deslauriers had taken a job as chief clerk to a lawyer at Troyes. He would save four thousand francs by living very economically and, even if he never received a penny from his mother's estate, he would still have enough to enable him to work on his own for three years while waiting for a position. They would, therefore, have to abandon their old plan of living together in the capital, at least for the present.

Frédéric bowed his head. It was the first of his dreams to crumble.

"Cheer up," said the captain's son, "life is long; we are young. I'll join you later. Don't worry about it!"

He took him by the hands and shook him gently; then, to distract him, asked about his journey.

Frédéric had little to tell. But his sorrow vanished at the memory of Madame Arnoux. A sense of delicacy prevented him from speaking of her. Instead he expanded on the subject of Arnoux himself, describing his conversation, his peculiarities, his connections, and Deslauriers strongly urged him to cultivate this acquaintance.

Frédéric had written nothing lately; his literary tastes had changed and he now prized passion above everything else; Werther, René, Franck, Lara, Lélia, and other, more mediocre figures inspired him with almost equal enthusiasm. Sometimes it seemed to him that music alone could express his interior turmoil, and then he dreamed of symphonies; or his imagination was gripped by the surface aspect of things, and then he longed to be a painter. He had, however, composed some verse; Deslauriers found one poem very beautiful, but did not ask to hear another.

As for him, he was no longer interested in metaphysics. Social economics and the French Revolution absorbed him. He was a tall, awkward fellow of twenty-two by now, thin, with a large mouth and a resolute air. This evening he was wearing a shoddy overcoat made of cheap cloth and his shoes were white with dust, for he had walked from Villenauxe to see Frédéric.

Isidore came up to them. Madame would like Monsieur to come home and she had sent him his cloak in case he was cold.

"Then stay!" said Deslauriers.

And they continued to stroll back and forth over the two bridges that led to the narrow island between the canal and the river.

On the Nogent side they faced a block of houses leaning slightly to one side; to the right, behind the sawmills with their closed sluice-gates, rose the church; and to the left the hedges along the bank marked the end of the barely visible gardens. On the opposite bank, toward Paris, however, the main road ran downhill in a straight line and the farther fields were lost in the evening mists. The night was silent and silvery clear. The scent of damp leaves rose toward them; the water falling from the weir a hundred yards away had the deep and gentle murmur of waves in the dusk.

Deslauriers stopped and said:

"It's amusing how soundly these good people sleep! Just wait! A new 'eighty-nine is coming! People are tired of constitutions, of charters, of subtleties, of lies! Oh, if I had a newspaper or a platform, how I'd shake it all up! But you've got to have money to do anything at all! What a curse it is to be a tavern-keeper's son and to waste years of youth earning enough to keep oneself alive!"

He bowed his head and bit his lips, shivering in his thin clothes.

Frédéric threw half his cloak around his friend's shoulders. They both wrapped themselves in it and, with their arms around one another's waists, walked along beneath it, side by side.

"How do you expect me to live in Paris without you?" asked Frédéric. His friend's bitterness had revived his own sadness. "I should have accomplished something if I had a woman who loved me . . . Why do you laugh? Love is the food and the very air that genius breathes. Sublime works are born of extraordinary emotions. And I will never search for the woman I need. In any case, if I ever found her she would reject me. I am one of the disinherited of this world, and I shall die with a treasure locked within me, never knowing whether it is paste or diamond."

A shadow fell on the paving stones, as someone said:

"Your servant, gentlemen!"

The speaker was a small man, wearing a loose brown overcoat and a cap, a pointed nose poking under its brim.

"Monsieur Roque?" said Frédéric.

"Yes," replied the voice.

The newcomer explained his presence by telling them that he was on his way back from inspecting the traps in his garden beside the water.

"And so you're back with us? Excellent! My little daughter told me you were. I hope your health is still good? You won't be leaving us again?"

And he went off, feeling, no doubt, rebuffed by Frédéric's welcome.

He was not, in fact, one of Madame Moreau's circle; Old Roque lived in concubinage with his maid and had little standing, even though he was croupier* of elections and Monsieur Dambreuse's steward.

"The banker who lives on the Rue d'Anjour?" asked Deslauriers. "Do you know what you ought to do, old boy?"

Isidore interrupted them again. He had definite orders to bring Frédéric back. Madame was becoming uneasy at his absence.

---

*A slang term indicating the degree of corruption in the electoral colleges under Louis-Philippe. Roque was electoral registrar.

"All right, all right. He's coming," said Deslauriers. "He won't spend the night out."

And, the servant having gone: "You should ask that old man to introduce you to the Dambreuses; a connection with a rich household is the most useful thing in the world! You have a tailcoat and white gloves—use them! You should get into that world! You can take me in later. Think of it, a millionaire! Do your best to please him, and his wife too. Become her lover!"

Frédéric protested.

"But it seems to me the advice I'm giving you is classic! Remember Rastignac, in *The Human Comedy!* I'm sure you'll succeed!"

Frédéric had so much confidence in Deslauriers that he felt shaken, and, either forgetting Madame Arnoux or including her in the prediction made about the other woman, he could not help smiling.

"One last word of advice: get through your examinations! A degree is always useful. And drop your Catholic and satanic poets; philosophically they're no more advanced than men of the twelfth century! Your despair is stupid. Some very great men have had more difficult starts in life, beginning with Mirabeau. Anyhow, we won't be separated for that long; I'll make my piker of a father cough up. It's time I went back. Good-bye. Have you got a hundred sous so that I can pay for my dinner?"

Frédéric gave him ten francs, the remnant of the sum he had taken from Isidore that morning.

Meanwhile, forty yards from the bridges, on the left bank, a light burned in the attic of a small house.

Deslauriers noticed it and, taking off his hat, said emphatically:

"Venus, Queen of the Heavens, your servant! But Poverty is the mother of Virtue. God knows we've been slandered enough on that score!"

This allusion to a mutual adventure filled them with joy. They shouted with laughter as they walked through the streets.

Then, having settled his bill at the inn, Deslauriers walked back with Frédéric to the crossroads in front of the hospital and, after a long embrace, the two friends separated.

Chapter Three

One morning two months later, Frédéric, alighting from the coach at the Rue Coq-Héron, thought immediately of paying his momentous call.

He had been lucky. Old Roque had brought him a packet of papers, asking him to deliver them personally to Monsieur Dambreuse, and had added an unsealed note introducing his young neighbor.

This seemed to surprise Madame Moreau, and Frédéric hid the pleasure that it gave him.

Monsieur Dambreuse's real name was the Count d'Ambreuse, but since 1825, gradually abandoning his rank and his party, he had turned to commerce; and with a contact in every office and a finger in every pie, always on the lookout for a good opportunity, canny as a Greek and hard-working as an Auvergnat, he had amassed what was said to be a considerable fortune. Moreover he was an officer of the Legion of Honor, a member of the departmental council of the Aube, a parliamentary deputy, and on his way to a peerage; on top of all of this he was an obliging man, who wearied the government with his endless requests for subsidies, for medals, for licenses to sell tobacco; and, in his feuds with those in power, he leaned to left of center. His wife, the pretty Madame Dambreuse, who figured constantly in the fashion magazines, ran charitable committees and appeased the rancor of the nobility by cajoling duchesses and leading them to believe that Monsieur Dambreuse might yet repent and be of service.

Frédéric made his way to their house in a state of some agitation.

"I should have worn my dress coat. They will probably

23

invite me to the ball next week. What will they say to me?" ran through his head.

He regained his self-possession by reflecting that Monsieur Dambreuse was nothing but a bourgeois, and he jumped briskly out of his cabriolet onto the sidewalk of the rue d'Anjou.

When he had pushed open one of the two carriage gates he crossed the courtyard, mounted the steps, and entered a hall paved with colored marble.

A double staircase, with a red carpet and brass stair-rods, ran up the high walls of glistening stucco. At the foot of the stairs stood a banana tree, whose broad leaves touched the velvet-covered banisters. Porcelain globes hung by chains from two bronze chandeliers, the yawning vents of the stoves emitted hot air, and nothing could be heard but the *ticktock* of a large clock, which stood beneath a panoply at the far end of the hall.

A bell rang; a servant appeared and showed Frédéric into a small room that held two strongboxes and some racks filled with box-files. Monsieur Dambreuse was in the center of the room writing at a roll-top desk.

He glanced through Roque's letter, cut the cloth surrounding the papers with his penknife, and examined them.

From a distance, because of his slim build, he might still pass for a young man. But his sparse gray hairs, his wasted limbs and, above all, the extraordinary pallor of his face, indicated a worn-out constitution. A pitiless energy shone in his glaucous eyes, which seemed colder than if they had been made of glass. His cheekbones were prominent and his knuckles were bony.

At last he rose to his feet and asked the young man some questions about mutual acquaintances, Nogent, and his studies; then he bowed and dismissed him. Frédéric left by a different corridor and found himself at the lower end of the courtyard, near the coachhouses.

A blue brougham, drawn by a black horse, was waiting in front of the steps. The door opened, a lady got in, and the carriage rumbled off over the sand.

Frédéric crossed the courtyard and reached the carriage entrance at the same time she did. There was not enough room to pass and he was forced to wait. Leaning out of the carriage window, the young woman spoke to the concierge in a low voice. He saw no more than her back, covered with a violet mantle. Meanwhile he peered inside the carriage, which was lined in blue rep with silk trimmings and fringes. The woman's clothes filled it, and from this small, quilted box came a scent of iris and a vague fragrance of feminine elegance. The coachman loosened the reins, the horse brushed abruptly around the corner pillar, and the carriage disappeared.

Frédéric returned on foot, by way of the boulevards. He regretted not having a chance to see Madame Dambreuse more clearly.

A little beyond the Rue Montmartre a tangle of carriages made him turn his head and opposite him, on the other side of the street, he read:

JACQUES ARNOUX

inscribed on a marble plaque.

Why had he not thought of her earlier? It was Deslauriers' fault. He crossed to the shop but did not go in; he waited for Her to appear.

Through the tall plate-glass windows could be seen an artfully arranged display of statuettes, drawings, prints, catalogues, and copies of "L'Art Industriel"; the subscription rates were set out on the door, which was decorated in the center with the editor's initials. Against the walls could be seen large pictures shining with varnish; at the end of the room stood two chests, laden with porcelain, bronzes, and intriguing curios; they were separated by a small staircase which ended at a doorway covered with a plush curtain; and an old Dresden chandelier, a green carpet on the floor, and a marquetry table made the place look like a drawing room rather than a shop.

Frédéric pretended to examine the drawings. After endless hesitation, he went in.

An assistant raised the curtain and answered that Monsieur would not be "at the shop" before five o'clock. But, if he could take a message . . .

"No, I will come back," replied Frédéric softly.

The following days were spent searching for lodgings, and he decided on a second-floor room in a furnished hotel on the Rue Saint-Hyacinthe.

He went to the first session of his law course carrying a brand-new blotter under his arm. Three hundred bareheaded young people filled an amphitheater where an old man in red robes held forth in a monotonous voice while pens scraped across the paper. The hall had the same dusty smell as his old classrooms, the same kind of chairs, the same boredom. He went back for two weeks, but he dropped the civil code before they reached Article Three, and he abandoned the Institutes of Justinian at the *Summa divisio personarum*.

The pleasures he had promised himself did not materialize and, when he had exhausted the resources of a library, surveyed the collections at the Louvre, and been to the theater several times in a row, he fell into a bottomless lethargy.

A thousand new things added to his melancholy. He had to count his laundry and put up with his concierge, a bumpkin who looked like a male nurse and came up to make his bed in the mornings smelling of alcohol and muttering to himself. His room, decorated with an alabaster clock, displeased him. The partitions were thin; he heard students making punch, laughing, singing.

Tired of this solitude, he looked up one of his old schoolmates, Baptiste Martinon, and found him in a bourgeois boardinghouse on the Rue Saint-Jacques, boning up on his rules of procedure in front of a coal fire.

Opposite him a woman in a calico dress was mending socks.

Martinon was what is described as a really good-looking man: big, plump, with regular features and goggling bluish eyes; his father, a large farmer, intended him to become a magistrate—and anxious to look grave, even now, he wore his beard trimmed in a fringe.

As Frédéric's sorrows had no reasonable basis, and he could not complain of any particular misfortune, Martinon found his lamentations about life incomprehensible. He himself went to the law school every morning, strolled in the Luxembourg gardens afterwards, drank a small cup of coffee at a café in the evenings, and was perfectly happy with fifteen hundred francs a year and the love of his working-class girl.

"What a notion of happiness!" exclaimed Frédéric to himself.

He had made another acquaintance at the law school, a Monsieur de Cisy, the scion of a great family, whose gentle manners made him seem girlish.

Monsieur de Cisy was interested in design, and loved the Gothic style. Several times they went to admire the Sainte-Chapelle and Nôtre-Dame together. But the young patrician's distinction concealed a feeble intellect. Everything surprised him; he laughed a great deal at the slightest joke, and exhibited a simplicity so complete that

Frédéric at first took him for a wag and ended up considering him a fool.

There was no one, therefore, in whom he could confide; and he was still waiting for an invitation from the Dambreuses.

On New Year's Day he sent them visiting cards, but none came in return.

He had gone back to "L'Art Industriel."

On his third visit he finally saw Arnoux, who was arguing in the midst of a group of five or six people and scarcely acknowledged his greeting. This hurt Frédéric's feelings but did not stop him from looking for a way to reach Her.

His first idea was to go often to the shop and haggle for some of the pictures. Then he thought of sending some controversial articles to the paper, which would lead to a relationship. Perhaps it would be better to go straight to his goal and declare his love? Thereupon he composed a twelve-page letter, full of lyrical passages and apostrophes; but he tore it up and did nothing, attempted nothing—paralyzed by the fear of failure.

On the first floor above Arnoux's shop there were three windows which were lighted every evening. Behind them moved shadows, one especially; it was hers—and he came a long way to look at those windows and gaze at that shadow.

A Negro woman whom he passed one day in the Tuileries, holding a little girl by the hand, reminded him of Madame Arnoux's servant. She must come there like everyone else; every time he crossed the Tuileries his heart beat faster in the hope of meeting her. On sunny days he continued his walk to the end of the Champs-Élysées.

Women sitting nonchalantly in barouches, their veils fluttering in the wind, paraded past him at the steady pace set by their horses, with an imperceptible swaying motion that made the varnished leather creak. The number of carriages increased and, slowing down after the Rond-Point, they took up the whole road. They were mane to mane, lantern to lantern; steel stirrups, silver curb-chains, brass buckles, glinted here and there among the knee breeches, the white gloves, and the furs that hung over the coats of arms on the doors. He felt as if he were lost in a remote world. His eyes strayed over the women's heads and a faint resemblance would remind him of Madame Arnoux. He pictured her among the others, in one of those little broughams, like that of Madame Dambreuse. But the sun was setting and a cold wind raised clouds of dust. The coachmen sank their chins into their cravats, the wheels turned faster, grating over the macadam; and all the carriages went off down the long avenue at a fast trot, jostling, passing, then, at the Place de la Concorde, dispersing. The sky behind the Tuileries turned the color of slate. The trees in the gardens formed two enormous masses, their tops tinged with violet. The gas lamps were lit and the Seine, greenish everywhere else, broke into silvery ripples against the piers of the bridges.

He went to have a forty-three-sou dinner in a restaurant on the Rue de la Harpe.

He looked disdainfully at the ancient mahogany counter, the stained napkins, the filthy cutlery, and the hats hanging on the wall. The other customers were students like himself. They gossiped about their teachers and their mistresses. A lot he cared about teachers! He had no mistress! He arrived as late as possible to avoid witnessing their cheerfulness. All the tables were covered with scraps of food. The two exhausted waiters slept in corners, and a smell of cooking, lamps, and tobacco filled the deserted room.

Then he went slowly back through the streets. The lamps swayed, and their long, yellowish reflections trembled on the mud. Shadows with umbrellas slid past on the edge of the sidewalks. The paving stones were slimy, the fog drew in, and he imagined that the damp gloom wrapped itself around him and soaked endlessly into his heart.

He was seized by remorse. He went back to the lectures. But, knowing nothing of the material already dealt with, he found very simple matters difficult.

He started work on a novel entitled *Silvio, the Fisherman's Son*. It was laid in Venice. He himself was the hero, the heroine was Madame Arnoux. She was called Antonia —and, to possess her, he assassinated several gentlemen, burned part of the town, and sang beneath her balcony where the red damask curtains of the Boulevard Montmartre fluttered in the breeze. He noticed the too frequent echoes of other writers in his work and was discouraged; he went no further, and the emptiness of his days redoubled.

It was then that he begged Deslauriers to come and share his rooms. They would manage to live on his two-thousand-franc allowance; anything would be better than

this intolerable existence. Deslauriers could not yet leave
Troyes. He urged him to forget his troubles, and to see
more of Sénécal.

Sénécal was a mathematics tutor, a strong-minded man,
a convinced republican, and according to the clerk, a
future Saint-Just. Frédéric climbed his five flights of stairs
three times, without receiving a single visit in return. He
did not go back.

He tried to enjoy himself. He went to the Opéra balls.
Their riotous gaiety froze him as soon as he came through
the door. Moreover, the state of his finances held him
back, for he imagined that to take a masked lady to
supper would be a great adventure, involving considerable
expense.

Yet it seemed to him that he should be loved. He woke
up sometimes with a heart filled with hope, dressed carefully, as if he were on his way to a rendezvous, and
walked endlessly around Paris. "There she is!" he said to
himself of every woman walking in front or coming toward him. Each time it was a fresh disillusionment. These
desires were strengthened by the thought of Madame
Arnoux. Perhaps she would cross his path; and, to enable
him to approach her, he imagined intricate dangers, extraordinary perils from which he would save her.

So the days went by, in recurrence of the same tedium
and the habits to which he had grown accustomed. He
thumbed over the pamphlets under the Odéon arcade,
went to a café to read the *Revue des Deux Mondes*,
dropped into a classroom at the Collège de France for
an hour and listened to a lecture on Chinese or political
economy. Every week he wrote a long letter to Deslauriers, he dined with Martinon from time to time, occasionally saw Monsieur de Cisy.

He rented a piano and composed German waltzes.

One evening, at the Théâtre du Palais-Royal, he saw
Arnoux beside a woman in a stage box. Was it she? Her
face was hidden by the green taffeta screen drawn up to
the edge of the box. At last the curtain went up and the
screen was lowered. It was a tall creature, about thirty
years old, faded and with thick lips which opened, when
she laughed, on splendid teeth. She chatted familiarly with
Arnoux, tapping him on the fingers with her fan. Then a
fair-haired girl, whose eyelids were a little red as if she
had just been crying, sat down between them. From then
on Arnoux talked to her, half-leaning on her shoulder,
while she listened without answering. Frédéric taxed his

ingenuity to discover the circumstances of these women, who were modestly clad in dark dresses with flat, turned-down collars.

At the end of the play he rushed into the corridor. It was filled with people. In front of him Arnoux descended the staircase step by step, a woman on either arm.

Suddenly he came under the light of a gas jet. He had a crepe band around his hat. Perhaps she was dead? This idea so tortured Frédéric that he hastened to "L'Art Industriel" the following day and, hurriedly purchasing one of the prints displayed in the window, asked the assistant how Monsieur Arnoux was.

The man answered:

"Why, he's very well!"

Frédéric, growing pale, added:

"And Madame?"

"Madame too!"

Frédéric forgot to take away his print.

Winter ended. He felt less sad in the spring, worked to prepare for his examination, and, having got through it with a mediocre grade, left for Nogent.

He did not go to Troyes to see his friend, so as to avoid his mother's comments. Later, at the beginning of the new term, he left his lodgings and took two rooms on the Quai Napoléon, which he furnished. He no longer hoped for an invitation to the Dambreuses; his sublime passion for Madame Arnoux was beginning to cool.

Chapter Four

One December morning, on his way to the course on procedure, Frédéric noticed that the Rue Saint-Jacques seemed more animated than usual. Students were hurrying out of cafés or shouting from house to house through the open windows; the shopkeepers watched anxiously from the middle of the sidewalk; shutters were being closed; and, when he reached the Rue Soufflot, he saw a great crowd around the Panthéon.

Irregular bands of five to twelve youths wandered about joining the larger clusters which formed here and there; at the end of the square, against the railings, speakers in workmen's smocks harangued the crowd while policemen, their three-cornered hats cocked over one ear and their hands behind their backs, strolled along by the walls, making the flagstones ring beneath their heavy boots. Everyone stood open-mouthed, a secretive look on each face; they were clearly expecting something to happen; there seemed to be a question on every lip.

Frédéric found himself next to a good-looking, fair young man, with the beard and moustache of a Louis XIII dandy. He asked him what had caused the disturbance.

"I have no idea," answered the other, "and neither have they! It's the fashion just now! What a farce!"

And he burst out laughing.

The electoral reform* petitions which were being cir-

---

*By lowering the financial qualifications for the franchise and extending the right to vote to certain categories of citizens, this proposed electoral reform would have increased the number of voters. The campaign in its favor was carried on by means of petitions and propagandist banquets known as "Reform Banquets."

culated in the National Guard, together with Humann's census* and various other events had led to inexplicable mob scenes in Paris during the past six months; in fact they happened so frequently that the papers no longer bothered to mention them.

"It lacks style and color," continued Frédéric's neighbor. "I'faith, messire, we have degenerated! In the good old days of Louis the Eleventh, nay even of Benjamin Constant, the scholars were more rebellious. God's Teeth, these are meek as sheep, nitwits, a pack of grocers! And this is what they call *The Students Population!*"

He threw open his arms with a sweeping gesture, like Frédéric Lemaître in *Robert Macaire*.

"Student Population, students, my blessing on you!"

Then, apostrophizing a rag-picker who was poking about among some oyster shells outside a wine-merchant's:

"Are you one of them, a member of the Student Population?"

The old man lifted a hideous face, where a red nose and two sodden, befuddled eyes could barely be distinguished in the midst of a gray beard.

"No! You seem to me more like 'one of those men with a ruffian's face who can be seen, in various groups, strewing gold by the handful . . .' Oh! strew away, my patriarch, strew away! Corrupt me with the treasures of Albion! *Are you English?* I do not reject the gifts of Artaxerxes! Let us discuss the customs union!"

Frédéric felt someone touch his shoulder: he turned around. It was Martinon, astoundingly pale.

"Well," he exclaimed with a heavy sigh, "another riot."

He was afraid of being compromised, and complained bitterly. The men in smocks frightened him more than anything else; he suspected them of belonging to secret societies.

"Are there really any secret societies!" said the young man in the moustache. "That's an old trick the government plays to frighten the bourgeois!"

Martinon begged him to drop his voice, for fear of the police.

"So you still believe in the police, do you? Anyhow, Monsieur, how do you know I'm not a police spy myself?"

And he gave him such a look that Martinon, terribly

*Humann was Minister of Finance. His census was designed to lead to a rise in taxes, and had caused riots in the provinces.

upset, took some time to realize that he was joking. The crowd was shoving them forward, and all three had been forced to climb onto the little staircase which led, through a passage, to the new amphitheater.

Soon the multitude divided of its own accord, and several people took off their hats; they were greeting the illustrious Professor Samuel Rondelot, who, muffled in his thick coat, holding his silver spectacles in the air, and panting from asthma, was calmly advancing to give his class. This man was one of the legal glories of the nineteenth century, rivaling the Zachariae and the Ruhdorffs. His recent elevation to the peerage had modified none of his habits. He was known to be poor and was greatly respected.

Meanwhile, from the end of the square, came cries of:

"Down with Guizot!"

"Down with Pritchard!"*

"Down with the traitors!"

"Down with Louis-Philippe!"

The crowd shifted restlessly and, pressing against the closed door of the courtyard, made it impossible for the professor to go forward. He stopped at the foot of the staircase. Soon he could be seen standing on the lowest of its three steps. He spoke, but his words were lost in a buzz of voices. A moment before he had been beloved; now they hated him as a symbol of Authority. Each time he tried to make himself heard the shouting started again. He made a sweeping gesture, urging the students to follow him. The response was a universal outcry. He shrugged his shoulders disdainfully and plunged into the passageway. Martinon had taken advantage of his position to disappear at the same time.

"What a coward!" said Frédéric.

"Merely prudent!" replied the other.

The crowd broke into applause. The professor's retreat had become a victory for them. There were curious spectators at every window. Some of them struck up the "Marseillaise"; others suggested going to Béranger's.

"To Laffitte's!"

"To Chateaubriand!"†

---

*Pritchard was an English consul who was alleged to have fomented an uprising against the French in Tahiti. Since we are now in 1841 and the Pritchard affair occurred in 1844, its mention here is one of Flaubert's rare anachronisms.

†Béranger was a republican critic of Louis-Philippe's government, Laffitte a member of the opposition, and Chateaubriand reconciled loyalty to the legitimate monarchy with democratic principles.

"To Voltaire's!" bellowed the young man with the blond moustache.

The policemen attempted to move through the mob saying, as persuasively as they could:

"Move along, gentlemen, move along please!"

Someone shouted:

"Down with the butchers!"

Since the troubles in September* it had become a common insult. Everyone took it up. The guardians of public order were booed and hissed; they began to grow pale; one of them could stand it no longer and, singling out a boy who ventured too close, mocking him to his face, he pushed him so roughly that his victim staggered back five paces and fell flat on his back in front of the wine-merchant's shop. Everyone drew back but, almost immediately, the policeman himself was felled by a sort of Hercules whose hair jutted out like a hank of tow beneath an oilcloth cap.

After pausing at the corner of the Rue Saint-Jacques for several minutes this man had suddenly abandoned the large box he was carrying to hurl himself at the policeman. Now, holding his victim down, he punched him heavily and repeatedly in the face. The other policemen rushed over. The redoubtable youth was so strong that it took at least four of them to control him. Two shook him by the collar, another two tugged at his arms, while a fifth kneed him in the kidneys; and they all called him a robber, a murderer, a rioter. Chest bare and clothes in shreds, he protested his innocence; he had not been able to stand calmly by and watch while a child was beaten up.

"My name is Dussardier! from Valinçart Brothers, laces and novelties, Rue de Cléry. Where is my box? I want my box!" He kept repeating, "Dussardier! . . . Rue de Cléry. My box!"

Nevertheless he calmed down and, with a stoical air, allowed himself to be led toward the police station in the Rue Descartes. The crowd flooded after him. Frédéric and the young man with moustaches walked immediately behind him, filled with admiration for the clerk and disgusted by the violence of the authorities.

As they advanced the crowd became steadily smaller.

From time to time the police turned around with a ferocious glare and, there being nothing more for the riotous ones to do or the curious to see, they all gradually melted away. The passersby along the way looked Dussardier over and made insulting comments in loud voices. One old woman standing in her doorway even shouted that he had stolen a loaf of bread, and this injustice increased the two friends' irritation. At last they arrived in front of the police station. No more than twenty people remained, and the sight of the policemen was enough to disperse them.

Frédéric and his companion boldly laid claim to the man who had just been imprisoned. The guard threatened that if they persisted they would be clapped into jail themselves. They demanded to see the head of the station and gave their names and position as law-students, asserting that the prisoner was a fellow student.

They were ushered into a completely bare room, with four benches against the smoke-stained plaster walls. A shutter over a window opened at the far end. Then Dussardier's robust face appeared. With its disordered hair, small frank eyes, and square-tipped nose, it was reminiscent of a good-natured dog.

"Don't you recognize us?" said Hussonnet.

This was the moustached young man's name.

"But . . ." stammered Dussardier.

"Stop playing the fool," replied the other. "They know you're a law-student like us."

In spite of their winks, Dussardier understood nothing. He seemed to be collecting his thoughts; then, suddenly, he blurted:

"Did they find my box?"

Frédéric lifted his eyes to heaven in discouragement. Hussonnet replied:

"Oh! The box where you keep your lecture notes? Yes, yes! Don't worry about that!"

They redoubled their pantomime. Dussardier finally understood that they had come to help him and kept quiet, frightened of compromising them. Moreover, he felt a kind of bashfulness seeing himself elevated to the social rank of a student and the equal of these young men whose hands were so white.

"Would you like to send a message to anyone?" asked Frédéric.

"No, thank you, no one!"

"But what about your family?"

He bowed his head without answering. The poor fellow was a bastard. His silence surprised the two companions.

"Have you got anything to smoke?" resumed Frédéric.

The prisoner patted himself, then brought out from the bottom of a pocket the remains of a pipe—a beautiful meerschaum pipe, with a stem of black wood, a silver cover, and an amber mouthpiece.

For three years he had worked to make it a masterpiece. He had always been careful to keep the bowl wrapped in a chamois-leather sheath, to smoke it as slowly as possible, never putting it down on marble, and every evening, to hang it at the head of his bed. Now he gave a shake to the fragments lying in his hand, with its bleeding nails; and, his chin on his chest and his eyes wide and fixed, he contemplated the ruins of his pride and joy with a look of ineffable sadness.

"What about giving him some cigars, eh?" murmured Hussonnet, with a gesture as if to reach for some.

Frédéric had already put a full cigar case on the sill of the little window.

"Take these, then! Good-bye, be brave!"

Dussardier threw himself on the two outstretched hands. He wrung them frantically, his voice caught by sobs.

"What? . . . For me! . . . For me!"

The two companions made their escape from his gratitude, left the building, and went off to lunch together at the Café Tabourey, in front of the Luxembourg.

While he was cutting up his steak, Hussonnet told his companion that he worked for some of the fashion magazines and designed advertisements for "L'Art Industriel."

"For Jacques Arnoux," said Frédéric.

"Do you know him?"

"Yes! No! . . . that is, I've seen him, I've met him."

He asked Hussonnet casually if he ever saw Arnoux's wife.

"Occasionally," replied the bohemian.

Frédéric dared not continue his questions; this man had just assumed a disproportionate place in his life. He paid the bill for lunch without any protest from his companion.

Their liking for each other was mutual; they exchanged addresses, and Hussonnet cordially invited Frédéric to accompany him as far as the Rue de Fleurus.

They were in the middle of the gardens when Arnoux's employee caught his breath, contorted his face in a hideous grimace, and started to crow. Immediately every cock in the neighborhood answered him with prolonged cock-a-doodle-doos.

"It's a signal," said Hussonnet.

They stopped near the Théâtre Bobino, in front of a house whose entrance was down an alleyway. A young woman appeared at the dormer window of an attic, bareheaded, in her corset, among the nasturtiums and sweet peas, leaning on the edge of the gutter with both arms.

"Hullo my angel, hullo my kitten," cried Hussonnet, blowing kisses in her direction.

He kicked open the gate and disappeared.

Frédéric waited for him all that week. He dared not visit him, for fear of seeming impatient to have his hospitality repaid, but he looked for him all over the Latin Quarter. One evening he ran into him and took him back to his room on the Quai Napoléon.

They talked for a long time, confiding in each other. Hussonnet's ambitions were for the fame and riches of the theater. He collaborated in unsuccessful vaudevilles, had masses of plans, turned out songs; he sang a few. Then, noticing a volume of Hugo and another of Lamartine in the bookcase, he launched into a string of sarcasms at the expense of the Romantics. Those poets were blessed with neither common sense nor accuracy and, above all, they were not French! He prided himself on his knowledge of the language and dissected the most beautiful passages with the peevish severity, the pedantic manner so characteristic of frivolous characters when they touch on serious art.

Frédéric's literary feelings were hurt; he wanted to break with Hussonnet. Then why not go right ahead and risk the request upon which his happiness depended? He asked the budding man of letters if he could take him to visit the Arnoux's.

Nothing could be easier, and they planned it for the following day.

Hussonnet did not turn up at the rendezvous; he missed three others as well. One Saturday, toward four o'clock, he appeared. Taking advantage of the carriage, however, he stopped first at the Théâtre-Français to buy a box seat; he wanted to stop off at a tailor's, then at a dressmaker's; he wrote notes which he left with porters. Finally they arrived at the Boulevard Montmartre. Frédéric crossed the shop and climbed the staircase. Arnoux recognized him in the mirror in front of his desk and, still writing, held out his hand to him over his shoulder.

There were five or six people standing about, filling

the narrow room, which was lighted by a single window giving onto the courtyard. At one end a sofa covered with brown wool damask stood in an alcove between two doorways hung with the same fabric. On the mantelpiece, covered with jumbled papers, a pair of candelabra with pink candles flanked a bronze Venus. To the right, near a file cabinet, a man was reading a newspaper in an armchair, his hat still on his head. The walls could hardly be seen for the prints and paintings, valuable engravings and sketches by contemporary masters embellished with dedications proclaiming the most sincere affection for Jaeques Arnoux.

"Everything still going well?" said the latter, turning toward Frédéric.

And, without waiting for an answer, he said to Hussonnet in a low voice:

"What's your friend's name?"

Then, aloud:

"Have a cigar. In the box, on the cabinet there."

"L'Art Industriel," lying in the very center of Paris, was a convenient meeting place; a neutral ground where rival groups rubbed elbows. Among those present on this occasion were Anténor Braive, the royal portrait painter; Jules Burrieu, whose drawings were beginning to popularize the wars in Algeria; Sombaz, the caricaturist; Vourdat, the sculptor; and a few others, not one of whom corresponded to the student's preconceived ideas. Their manners were simple and their conversation free. Lovarias, the mystic, told a dirty story, and the famous Dittmer, who had invented the Oriental landscape, wore a knitted vest under his waistcoat and went home by bus.

The first subject of conversation was a certain Apollonie, an ex-model, whom Burrieu claimed to have seen on the boulevard in a carriage with postilions. Hussonnet explained this metamorphosis by running through the list of her successive protectors.

"How this fellow knows the women of Paris!" exclaimed Arnoux.

"After you, Sire, if there are still some left," replied the bohemian, with a military salute, parodying the grenadier offering his flask to Napoléon.

Then they discussed some canvases in which Apollonie's head had been used. Their absent colleagues were criticized. There was astonishment at the amount their work fetched, and everyone was complaining of not earning enough when a man came into the room. He was of middle height, his coat was held together by a single button, his eyes were bright, and he looked a little mad.

"What a pack of bourgeois you are!" he said. "Good Lord, what does it matter! The old fellows who turned out the masterpieces didn't worry about the millions. Correggio, Murillo . . ."

"Don't forget Pellerin," said Sombaz.

But, taking no notice of this witticism, he continued to hold forth with so much vehemence that Arnoux was constrained to repeat twice:

"My wife is counting on you for Thursday. Don't forget!"

This remark brought Frédéric's thoughts back to Madame Arnoux. Her quarters were probably through the small room next to the divan. Arnoux had just opened the door to get a handkerchief and Frédéric had noticed a washstand at the end. But a kind of growl came from beside the fire; it was the personage who had been reading his newspaper in the armchair. He was five-foot nine, with slightly drooping eyelids, gray hair, and a majestic look—his name was Regimbart.

"What is it, Citizen?" said Arnoux.

"Another despicable action by the government!"

He was referring to the dismissal of a schoolmaster. Pellerin resumed his parallel between Michelangelo and Shakespeare. Dittmer left. Arnoux ran after him to put two bank notes into his hand. Then Hussonnet, thinking this a favorable moment, said:

"Could you, my dear patron, advance me . . ."

But Arnoux had regained his seat and was berating a shabby old man in blue spectacles.

"Oh, you're a nice one, Isaac. Three works discredited, lost! Everyone is laughing at me! And now they're known! What do you expect me to do with them? I shall have to send them off to California! —Go to the devil! No, shut up!"

The old man specialized in forging old master's signatures on the bottom of pictures. Arnoux refused to pay him, and dismissed him brutally. Then, changing his tone, he greeted a stiff gentleman, with a white cravat and whiskers, who wore a decoration in his buttonhole.

He talked to him in honeyed tones for a long time, his elbow on the window latch. Finally he burst out:

"Ah, I have no trouble finding agents, Monsieur le Comte!"

The gentleman gave in; Arnoux paid him twenty-five louis and, as soon as he left the room:

"What bores they are, these grandees!"

"All scoundrels!" murmured Regimbart.

As time went on, Arnoux's became busier; he sorted out articles, opened letters, checked accounts; at the sound of hammering in the shop he went out to oversee the packing, then resumed his work and, even while scribbling away with his metal pen, he parried the others' jokes. He was dining with his lawyer that evening, and leaving for Belgium the next morning.

The others chatted about the topics of the moment; Cherubini's portrait, the hemicycle at the Beaux Arts; the forthcoming Exhibition. Pellerin railed at the Institut. Scandalous stories and serious discussions mingled. The low-ceilinged room was so crowded that it was impossible to move, and the light of the pink candles shone through the cigar smoke like the rays of the sun through a fog.

The door by the sofa opened and a tall, thin woman came in—her abrupt movements made all the trinkets on her watch chain jingle against her black taffeta dress.

It was the woman he had caught sight of the previous summer at the Théâtre du Palais-Royal. Some of the guests shook hands with her, calling her by name. Hussonnet had finally managed to extract his fifty francs; the clock chimed seven, everyone left.

Arnoux asked Pellerin to wait and led Mademoiselle Vatnaz into the dressing room.

They whispered and Frédéric could not hear what they said. However, the woman's voice rose at one point:

"It's six months now since the business was taken care of and I'm still waiting!"

There was a long silence and Mademoiselle Vatnaz reappeared. Arnoux had again promised her something.

"Oh, we'll see later on!"

"Good-bye, lucky man!" she said as she left.

Arnoux darted back into the dressing room, smeared pomade onto his moustache, hitched his suspenders to tighten his trouser straps, and, in the middle of washing his hands, called out:

"I need two panels to go over doors, at two hundred and fifty each, in the style of Boucher. All right?"

"All right," said the artist, red-faced.

"Good! And don't forget my wife!"

Frédéric accompanied Pellerin as far as the Boulevard

Poissonnière and asked his permission to come and see him sometimes, a favor which was graciously granted.

Pellerin read all the books on aesthetics in an effort to discover the true theory of Beauty, convinced that, when he had found it, he would be able to paint masterpieces. He had surrounded himself with every imaginable aid—drawings, plaster casts, models, engravings; and he searched and fretted, blaming the weather, his nerves, his studio; he would go out into the street in search of inspiration, thrill at having seized it, then abandon his picture and dream of another which was bound to be more beautiful. Thus, tormented by his thirst for glory and wasting his time in argument, putting his faith in all sorts of nonsense, in systems, in analyses, in the importance of a set of rules or a reform in the field of art he had, at fifty, produced nothing but preliminary sketches. His robust conceit spared him from even the slightest discouragement, but he was always irritated and in that exalted state, artificial and natural at the same time, which is characteristic of actors.

On entering his studio one noticed two large pictures whose base colors, laid on here and there, made patches of brown, red, and blue on the white canvas. A skein of chalk lines spread over them like the much-mended meshes of a net, so that it was impossible to make out any form at all. Pellerin described the subjects of these two compositions, sketching in the missing parts with his thumb. One represented the "Madness of Nebuchadnezzar," the other "The Burning of Rome by Nero." Frédéric admired them.

He admired whole academies of disheveled women, of landscapes full of trees writhing before the tempest, and, especially, several pen and ink sketches reminiscent of Callot, Rembrandt, or Goya, whose originals he did not know. Pellerin no longer valued these youthful works; now he was enamored of the grand style. He spoke eloquently and dogmatically of Phidias and Winckelmann. The objects around him lent force to his words; there was a death's-head on a prie-dieu, some yataghans, a monk's habit; Frédéric tried it on.

When he came early he would find him in his wretched trestle bed, screened off by a fragment of tapestry, for Pellerin went to bed late, being an assiduous theatergoer. He was looked after by an old woman dressed in rags; he dined at a cookshop and had no mistress. His paradoxes drew flavor from the hoard of miscellaneous information he had picked up here and there. His hatred of the vulgar and the commonplace overflowed in magnificent lyrical sarcasms and his reverence for the old masters was such that it almost succeeded in lifting him to their level.

But why did he never mention Madame Arnoux? Her husband he described sometimes as a good fellow and sometimes as a charlatan. Frédéric waited for Pellerin to confide in him.

One day, leafing through one of Pellerin's portfolios, Frédéric found a portrait of a gypsy with something of Mademoiselle Vatnaz to her; and as that lady interested him, he asked about her circumstances.

She had, Pellerin believed, once been a provincial schoolteacher; now she gave lessons and tried to write for the little magazines.

Her manner toward Arnoux might, according to Frédéric, lead one to suppose that she was his mistress.

"Oh! Well. He has others!"

Turning away his face, which was red at the infamy of his thoughts, the young man then added with a swagger:

"And his wife probably pays him back in kind?"

"Not at all! She's a virtuous woman!"

Frédéric was filled with remorse and became an even more conscientious visitor at the office.

The large letters that spelled out Arnoux's name on the marble plaque above the shop seemed to him extraordinary and full of significance, like a sacred script. The broad sidewalk sloped downwards to facilitate his advancing steps; the door almost opened of its own accord, and its handle, smooth to the touch, had the sweetness, almost the understanding of a hand in his own. Gradually, he became as regular as Regimbart.

Every day Regimbart installed himself in his armchair next to the fire, picked up the *National*, from which he was henceforth inseparable, and expressed his thoughts by exclamations or simply by shrugging his shoulders. From time to time he mopped his forehead with the rolled-up sausage of his handkerchief, which he kept stuffed into his breast between two buttons of his green coat. He wore creased trousers, Blucher boots, and a scarf; and his hat, with its turned-up brim, made him easy to pick out of the crowd at a distance.

Each morning at eight he came down from the heights of Montmartre to drink white wine in the Rue Nôtre-Dame-des-Victoires. His lunch, followed by several games of billiards, took him till three o'clock. Then he would proceed to the Passage des Panoramas for some absinthe. After the session at Arnoux's he used to go to a bar called the Bordelais for some vermouth; then, instead of rejoining his wife, he often chose to dine alone in a little café on the Place Gaillon where he would ask to be given "home cooking, natural food!" Finally he would go to another billiard saloon and stay there till midnight, till one, till the moment when, with the lights turned out and the shutters up, the exhausted proprietor would beg him to leave.

And it was not a taste for liquor which drew Citizen Regimbart to these places but his earlier habit of talking politics there. With the onset of old age his fervor had ebbed, leaving him silent and morose. To see his grave face you would have thought he was weighing the problems of the world, but he disclosed nothing; and no one, not even his friends, had ever seen him working, although he indicated he had an office.

Arnoux seemed to have the greatest respect for him. He said to Frédéric one day:

"He's a deep one, you know! A real brain!"

On another occasion Regimbart covered his desk with papers about some clay pits in Brittany; Arnoux greatly valued his experienced opinion.

Frédéric treated him more ceremoniously, to the point of buying him an absinthe from time to time; and although he considered Regimbart stupid, he often spent a good hour in his company purely because he was Jacques Arnoux's friend.

After helping to launch some contemporary masters, Arnoux the picture dealer, not the man to rest on his laurels, had attempted to increase his financial profits without abandoning his artistic standing. His goal was the emancipation of the arts, bargains in the sublime. All the Parisian luxury trades had felt his influence, which was good in small matters and pernicious in important ones. With his passion for gratifying existing tastes, he deflected able artists from their true paths, corrupted the strong, exhausted the weak, and made the mediocre famous, his power over them springing from his connections and his magazine. The art students were ambitious to have their pictures in his shop window, and his furniture was copied by the upholsterers. Frédéric looked on him as a millionaire, a dilettante, and a man of action all at once. There were, however, plenty of things that surprised him, for Arnoux was, commercially speaking, a rogue.

A canvas would arrive from the depths of Germany or

Italy which had cost him fifteen hundred francs in Paris and, producing an invoice valuing it at four thousand, he would resell it as a favor for three thousand five hundred. One of his usual tricks with painters was to demand a small copy of their picture as a bonus, on the pretext of publishing it as a print. He invariably sold the copy and the print never appeared. To those who complained that they had been exploited, his reply was a cheerful dig in the ribs. But he excelled in other respects: he was lavish with his cigars, friendly with strangers, quick to enthusiasm for a man or a picture; and then, stubbornly committed, he would give it the unreserved support of a flood of calls, letters, and advertisements. He regarded himself as a truly honest man, and his expansive nature led him to tell stories of his shady dealings with complete naïveté.

Once, to annoy a colleague who was giving a large banquet to inaugurate a new art magazine, he asked Frédéric to sit down under his eye and write notes cancelling the guests' invitations just before the scheduled hour.

"There's nothing dishonorable in it, you know."

And the young man did not dare to refuse.

The next day, as he and Hussonnet entered the office, Frédéric glimpsed the hem of a dress disappearing through the door that led to the staircase.

"I beg your pardon!" said Hussonnet. "If I'd known there were women here . . ."

"Oh, it was only my wife," replied Arnoux. "She was passing by and dropped in for a little visit."

"What?" said Frédéric.

"Oh yes, she's on her way back home, to the house."

The surrounding objects suddenly lost their charm. The presence he had felt vaguely diffused through these rooms had vanished—or rather had never been there. He was filled with a boundless astonishment and something resembling the grief of a betrayal.

Arnoux, rummaging through his drawer, smiled. Was he mocking him? The clerk put a bundle of damp papers down on the table.

"Ah! The posters," exclaimed the dealer. "Dinner is still a long way off this evening."

Regimbart picked up his hat.

"What, are you leaving?"

"Seven o'clock," said Regimbart.

Frédéric followed him.

At the corner of the Rue Montmartre he turned around, looked at the second-floor windows, and gave a silent laugh of self-contempt, remembering the ardor with which he had so often gazed at them. Then, where did she live? How was he to meet her now? And a deeper gulf of solitude than ever reopened around his desire.

"Do you want it?" said Regimbart.

"Want what?"

"Some absinthe!"

And, yielding to Regimbart's obsession, Frédéric allowed himself to be led off to the Bordelais. While his companion, leaning on his elbow, contemplated the carafe, Frédéric looked around. He caught sight of Pellerin's profile on the sidewalk and rapped vigorously on the window-pane; the painter had not even had time to sit down before Regimbart asked why he had stopped visiting "L'Art Industriel."

"I'll be damned if I'll go back! He's a savage, a bourgeois, a swindler, a know-nothing!"

These insults gratified Frédéric's anger. Yet, he was wounded by them, for they seemed to reflect a little on Madame Arnoux.

"What on earth has he done to you?" asked Regimbart.

Pellerin stamped his foot on the floor and breathed heavily instead of answering.

He did some clandestine work, such as charcoal-and-chalk portraits, or pastiches of the great masters for ignorant collectors; and, since it humiliated him, he generally preferred to keep quiet about it. But Arnoux's "filthy behavior" infuriated him beyond all bounds. He relieved his feelings.

To fill the order which Frédéric had witnessed, he had brought Arnoux two pictures. The dealer had then presumed to be critical! He had found fault with the composition, the color, the draftsmanship, especially with the draftsmanship; in short he wouldn't have them at any price. But a note which fell due at that moment obliged Pellerin to sell them to Isaac the Jew; two weeks later Arnoux himself sold them to a Spaniard for two thousand francs.

"Not a penny less! What a dirty trick! And he's played plenty of others, by God! One of these days we'll see him in court."

"How you exaggerate!" said Frédéric in a timid voice.

"Oh, so I exaggerate, do I!" cried the artist, thumping on the table with his fist.

His violence restored the young man's self-confidence. Certainly some people would have behaved better; however, if Arnoux found the two canvases . . .

"Bad! Say what you mean! Have you seen them? Is this your profession? Well, I'll tell you something, young man; I can't stand amateurs."

"Oh, it's none of my business," said Frédéric.

"Why should you defend him then?" replied Pellerin coldly.

"But . . . because he's my friend," stammered the young man.

"Give him a kiss from me! Good night!"

And the painter stomped out without, of course, mentioning the bill for his drink.

Frédéric had convinced himself by his defense of Arnoux. In the heat of his eloquence he was filled with tenderness for this good and intelligent man, maligned by his friends, who at this moment was toiling away, alone and abandoned. He gave in to an extraordinary desire to see him at once. Ten minutes later he pushed open the door of the shop.

Arnoux and his clerk were working on some monster posters for an exhibition of paintings.

"Well, well! What brings you back?"

This simple question embarrassed Frédéric and, not knowing how to reply, he asked if they had by any chance found his notebook, a small blue leather notebook.

"The one where you keep your letters from women?" said Arnoux.

Blushing like a virgin, Frédéric denied any such supposition.

"Your poetry, then?" asked the dealer.

He leafed through the pile of specimen copies, discussing their shape, their color, their borders; and Frédéric found himself becoming more and more irritated by his meditative air and, above all, by the hands which moved amongst the papers—coarse hands, a little flabby, with flattened nails. At last Arnoux got up and, exclaiming "That's finished," he chucked Frédéric familiarly under the chin. Frédéric was offended by this intimacy; he recoiled, then crossed the threshold of the office for, he thought, the last time. Madame Arnoux herself was diminished by the vulgarity of her husband.

That same week he received a letter from Deslauriers announcing his arrival in Paris the following Thursday. He experienced a violent reaction toward this higher and more solid affection. A man like that was worth more than all the women in the world! He would no longer need Regimbart, Pellerin, Hussonnet, or anyone else! To make his friend more comfortable, he bought an iron bedstead and a second armchair and divided his supply of bedding in two; and on Thursday morning he was getting dressed to go to meet Deslauriers when his doorbell rang. In came Arnoux.

"Just a word! I was sent a beautiful trout from Geneva yesterday; we're counting on you this evening, at seven on the dot . . . It's Rue de Choiseul, twenty-four-A. Don't forget!"

Frédéric was forced to sit down. His knees were trembling. He kept repeating to himself, "At last! At last!" Then he wrote to his tailor, his hatter, his bootmaker; and he sent off the three notes by three different messengers. The key turned in the lock and the concierge appeared with a trunk on his shoulder.

At the sight of Deslauriers, Frédéric began to tremble like an adulteress before her husband.

"What on earth's wrong with you?" said Deslauriers. "You must have received my letter?"

Frédéric had not enough strength to lie to him. He threw his arms around his friend and hugged him close.

Then the clerk told his story. His father had not wanted to render an account of his trusteeship, imagining that such accounts were no longer required after ten years. But, strong in his knowledge of legal procedure, Deslauriers had finally wrested from him the whole sum he had inherited from his mother, seven thousand francs net, which he was carrying on him in an old portfolio.

"It's a reserve in case of bad luck. I must see about investing it and finding a situation for myself starting tomorrow morning. Today is a total holiday and I'm all yours, old boy!"

"Oh, don't stand on ceremony!" said Frédéric. "If you have something important to do this evening . . ."

"Nonsense! What an unfeeling dog I'd be . . ."

These random words cut Frédéric to the quick, as if they had been a deliberate comment on him.

On the table beside the fire the concierge had laid out some cutlets, galantine, a lobster, dessert, and two bottles of Bordeaux. Deslauriers was touched by this reception.

"My word, you're treating me like a king!"

They talked of their past, of the future, and from time to time, they grasped hands across the table, looking tenderly at each other for a moment. But an errand boy brought in a new hat. Deslauriers remarked aloud on how the lining shone. Then the tailor himself brought back the coat which he had pressed.

"Anyone would think you were getting married," said Deslauriers.

An hour later a third individual came in and drew a resplendent pair of glossy boots out of a large black bag. While Frédéric tried them on, the bootmaker looked contemptuously at the provincial's footwear.

"Do you need anything, sir?"

"No, thank you," replied the clerk, tucking his old laced shoes under his chair.

This humiliating incident made Frédéric feel uncomfortable. He delayed the moment of his confession. At last, as if the idea had just struck him, he cried:

"Oh! Damn it, I forgot!"

"What?"

"I'm going out to dinner this evening."

"At the Dambreuses'? Why is it you never mention them in your letters?"

It was not at the Dambreuses' but at the Arnoux's.

"You should have let me know!" said Deslauriers. "I could have come a day later."

"Impossible!" replied Frédéric curtly. "They only invited me this morning."

And, to redeem his mistake and distract his friend's attention from it, he unknotted the tangled cords around his trunk, arranged all his things in the chest of drawers, tried to make Deslauriers take his own bed while he slept in the closet which had formerly been used for storing firewood. Then, at four o'clock, he began to get ready.

"You've got plenty of time!" said the other.

Eventually he finished dressing and left.

"What it is to be rich!" thought Deslauriers.

And he went off to dinner in a little restaurant he knew in the Rue Saint-Jacques.

Frédéric's heart was beating so fast that he paused several times on the staircase. One of his gloves was too tight; it burst, and while he was pulling his shirt cuff down over the tear, Arnoux, climbing the stairs behind him, took his arm and led him in.

The anteroom was decorated in Chinese style, with a painted lantern hanging from the ceiling and bamboos in the corners. On his way across the drawing room Frédéric stumbled over a tiger skin. The candles had not been lighted, but two lamps shone in the boudoir at the far end.

Mademoiselle Marthe came in to tell them that her mother was dressing. Arnoux swung her up in the air to kiss her; then, wishing to pick out certain bottles of wine for himself, he went down to the cellars, leaving Frédéric with the child.

She had grown a lot since the journey to Montereau. Her brown hair fell over her bare arms in long, crimped ringlets. The rosy calves of her legs showed beneath her dress, more bouffant than a dancer's skirt, and her whole fresh little body smelt as sweet as a bouquet. She accepted the gentleman's compliments coquettishly, fixed her dark eyes on him for a moment, then slipped away among the furniture and disappeared like a cat.

He no longer felt uneasy. Through their lacy paper shades the lamps shone with a milky light, which softened the color of the mauve satin on the walls. Through the slats of the fire screen, which looked like an enormous fan, he could see the glowing coals on the hearth; next to the clock stood a little box with silver clasps. Personal belongings were scattered here and there: a doll in the middle of the little sofa, a scarf over the back of a chair, and, on the worktable, some knitting from which two ivory needles dangled, points downward. The general effect of the room was peaceful, unpretentious, and comfortable.

Arnoux returned and Madame Arnoux appeared through the other door. She was half hidden in the shadows, and at first he could distinguish only her head. She wore a black velvet dress and, over her hair, a long Algerian net of red silk which was caught by her comb and fell onto her left shoulder.

Arnoux introduced Frédéric.

"Oh, I remember Monsieur extremely well," she replied.

Then, at almost the same moment, all the guests arrived: Dittmer, Lovarias, Burrieu, the composer Rosenwald, the poet Theophile Lorris, two art-critic colleagues of Hussonnet's, a paper manufacturer, and, finally, the eminent Pierre-Paul Meinsius, the last representative of the grand tradition in painting, who carried his glory as lightly as his eighty years and his great belly.

When they went into the dining room, Madame Arnoux took his arm. There was a place set for Pellerin. Arnoux was fond of him, even though he exploited him. Moreover, he was afraid of his biting tongue—so much so that, to pacify him, he had published his portrait in "L'Art Industriel" accompanied by hyperbolical eulogies; and Pellerin, to whom fame was more important than money, turned up about eight o'clock completely out of breath. Frédéric imagined that they had been reconciled for a long time.

The company, the food, everything pleased him. The dining room was hung with stamped leather, like a medieval parlor; a Dutch dresser stood opposite a rack of Turkish pipes; and the variously colored Bohemian glasses around the table, amid the flowers and fruit, gave the effect of an illuminated garden.

He had a choice of ten varieties of mustard. He ate gazpacho, curry, ginger, songbirds from Corsica, Roman lasagna; he drank extraordinary wines, lip-fraoli and tokay. Arnoux in fact prided himself on his dinners. With his table in mind he paid court to all the stagecoach drivers and developed contacts among the cooks of the great houses, who gave him recipes for sauces.

But Frédéric took his greatest pleasure in the conversation. His taste for travel was gratified by Dittmer, who spoke of the Orient; he slaked his curiosity in theatrical matters listening to Rosenwald discussing the opera; and the miseries of the bohemian life seemed amusing when seen through the gaiety of Hussonnet, who gave a picturesque description of how he had spent an entire winter with nothing to eat but Dutch cheese. Then Lovarias and Burrieu discussed the Florentine School, told him of masterpieces, widened his horizons; and he could barely contain his enthusiasm when Pellerin exclaimed:

"Stop talking to me about your hideous reality! What does it mean, reality? Some people see black, some see blue, and most see stupid! Nothing could be less natural than Michelangelo, nothing could be more powerful. This concern with exterior reality is a sign of the baseness of our times; if it goes on like this art will degenerate into heaven knows what kind of paltry affair, less poetic than religion and less interesting than politics. You cannot attain its goal—yes, its goal!—which is to make us feel an impersonal exaltation, by means of little works, no matter how exquisitely wrought they are. Look at Bassolier's paintings, for example: they are pretty, elegant, neat, and they don't weigh too much! You can put them in your pocket, take them along on a trip. Accountants buy them for twenty thousand francs; the concept is not worth three sous, and without a grand concept you can have nothing great! And beauty cannot exist without greatness! Olympus is a mountain! The pyramids will always be the mightiest monument. Exuberance is worth more than taste, the desert than the pavement, and a savage than a hairdresser!"

Frédéric listened to all this while watching Madame Arnoux. The words fell into his spirit like metal into a furnace, fused with his passion, and were transformed into love.

He was sitting on the same side of the table as she was, three places lower. From time to time she leaned forward a little, turning her head to say a few words to her small daughter; she smiled at these moments so that a dimple appeared in her cheek, which made her face seem kinder and more tender than ever.

When the liqueurs were brought in she disappeared. The conversation then became very bawdy; Monsieur Arnoux excelled in this kind of talk, and Frédéric was astounded by the cynicism of these men. However, their preoccupation with women seemed to put them on the same level as himself, which raised him in his own esteem.

When they returned to the salon, he picked up one of the albums lying on the table to give himself something to do. The great artists of the day had illustrated it with their drawings, had filled it with prose, or with verse, or simply with their signatures; there were plenty of unknown names among the famous ones, and the few unusual ideas were awash in a flood of nonsense. All the entries paid homage, more or less directly, to Madame Arnoux; Frédéric would have been frightened to write a line beneath them.

She went into her boudoir to fetch the box with silver clasps which Frédéric had already noticed on the mantelpiece. It was a present from her husband, a Renaissance piece. Arnoux's friends complimented him, his wife thanked him; he was touched, and kissed her in front of everyone.

After this they broke up into conversational groups; old Meinsius sat near Madame Arnoux in an easy chair beside the fire; she leaned over to speak into his ear, their heads touched—and Frédéric would gladly have become deaf, infirm, and ugly if he could have had a famous name and white hair—anything, in fact, which would enthrone him in such an intimacy. He ate his heart out, furious at his own youth.

But she came over to the corner of the drawing room where he was standing, asking him if he knew any of the guests, if he liked painting, how long he had been studying in Paris. Each word she let fall seemed to Frédéric something newly created, belonging exclusively to her. He gazed intently at the tapering mass of her hair, whose ends caressed her bare shoulder, and, never turning his eyes away for a moment, he buried his soul in the whiteness of her woman's flesh; he was not, however, bold enough to look up directly into her face.

Rosenwald interrupted them, asking Madame Arnoux to sing something. He played a prelude, she waited; then her lips opened and a pure, long-drawn-out note rose into the air.

The words were Italian and Frédéric understood nothing.

It started with a solemn rhythm, like an ecclesiastical chant; then mounting to a crescendo of animation, the sonorous peals came thick and fast, suddenly subsided, and the melody crept amorously back with a broad, insolent lilt.

She stood erect near the keyboard, her arms by her sides, her gaze unseeing. Occasionally she blinked and leaned forward for a moment to read the music. Her contralto voice took on a mournful intonation on the low notes which chilled her audience, and at those moments her beautiful head with its arched eyebrows inclined toward her shoulder; her bosom swelled, she opened her arms and her throat, the source of these roulades, lolled languidly backwards, as if caressed by aerial kisses; she loosed three high notes, her voice sank again, then came another even higher, and, after a silence, she finished with a sustained cadence.

Rosenwald did not leave the piano but continued to play to himself. From time to time one of the guests would disappear. At eleven o'clock, as the last ones were leaving, Arnoux went out with Pellerin, on the pretext of seeing him home. He was the sort of man who announces he feels ill if he has not had his "constitutional" after dinner.

Madame Arnoux had come out into the hall; Dittmer and Hussonnet bade her good-night and she offered her hand; she offered it to Frédéric too, who felt a piercing sensation in every atom of his skin.

He wanted to be alone and left his friends. His heart was overflowing. Why had she given him her hand? Was it a thoughtless gesture or an encouragement? "Nonsense! I must be going mad!" In any case, what did it matter?—since now he could call on her whenever he chose, live in her atmosphere.

The streets were deserted. From time to time a heavy cart passed, shaking the pavement. The houses filed past with their gray façades and shuttered windows, and he thought disdainfully of all the human beings asleep behind those walls who lived out their lives without seeing her, not one of whom even suspected her existence. He was no longer aware of his surroundings, of space, of anything at all, and, stamping his heels on the pavement and rattling his stick against the shutters of the shops, he moved blindly forward at random, distracted, overwhelmed. A breath of damp air enfolded him and he realized he had reached the quays.

The street lamps stretched away to infinity in two straight lines, and long, red flames wavered in the depths of the water. The river was slate-colored while the lighter sky seemed to rest on two great walls of shadow which rose on either side of the flow. The darkness was deepened by unseen buildings. Farther off a luminous mist floated above the roofs; all the sounds melted into one murmur; a light breeze blew.

He had paused in the middle of the Pont-Neuf and, bareheaded and with his coat open, he breathed deeply. At this moment he felt an inexhaustible spring welling up within him, a flood of tenderness which undid him like the movement of the waves before his eyes. A church clock struck the hour, slowly, like a voice calling to him.

Suddenly he was gripped by one of those moods when one seems to have been transported to a higher world. An extraordinary ability, whose purpose he did not know, had come upon him. He considered seriously whether he should become a great painter or a great poet—and decided on painting, as the demands of that career would draw him closer to Madame Arnoux. So he had discovered his vocation! The goal of his existence was clear now, the future infallible.

When he shut the door behind him he heard someone snoring in the small dark closet next to his bedroom. It was his friend. He had forgotten all about him.

He noticed his face, reflected in the mirror. He found it handsome—and stayed there for a minute gazing at himself.

Chapter Five

Before noon the next day he had bought himself a box of paints, some brushes, and an easel. Pellerin agreed to give him lessons, and Frédéric took him over to his lodgings to see if he had all the necessary equipment.

Deslauriers was in. The second armchair was occupied by a young man. The clerk pointed toward him and said:

"That's him! Here he is! Sénécal!"

Frédéric thought him an unattractive fellow. His crew-cut hair exaggerated the height of his forehead. His gray eyes seemed hard and cold, and his long, black frock coat, all his clothes, in fact, reeked of the pedagogue and ecclesiastic.

At first they chatted about the topics of the moment, among others Rossini's *Stabat;* in answer to a question, Sénécal declared that he never went to the theater. Pellerin opened the paint box.

"Is all that stuff for you?" asked Deslauriers.

"Yes, of course."

"Well! What an odd idea!"

And he bent over the table, where the mathematics teacher was leafing through a book by Louis Blanc. He had brought it with him and read out passages in a low voice while Frédéric and Pellerin examined the palette, the knife, and the paint tubes; then they started chatting about Arnoux's dinner party.

"The picture dealer?" asked Sénécal. "He's a charming type, I must say!"

"Why?" said Pellerin.

Sénécal replied:

"A man who makes money out of political chicanery!"

And he started talking about a celebrated lithograph

that showed the entire royal family engaged in edifying pursuits: Louis-Philippe held a legal code, the queen a prayer book, the princesses were embroidering, the Duc de Nemours was buckling on his saber, Monsieur de Joinville showing his younger brothers a map; in the background was a double bed. This picture, entitled "A Good Family," had delighted the bourgeois and disgusted the republicans. Pellerin, sounding as piqued as if he had painted it himself, replied that one opinion was as good as another; Sénécal protested. The only aim of art should be the improvement of the morality of the masses! Only subjects inspiring virtuous actions should be represented; all others were harmful.

"But doesn't that depend on how they are painted?" cried Pellerin. "I might produce masterpieces!"

"So much the worse for you, Monsieur. You have no right . . ."

"What?"

"No, Monsieur, you have no right to engage my interest in things that I deplore! What need have we of overworked trifles that cannot possibly benefit anyone—those Venuses, for example, and all your landscapes? I fail to perceive what the people can learn from them! Show us their miseries instead! Excite us over their sacrifices! Good Lord, there's no shortage of subjects: the farm, the workshop . . ."

Pellerin, stammering with indignation at all this, believed that he had found an argument.

"Do you admire Molière?"

"Certainly! I admire him as a precursor of the French Revolution!"

"Oh, the Revolution! What art! There has never been a more pitiable period!"

"There has never been a greater, Monsieur!"

Pellerin crossed his arms and, looking him in the eye, retorted:

"You sound to me like an ideal member of the National Guard!"

Used to arguments, his antagonist replied:

"I am not one of *them*. And I detest them as much as you do. But it is principles like that that corrupt the people and it plays into the hands of the government, which would not be so strong without the complicity of a pack of rascals like that man, Arnoux."

The painter, exasperated by Sénécal's opinions, took up the dealer's defense. He even had the face to insist that

Jacques Arnoux really had a heart of gold, was devoted to his friends, and cherished his wife.

"Oh, yes indeed! If you offered him a large enough fee he'd hand her over as a model."

Frédéric grew pale:

"He must have offended you very deeply, Monsieur?"

"Me? No! I once saw him with a friend in a café, that's all."

Sénécal was speaking the truth. But the advertisements for "L'Art Industriel" were a constant irritation to him. To his mind, Arnoux represented all that was fatal to democracy. An austere republican, he suspected all elegance of having a corrupting influence; he himself wanted nothing and was a man of inflexible probity.

It was difficult to continue the conversation. The painter soon remembered an appointment, the teacher his pupils; when they had left, Deslauriers, after a long silence, asked various questions about Arnoux.

"You'll introduce me to him later, won't you, old man?"

"Of course!" said Frédéric.

They then turned their attention to their living arrangements. Deslauriers had had no trouble finding a position as second clerk in a barrister's office; he enrolled at the law school, bought the indispensable books—and the life of which they had dreamed so long began.

It proved delightful, thanks to their youthful grace. Deslauriers had not mentioned financial arrangements, so neither did Frédéric. He paid all expenses, kept their larder filled, took charge of the housekeeping; but if it was necessary to reprimand the concierge, the clerk would do it, continuing the role of elder and protector he had assumed at school.

After being separated all day they would meet again in the evening. Each took his place beside the fire and set to work. It never lasted long. There were endless confidences, fits of unprovoked gaiety, and sometimes wrangles about a flaring lamp or a mislaid book, quarrels that lasted only a minute, to be drowned in laughter.

They left the door of the wood closet open and talked across the room after they had gone to bed.

In the mornings they would stroll on their terrace in shirtsleeves. The sun rose, a light mist drifted over the river, shouts rose from the nearby flower market—and the smoke from their pipes curled upwards in the pure air that caressed their eyes, still puffy from sleep; breathing it, they felt that the world was filled with enormous hope.

On Sundays when it was not raining they went out together and wandered through the streets arm in arm. Almost always the same thought came to them simultaneously or they would be so deep in conversation that they noticed nothing around them. Deslauriers wanted money, as a means of power over men. He would like to make a great stir in the world, to be a celebrity, to have three secretaries awaiting his orders, and give an important political dinner party once a week. Frédéric created a Moorish palace for himself where he could dream away his life reclining on cashmere couches, the murmur of a fountain in his ears, tended by Negro page boys; in the end these visions became so clear that he was as saddened as if they had actually existed and he had lost them.

"What's the use of talking about all that," he said. "We'll never get it."

"Who knows?" replied Deslauriers.

In spite of his democratic opinions the latter urged his friend to make his way into the Dambreuse circle. Frédéric objected, citing his previous attempts.

"Bah! Go back! They'll invite you!"

Toward the middle of March a collection of fairly heavy bills arrived, among them those from the restaurant that sent in their dinners. Frédéric was unable to meet them and borrowed a hundred écus from Deslauriers; a fortnight later he made the same request and the clerk scolded him for the amount he spent at Arnoux's.

It was true that he had been extravagant there. Views of Venice, Naples, and Constantinople hung in the center of the three walls, and equestrian subjects by Alfred de Dreux here and there; a Pradier group on the mantelpiece; copies of "L'Art Industriel" on the piano, and the folios in the corners cluttered the place to such an extent that it was hard to put down a book or move an elbow. Frédéric claimed that he needed all this stuff for his painting.

He worked at Pellerin's. But Pellerin was often out, since he made a habit of attending all funerals and other events which would be reported in the papers—and Frédéric spent hours entirely alone in the studio. The peace of this enormous room—where the only sound was the rustling of mice—the light streaming down from the skylight, and even the purring of the stove, combined, at first, to plunge him into a state of intellectual well-being. But eventually his eyes, wandering from his work, would stray over the flaky plaster of the walls, among the knicknacks on the dresser, along torsos where the accumulated dust looked like scraps of velvet and, like a traveler lost in the woods who finds that every path continually leads him back to the same place, he found that every idea ended in the recollection of Madame Arnoux.

He would plan to visit her on certain days; when he arrived at her door on the third floor he would hesitate before ringing. Steps approached from the other side; the door opened and the words "Madame is not at home" were a relief, as if one burden less weighed on his heart.

Sometimes, however, she was in. The first time there were three ladies with her; another afternoon Mademoiselle Marthe's writing master arrived. Moreover, the men who came to dinner at Madame Arnoux's house never called on her. He was discreet and did not return.

But, in order to be invited to the Thursday dinner parties, he never missed his regular visit to "L'Art Industriel" on Wednesday, and he would stay after all the others had left, longer than Regimbart, until the last possible moment, pretending to examine an engraving or skim through a newspaper. Finally Arnoux would say: "Are you free tomorrow evening?" He would accept before the sentence was out. Arnoux seemed to have become fond of him. He taught him to recognize wines, to brew punch, to make a salmis of woodcock; Frédéric followed his instructions obediently—his love was great enough to embrace everything connected with Madame Arnoux, her furniture, her servants, her house, her street.

He hardly spoke during these dinner parties; he gazed at her. She had a little mole at her right temple; the smooth tresses surrounding her face were darker than the rest of her hair and always seemed a little damp at the edges; from time to time she would pat them into place, using only two fingers. He knew the shape of each of her nails, he delighted in listening to the rustle of her silk dress when she passed the door, he secretly breathed in the scent on her handkerchief; her comb, her gloves, her rings had a special significance for him; they were as important as works of art, alive almost, as if they were people; everything took possession of him and deepened his passion.

He had not had the strength to hide it from Deslauriers. When he returned from Madame Arnoux's he would wake him up, as if by accident, so that he could talk about her.

Deslauriers, who slept in the closet near the cistern

which had been used for storing firewood, would let out a great yawn. Frédéric would sit down at the foot of his bed. At first he spoke of the dinner, then he recounted a thousand insignificant details in which he saw signs of disdain or affection. Once, for instance, she had refused to take his arm and accepted Dittmer's and Frédéric was miserable.

"Don't be such a fool!"

Or perhaps she had called him her "friend."

"Go ahead and try your luck, then."

"But I daren't," said Frédéric.

"Then, forget it! Good night."

Deslauriers turned toward the wall and went to sleep. He did not understand anything about this love, regarding it as a final weakness of adolescence; and feeling that Frédéric no longer found his friendship sufficient, he had the idea of inviting their mutual friends in once a week.

They used to come on Saturdays, about nine o'clock. The three Algerian curtains were carefully drawn, the lamp and the four candles lighted, the tobacco jar, full of pipes, was set in the middle of the table among bottles of beer, the teapot, a flask of rum, and some petit-fours. They discussed the immortality of the soul and compared their professors.

One evening Hussonnet brought a tall young man with an awkward air wearing a frock coat whose sleeves were too short for him. It was the youth they had laid claim to at the police station the year before.

As he was unable to return the box of lace he had lost in the scuffle to his employer, the latter had accused him of theft and threatened to take him to court; now he was working as a clerk in a transport office. Hussonnet had run into him on a street corner that morning and had brought him along because Dussardier, moved by gratitude, wanted to see "the other one."

He held out the cigar case to Frédéric, still full; he had kept it religiously in hopes of returning it. The young men invited him to come again. He took them at their word.

They were a congenial group. For one thing, their hatred of the government had attained the stature of an indisputable dogma. Martinon was the only one who attempted to defend Louis-Philippe. They overwhelmed him with the common charges to be found in every newspaper: the turning of Paris into a Bastille, the September laws, Pritchard, "Lord" Guizot*——to such effect that Martinon held his peace, frightened of offending anyone. In seven years at school he had not earned a single demerit, and he knew how to please the professors at the law school. Normally he wore a thick, putty-colored frock coat and rubber overshoes, but one evening he turned up dressed like a bridegroom: a velvet shawl waistcoat, a white cravat, a gold chain.

Their astonishment increased when they learned that he had come from Monsieur Dambreuse's. Dambreuse, the banker, had in fact just bought a large tract of woodland from Martinon's father. The old man having introduced him to his son, he had invited them both to dinner.

"Were there plenty of truffles?" asked Deslauriers, "and did you hug his wife between two doors *sicut decet?*"

Then the conversation turned to women. Pellerin would not allow that there were such things as beautiful women (he preferred tigers); anyhow, the female of the human species held an inferior place in the aesthetic hierarchy.

"The things that attract you are those which particularly degrade her as an ideal; I mean the breasts, the hair . . ."

"But still," objected Frédéric, "long black hair with large, dark eyes . . ."

"Oh, we know all about that!" cried Hussonnet. "Enough of these Andalusians! A touch of the antique? No, thanks! Look, now, let's be frank! A whore is more fun than the Venus de Milo! Let us be Gallic, for goodness' sake! And Regency, if we can! *'Pour out, ye good wines; ladies, bless us with your smiles.'* We must move from brunette to blonde! Isn't that your view, Dussardier, old man?"

Dussardier made no reply. Everyone urged him to disclose his taste.

"Well," he said blushingly, "I'd like to love the same one, forever."

He said this in such a way that there was a moment of silence, some being surprised by his ingenuousness and

---

*In 1833, the Chamber of Deputies had refused a governmental request for money to construct a ring of forts around Paris which, it was generally believed, would be used against the populace rather than a foreign enemy. The laws passed in September, 1835, repressed republicanism and imposed a severe censorship on the press. For the Pritchard affair, see note, page 33. Guizot, who had been Louis-Philippe's chief minister since 1840, was nicknamed "Lord" because of his supposed predilection for England.

others, perhaps, discovering in it the secret longing of their own hearts.

Sénécal set his mug of beer down on the chimney piece and declared dogmatically that, as prostitution was a tyranny and marriage immoral, it was better to abstain. Deslauriers maintained that women were a useful distraction, nothing more. Monsieur de Cisy was frightened of everything connected with them.

Brought up under the supervision of a pious grandmother, he found the company of these young men as alluring as a visit to a house of ill fame and as educational as the Sorbonne. They did not spare their lessons and he showed himself a zealous pupil, to the point of insisting on smoking in spite of the nausea which it invariably brought on. Frédéric lavished attention on him. He admired the tones of his cravats, the fur on his overcoat, and, above all, his boots, which were as thin as gloves and almost insolent in their delicacy and cleanliness; his carriage used to wait for him in the street below.

One snowy evening when he had just left, Sénécal began pitying his coachman. Then he denounced the dandies of the Jockey Club. He valued a workingman more highly than a gentleman.

"At least I work! I am poor!"

"That's self-evident," Frédéric finally exclaimed impatiently.

The tutor held a grudge against him for this remark.

But, as Regimbart had once said that he knew Sénécal slightly, Frédéric, wishing to be polite to Arnoux's friend, asked him to the Saturday gatherings; the two patriots enjoyed their meeting.

They had, however, different points of view. Sénécal —who had a pointed skull—valued nothing but systems. Regimbart, on the contrary, saw nothing in facts but facts. His chief worry was the Rhine frontier.* He had set himself up as an expert on artillery and had his clothes made by the Polytechnic tailor.

The first time he came he shrugged his shoulders disdainfully when offered some cakes, remarking that they were all right for women; and he was hardly more gracious on later occasions. As soon as the conversation reached a certain level he would murmur: "Oh please, no Utopias, no dreams!" As far as art was concerned

---

*There was a strong movement in France from 1830 on to abrogate the treaties imposed in 1815 and occupy the left bank of the Rhine.

(although he was a frequent visitor to studios, where he sometimes obliged by giving a fencing lesson), his opinions were far from transcendent. He compared Monsieur Marrast's* style to that of Voltaire, and Mademoiselle Vatnaz to Madame de Staël because of an ode on Poland "that showed real feeling." To sum up, Regimbart bored everyone, and, since he was a friend of Arnoux's, particularly Deslauriers. Now the clerk's ambition was to become a frequent guest at that house, hoping to strike up some profitable friendships there. "Well, when are you going to take me?" he would ask Frédéric. Arnoux was terribly overworked, or he was leaving for a journey; then it wasn't worthwhile since the dinners were on the point of finishing.

If the occasion had arisen to risk his life for his friend, Frédéric would have done so. But, concerned as he was to make the best impression possible, scrutinizing his language, his manners, and his dress even to the extent of always being irreproachably gloved when he visited the offices of "L'Art Industriel," he was afraid that Madame Arnoux would dislike Deslauriers with his old black suit, his lawyer's manner, and his overweening conversation, and that this dislike might compromise him and lower him in her estimation. He could accept the others, but Deslauriers, precisely, would have embarrassed him a thousand times more than anyone else could. The clerk saw that he did not want to keep his promise, and Frédéric's silence seemed to him an aggravation of the insult.

He would have liked to control him completely, to see him develop on the lines of their youthful ideals, and his companion's idleness disgusted him as a kind of disobedience and treason. Besides, Frédéric, obsessed with Madame Arnoux, often talked about her husband; and Deslauriers began an intolerably annoying trick of repeating the latter's name a hundred times a day, at the end of every sentence, like an idiot's tic. When someone knocked at the door he replied, "Come in, Arnoux." In a restaurant he would ask for a Brie cheese "the kind Arnoux likes," and at night, pretending to have a bad dream, he would awaken his companion with screams of "Arnoux! Arnoux!" Eventually one day the exhausted Frédéric said in a mournful voice:

*Marrast was a republican journalist who wrote first for the *Tribune* and then for the *National*. Despite his fierce attacks on Louis-Philippe and his government, he was no Voltaire.

"Oh, do stop bothering me about Arnoux!"

"Never!" replied the clerk, and declaimed:

> *Always him! Everywhere! Scorching or icy*
> *The image of Arnoux . . .*

"Shut up!" shouted Frédéric, clenching his fist. Then, gently:

"You know very well that the subject is painful for me."

"Oh, I apologize, old boy," replied Deslauriers, bowing very low. "From henceforth Mademoiselle's nerves will be respected! I apologize yet again! A thousand pardons!"

Thus the joke came to an end.

However, one evening three weeks later, he said:

"Well, I've just seen her, Madame Arnoux!"

"Where?"

"At the law courts, with Balandard, the attorney. A brunette, isn't she, medium height?"

Frédéric made a gesture of assent. He waited for Deslauriers to continue. He was prepared to cherish the slightest word of praise, and would have poured out his heart if it had been forthcoming, but the other held his peace; at last Frédéric could stand it no longer and inquired, offhandedly, what he had thought of her.

Deslauriers found her "not bad, but nothing extraordinary about her."

"Oh! You think so?" said Frédéric.

August, the month of his second examination, arrived. According to general opinion, two weeks' preparation should be ample. Frédéric, confident of his ability, swallowed in one gulp the four first volumes of the procedural code, the first three of the penal code, several fragments of criminal investigation, and part of the civil code annotated by Monsieur Poncelet. On the eve of the examination Deslauriers made him go through a review that lasted till morning, and he put the final quarter-hour to use by continuing to question him as they walked along the street.

As several examinations were taking place simultaneously, the courtyard was full of people, including Hussonnet and Cisy; one always attended these tests when a friend was involved. Frédéric put on the traditional black gown; then he and three other students, followed by the crowd, went into a large room lighted by uncurtained windows and furnished with benches along the walls. In the middle stood a table surrounded by leather-covered chairs and decorated with a green cloth. It separated the candidates from the examiners, who all wore red robes, and ermine bands on their shoulders and tall hats trimmed with gold braid.

Frédéric was the last but one in the group, a bad position. In answer to the first question, on the difference between a covenant and a contract, he defined the one as the other and the professor, a kind man, said: "Don't worry, Monsieur, compose yourself!" Then, having asked two easy questions that evoked confused replies, he at last turned to the fourth candidate. This wretched beginning demoralized Frédéric. Deslauriers, who was opposite him in the public section, signaled that all was not yet lost; and he did reasonably well at the second interrogation, on criminal law. However, after the third, on sealed wills, with the examiner remaining impassive throughout, his anguish redoubled, for Hussonnet made as if to applaud while Deslauriers repeatedly shrugged his shoulders. Finally the moment arrived when he had to face the questions on procedure! The subject was intervention by a third party. The professor, offended at hearing theories that contradicted his own, asked brusquely:

"And you, Monsieur, is that your view? How do you reconcile Article 1351 of the civil code with this extraordinary line of attack?"

Frédéric's head ached unbearably from his sleepless night. A sunbeam, passing through a chink in one of the shutters, shone directly into his face. Standing behind the chair he shifted from one foot to the other, pulling at his moustache.

"I am still waiting for your answer," said the man in the gold-braided hat.

And, probably irritated by Frédéric's fidgeting, he added:

"You will not find it in your beard!"

This sarcasm raised a laugh in the auditorium. The flattered professor's irritation subsided. He asked two further questions on adjournments and summary proceedings, then nodded his head in approbation. The public examination was over. Frédéric went back to the vestibule.

While the beadle stripped him of his gown, which was immediately handed on to someone else, his friends surrounded him, completing his confusion with their conflicting opinions on the result of the examination. Soon it was proclaimed in a sonorous voice from the threshold of the room: "The third has . . . failed."

"That's that!" said Hussonnet. "Let's go."

In front of the porter's lodge they ran into Martinon, flushed with excitement, beaming, his head encircled with a halo of triumph. He had just passed his final examination without a hitch. All that remained was the thesis. In two weeks he would have his license. His family knew a minister and a "fine career" lay before him.

"Well, he beat you all right," remarked Deslauriers.

There is nothing so humiliating as to see fools succeed where one has failed oneself. Frédéric, vexed, replied that he couldn't care less. He was aiming at something higher; and as Hussonnet seemed to be on the point of leaving, he drew him aside and said:

"You won't mention all this to *them*, of course."

It would be easy to keep the secret, for Arnoux was leaving for Germany the next day.

When he returned home that evening, the clerk found his friend in a strangely different mood; he pirouetted, whistled, and, when the other expressed his astonishment at this change, Frédéric declared that he was not going home, he would spend his vacation working.

The news of Arnoux's departure had filled him with joy. He could call at the house as often as he pleased, without fear of his visits being interrupted. The conviction that he was absolutely secure would give him courage. Above all, he would not be far away, would not be separated from Her. Something stronger than an iron chain attached him to Paris; an interior voice cried out to him to remain.

There were obstacles. He overcame them by writing to his mother; first he confessed his failure, due to changes in the syllabus—an accident, an injustice—anyhow all the great lawyers (he mentioned their names) had failed examinations. But he was planning to try again in November. So, having no time to lose, he was not coming home this year, and, in addition to his term's allowance, he asked for two hundred and fifty francs for a course of private tutoring in law that would be very helpful—all this garnished with apologies, condolences, cajoleries, and protestations of filial love.

Madame Moreau, who had been expecting him the following day, was doubly grieved. She concealed her son's mishap and answered that he should "come all the same." Frédéric did not give way. There was a quarrel.

At the end of the week, however, he received his money for the term plus the sum intended for special tutoring, which he spent on a pair of pearl-gray trousers, a white felt hat, and a gold-knobbed cane.

After he had acquired all these things, he thought:

"Perhaps there is something vulgar about this scheme?"

And he fell prey to terrible indecision.

To determine whether he should visit Madame Arnoux he tossed a coin three times. Each time the omen was favorable. It was, therefore, the will of fate. He took a cab to the Rue de Choiseul.

He climbed quickly up the stairs and rang the bell; there was no sound; he felt as if he were about to faint.

He tugged savagely at the heavy red silk tassel. A chime of bells rang out, gradually grew fainter, and lapsed into silence. Frédéric was frightened.

He put his ear to the door; not a murmur! He looked through the keyhole but could see nothing but the points of two reeds among the flowers on the wallpaper. He was finally turning away when he changed his mind. This time he gave a short, gentle pull. The door opened and Arnoux himself appeared on the threshold, his hair tousled, his face crimson, and looking thoroughly cross.

"Well, well! What the devil are you doing here? Come in!"

He took him not to the boudoir or to his own room but to the dining room, where a bottle of champagne and two glasses stood on the table, and said bluntly:

"Is there something I can do for you, my dear boy?"

"No, nothing, nothing!" babbled the young man, trying to think of a pretext for his visit. Finally he explained that he had come to ask for news of him, having heard from Hussonnet that he was in Germany.

"No such thing!" responded Arnoux. "What a hare-brain he is, always getting everything backwards!"

Frédéric paced up and down the room to hide his confusion. He accidentally kicked the leg of a chair and knocked off the parasol which lay on it; the ivory handle broke.

"Oh dear!" he exclaimed. "I'm so sorry, I've broken Madame Arnoux's parasol."

On hearing these words, the dealer lifted his head and smiled strangely. Frédéric, seizing the opportunity to speak of her, added timidly:

"Could I see her?"

She was in the country with her mother, who was sick.

He dared not ask how long she was to be away. He merely inquired whereabouts in the country she came from.

"Chartres! Does that surprise you?"

"Me? No! Why? Not in the slightest!"

After this they found nothing whatever to say. Arnoux, who had rolled himself a cigarette, strolled around the table, puffing. Frédéric, leaning against the stove, contemplated the walls, the dresser, the parquet floor, while a series of charming images passed through his memory, or more correctly, before his eyes. At last he took his leave.

A piece of newspaper, rolled into a ball, lay on the floor of the vestibule. Arnoux picked it up and, standing on tiptoe, stuffed it into the bell so that, he said, he could continue his interrupted siesta. Then, shaking his hand:

"Would you please tell the porter that I am out!"

And he slammed the door behind Frédéric.

Frédéric went down the stairs one step at a time. This unsuccessful first attempt discouraged him from trying his luck again. So began three months of boredom. Having no work, his idleness aggravated his melancholy.

He spent hours high on his balcony watching the river flowing between the gray quays, blackened in places by the waste from the sewers, with a laundry barge moored at the bank where urchins sometimes amused themselves bathing a poodle in the mud. His eyes, leaving the stone bridge of Nôtre-Dame and the three suspension bridges to the left, turned invariably toward the Quai aux Ormes and rested on a clump of old trees like the lime trees at the port of Montereau. The tower of Saint-Jacques, the Hôtel de Ville, Saint-Gervais, Saint-Louis, Saint-Paul rose opposite him, amid a confusion of roofs, and the genie on the column commemorating the Fourteenth of July shone in the east like a great golden star, while in the opposite direction the massive blue dome of the Tuileries thrust its rounded silhouette into the sky. Beyond it must lie Madame Arnoux's house.

He would go back to his room and, lying on his bed, abandon himself to a garbled meditation: work schedules, plans of action, projections into the future. Eventually, to escape his own company, he would go out.

He wandered aimlessly through the Latin Quarter, normally swarming with activity but deserted at this time of the year when all the students had left for their homes.

The great walls of the colleges which seemed longer in the silence, looked gloomier than ever; all sorts of peaceful sounds could be heard, the fluttering of wings in cages, the purring of a lathe, a cobbler's hammer; and the old-clothes men, from the center of the street, eyed every window questioningly to no avail. Inside the empty cafés, the barmaids yawned among their full decanters; the newspapers stayed tidy on the tables in the reading rooms; in the ironing rooms of the laundries, the linens quivered before the gusts of a warm breeze. From time to time, Frédéric paused at the window of a secondhand bookshop; an omnibus, grazing the sidewalk on its way down the street, made him turn; once he had reached the Luxembourg, he went no farther.

Sometimes the hope of finding some distraction would draw him to the boulevards. Leaving the dark alleys exhaling a cool dampness, he would reach the great empty squares, dazzling with light, where statues threw a lacework of black shadow on the edge of the pavement. But the carts and shops began again and the crowds stupefied him—especially on Sundays when, from the Bastille to the Madeleine, an immense flood rippled over the asphalt, in a cloud of dust and a perpetual din; he was nauseated by the meanness of the faces, the silliness of the remarks, the imbecile smugness oozing out on their sweaty foreheads! However, the consciousness of being worth more than these men alleviated the ordeal of watching them.

He visited "L'Art Industriel" every day; and, in order to discover the date of Madame Arnoux's return, he inquired about her mother in great detail. Arnoux's reply never varied: she was "doing better daily"; his wife and the child would be back the following week. The longer she stayed away the more anxiety Frédéric showed, so much so that Arnoux, touched by such affection, took him to restaurants for dinner five or six times.

During these long conversations Frédéric began to realize that the art dealer was not very intelligent. It was possible that Arnoux had noticed his growing coolness; anyhow it was time to pay back a small part of his hospitality.

Determined to do things in grand style, he sold all his new clothes to a secondhand dealer, who gave him eighty francs for the lot; he added this to the hundred he still had, and went around to Arnoux's to ask him out to dinner. Regimbart happened to be there. They went to the Trois-Frères-Provençaux.

The Citizen began by removing his coat and, confident the others would defer, he planned the meal. But it was in vain that he visited the kitchen to talk personally to the chef, went down to the cellar, which he knew inside out, summoned the owner of the establishment and gave him "a talking-to"—he was satisfied with neither the food, the wine, nor the service! With each new dish, each different bottle, at the first mouthful, the first sip, he put down his fork or thrust away his glass; then, leaning on the table with his arms stretched out before him, he would cry that it was no longer possible to dine in Paris! Finally, not knowing what to eat, he ordered kidney beans in oil, "absolutely plain," and this, although no more than half-right, appeased him a little. After this he had a conversation with the waiter about former waiters at the Provençaux: "What had become of Antoine? And that Eugène? And young Théodore, who always worked downstairs? In those days the fare had been very different, and that kind of Burgundy would not be seen again!"

After this the conversation turned to suburban land values, one of Arnoux's infallible speculations. While waiting for them to rise, he was losing the interest he might earn on his investment. As he refused to sell at any old price, Regimbart undertook to find someone for him, and the two gentlemen occupied themselves with penciled calculations until after the dessert.

They went to a mezzanine taproom on the Passage de Saumon for coffee. Frédéric stood and watched endless billiard games, washed down with innumerable beers—and he stayed there till midnight without knowing why, through cowardice, through stupidity, in the confused hope that something favorable to his love might happen.

When would he see her again? Frédéric was in despair. But one evening, toward the end of November, Arnoux said to him:

"My wife came back yesterday, you know!"

He called on her at five o'clock the following afternoon.

He began by congratulating her on her mother's recovery from such a serious illness.

"Why no! Who told you so?"

"Arnoux!"

She said "Ah" softly to herself, then added that at first she had been seriously worried but that her fears had proved groundless.

She sat in the small tapestry armchair beside the fire. He was on the sofa, holding his hat between his knees, and the conversation was difficult; she kept letting it drop and Frédéric could find no opening whereby he might introduce his feelings. However, when he complained of being forced to study legalistic deviousness, she replied, "Yes . . . I understand . . . business!" and bowed her head, suddenly absorbed in her own thoughts.

He longed to know what they were, so much so that he could think of nothing else. The shadows of twilight gathered around them.

She rose, having an errand to attend to, then reappeared in a velvet hood and a black mantle edged with Siberian squirrel. He summoned up his courage and asked if he could accompany her.

It was impossible to see anything; the weather was cold and a thick, reeking fog obscured the fronts of the houses. Frédéric breathed it in joyfully; for through the thickness of his clothes he could feel the shape of her arm; and her hand, in a chamois glove with two buttons, her little hand which he would have liked to cover with kisses, rested on his sleeve. The slickness of the sidewalk made them sway a little; to Frédéric it seemed that they were both being rocked by the wind in the midst of a cloud.

The glare of the lights on the boulevard brought him back to reality. It was a good opportunity and he had not much time. He decided to declare his love before they reached the Rue de Richelieu. But she stopped almost immediately, in front of a china shop, saying:

"Here we are! Thank you. Until Thursday, then, as usual?"

The dinners started again and the more he saw of Madame Arnoux the more he languished.

The contemplation of this woman enfeebled him like the use of too strong a perfume. Sinking into the depths of his character it became almost a general way of apprehending reality, a new mode of existence.

The prostitutes he encountered beneath the gas lamps, the singers trilling roulades, the horsewomen on their galloping mounts, the prosperous housewives on foot, the working girls leaning out of their windows, all women reminded him of this one by similarities or by violent contrasts. As he passed the shop windows he looked at the cashmere shawls, the laces, the jeweled pendants, and imagined them draped around the curve of her back, sewn into the top of her dress, sparkling in her dark hair. The flowergirls' baskets blossomed so that she could choose from them as she went past, in the shoemakers' windows the little satin slippers trimmed with swansdown seemed to be waiting for her feet; her house lay at the end of every road, and the cabs stood waiting in the squares only to take one there more quickly; everything in Paris existed in relation to her, and all the voices of the great city rose around her like an immense orchestra.

The sight of a palm tree when he visited the Botanical Gardens would transport him to faraway places. They traveled together, on the backs of dromedaries, on canopied elephants, in the cabin of a yacht among the blue archipelagoes, or rode side by side on two mules, their harnesses adorned with little bells, who stumbled over broken columns lying in the grass. Sometimes he paused in front of the ancient pictures in the Louvre and his love, reaching out to her even in the vanished centuries, substituted her for the people in the paintings. Wearing a wimple she knelt in prayer before a leaded window. A lady of Castille or Flanders, she sat in a starched ruff and a whalebone bodice with enormous puffed sleeves. Then, surrounded by senators, she descended some great porphyry staircase in a brocade robe under a canopy of ostrich plumes. At other times he imagined her in yellow silk trousers on the cushions of a harem; and anything beautiful—the light of the stars, certain melodies, a perfect phrase, a contour—would bring her abruptly and effortlessly to his mind.

As for trying to make her his mistress, he was certain that any attempt would be in vain.

One evening Dittmer kissed her on the forehead on arrival; Lovarias followed suit saying:

"You'll allow me, won't you? It's a friend's privilege."

Frédéric stammered:

"It seems to me that we are all friends?"

"But not all old friends!" she replied.

She had repulsed him in advance, indirectly.

Anyhow, what could he do? Tell her that he loved her? He had no doubt that she would refuse him or perhaps, indignant, turn him out of the house! Well, he would prefer any pain to the terrible risk of not seeing her again.

He envied the pianists their talent, the soldiers their scars. He longed to fall dangerously ill, hoping that this might attract her interest.

One thing astonished him—that he felt no jealousy for Arnoux; also he was unable to picture her other than fully dressed, so natural did her modesty seem and so dense a veil of mystery did it cast around her sex.

Nevertheless he dreamed of the joy of living with her, of talking intimately with her, of slowly stroking her hair, or of kneeling at her feet, his arms around her waist, reading her soul in her eyes. To accomplish this he would have to overthrow destiny; and incapable of action, cursing God, and accusing himself of cowardice, he fretted in the prison of his desire like a captive in his cell. A perpetual agony suffocated him. He spent hours immobile, or he would burst into tears; and one day, when he had not had the strength to contain himself, Deslauriers exclaimed:

"Good Lord! What's the matter with you?"

Frédéric's nerves were overstrained. Deslauriers would have none of that. Confronted by such suffering he had felt his tenderness revive, and he did his best to comfort his friend. What foolishness for a man like him to let himself become discouraged! All very well when you are still young, but later what a waste of time.

"You're spoiling my Frédéric. I want the old one back. Waiter, the same again. I liked him. Come on, have a smoke, you idiot! Pull yourself together, you're depressing me!"

"It's true," said Frédéric, "I'm mad!"

The clerk continued:

"Ah, my old troubadour, I know what your trouble is! Your heart? Be honest! Bah! There are more fish in the sea! We console ourselves from virtuous women, with the other kind. Do you want me to introduce you to some? Just come to the Alhambra." (This was a public amusement garden which had recently opened near the top of the Champs Élysées, and which went bankrupt after its second season because of its luxury, premature for this type of establishment.) "I hear it's great fun. Let's go. You can bring your friends if you like; I'll even let you have Regimbart!"

Frédéric did not invite the Citizen. Deslauriers did without Sénécal. They took only Hussonnet, Cisy, and Dussardier, and the same cab set them all down at the door of the Alhambra.

On the right and left extended two parallel Moorish arcades. Opposite them the wall of a house filled the entire end of the garden, and the fourth side (where the restaurant stood) represented a Gothic cloister, complete with stained-glass windows. The stage where the musicians played was sheltered by a kind of Chinese roof; the surrounding area was covered with asphalt, and Venetian lanterns hung from posts and, from a distance, formed a crown of multicolored fire above the lines of dancers. Here and there a pedestal supported a stone basin from which rose a thin jet of water. Plaster statues could be glimpsed among the leaves, Hebes or Cupid, glistening with oil paint; and the numerous walks, covered with very yellow sand which had been carefully raked, made the garden seem much larger than it really was.

Students strolled about with their mistresses; salesmen strutted like peacocks, cane in hand; schoolboys smoked cigars; elderly bachelors caressed their dyed beards with combs; there were Englishmen, Russians, South Americans, and three Orientals wearing tarbooshes. Courtesans, working girls, prostitutes had come in the hope of finding a protector, a lover, a piece of gold, or simply for the fun of dancing; and their tunic dresses of sea-green, blue, cherry, or violet swayed and fluttered among the laburnums and the lilac. Almost all the men were in checks; a few wore white trousers in spite of the coolness of the evening. The gas jets were being lighted.

Hussonnet, through his connections with the fashion magazines and the little theaters, knew a great many women; he blew them kisses and sometimes left his friends and went off to chat with them.

Deslauriers was jealous of this behavior. He cynically accosted a large blonde in a nankeen dress. After looking him over in a disagreeable way, she said: "No! I don't like the look of you!" and turned on her heel.

He tried again with a plump brunette, who was probably unbalanced, for she jumped at his first words and threatened to call the police if he persisted. Deslauriers forced a laugh; then, noticing a girl sitting by herself beneath a lamp, he asked her to dance a quadrille with him.

The musicians, perched on the stage like so many monkeys, blew and scraped vehemently. The conductor stood and beat time automatically. People were packed together and enjoying themselves. Loosened hat-ribbons brushed against cravats, boots pushed their way in under skirts, everything bounced in the same rhythm. Deslauriers pressed the little woman to him and, swept up in the delirium of the can-can, threw himself about among the dancers like a great marionette. Cisy and Dussardier walked on; the young aristocrat ogled the girls and, in spite of his companion's exhortations, dared not speak to them, imagining that, with that type of girl, there was always "a man hidden in the cupboard with a pistol who popped out and forced you to sign promissory notes to him."

They returned to where Frédéric was standing. Deslauriers had finished dancing, and they were all wondering how to bring the evening to an end when Hussonnet exclaimed:

"Look! There's the Marquise d'Amaëgui!"

She was a pale woman, with a turned-up nose, mitts to her elbows, and long, black curls that fell at either cheek like a dog's ears. Hussonnet said to her:

"How about a little party at your place, an Oriental revel? Try and collect some of your sweet friends for these cavaliers of France. Well, what's bothering you? Are you waiting for your hidalgo?"

The Andalusian bowed her head; knowing her friend's far-from-extravagant habits she was afraid of having to pay for the refreshments. Finally, when she mentioned money, Monsieur de Cisy offered five napoléons, all that he had in his purse, and the thing was settled. But Frédéric had disappeared.

He thought that he had recognized Arnoux's voice, had glimpsed a woman's hat, and he had plunged as fast as he could into the neighboring grove.

Mademoiselle Vatnaz was alone with Arnoux.

"I'm so sorry. Am I disturbing you?"

"Not in the slightest," replied the dealer.

From what he had overheard of their conversation, Frédéric gathered that Arnoux had rushed to the Alhambra to discuss some urgent matter with Mademoiselle Vatnaz, and he was obviously not completely reassured, for he said anxiously:

"You're quite certain?"

"Quite! She loves you! Oh! What a man!"

And she made a face at him, pouting with her thick lips, which were so red they almost seemed to be bleeding. But she had wonderful eyes, like a wild animal's, with golden flecks in the pupils, full of wit, love, and sensuality. They lit her thin, sallow face like two lamps.

Arnoux seemed amused by her scolding. He leaned toward her, saying:

"How sweet you are, give me a kiss!"

She took him by the ears and kissed him on the forehead.

Just then the dance music stopped and the conductor's place was taken by a handsome young man, over-plump and as pale as wax. He had long black hair arranged like Christ's and a blue velvet waistcoat decorated with large golden palms; he looked proud as a peacock and stupid as a goose. When he had greeted his public he began to sing. It was a countryman telling the story of his visit to the capital; the artiste spoke in Norman dialect and mimicked a drunkard. The chorus:

> Ah! how I laughed there, how I laughed,
> In that foul hole called Paris.

brought an enthusiastic stamping of feet. Delmas, "the singer with a heart," was too clever to allow them time to cool off. He was quickly handed a guitar and sobbed out a romance entitled "The Albanian's Brother."

The words reminded Frédéric of those sung by the ragged harpist beside the paddle-wheel of the steamer. Unconsciously his eyes became fixed on the hem of the dress spread out in front of him. After each couplet there was a long pause—and the sighing of the wind in the trees was like the sound of waves.

Mademoiselle Vatnaz, with one hand holding back the branches of a privet bush that obstructed her view of the platform, gazed steadfastly at the singer, her nostrils dilated and her eyes narrowed, as if absorbed in a grave delight.

"Well, well!" said Arnoux. "Now I understand why you came to the Alhambra tonight! Delmas appeals to you, my dear."

She would admit nothing.

"Oh, what modesty!" and, pointing to Frédéric:

"Because of him? You would be wrong. Most discreet fellow around!"

The others came into the little glade in search of their friend. Hussonnet introduced them. Arnoux distributed cigars and bought sherbets all around.

Mademoiselle Vatnaz had blushed on seeing Dussardier. She soon got up and, holding out her hand, said:

"Don't you recognize me, Monsieur Auguste?"

"How do you happen to know her?" asked Frédéric.

"We used to work in the same place!" Dussardier replied.

Cisy tugged at his sleeve; they went off and were hardly out of sight before Mademoiselle Vatnaz began eulogizing his character. She even added that he had "a genius for loving."

Then they talked about Delmas, who was a likely bet for the theater as a mime, and this was followed by a discussion that touched on Shakespeare, censorship, style, the people, the revenue at the Porte-Saint-Martine, Alexandre Dumas, Victor Hugo, and Dumersan. Arnoux had known several famous actresses; the young men leaned forward to listen to him. But his words were drowned by the music, and no sooner had a polka or a quadrille finished than everyone fell upon the tables, laughing and shouting for the waiters; bottles of beer and fizzy lemonade detonated among the leaves; the women screamed like so many chickens; from time to time two of the men would start to fight; a thief was arrested.

When the time came for the galop, the dancers invaded the paths.

Panting, smiling, red in the face, they swept past in a whirlwind that whisked the dresses and the coattails into the air; the trombones wailed louder, the rhythm beat faster; there was a crackling behind the medieval cloister, fireworks burst, suns revolved; for a moment the whole garden was bathed in the emerald light of Bengal fire—and, at the final rocket, a great sigh rose from the crowd.

The mob drifted slowly away. A cloud of gunsmoke floated in the air. Frédéric and Deslauriers were moving step by step in the midst of the throng when they were halted by the sight of Martinon collecting his change at the cloakroom; he was escorting a woman in her fifties, ugly, magnificently dressed, and of an uncertain social rank.

"That fellow," said Deslauriers, "is not as simple as you might think. But where's Cisy?"

Dussardier pointed toward the wine shop, where they saw the descendant of warriors at a punch bowl in the company of a pink hat.

Hussonnet, who had left them five minutes earlier, reappeared at that moment.

A young woman hung on his arm, addressing him aloud as her "little duck."

"No, no!" he remonstrated. "Not in public! You'd bet-

ter call me 'Viscount'! That conjures up an image of a
Louis XIII cavalier in soft leather boots that pleases
me! Yes, my boys, an old friend! Isn't she sweet?"
He took her by the chin. "Say 'how do you do' to the
gentlemen! Their fathers are peers of France, and I associate with them so that they'll name me ambassador!"

"What a lunatic you are!" sighed Mademoiselle Vatnaz.

She asked Dussardier if he would escort her home.

Arnoux gazed after their receding figures; then, turning to Frédéric, asked:

"Do you find La Vatnaz attractive? But actually you're
not very open on that subject. I believe you keep your
love affairs quiet, don't you?"

Frédéric, turned pale, swore that he had nothing to
hide.

"It's because no one knows if you've got a mistress,"
replied Arnoux.

Frédéric felt an impulse to produce a name at random.
But the story might reach *her* ears. He answered that
in fact, he had none.

The dealer reproached him.

"This evening was a good opportunity! Why didn't you
behave like the others—every one of them left with a
woman!"

"Well, what about you?" said Frédéric, irritated by such
persistence.

"Oh, that's different, my boy! I'm going back to mine
now!"

He hailed a cab and disappeared.

The two friends set off on foot. There was an east
wind blowing. Neither of them spoke. Deslauriers was unhappy at not having shone in front of the editor of a
paper, and Frédéric was sunk in gloom. Finally he remarked that the dance hall had struck him as stupid.

"Well, whose fault was that? You shouldn't have
dropped us for your Arnoux!"

"Bah! Anything I did would have been pointless."

But the clerk had certain theories. To get what you
wanted you had only to want it strongly enough.

"But a few minutes ago you yourself—"

"I didn't care!" cried Deslauriers, cutting short the allusion. "Why should I want to get mixed up with women!"

And he railed against their archness, their stupidity.
In short, he disliked them.

"Stop posing!" said Frédéric.

Deslauriers held his peace. Then, suddenly:

"Do you want to bet a hundred francs that I make the first woman we meet?"

"Yes! You're on!"

The first woman to pass was a hideous beggar, and they were beginning to lose faith in chance when, in the middle of the Rue de Rivoli, they saw a tall girl with a small package in her hand.

Deslauriers accosted her under the arcades. She veered suddenly toward the Tuileries and soon turned down the Place du Carrousel, glancing to left and right. She ran after a cab; Deslauriers caught up with her again. He walked beside her, talking and gesticulating with great expression. At last she accepted his arm and they continued along the quays. Then, when they were level with the Châtelet, they spent at least twenty minutes walking up and down the sidewalk, like sailors on watch. But suddenly they crossed the Pont au Change, the Marché aux Fleurs, the Quai Napoléon. Frédéric followed them in. Deslauriers gave him to understand that he would be in the way and had only to follow his example.

"How much do you have left?"

"Two hundred-sou pieces."

"That's enough! Good night!"

Frédéric was overcome by the astonishment one feels when a prank works. "He's fooling me," he thought. "Suppose I went up?" Perhaps Deslauriers would think that he envied him his love? "As if I didn't have one of my own, a hundred times rarer, nobler, stronger!" Driven by a kind of anger he arrived at Madame Arnoux's door.

None of the windows on the street belonged to her apartment. He waited nevertheless, his eyes glued to the façade—as if he believed this contemplation might pierce the walls. At this moment she must be lying tranquil as a sleeping flower, her beautiful black hair mingled with the lace on the pillow, her lips parted, her head on her arm.

He had a vision of Arnoux's face and moved away to escape this apparition.

He remembered Deslauriers' advice; it was repugnant to him. So he wandered about the streets.

When a passerby approached, he tried to make out his features. From time to time a ray of light passed between his legs, describing an immense quarter circle on the pavement; and a man materialized in the shadows, his basket on his back carrying a lantern. Here and there a tin chimney pipe rattled in the wind, sounds rose in the distance to mingle with the buzzing in his ears, and he thought he could hear the diffuse strains of a quadrille on the breeze. The rhythm of his steps sustained this trance; he found himself on the Pont de la Concorde.

Then he remembered that evening of a winter earlier when, leaving her house for the first time, he had been forced to stop short, his heart beat so fast in the grip of his hopes. They were all dead now!

Dark clouds scudded across the face of the moon. He gazed at them, musing on the grandeur of space, the misery of life, the nullity of everything. Dawn broke; his teeth were chattering and, half asleep, sodden with mist and full of tears, he asked himself why he should not end it all! A simple movement, it would take no more! The weight of his forehead drew him downwards, he saw his corpse floating in the water; Frédéric leaned over. The parapet was rather broad and it was lassitude that kept him from making the effort to cross it.

Terror seized him. He turned back to the boulevards and collapsed onto a bench. Some policemen woke him up, convinced that he had "made a night of it."

He started walking. But, as he was very hungry and all the restaurants were closed, he went to have supper in a tavern in Les Halles. After which, judging that it was still too early, he strolled around near the Hôtel de Ville till a quarter past eight.

Deslauriers had sent his girl away long since and was writing at the table in the middle of the room. About four o'clock Monsieur de Cisy came in.

Thanks to Dussardier, he had met a lady the previous evening, had even escorted her, with her husband, in a carriage to the door of her house where she had given him an assignation. He had just come from there. She was not a woman of bad reputation!

"What do you want me to do about it?" said Frédéric.

At this point Cisy beat about the bush; he talked about Mademoiselle Vatnaz, the Andalusian, and all the others. Finally, with many circumlocutions, he came to the point of his visit: trusting in his friend's discretion he had come to ask his help in an enterprise after which he would definitively regard himself as a man; Frédéric did not refuse. He told the story to Deslauriers, casting himself as the hero.

The clerk decided that "he was doing very well now." This deference to his advice increased his good humor.

It was by virtue of this good humor that he had, the first day they met, seduced Mademoiselle Clémence Daviou, a needleworker who embroidered military uniforms with gold thread. She was the gentlest person on earth, and slim as a reed, with great blue eyes forever filled with wonder. The clerk abused her simplicity to the point of telling her that he had a decoration; he stuck a red ribbon in his buttonhole during their tête-à-têtes but removed it in public—in order not to humiliate his employer, he said. For the rest he kept her at a distance, let himself be caressed like a pasha, and addressed her as "daughter of the people" by way of a joke. Every time she came, she brought him a little bunch of violets. Frédéric had no wish for this kind of love.

Nevertheless, when they set off arm in arm for a room at Pinson's or Barillot's, Frédéric felt oddly sad. He had no idea how much he had made Deslauriers suffer every Thursday for the past year, as he brushed his nails before leaving for dinner at the Rue de Choiseul.

One evening, when he was on his balcony watching them leave, he saw Hussonnet in the distance on the Pont d'Arcole. The bohemian started signaling for him to come down and, when Frédéric had reached the foot of his five flights of stairs:

"Look, it's about next Saturday, the twenty-fourth. It's Madame Arnoux's name day."

"How can it be? Her name's Marie."

"Angèle, too, what does it matter! They're having a party at their country house, at Saint-Cloud; I was asked to let you know. You'll find a carriage at the newspaper office at three o'clock! There, that's settled! Sorry to have bothered you, but I have so many errands to do!"

Frédéric had hardly turned around when his porter brought him a letter:

"Monsieur and Madame Dambreuse hope that Monsieur F. Moreau will do them the honor of dining with them on Saturday the twenty-fourth of this month. R.S.V.P."

"Too late," he thought.

Nevertheless he showed the note to Deslauriers, who cried:

"Ah, at last! But you don't seem pleased! Why not?"

After a slight hesitation Frédéric told him that he had another invitation for the same day.

"Do me the favor of sending the Rue du Choiseul

packing. Don't be absurd! I'll answer for you, if that's what's worrying you."

And the clerk wrote an acceptance in the third person.

Having seen the world exclusively through the fever of his covetousness, he conceived it to be an artificial creation, functioning in obedience to mathematical laws. A dinner party in the capital, the acquaintance of an official, a smile from a pretty woman could, by a series of events each deriving from its forerunner, produce enormous results. Certain Parisian salons were like those machines that take raw material and increase its value a hundredfold. He believed in courtesans advising diplomats, in rich marriages stemming from intrigue, in the genius of criminals, and in fortune's docile submission to an iron will. In short, he counted a friendship with the Dambreuses so useful, and he argued his case so persuasively, that Frédéric no longer knew what to decide.

In any case, since it was Madame Arnoux's name day, he should give her a present; he thought, naturally, of a parasol, to make up for his clumsiness. Now, he had discovered a marquise sunshade in pigeon-gray silk with a little carved ivory handle, which had just come in from China. But it cost a hundred and seventy-five francs and he hadn't a penny, he was even living on credit against his next term's allowance. However, he wanted it, he was determined to have it, and despite his repugnance, he turned to Deslauriers.

Deslauriers replied that he had no money.

"I need it," said Frédéric. "I need it very much."

And, when his friend repeated the same excuse, he burst out:

"You might at least, sometimes . . ."

"What?"

"Nothing."

The clerk understood. He took the necessary sum from his reserve and, when he had counted it out, bit by bit:

"I won't ask for a receipt, since I live off you!"

Frédéric threw his arms around his neck with a thousand cries of affection. Deslauriers remained cold. Then, the following day, noticing the parasol on the piano:

"Ah! It was for that."

"Perhaps I'll send it," said the cowardly Frédéric.

Fortune favored him, for he received a note that evening from Madame Dambreuse announcing the death of an uncle and excusing herself for deferring to a later date the pleasure of making his acquaintance.

He was at the offices of the paper by two o'clock. Instead of waiting to take him along in his carriage, Arnoux had left the previous day, unable to resist his longing for fresh air.

Every year when the first leaves appeared, he left home several mornings in a row, took long walks across country, drank milk at the farms, bantered with the village girls, inquired about the state of the crops, and returned with his kerchief full of salad plants. Finally, fulfilling an ancient dream, he had bought a house in the country.

Mademoiselle Vatnaz arrived while Frédéric was talking to the clerk and was disappointed not to see Arnoux. He might possibly stay at Saint-Cloud for two days. The clerk advised her to "go out there"—she could not; to write a letter—she was afraid a letter might go astray. Frédéric offered to deliver it himself. She quickly scribbled a note and asked Frédéric to hand it over when no one was watching.

Forty minutes later he disembarked at Saint-Cloud. The house was halfway up the hill, a hundred yards beyond the bridge. The garden walls were concealed by two rows of lime trees, and a broad lawn dipped to the river's edge. The gate was open, so Frédéric walked in.

Arnoux, lying on the grass, was playing with a litter of kittens. He seemed completely absorbed. Mademoiselle Vatnaz's letter roused him from his torpor.

"Damn! Dammit! What a nuisance! She's right, I must leave."

Then, having stuffed the letter into his pocket, he took pleasure in displaying his domain. He showed Frédéric everything, the stable, the cart-house, the kitchen. The drawing room was on the left, and on the side toward Paris it looked out onto a trellised pavilion with clematis growing up it. But a run of notes rang out above their heads; Madame Arnoux, believing herself alone, was passing the time by singing. She sang scales, trills, arpeggios. There were long notes that seemed suspended in the air, others that fell precipitately, like drops from a waterfall, and her voice, from behind the lattice, clove the enormous silence and soared into the blue sky.

She stopped suddenly when Monsieur and Madame Oudry, their neighbors, arrived.

Then she appeared herself on the landing, and as she descended the steps he caught a glimpse of her foot. She wore little open shoes in bronze leather, with three crossstraps that traced a golden network on her stockings.

The guests arrived. Except for Monsieur Lefaucheur, a lawyer, they were the usual Thursday crowd. Each had brought a present: Dittmer a Syrian scarf, Rosenwald an album of songs, Burrieu a watercolor, Sombaz a caricature of himself, and Pellerin a charcoal drawing of a sort of dance of death, a hideous fantasy poorly executed. Hussonnet had come without bringing a gift.

Frédéric waited till after the others before offering his. She thanked him warmly. He replied,

"But . . . it's almost a debt. I was so angry with myself."

"But what about?" she asked. "I don't understand."

"Let's eat!" exclaimed Arnoux, seizing him by the arm. Then, in his ear: "You're not very bright, are you?"

Nothing could have been pleasanter than the dining room, which had been painted a sea-green. At one end, a stone nymph dabbled her toes in a shell-shaped basin. Through the open windows you could see the entire garden, with the long lawn flanked by an old Scotch pine, three-quarters leafless; banks of flowers gave it an asymmetrical outline, and, on the far side of the river, the Bois de Boulogne, Neuilly, Sèvres, and Meudon formed a great semicircle. A little sailing boat tacked to and fro beyond the railings.

First they talked of the view before them, then of the countryside in general; they were starting to argue when Arnoux ordered the servant to have the phaeton ready at nine-thirty. A letter from his chief cashier had summoned him back to town.

"Would you like me to go back with you?" Madame Arnoux asked.

"But of course!" and, making her a low bow: "You are well aware, Madame, that it is impossible to exist without you!"

Everyone congratulated her on having such a good husband.

"Ah, it's because I am not the only one!" she replied gently, pointing to her little daughter.

The conversation then turned to painting; someone mentioned a Ruysdael for which Arnoux hoped to obtain a considerable sum, and Pellerin asked if it was true that the famous Saul Mathias of London had come over the previous month to offer him twenty-three thousand francs.

"Perfectly true!" he said, turning to Frédéric: "He was the man I had with me at the Alhambra the other night; against my will, I assure you, for these Englishmen are not much fun!"

Frédéric, suspecting that the letter from Mademoiselle Vatnaz was connected with some amorous intrigue, had admired the dexterity with which Arnoux had found a legitimate excuse for packing up, but this new and absolutely pointless lie made him gape.

The dealer added innocently:

"What's his name again, that tall young man, your friend?"

"Deslauriers," said Frédéric eagerly.

And, to make up for the wrongs he felt he had done him, Frédéric praised him as a superior intellect.

"Oh, really? But he doesn't seem as nice a fellow as the other, the clerk from the transport company."

Frédéric cursed Dussardier. She would believe that he associated with the lower classes.

After that they talked about the improvements in the city, the new districts, and the old Oudry mentioned Monsieur Dambreuse as one of the important speculators.

Frédéric, seizing the chance to enhance his prestige, said that he knew him. But Pellerin launched into a Catiline oration denouncing grocers; he saw no difference between those who sold candles and those who sold money. Then Rosenwald and Burrieu chatted about porcelain; Arnoux talked gardening with Madame Oudry while Sombaz, a wag of the old school, amused himself by teasing her husband; he called him Odry, like the actor, and declared that he must be descended from Oudry, the painter who specialized in dogs, for the bump of zoology was visible on his forehead. He even wanted to feel his head; the other, fearful for his wig, fended him off; and dessert ended in roars of laughter.

After coffee and a cigar under the lime trees, and several turns around the garden, they went for a stroll along the river.

The group stopped in front of a fisherman who was cleaning eels in a bin. Mademoiselle Marthe wanted to see them. He emptied his box onto the grass, and the little girl fell to her knees to capture them, laughing with pleasure and screaming with fright. They were all lost; Arnoux paid for them.

Then he thought of going for a boat ride.

On one side the horizon had begun to grow pale while on the other a broad orange band spread across the sky, turning purple above the crests of the hills which had become completely black. Madame Arnoux sat down on a large rock with her back to this fiery glow. The others strolled about; and from the bank Hussonnet was skipping stones over the water.

Arnoux returned, followed by an ancient boat into which, despite wiser protests, he insisted on piling his guests. It foundered; they were forced to disembark.

The candles were already burning in the chintz-hung drawing room with its crystal candelabra. Old Madame Oudry went quietly off to sleep in an armchair and the others listened to Monsieur Lefaucheur while he expatiated on the glories of the legal profession. Madame Arnoux was alone near the window; Frédéric joined her.

They discussed what the others were saying. She admired orators; he preferred the rewards of a writer. But, she objected, there must be greater gratification in swaying a crowd in person and seeing their souls open to all one's own emotions. Such triumphs did not tempt Frédéric, who had no ambition.

"Oh, why?" she asked. "Everyone needs a little ambition."

They stood near each other in the window recess. Before them the night spread out like an enormous dark veil sprinkled with silver. It was the first time that they had spoken of anything that was not insignificant. He even discovered her antipathies and her tastes; she detested certain scents, was interested in books about history, believed in dreams.

He broached the subject of affairs of the heart. She pitied the victims of disastrous passions but was revolted by hypocritical baseness; and this uprightness of spirit accorded so well with the beauty of her regular features that the one seemed to derive from the other.

Sometimes she smiled, allowing her eyes to rest on him for a moment. Then he felt her gaze penetrating as a bright ray of sun reaches to the bottom of the water. He loved her without reservation, without hope of his affection being returned, absolutely; and, in these moments of silent ecstasy which resembled transports of gratitude, he would have liked to cover her forehead with kisses. At the same time he was enraptured by a secret desire; it was a longing to sacrifice himself, a wish to consecrate himself to her immediately, all the stronger for being impossible to fulfill.

He and Hussonnet did not leave with the others. They were to return to Paris in the carriage, and the phaeton was waiting at the foot of the steps when Arnoux went down into the garden to pick some roses. Then, as the stems stuck out untidily after he had tied some string round them, he rummaged in his pockets which were full of papers, took the first that came to hand, wrapped it round the flowers, consolidated his creation with a large pin, and presented it to his wife with some emotion.

"Here you are, dearest. Forgive me for having forgotten you!"

But she gave a little cry; she had pricked herself on the clumsily placed pin and went back up to her room. They waited for almost a quarter of an hour. Finally she reappeared, picked up Marthe, and flung herself into the carriage.

"What about your bouquet?" asked Arnoux.

"No! No! It's not worth it!"

Frédéric ran up to fetch it; she called after him:

"I don't want it!"

But he brought it down in a few minutes, explaining that he had had to rewrap it, having found the flowers on the floor. She thrust them into the leather apron beside the seat and they set off.

Frédéric, who was sitting next to her, noticed that she was trembling violently. Then, when they had crossed the bridge and Arnoux made as if to turn to the left:

"No, no! You're mistaken! That way, to the right!"

She seemed in an irritable frame of mind; everything annoyed her. Finally, when Marthe had shut her eyes, she picked up the bouquet and threw it out of the window, then caught Frédéric's arm and signaled to him with her other hand that he was never to mention it.

After this she pressed her handkerchief to her lips and did not move again.

The other two, on the box, were talking about printing and posters. Arnoux, who was paying no attention to his driving, lost his way in the middle of the Bois de Boulogne. They moved along little lanes. The horse slowed to a walk, branches from the trees brushed against the hood. All Frédéric could see of Madame Arnoux was two eyes in the shadow. Marthe had stretched out across her lap and he supported her head.

"She is tiring you!" said her mother.

He answered:

"No! Oh, no!"

The dust rose in slow eddies, they passed through Auteuil. All the houses were shuttered, here and there the angle of a wall was lighted by a street lamp, then the darkness returned; once he noticed that she was in tears. Was it remorse? Longing? What could it be? This unknown sorrow interested him as if it were his own; there was a new bond between them now, a kind of complicity, and he asked her in his most caressing voice:

"Are you feeling ill?"

"Yes, a little," she replied.

The carriage rolled on, and the honeysuckle and syringa overhanging the garden fences filled the night with soft waves of fragrance. The many folds of her dress hid her feet. He seemed to himself to communicate with her whole person through the child stretched between them. He leaned over the little girl and, parting her pretty brown hair, kissed her gently on the forehead.

"How good you are!" said Madame Arnoux.

"Why?"

"Because you love children."

"Not all children!"

He said nothing further but held out his open left hand in her direction, imagining that she might perhaps do the same and that their hands would meet. Then he felt ashamed and withdrew it.

Soon they reached the paved streets. The carriage moved faster, the gas lamps multiplied, they were in Paris. Hussonnet jumped down from the box in front of the Garde-Meuble. Frédéric waited till they reached the courtyard before getting out; then he posted himself at the corner of the Rue de Choiseul and saw Arnoux making his way slowly back toward the boulevards.

He set to work the following day and from then on studied as hard as he could.

He visualized himself in court, on a winter evening, with the final addresses drawing to an end, the jurors pale, and the partitions of the courtroom cracking from the pressure of the breathless crowd, he having already spoken for four hours, reviewing all his arguments, revealing new ones, and at each phrase, at each word, at each gesture, feeling the blade of the guillotine hanging behind him gradually recede; then in parliament, an orator on whose lips depends the salvation of a whole people, drowning his adversaries in his magniloquence, flattening them with a retort, his voice charged with thunder, full of musical intonations, ironic, pathetic, passionate, sublime. She would be there, somewhere, among the others, hiding her tears of enthusiasm under her veil; they would meet afterwards—and discouragement, calumny, and insult could not touch him if she said: "Oh! That was meet afterwards—and discouragement, calumny, and insult

could not touch him if she said: "Oh! That was wonderful!"
while she stroked his forehead with her gentle fingers.

These images flashed like beacons on the horizons of
his life. His aroused mind became nimbler and stronger.
He shut himself up with his books until August and
passed his final examination.

Deslauriers, who had had great difficulty cramming him
for the second examination at the end of December and
for the third in February, was astounded by his enthusiasm. The old hopes returned. Frédéric would be a
deputy in ten years, a minister in fifteen; why not?
With his father's money, which he would soon inherit, he
could begin by founding a newspaper; that would be the
start, and afterwards they would see. As for himself, his
ambition was still a chair at the law school, and he defended his doctoral thesis in so remarkable a manner that
he was complimented by the professors.

Frédéric defended his own three days later. Before
leaving for vacation he proposed a picnic for the last of
the Saturday gatherings.

He was in a gay mood. Madame Arnoux was at Chartres with her mother but he would soon be seeing her
again and, in the end, he would become her lover.

Deslauriers, who had been admitted that very day
to the Orsay debating society, had made a speech which
had won great applause. In spite of his normal sobriety
he got drunk, and over dessert he said to Dussardier:

"You're a good man! When I'm rich I shall make you
my steward."

All of them were happy: Cisy was not going to finish
law school; Martinon would pursue his career in the
provinces, where he was to be appointed a deputy prosecutor; Pellerin was getting to work on a large picture
entitled "The Spirit of the Revolution"; Hussonet was to
read the outline of a play to the director of *Délassements*
the following week and fully expected success:

"For," he observed, "everyone admits that I can put a
plot together! I have been around enough to know the
passions inside out; as for witty lines, that's my métier!"

He jumped into the air, landed on his hands, and
walked round the table for a few minutes with his legs
in the air.

This prank did not divert Sénécal. He had just been
thrown out of his school for beating the son of an aristocrat. He blamed his growing poverty on the social order,
cursing the rich; and he poured out his heart to Regim-

bart, who had become more and more disillusioned, saddened, and disgusted. The Citizen was now turning his
attention to economic questions and accused the Camarilla
of throwing away millions in Algeria.*

As Regimbart could not sleep without stopping in at
Alexandre's bar, he took himself off at eleven o'clock.
The others left later, and Frédéric, while saying good-bye
to Hussonnet, learned that Madame Arnoux had been expected back the previous evening.

He therefore went to the coach office to change his seat
to one for the next day and called on Madame Arnoux at
six in the evening. The concierge told him that her return
had been postponed for a month. Frédéric dined alone,
then strolled along the boulevards.

Pink clouds stretched like scarves above the roofs; they
were beginning to roll up the awnings in front of the
shops; the water carts sprinkled their raindrops on the
dust and an unexpected freshness mingled with the odors
from the cafés, through whose half-open doors one could
see, amid the silver plate and gilding, sheaves of flowers
reflected in the tall looking-glasses. The crowd moved
slowly. There were groups of men chatting in the middle
of the sidewalk; and women passed, with soft eyes and
that camellia-like complexion which the lassitude of summer heat lends to the female skin. Some enormous power
enveloped the city and covered the houses. Paris had never
seemed so beautiful to him. Looking into the future he
saw nothing but an unending procession of years brimming with love.

He stopped in front of the Théâtre du Porte-Saint-
Martine to look at the posters and, for want of anything
better to do, bought a ticket.

They were putting on an old charade. The audience
was sparse. The gallery windows cut the daylight into
small blue squares while the footlights merged into a single
line of glowing yellow. The scene, a slave-market in Peking,
complete with little bells, drums, sultanas, and pointed hats,
was delivered in puns. When the curtain fell, he wandered
around the foyer alone and admired a large green landau,
drawn by two gray horses held by a coachman in knee-
breeches, which was standing in the boulevard at the foot
of the steps.

While he was on his way back to his seat, a lady and
gentleman entered the first stage box in the balcony. The
husband had a pale face fringed with a strip of gray

*An allusion to the 1844 campaign against the Moroccans.

beard, the rosette of an officer of the Legion of Honor, and the glacial expression usually attributed to diplomats.

His wife, a good twenty years younger, neither tall nor short, pretty nor ugly, wore her blonde hair in corkscrews like an Englishwoman; her dress had a flat bodice and she carried a large, black lace fan. People of this type attending the theater out of season could only be explained by some accident, or by the boredom of spending the evening tête-à-tête. The lady nibbled at her fan and the gentleman yawned. Frédéric could not remember where he had seen his face before.

While he was crossing a corridor during the next intermission he saw both of them; when he gave them a vague bow, Monsieur Dambreuse, recognizing him, came up and immediately excused himself for his unpardonable negligence. This was an allusion to the innumerable visiting cards sent on Deslauriers' advice. However, he muddled the dates, thinking that Frédéric was in his second year at law school. Then he said that he envied his leaving for the country. He needed a rest himself but business kept him in Paris.

Madame Dambreuse, leaning on his arm, inclined her head slightly; and the agreeable and intelligent expression of her face contrasted with her earlier fretfulness.

"Well, at least we have some delightful entertainments!" she said at her husband's last words. "What a stupid play this is! Don't you agree with me, Monsieur?" And the three of them stood chatting about the theater and the new plays.

Frédéric, used to the grimaces of provincial middle-class women, had never met a woman with such unaffected manners—with that simplicity which is itself a refinement and which the naïve take as an indication of immediate friendship.

They were counting on seeing him as soon as he returned; Monsieur Dambreuse asked him to give his regards to Old Roque.

Frédéric, when he got home, did not fail to tell Deslauriers of this reception.

"Wonderful!" said the clerk, "and don't let your Mamma get around you. Come straight back!"

The day following his arrival, Madame Moreau took her son out into the garden after lunch.

She told him that she was glad he had a profession, for they were not as rich as people believed; their land brought in very little, the farms paid badly; she had even been forced to sell her carriage. Finally, she described their situation.

When she had found herself in difficulties soon after her husband's death, Monsieur Roque, an astute man, had made her loans which he had renewed and prolonged against her wishes. He had suddenly demanded repayment and she had submitted to his terms and sold him the Presles farm at a contemptible price. Ten years later, her capital had disappeared in the failure of a Melun bank. Mortgages horrified her, and she wanted to keep up appearances for the sake of her son's future, so when Old Roque appeared again, she let herself be persuaded a second time. But now she was free of debt. In short, they had an annual income of about ten thousand francs, of which twenty-three hundred belonged to him—his entire inheritance.

"That's impossible!" cried Frédéric.

She nodded her head to indicate that it was very possible.

But his uncle would leave him something?

Nothing could be less certain.

And they circled the garden without speaking. At last she put her arms around him and, in a voice choked with tears, said:

"My poor boy, I have had to give up many dreams!"

He sat down on a bench in the shade of the big acacia.

What she advised him to do was to take a position as a clerk with Monsieur Prouharam, the lawyer, who would sell him his practice; if he made it pay he would be able to resell it and make a good match.

Frédéric was no longer listening. He gazed unseeingly over the fence into the garden opposite.

A little girl of about twelve with red hair was the only person there. She had made herself earrings of rowan berries; her bare shoulders, slightly sunburned, rose out of a gray toile bodice, her white skirt was spotted with jam stains—and her whole person emanated the grace of a young savage, at once supple and high-strung. The presence of a stranger startled her, it seemed, for she stopped short, her watering can in hand, and gave him a piercing look from her clear blue-green eyes.

"It is Monsieur Roque's daughter," said Madame Moreau. "He has just married his servant and legitimized his child."

Chapter Six

Ruined, stripped, finished!

He had remained on the bench stupefied as if by shock. He cursed his fate; he longed to beat somebody, and to add to augmenting his despair, he felt weighed down by a sort of dishonor, a stain on his good name. Frédéric had imagined that his inheritance from his father would one day amount to fifteen thousand francs a year and, indirectly, he had indicated as much to Monsieur and Madame Arnoux. Now he would be put down as a fraud, a rascal, a cheap charlatan who had wormed his way into their lives with some purpose in mind! And Madame Arnoux—how was he to see her again now?

It would be completely impossible, in any case, with an income of only three thousand francs! He could not live forever on the fourth floor, with no servant but the porter, and turn up in cheap black gloves going blue at the tips, a greasy hat, the same coat for a whole year! No! No! Never! But existence without her was intolerable. There were plenty of people who lived comfortably without being rich, Deslauriers among them—and he felt he was ignoble to attach so much importance to such trivial things. Poverty might strengthen his abilities a hundredfold. He grew excited at the thought of all the great men who had worked in garrets. A spirit like Madame Arnoux's would be moved at the spectacle, and she would soften toward him. So this catastrophe would turn out for the best after all; like those earthquakes which expose treasures, it had revealed the secret riches of his own nature to him. But there was only one place in the world where he could make them count: Paris! For to his mind, art, science, and love (the three faces of God, as Pellerin had said) had their sole source in the capital.

That evening he told his mother that he would return there. Madame Moreau was surprised and indignant. It was mad, absurd. He would do better to follow her advice, that is to stay and take a practice near her. Frédéric shrugged his shoulders: —"Please!"—insulted by the suggestion.

Then the good lady tried a different approach. In a tender voice, interspersed with little sobs, she began to speak of her loneliness, her old age, the sacrifices she had made. Now that she was worse off than ever, he was going to abandon her. Then, alluding to her approaching end:

"Have a little patience! You will soon be free!"

These lamentations were renewed twenty times a day for three months and, at the same time, he was being seduced by the comforts of home; he enjoyed his softer bed, the untorn napkins; so that weary, enervated, finally vanquished by the terrible power of indulgence, Frédéric let himself be taken to Monsieur Prouharam's.

Once there he showed neither learning nor aptitude. He had till then been considered a young man of great ability, who would one day be the glory of the district. It was a public disillusionment.

At first he told himself: "I must let Madame Arnoux know," and for a week he devoted much thought to dithyrambic letters and brief notes in a sublime and lapidary style. He was restrained by the fear of exposing his situation. Then it occurred to him that it would be better to write to the husband. Arnoux knew the world and would be able to understand. Finally, after a fortnight's hesitation:

"Bah! I shall never see them again; let them forget me! At least she will not remember me as a failure! She will assume I am dead and miss me—perhaps."

As extravagant resolutions cost him little, he swore never to return to Paris, and even never to inquire after Madame Arnoux.

And yet, he missed even the smell of gas and the racket of the buses. He dreamed over every word she had said to him, the tone of her voice, the light in her eyes—and, regarding himself as a dead man, he no longer did anything at all.

He got up very late and watched the passing wagon teams from his window. The first six months were particularly abominable.

On some days, however, he would be filled with self-disgust. Then he would go out. He walked in the meadows, half covered in winter by floodwater from the Seine. Lines of poplar trees divided them. Small bridges stood here and there. He would wander around till the evening, brushing through the yellow leaves, breathing in the mist, jumping the ditches; as the blood ran more swiftly through his veins a yearning for violent action overcame him; he thought of becoming a trapper in America, taking service with a pasha in the East, signing on as a sailor; and he vented his melancholy in long letters to Deslauriers.

The latter was striving to make his way. His friend's spineless behavior and eternal jeremiads struck him as stupid. Soon their correspondence waned to nothing. Frédéric had given all his furniture to Deslauriers, who had kept on the apartment. His mother asked him about it from time to time. One day he finally admitted his gift, and she was scolding him when a letter arrived.

"What's wrong?" she said. "You're trembling."

"There's nothing the matter with me!" replied Frédéric.

He had just learned from Deslauriers that the latter had taken in Sénécal and they had been living together for the last two weeks. So now Sénécal sat at his ease among the things which had come from Arnoux's shop. He could sell them, make remarks about them, ridicule them. Frédéric was wounded to his very heart. He went up to his room, wishing he were dead.

His mother called him. She wanted to consult him about some planting in the garden.

The garden, modeled on an English park, was divided in two by a wooden fence, and the other half belonged to Old Roque, who also owned a vegetable patch beside the river. The two neighbors, who were not on good terms, refrained from going into the garden at the same time. Since Frédéric's return, however, the old man appeared there more frequently, and spared no effort to be polite to Madame Moreau's son. He commiserated with him on living in a small town. One day he told him that Monsieur Dambreuse had asked after him. Another time he expatiated on the customs of Champagne, where nobility was inherited through the female line:

"In those days you would have been a lord, since your mother's name was de Fouvens. And, whatever they say, a name is worth something. After all," he added, with a cunning look, "it all depends on the Keeper of the Seals."

This interest in the aristocracy was singularly at odds with his appearance. He was small, and his big brown frock coat exaggerated the length of his trunk. When he took off his cap, you noticed that his face was almost feminine, with a very pointed nose; his yellow hair resembled a wig; he greeted everyone with a low bow, staying close to the wall.

Until he was fifty, he had been content with the services of Catherine, a woman from Lorraine of the same age as himself, badly scarred with smallpox. But about 1834 he brought back from Paris a beautiful blonde with a face like a sheep and "the carriage of a queen." She was soon peacocking about in large earrings and everything was explained by the birth of a daughter, registered under the name Élizabeth-Olympe-Louise Roque.

The jealous Catherine expected to detest the child. On the contrary, she adored her. She surrounded her with care, attention, and caresses, so as to supplant her mother and make her odious to the child—an easy task, as Madame Eléonore neglected the little girl completely, preferring to gossip with the tradesmen. As soon as she was married, she went to call at the sub-prefecture, stopped speaking familiarly to the servants, and believed she should demonstrate her status by strictness with her child. She attended her lessons; the tutor, an old bureaucrat from the town hall, had no idea how to teach. The pupil rebelled, was slapped, and went off to sob on the lap of Catherine, who invariably took her part. Then the two women would quarrel. Monsieur Roque imposed silence. He had married out of affection for his daughter and did not want her tormented.

She often wore a ragged white dress with lace-trimmed pantaloons; and on holidays she went out dressed like a princess to show up the bourgeois, who would not let their children play with her because of her illegitimate birth.

She led a solitary existence in her garden, playing on the swing, running after butterflies, then suddenly stopping to watch the beetles settling on the roses. It was probably these habits that made her expression both bold and pensive. Moreover, she so resembled Marthe that Frédéric, the second time they talked, asked her:

"Would you allow me to kiss you, Mademoiselle?"

The little thing lifted her head and answered:

"I'd like it!"

But they were separated by the wooden fence.

"I shall have to climb over," said Frédéric.

"No, lift me up!"

He leaned over the fence and, catching her under the arms, he pickd her up and kissed her on both cheeks, then put her back by the same method, which was repeated at their subsequent encounters.

With no more reserve than a child of four she would run to meet her friend as soon as she heard him coming, or else, hiding behind a tree, she would yap like a dog to startle him.

One day when Madame Moreau was out, he took her up to his mother's room. She opened all the bottles of perfume, poured pomade onto her hair with a lavish hand; then, without the least self-consciousness, she lay down on the bed and stretched out full length, wide awake.

"I'm pretending to be your wife," she said.

Next day he found her in tears. She admitted that she was "weeping for her sins," and when he tried to find out what they were, she replied, with downcast eyes:

"Don't ask anything more!"

It was nearly time for her first communion and she had been taken to confession that morning.

The sacrament had no effect on her behavior. Sometimes she would have terrible fits of rage and they would send for Monsieur Frédéric to calm her.

He often took her with him on his walks. While he walked along, lost in his dreams, she picked poppies on the edge of the wheat fields and, when she noticed that he was more melancholy than usual, she did her best to console him. His heart, starved of love, fell back on this friendship with a child; he drew pictures for her, told her stories, and began reading to her.

He started with the *Annales romantiques,* a collection of verse and prose well known in those days. Then, so taken with her intelligence that he forgot her age, he read *Atala, Cinq-Mars, Les Feuilles d'automne.* But one night (that very evening she had listened to *Macbeth* in Letourneur's simple translation) she woke up screaming, "The spot! The spot!" Her teeth were chattering, she trembled and rubbed her right hand, looking at it in terror and muttering: "There is still a spot!" The doctor finally arrived and advised that she should avoid overexcitement.

The bourgeoisie saw nothing in all this but an unfavorable prognostic for her morals. It was rumored that the "Moreau boy" meant to make her an actress when she was older.

Soon another event occurred—to wit, the arrival of Uncle Bathélemy. Madame Moreau put him in her own bedroom and, in her desire to please, went so far as to serve meat on days of abstinence.

The old man was hardly pleasant. He perpetually compared Le Havre to Nogent, where he found the air heavy, the bread bad, the streets ill-paved, the food undistinguished, and the inhabitants lazy. "How bad business is here!" He censured his late brother's extravagances; whereas he, on the other hand, had amassed an income of twenty-seven thousand francs a year! At the end of a week he finally left and, on the step of the carriage, remarked unreassuringly:

"Well, I'm glad to know you're nicely off."

"You won't get a thing!" said Madame Moreau, on re-entering the drawing room.

He had only come because of her entreaties; and for eight days she had made opportunities for him to confide in her, perhaps too openly. She regretted her behavior and stayed in her armchair, with bowed head and tightly compressed lips. Sitting opposite, Frédéric watched her; and they both kept silent, as they had done five years earlier on his return from Montereau. This parallel occurred to him too and reminded him of Madame Arnoux.

At that moment he heard the crack of a whip under the window and a voice calling him.

It was Old Roque, alone in his van. He was off to La Fortelle, to spend the whole day with Monsieur Dambreuse, and cordially invited Frédéric to accompany him.

"You don't need an invitation if you're with me; don't worry!"

Frédéric was tempted to accept. But how could he explain his permanent residence at Nogent? He had no suitable summer clothes. And finally, what would his mother say? He refused.

From then on their neighbor was less friendly. Louise was growing up; Madame Eléonore fell dangerously ill and the connection came to an end, to the great relief of Madame Moreau, who feared the effect on her son's career of associating with such people.

She dreamed of buying him the post of clerk at the law court; Frédéric did not oppose this idea too vehemently. He now accompanied her to mass and played a few hands of cards in the evenings; he was growing accustomed to provincial life, becoming a part of it—and even his love had taken on a kind of mournful sweetness, a lulling charm. What with continually pouring out his sorrow in letters, mingling it with his reading, with his walks, spreading it everywhere, he had almost exhausted it, so that Madame Arnoux seemed to him like someone who had died, the whereabouts of whose grave he was surprised not to know, so tranquil and resigned had his affection become.

One day, December 12, 1845, about nine o'clock in the morning, the cook brought a letter up to his room. The address was written in large letters in a hand he did not recognize and, being drowsy, he was in no hurry to open it. Finally he read:

> Justice of the Peace, Le Havre, III°
> Monsieur,
> Your uncle, M. Moreau, having
> died intestate . . .

The legacy was his! He jumped out of bed, barefoot and in his nightshirt, as if a fire had suddenly broken out on the other side of the wall: he passed his hand over his face, doubting his eyes, half convinced he was still asleep and, to confirm that this was really happening, threw open the window as far as it would go.

There had been a fall of snow; the roofs were white; he even recognized a washtub in the courtyard over which he had stumbled the previous evening.

He read the letter over three times running. Could it be true? The whole of his uncle's fortune! Twenty-seven thousand livres a year! And he was shaken by a frantic joy at the thought of seeing Madame Arnoux again. With the clarity of a hallucination he saw himself with her, in her home, bringing her some gift wrapped in tissue paper, while his tilbury waited at the door, no, a brougham would be better! A black brougham with a servant in brown livery; he could hear the pawing of his horse, and the chinking of the curb merged with the murmur of their kisses. This would happen every day, endlessly. He would ask them to visit him, at his house; the dining room would be hung with red leather, the boudoir with yellow silk, there would be divans everywhere! And such cabinets, such Chinese vases! Such carpets! The images flashed into his mind with such turbulence that he felt his head spinning. Then he remembered his mother and went downstairs, still holding the letter.

Madame Moreau tried to contain her emotion and fainted. Frédéric held her in his arms and kissed her forehead:

"Dear Mother, now you can buy back your carriage; so laugh, don't cry anymore. Be happy!"

Ten minutes later the news had reached even to the outskirts of the town. Then Monsieur Benoit, Monsieur Gamblin, Monsieur Chambion, all their friends, rushed to see them. Frédéric escaped for a moment to write to Deslauriers. More visitors arrived. The afternoon passed in congratulations in which Roque's wife was forgotten, though she was "very low."

When they were alone together that evening Madame Moreau told her son that she would advise him to establish himself as a lawyer at Troyes. Being better known in his own district than elsewhere it would be easier for him to make a good match there.

"Oh, this is too much!" cried Frédéric.

Hardly had he laid hands on his happiness than they wanted to snatch it away! He declared his explicit resolution to live in Paris.

"What will you do there?"

"Nothing!"

Madame Moreau, surprised by his manner, asked him what he wanted to become.

"A minister!" replied Frédéric.

And he declared that, far from joking, he intended to become a diplomat, that his instincts and training drew him to that career. He would start by joining the Conseil d'État under the auspices of Monsieur Dambreuse.

"Then you know him?"

"Yes, of course! Through Monsieur Roque!"

"How strange," said Madame Moreau.

He had reawakened the old ambitious visions in her heart. She gave herself over to them and did not speak of the alternatives again.

If he had given in to his impatience, Frédéric would have left immediately. The following day all the places on the stagecoach were filled; he fretted until seven o'clock the day after.

They were sitting down to dinner when three strokes sounded from the church bell and the maid came in to announce that Madame Eléonore had just died.

Her death was, after all, a misfortune for no one, not

even for her daughter. The girl would find later that she had only benefited from it.

As the two houses adjoined, they could hear a great commotion and the sound of voices; the idea of the nearby corpse threw a funereal shadow over their parting. Madame Moreau wiped her eyes two or three times. Frédéric's heart was heavy.

After the meal, Catherine caught him as he crossed the hall. Mademoiselle absolutely had to see him. She was waiting for him in the garden. He went out, climbed over the fence and, occasionally bumping into the trees, made his way toward Monsieur Roque's house. There were lights in one of the second-floor windows; then a form emerged from the shadows and a voice whispered:

"It's me."

She seemed taller than usual to him, no doubt because of her black dress. Not knowing how to greet her, he merely took her hands and sighed:

"Oh! My poor Louise."

She made no reply. She looked at him searchingly for a long time. Frédéric was afraid of missing the coach; he thought he heard a rumble of wheels in the distance and, to bring the meeting to an end, he said:

"Catherine told me you had something . . ."

"Yes, that's right. I wanted to tell you . . ."

He was astounded to hear her use the formal mode of address and, as she again fell silent:

"Well, what?"

"I don't know—I can't remember . . . Is it true you're leaving?"

"Yes, in a few minutes."

She repeated:

"In a few minutes? . . . For good? . . . We won't see each other again?"

Her tears choked her.

"Good-bye! Good-bye! Then kiss me!"

And she clutched him passionately.

PART TWO

Chapter One

When he had taken his place in the back of the coupé and the coach began to move, the five horses springing forward all at once, he felt a wild joy flood over him. Like an architect drawing up the plans of a palace, he settled his life in advance. He filled it with luxuries and splendors; it rose up to the sky; a profusion of things appeared to him, and he was so deep in their contemplation that the outside world disappeared.

When they reached the foot of the Sourdun hill he realized where they were. They had come only five kilometers! He was indignant. He let down the window to see the road. He asked the coachman several times exactly when they would arrive. However, he eventually calmed down and sat back in his corner, his eyes open.

The lantern hanging from the postilion's seat lit up the wheel-horses' hindquarters. Beyond them he could see nothing but the manes of the others horses, undulating like white waves; their breath hung like a fog on either side of the team; the iron pole-chains jingled, the windows shook in their frames, and the heavy carriage rolled over the pavement at a steady speed. Here and there, one could pick out the wall of a barn or perhaps a solitary inn. Sometimes, as they passed through a village, a baker's oven would throw out a lurid glow like a burning house and the monstrous silhouette of the horses would be projected onto the opposite wall. At the posting-house, when they had unhitched the team, there was a moment of complete silence. Someone moved about on top, under the tilt, while a woman stood in a doorway, a candle cupped in her hand. Then the driver jumped onto the footboard and the stagecoach set off again.

At Mormans they heard a quarter past one striking. "So it's today," he thought, "this very day, quite soon!"

But little by little his hopes and memories, Nogent, the Rue de Choiseul, Madame Arnoux, his mother, all grew confused in his mind.

He was awakened by the sound of the coach rumbling over planks. They were crossing the Pont de Charenton; they were in Paris. One of his companions then took off his cap and the other his kerchief; they both put on their hats and started chatting. The first, a fat, red-faced man in a velvet frock coat, was a businessman; the second had come to the capital to consult a doctor, and, fearful that he might have cause him some discomfort during the night, Frédéric made a spontaneous apology, such was the softening effect of happiness upon his heart.

The Quai de la Gare must have been flooded, for they kept straight on and found themselves back in the country. Tall factory chimneys smoked in the distance. Then they took a turning in Ivry. They drove up a street and he suddenly caught sight of the dome of the Panthéon.

The plowed-up plain resembled some empty ruin. The enclosing fortifications formed a horizontal ridge; and on the dirt sidewalks bordering the road grew small trees without branches, protected by laths bristling with nails. Chemical factories alternated with lumberyards. Tall gates like those on farms stood ajar, to show squalid courtyards full of filth, with pools of dirty water in the middle. Long red-brown taverns displayed between their first-floor windows two crossed billiard cues encircled by a garland of painted flowers; here and there a half-built plaster shack had been abandoned. Then the double row of houses became continuous, with an occasional gigantic tin cigar standing out from their blank facades to mark a tobacco shop. The midwives' signs depicted a matron in a bonnet dandling a baby in a lace-trimmed wrap. The walls at the street corners were covered with tattered posters that trembled like rags in the wind. They passed workmen in their smocks, brewers' drays, laundry carts, butchers' vans; there was a fine rain falling, it was cold, and the sky was pale, but two eyes which meant as much to him as the sun shone beyond the haze.

The gateway to Paris was blocked by poultry vendors, waggoners, and a flock of sheep, so they had to wait a long time. The sentry, his hood thrown back, walked to and fro in front of his box to keep warm. The toll collector climbed onto the roof of the coach and a fanfare of cornets sounded. They descended the boulevard at a spanking trot, the swing-bars threshing, the traces streaming. The long whip's lash cracked in the damp air. At the driver's ringing cry: "Make way! Make way! Hey!" the sweepers stood aside, the pedestrians jumped back; mud splashed on the windows, they passed dust carts, cabriolets, omnibuses. Finally they saw the railings of the Jardin des Plantes.

The yellowish Seine was almost touching the arches of the bridges. A breath of freshness came from it. Frédéric drew it deep into his lungs, savoring the good Parisian air, which seems to contain amorous effluvia and intellectual emanations; his heart leaped when he saw the first cab. His affection extended even to the straw-strewn thresholds of the wine shops, the shoeblacks with their boxes, the grocers' boys shaking their coffee-roasters. Women trotted past beneath their umbrellas, and he leaned forward to see their faces; some chance might have brought Madame Arnoux out.

The shops slid past, the crowd became denser, the noise grew louder. After the Quai Saint-Bernard, the Quai de la Tournelle, and the Quai Montebello, they went down the Quai Napoléon; he tried to see his windows but they were a long way off. Then they recrossed the Seine by the Pont-Neuf, went down as far as the Louvre and then by way of the Rue Saint-Honoré, Rue Croix-des-Petits-Champs, and Rue du Bouloi, they reached the Rue Coq-Héron, where they drew up in the courtyard of the hotel.

Frédéric dressed as slowly as possible so as to prolong his pleasure, and even went so far as to walk on foot to the Boulevard Montmartre; he smiled to himself at the idea of shortly seeing once more the marble plaque inscribed with the cherished name. He raised his eyes. No more show windows, no pictures, nothing!

He rushed to the Rue de Choiseul. Monsieur and Madame Arnoux did not live there and a neighbor was tending the lodge; Frédéric waited for the porter; finally he arrived, but it was a different man. He had no idea of their address.

Frédéric went to a café and, while he ate, consulted a business directory. There were three hundred Arnoux's, but no Jacques Arnoux! Where could they be living then? Pellerin must know.

He went to his studio, at the top of the Faubourg

Poissonnière. There was neither a knocker nor a bell, so he hammered on the door with his fist, called out, shouted. Silence was his only answer.

Next he thought of Hussonnet. But where would you find a man like that? He had once accompanied him to his mistress's house in the Rue de Fleurus. Having arrived at the Rue de Fleurus, Frédéric realized that he did not know the young lady's name.

He tried the Prefecture of Police. He wandered from staircase to staircase, from office to office. The information bureau was closing. He was told to come back the next day.

Then he visited all the art dealers he could find, to see if they knew anything about Arnoux. Monsieur Arnoux was no longer in business.

Finally, discouraged, worried, ill, he returned to his hotel and went to bed. As he stretched out between the sheets he was struck by an idea that made him start with joy:

"Regimbart! What a fool I am not to have thought of him earlier!"

At seven the next morning, he arrived in front of a grog shop in the Rue Nôtre-Dame-des-Victoires where Regimbart habitually took a glass of white wine. It was not yet open; he walked around the neighborhood for half an hour, then returned. Regimbart had just left. Frédéric dashed into the street. He even thought he saw his hat in the distance, but a hearse and the cortège of carriages came between them. When the jam cleared, the vision had disappeared.

Luckily he remembered that the Citizen lunched every day at precisely eleven o'clock at a little restaurant in the Place Gaillon. It was only a matter of patience, and, after an interminable stroll from the Bourse to the Madeleine, and the Madeleine to the Gymnase, Frédéric entered the restaurant at exactly eleven o'clock, certain that he would find his Regimbart there.

"Don't know him!" said the cook-shopkeeper haughtily.

Frédéric persisted; he replied:

"I no longer know him, Monsieur!" arching his eyebrows majestically and wagging his head in a manner which betrayed some mystery.

But the Citizen had spoken of Alexandre's bar at their last meeting. Frédéric swallowed a roll and, jumping into a cab, asked the driver if, somewhere on the heights of Sainte-Geneviève, there was not a certain café Alexandre.

The cabbie drove him to an establishment of that name in the Rue des Francs-Bourgeois-Saint-Michel and, in response to his inquiry: "Monsieur Regimbart, please?" the proprietor answered with an ingratiating smile:

"He has not been in yet, Monsieur," throwing a glance of complicity to his wife, seated behind the cash desk.

Then immediately, turning toward the clock:

"But he will be arriving, I hope, in the next ten minutes, a quarter of an hour at the most—Célestin, bring the papers, quick! What would Monsieur like to drink?"

Although he had no desire to drink anything, Frédéric swallowed a glass of rum, then a kirsch, then a curaçao, then different grogs, some hot, some cold. He read and reread the whole of that day's *Siècle;* he examined the caricature in *Charivari* till he knew the very grains of the paper; in the end he could have recited the advertisements from memory. From time to time he would hear footsteps on the sidewalk: it was he! Someone's profile would appear outside the window-pane, but it always passed by.

To relieve his boredom, Frédéric shifted from place to place; he went and sat at the back of the room, then on the right, then on the left, and finally he stayed in the center of the banquette, his arms spread out on either side. But a cat, padding delicately over the velvet on the back of the seat, startled him by suddenly leaping to lick the splashes of syrup on the tray; and the proprietor's child, an intolerable brat of four, played with a rattle on the steps of the cash desk. Its mother, a pale little woman with bad teeth, smiled stupidly. What could have happened to Regimbart? Frédéric waited, sunk in unfathomable gloom.

Rain rattled like hail on the hood of his cab. When he drew back the muslin curtain he could see the wretched horse standing in the street, as motionless as if he were carved of wood. The enormously swollen stream of water in the gutter ran between two spokes of the wheels and the driver dozed in the shelter of the cover but, fearful that his fare might slip away, he half-opened the café door from time to time, streaming with water—and, if objects could be worn down by looks, the clock would have dissolved under Frédéric's steady gaze. It ticked on however. Master Alexandre walked up and down repeating: "He'll be along. I'm sure he'll be along!" and, to distract Frédéric, he started a conversation, discussed politics. His desire to please even led him to suggest a game of dominos.

Finally, at half-past four, Frédéric, who had been there since noon, jumped up and declared that he would wait no longer.

"I can't understand it myself," responded the café owner with an ingenuous air. "It's the first time Monsieur Ledoux has missed!"

"What do you mean, Monsieur Ledoux?"

"That's right, Monsieur!"

"I said Regimbart!" cried the exasperated Frédéric.

"Oh, I'm very sorry, you're mistaken! —Isn't that right, Madame Alexandre, didn't Monsieur say Monsieur Ledoux?"

And, appealing to the waiter:

"You must have heard what I did?"

But, probably to avenge himself on his master, the waiter merely smiled.

Frédéric had taken himself back to the boulevards, indignant at the loss of time, furious with the Citizen, imploring his presence like that of a god, and resolute in his determination to extract him from the depths of the furthermost cellar. His carriage annoyed him, so he sent it away; his thoughts tumbled in confusion; then the name of every café he had heard that imbecile mention flashed into his mind at once, like the thousand components of a fireworks display: café Gascard, café Grimbert, café Halbourt, estaminet Bordelais, Havanai, Havrais, Boeuf-à-la-mode, brasserie Allemande, Mère Morel, and he repaired to each of them in turn. But at one Regimbart had just left, at another he might be coming, at a third he had not been seen for six months, somewhere else he had ordered a leg of lamb yesterday for Saturday. Finally, at Vautier's coffeehouse, he bumped into a waiter as he opened the door:

"Do you know Monsieur Regimbart?"

"What do you mean, do I know him, Monsieur? It is I who have the honor of waiting on him. He is upstairs; he has just finished dinner."

And the proprietor himself came up, a napkin over one arm:

"You were asking for Monsieur Regimbart, Monsieur? He was here a moment ago."

Frédéric swore, but the coffeehouse keeper assured him that he would undoubtedly find his quarry at Bouttevilain's:

"I give you my word of honor! He left a little earlier than usual because he had a business appointment with some gentlemen. But I repeat that you will find him at Bouttevilain's on Rue Saint-Martin, number ninety-two, second staircase on the left, at the far end of the courtyard, the mezzanine, the door on the right!"

At last he saw him through the pipe smoke, alone, in the back bar next to the billiard room, a glass in front of him, his chin sunk on his chest in an attitude of meditation.

"Ah, I've been looking for *you* for a long time!"

Regimbart held out two fingers only, with no display of emotion, and, as if he had seen him the day before, let fall several insignificant remarks on the opening of the parliamentary session.

Frédéric interrupted, asking, as naturally as he could: "Is Arnoux well?"

The answer came slowly; Regimbart was gargling with his liquor.

"Yes, not bad."

"Where does he live now?"

"But . . . Rue Paradis-Poissonnière," replied the Citizen, astonished.

"What number?"

"Thirty-seven. My word, you are strange!"

Frédéric got up.

"What, are you leaving?"

"Yes, yes, I've got an errand, something I'd forgotten. Good-bye!"

Frédéric traversed the distance from the tavern to Arnoux's as if borne by a soft wind, with the extraordinary ease of actions in dreams.

He soon found himself on a second-floor landing in front of a door whose bell was ringing; a maid appeared, a second door opened; Madame Arnoux was sitting near the fire. Arnoux jumped up and embraced him. She had a little boy of about three on her knee; her daughter, now as tall as she, stood on the other side of the fireplace.

"Allow me to introduce you to this gentleman," said Arnoux, taking his son by the armpits.

And for several minutes he amused himself by throwing him up into the air as high as he could and catching him at arm's length.

"You'll kill him! Oh, goodness, do stop!" cried Madame Arnoux.

But Arnoux, swearing that it was quite safe, continued

and even lisped out endearments in the dialect of Marseilles, his native tongue: "There you go, that's my boy!" Then he asked Frédéric why he had not written for such a long time, what on earth he could have been doing down there, what brought him back!

"As for me, I sell chinaware now. But tell us about you."

Frédéric adduced a long lawsuit, his mother's health; he emphasized this to make himself interesting. In short, he had come to Paris for good this time; he said nothing about his inheritance, for fear of betraying his past.

The curtains and upholstery were in dark brown wool damask; two pillows lay side by side against the bolster; a kettle simmered on the coals; and the shade over the lamp, which stood on the edge of the bureau, made the room gloomy. Madame Arnoux was wearing a dark blue merino dressing gown. Her eyes on the embers and one hand on the little boy's shoulder, she undid the laces of his vest with the other. The brat, in his shirt, cried as he scratched his head, just like Monsieur Alexandre, Jr.

Frédéric had expected paroxysms of joy—but passions are enfeebled by a change of location and, not finding Madame Arnoux in the surroundings where he had originally known her, she seemed to him to have lost something, to be somehow degraded, in fact not to be the same. He was astounded at the calm of his emotions. He inquired after the old friends, Pellerin among others.

"I don't see him very often," said Arnoux.

She added:

"We don't entertain as we used to!"

Was this a warning that he would not be invited? But Arnoux continued to be cordial, and reproached him for not having come to dinner with them on the spur of the moment. He explained why he had changed businesses:

"What can you do in a decadent time like ours? Great painting is unfashionable! Anyhow, you can introduce art anywhere. You know how I love Beauty! One of these days I must take you out to my factory."

And he wanted to show him some of its products at once, in his shop on the mezzanine.

The floor was covered with dishes, soup tureens, plates, and basins. Leaning against the walls were large square tiles for bathrooms and lavatories, decorated with mythological subjects in Renaissance style, while in the middle of the room a double set of shelves, reaching to the ceiling, held pots intended for ice, flower vases, candelabras, little jardinières, and large polychrome statuettes of blackamoors or Pompadour shepherdesses. Arnoux's tour bored Frédéric, who was cold and hungry.

He hurried to the café Anglais and had a magnificent supper, saying to himself as he ate:

"What an idiot I was, back home, with my aching heart! She hardly recognized me! What a bourgeoise!"

And, in a sudden surge of healthiness, he resolved to live for himself. He felt that his heart was as hard as the table under his elbows. So now he could throw himself fearlessly into society. The thought of the Dambreuses occurred to him; he would make use of them. Then he remembered Deslauriers: "Oh, what a nuisance!" However, he sent him a note by messenger arranging to meet at the Palais-Royal the following day, for lunch together.

Fortune had not smiled so sweetly on Deslauriers.

He had entered the competitive examination for a fellowship with a thesis on "the rights of testamentary disposition," wherein he had argued that they should be restricted as far as possible and, when his opponent provoked him into making stupid remarks, he had made a great many without the examiners flinching. Then, luck had it that he drew "the Statute of Limitations" as the subject of his extemporaneous lecture. At this point Deslauriers had voiced some deplorable theories; ancient litigation should be dealt with on the same basis as new; why should an owner be deprived of his property because he could not furnish proof of title until thirty-one years had elapsed? This was to hand over an honest man's security to the heir of a successful thief. All kinds of injustices were enshrined by the extension of this right, which was tyrannous, an abuse of force! He had even cried:

"Abolish it and the Franks will no longer oppress the Gauls, the English the Irish, the Yankees the Red-Skins, the Turks the Arabs, the whites the blacks, Poland . . ."

The President had interrupted him:

"All right! All right! We are not concerned with your political opinions, Monsieur! You can present yourself again later!"

Deslauriers had chosen not to present himself again. But that accursed Title XX of the third book of the civil code had become a mountainous stumbling block as far as he was concerned. He was drafting a great work on "The Statute of Limitations, considered as the Base of the Civil and Natural Rights of Peoples"; and he had plunged into Dunod, Rogérius, Balbus, Merlin, Vazeille, Savigny, Troplong, and other lengthy studies. So as to have more time to devote to it, he had given up his job as chief clerk. He lived by giving private lessons and writing theses; and, at sessions of the legal debating society, his virulence frightened the conservatives, all the doctrinaire sons of Professor Guizot—so that in certain circles he had attained a kind of celebrity tinged with a little mistrust.

He arrived at the rendezvous in a thick overcoat lined with red flannel, like the one Sénécal used to wear.

Out of respect for the sensibilities of the passersby they cut short their embraces; and they went off arm in arm to chez Véfour, chuckling with pleasure but each with a tear in the corner of his eye. As soon as they were alone, Deslauriers cried:

"By God, we're going to have a fine time now!"

Frédéric was far from pleased by Deslauriers' way of immediately associating himself with his fortune. His friend displayed too much pleasure for the both of them, and not enough for Frédéric alone.

Afterwards Deslauriers told Frédéric about his failure and, little by little, about his work, his existence, speaking stoically of himself and bitterly of others. Nothing pleased him. There was not a man in office who was not a rogue or a cretin. He let fly at the waiter because a glass had not been properly washed and, to Frédéric's mild reproaches, he replied:

"As if I should worry about fellows like that, who earn up to six or eight thousand francs a year; they've got the vote! They can probably even stand for election! Oh no!"

Then, playfully:

"But I forget that I'm speaking to a capitalist, to a Mondor—for you are a Mondor now!"

And, returning to the subject of the inheritance, he expressed the view that collateral succession (in itself unjust, although he was delighted by this instance of it) would be abolished one of these days, in the forthcoming revolution.

"You think it will come?" said Frédéric.

"You can count on it!" replied the other. "Things can't go on like this! There is too much suffering! When I see men like Sénécal living in poverty . . ."

"Still Sénécal!" thought Frédéric.

"Well, what other news do you have? Are you still in love with Madame Arnoux? That's over, eh?"

Frédéric, not knowing how to answer, closed his eyes and bowed his head.

With regard to Arnoux, he learned from Deslauriers that his paper now belonged to Hussonnet, who had transformed it. It was entitled *"Art,* a literary institution incorporated in shares of one hundred francs each; company capital: forty thousand francs," each shareholder having the right to submit his copy; for "the aim of the company is to publish work by beginners, to protect talent, perhaps genius, from those painful crises which overwhelm, etc. . . ." You know the game! Something, however could be done; the tone of the journal could be raised, then, suddenly, keeping the same editors and promising to keep up the serial, they could serve up a political paper to the subscribers. It would not require an enormous amount.

"Well, what do you think? Do you want to take it on?"

Frédéric did not turn the proposition down. But he would have to wait for the settlement of his affairs.

"Then, if you need anything . . ."

"No thank you, old boy!" said Deslauriers.

Then they smoked cheroots, their elbows on the velvet windowsill. The sun shone, the air was warm, flocks of birds flew down and lit in the garden, the rain-washed bronze and marble statues shone; maids in aprons gossiped on the chairs; they could hear the laughter of children and the continuous murmur from the fountain.

Deslauriers' bitterness had made Frédéric uneasy, but under the influence of the wine circulating in his veins, half asleep, torpid, with the light beating full on his face, he felt nothing but an immense sense of well-being, a voluptuous stupidity, like a plant saturated with warmth and moisture. Deslauriers gazed vaguely into the distance through half-shut eyelids. His chest swelled and he said:

"Oh, how much nobler were the days when Camille Desmoulins, standing on a table over there, urged the people on to the Bastille! A man was *alive* in those days, he could assert himself, show his worth. Simple lawyers gave orders to generals, beggars conquered kings, while nowadays . . ."

He fell silent, then, suddenly:

"Bah! The future will bring great things!"

And, drumming out the charge on the windowpane, he declaimed Barthélemy's lines:

That the terrible Assembly will appear
once again,
That after forty years still sets you trembling—
A Colossus striding forth fearless.

"I've forgotten the rest! But it's getting late, shall we leave?"

And he continued to expound his theories in the street.

Frédéric, who was not listening, watched the show windows for fabrics and furniture for his new house, and it may have been the thought of Madame Arnoux that made him stop in front of three faïence dishes in the window of a curiosity shop. They were decorated in yellow arabesques with metallic glints and cost a hundred écus each. He had them put aside.

"If I were in your position," said Deslauriers, "I would buy silver," by this taste for the luxurious revealing the man of mean origins.

As soon as he was alone, Frédéric went to the famous Pomadère, where he ordered three pairs of trousers, two coats, a fur pelisse, and five waistcoats; then he visited a bootmaker's, a shirtmaker's, a hatter's, leaving instructions everywhere to have his purchases ready as soon as possible.

Three days later, on his return from Le Havre in the evening, he found that his complete wardrobe had arrived and, impatient to make use of it, he determined to visit the Dambreuses immediately. But it was too early, barely eight o'clock.

"Suppose I went to see the others?" he said to himself.

Arnoux was alone, shaving himself in front of his mirror. He suggested taking Frédéric to a place where he would enjoy himself and, when Monsieur Dambreuse was mentioned:

"Oh, all the better! You'll see some of his friends there. Come along! It will be fun."

Frédéric made his excuses. Madame Arnoux recognized his voice and greeted him through the partition, for her daughter was unwell, she herself was ailing, and they could hear the clink of a spoon on a glass and all the rustling of things being gently moved about that comes from a sickroom. Then Arnoux disappeared to say good-bye to his wife. He piled one excuse on another:

"You know it's important! I must go, I have business there and they are expecting me."

"Go, go, my dear. Have a good time!"

Arnoux hailed a cab.

"Palais-Royal! Galerie Montpensier, seven."

And, sinking back into the cushions:

"Oh, I'm dying of exhaustion, old man! Anyhow, I can certainly tell *you*."

He leaned forward and whispered mysteriously into his ear:

"I'm trying to rediscover the copper red the Chinese used."

And he explained about glaze and slow-firing.

When they reached Chevet's, he was given a large basket which he had taken out to the cab. Then he chose grapes, pineapples, and other delicacies for "his poor wife" and asked that they should be delivered early the following morning.

Next they went to a costumier, for they were on their way to a ball. Arnoux chose a pair of blue velvet breeches, a jacket in the same material, and a red wig; Frédéric a domino; and they alighted from their cab in the Rue de Laval, in front of a house whose second story was decorated with colored lanterns.

From the foot of the stairs they could hear the sound of violins.

"Where the devil are you taking me?" asked Frédéric.

"To call on a nice girl! Don't be frightened!"

A page opened the door for them and they entered a hall whose chairs were heaped with overcoats, cloaks, and shawls. A young woman in the costume of a Louis XV dragoon was crossing it at that moment. This was Mademoiselle Rose-Annette Bron, the mistress of the place.

"Well?" said Arnoux.

"It's all arranged!" she replied.

"Ah! Thank you, my angel!"

And he tried to embrace her.

"Be careful, you idiot, you'll spoil my makeup!"

Arnoux introduced Frédéric.

"Go right in, Monsieur! You're very welcome!"

She thrust aside a door-curtain behind her and shouted bombastically:

"Messire Arnoux, the scullion, and one of his princely friends!"

At first Frédéric was dazzled by the lights; he could see nothing but silks, velvets, bare shoulders, a mass of colors that swayed to the sound of a band hidden behind some plants, between walls hung in yellow silk with pastel portraits here and there and crystal sconces in the Louis XVI style. Tall lamps, whose frosted globes resembled snowballs, overhung baskets of flowers on the tables in the corners and, opposite, beyond a smaller second room, a bed with twisted columns and a Venetian looking-glass at its head could be glimpsed in a third.

The music stopped and there was a joyful hubbub of applause at the sight of Arnoux advancing with his basket on his head.

"Watch out for the chandelier!"

Frédéric looked up; it was the antique Dresden chandelier that used to hang in the "L'Art Industriel" shop: memories of the old days flooded into his mind; but a line-infantryman, in undress uniform and with the half-witted look traditionally ascribed to conscripts, took a stance before him, throwing wide his arms to show his astonishment. And despite the appalling black moustaches, with their exaggerated points that disfigured him, Frédéric recognized his old friend Hussonnet. The bohemian overwhelmed him with congratulations in a half-Alsatian, half-Negro gibberish, addressing him as "Colonel." Frédéric, abashed before all these people, could think of no response. There was a rap of a fiddlestick on a music stand and the dancers took their places.

There were about sixty of them, most of the women being dressed as villagers or marquises. The men, who were nearly all elderly, were attired as waggoners, stevedores, or sailors.

Frédéric, who had placed himself against the wall, watched the quadrille before him.

An elderly beau dressed in a long purple silk gown, like a Venetian Doge, was dancing with Mademoiselle Rosanette, who wore a green coat, knitted breeches, and soft leather boots with golden spurs. The couple opposite consisted of an Albanian hung with scimitars and a blue-eyed Swiss Girl, white as milk, plump as a quail, in a long-sleeved shirt and a red bodice. A big blonde dancer from the Opéra had got herself up as a Savage to draw attention to her hair, which fell to her knees; she wore nothing over her brown tights but a leather loincloth, some glass bracelets, and a tinsel diadem from which there rose a tall sheaf of peacock feathers. In front of her a Pritchard,* rigged out in a grotesquely large black coat, beat time with his elbow on his snuffbox. A little Watteau Shepherd, in moonlight shades of blue and silver,

*See note page 33.

struck his crook against the thyrsus of a grape-crowned Bacchante wearing a leopard skin over her left shoulder and gold-laced buskins. On the other side, a Polish Woman in a spencer of orange velvet swung a gauze petticoat over pearl-gray stockings that disappeared into short pink boots hooped with white fur. She was smiling at a pot-bellied quadragenarian disguised as a Choirboy, who was leaping high in the air, lifting up his surplice with one hand and holding onto his red skullcap with the other. But the queen, the star, was Mademoiselle Loulou, the famous dancer who performed at the public balls. She was rich now, so she wore a broad lace collar over her plain black velvet jacket; and her wide, flame-colored silk trousers, tight across the buttocks and tied at the waist with a cashmere scarf, had small fresh white gardenias all down the seams. Her pale puffy face, with its retroussé nose, was rendered still saucier by the disorder of her wig, and a man's gray felt hat clapped into place over her right ear; when she jumped her diamond-buckled pumps almost reached the nose of her neighbor, a big medieval Baron much hampered by his iron armor. There was also an Angel, a golden sword in her hand, two swan's wings on her back who, not having the faintest comprehension of the figures of the dance, moved back and forth, forever losing touch with her partner, a Louis XIV, and snarling up the set.

Frédéric, looking at these people, felt neglected and ill at ease. He was still thinking of Madame Arnoux and he felt he was taking part in some hostile plot aimed at her.

When the quadrille had finished Mademoiselle Rosanette came up to him. She was panting a little, and her collar plate, as polished as a mirror, rose and fell gently beneath her chin.

"What about you, Monsieur?" she said. "You're not dancing?"

Frédéric made his excuses; he did not know how to dance.

"Really? But with me? Are you quite sure?"

And she looked at him for a moment, all her weight on one foot, the other drawn slightly back, caressing her mother-of-pearl sword-hilt with her left hand, her manner half-supplicant, half-jeering. Finally she said "Good night!" pirouetted, and disappeared.

Frédéric, dissatisfied with himself and not knowing what to do, began wandering about the house.

He went into the boudoir, which was quilted in pale
blue silk with bouquets of wild flowers; on the ceiling,
in a circular frame of gilded wood, Cupids, emerging
from an azure sky and frolicking on clouds like down
cushions. All these elegant touches, which would be mere
trifles to one of Rosanette's modern counterparts, dazzled
him and he admired it all: the artificial convolvulus around
the edge of the mirror, the curtained fireplace, the Turkish divan and, in an alcove, a sort of white muslin tent
lined with pink silk. The bedroom furniture was black
with brass marquetry; the great bed, with its canopy and
ostrich plumes, stood on a platform covered with swans
skin. Pins with jeweled heads stuck into pincushions,
rings lying about on trays, gold-rimmed lockets and silver
caskets could be distinguished in the dim light coming
from a Bohemian urn which hung from three chains.
A small door stood ajar on a winter garden that filled
the entire width of a terrace with an aviary at the
farther end.

The whole establishment had certainly been designed
to please. In a sudden surge of youthful feeling, he determined to take advantage of it; he took heart and returned to the drawing room door. There were more people now and everyone moved in a kind of luminous haze;
he stood watching the quadrilles, blinking to see better
and breathing in the soft scent of women that spread
on the air like an enormous diffused kiss.

But near him, on the other side of the doorway, stood
Pellerin—Pellerin in full evening dress, his left hand in
the bosom of his coat, and holding his hat and a torn
white glove in his right.

"Hullo, it's a long time since we've seen you! Where
the devil have you been? traveling? in Italy? Hackneyed,
Italy, isn't it? not as exciting as they say? Anyway, come
and bring me your sketches one of these days."

And, without waiting for an answer, the artist began
talking about himself.

He had made great progress, having definitely recognized the stupidity of Line. We should be less concerned
with Beauty and Unity in a work, more with the character and diversity of things.

"For everything exists in nature, so everything is
legitimate, everything is paintable. It's just a question of
striking the right note! I've discovered the secret." And,
giving him a nudge with his elbow, he repeated several
times: "I've discovered the secret, you see! For instance

look at that little woman in a sphinx headdress dancing with a Russian Postilion; sharp, dry, definite, all flat surfaces and crude colors. Indigo under the eyes, a patch of cinnabar on the cheek, bistre on the temples—pif! paf!" and he sketched brushstrokes in the air with his thumb. "While that fat one over there," he continued—pointing to a Fishwife in a cherry-red dress with a gold cross around her neck and a knotted linen kerchief hanging down her back—"she's all curves; the nostrils are flared like the wings of her bonnet, the mouth turns up at the corners, the chin droops; it's all lush, melting, abundant, calm and sunny, a real Rubens! Yet they are both perfect! Then what's the ideal?" He was becoming heated. "What is a beautiful woman? What is beauty? Ah, beauty! you'll say . . ." Frédéric interrupted him to ask about a Pierrot with a profile like a billy goat, who was giving his benediction to all the dancers in the midst of a quadrille.

"No one of any interest! A widower, the father of three boys. He leaves them in rags, spends his time at the club, and sleeps with the maid."

"And the one dressed as a Bailiff, talking to the Pompadour Marquise over in the window recess?"

"The Marquise is Madame Vandael, who used to be an actress at the Gymnase; she is the mistress of the Doge, the Comte de Palazot. They've been together for twenty years now; nobody can understand why. What beautiful eyes that woman had once! As for the man next to her, they call him Captain d'Herbigny, an old soldier whose only fortune is his Legion of Honor and his pension. He plays uncle to the good-time girls on solemn occasions, arranges duels, and dines out."

"A rogue?" asked Frédéric.

"No! A good man!"

"Oh!"

The artist pointed out other people; then, noticing a man wearing a long robe of black serge like one of Molière's Doctors but wide open from top to bottom to show off the trinkets on his watch chain:

"There you have Doctor Des Rogis, who is furious at not being famous, the author of a book of medical pornography, an assiduous boot-licker, discreet; these ladies adore him. He and his wife (that thin Châtelaine in a gray dress) trail around together in all sorts of places, public and otherwise. In spite of the impoverished state

of their household they have an 'at home' day—artistic
teas where they recite poetry—watch out!"

Indeed the Doctor was approaching, and soon the
three of them were gossiping in a group at the entrance
of the drawing room. They were joined by Hussonnet
and then by the Lady Savage's lover, a young poet whose
short François I mantle revealed a puny anatomy, and
finally by a witty young man disguised as a Turkish Pedlar.
But his yellow-braided jacket had seen the world from
the back of so many traveling dentists, the red of his large
pleated trousers was so faded, his turban, twisted like
a grilled eel, was so shabby, in fact his whole costume
was so hideous and authentic that the women did not
hide their disgust. The Doctor consoled him by praising
his mistress, a Stevedore. This Turk was the son of a
banker.

In the interval between two quadrilles, Rosanette went
over to the fireplace, where a fat, elderly little man in a
brown coat with gold buttons was installed in an armchair. Despite his withered cheeks dropping over his high
white cravat, his hair was still blond and curled naturally like a poodle's coat, which gave him a sprightly air.

She bent over and listened to him. Then she brought
him a glass of cordial; and nothing could have been prettier than her hands under their lace cuffs, beneath the
sleeves of her green coat. When the old man had finished his drink he kissed them.

"But it's Monsieur Oudry, Arnoux's neighbor!"

"Ex-neighbor!" said Pellerin with a laugh.

"What?"

A Postilion from Longjumeau* put his arm around
her waist as a waltz started. All the women sitting
on the padded benches around the room jumped up, one
after the other, and their skirts, sashes, and headdresses
began to revolve.

They passed so close to him that Frédéric could see
the beads of moisture on their foreheads; and this gyra-
tory movement which grew steadily faster and more regular, producing a kind of intoxication in his thoughts, evoked
other images; as they all spun past in the same dizzy
fashion, each one aroused a separate excitement according to her type of beauty. The Polish Woman, languour-
ously given up to the dance, inspired him with a longing

---

*A man dressed as the hero of Adam's operetta *Le Postillon de
Longjumeau*.

to press her to his heart as they drove in a sleigh over a snow-covered plain. The Swiss Girl waltzed with downcast eyes and erect body, and prospects of peaceful delight in a lakeside chalet spread before her feet. Then the Bacchante, her brown head thrown back, suddenly turned his thoughts to devouring caresses in oleander woods in a ranging storm, to the confused sound of tambourines. The Fishwife, out of breath from dancing too fast, was laughing; he would have liked to drink with her at Porcherons and rumple her kerchief with both hands, as they did in the good old days. But the Stevedore's nimble toes scarcely brushed the floor—the suppleness of her limbs and the gravity of her face seemed to embody all the refinements of modern love, which has the exactitude of a science and the mobility of a bird. Rosanette revolved with her hand on her hip, her knotted wig bouncing on her collar and scattering orris-root powder about her, and at every turn she just missed Frédéric with the tips of her golden spurs.

With the last strains of the waltz, Mademoiselle Vatnaz appeared. She had an Algerian kerchief on her head, a string of piastres across her forehead, antimony around her eyes, and a sort of loose, black cashmere coat over a light-colored skirt of silver lamé; she carried a tambourine in her hand.

Behind her walked a tall young man in classical Dante costume who was (she no longer tried to conceal it) the former singer at the Alhambra who, born Auguste Delamare, had originally called himself Anténor Dellamarre, then Delmas, then Belmar, and finally Delmar, thus adjusting and perfecting his name to match his growing fame; for he had left the dance halls for the theater and had just made a spectacular debut in *Gaspardo le Pêcheur* at the Ambigu.

Hussonnet scowled at the sight of him. Since the rejection of his play he detested actors. The conceit of those fellows was inconceivable—and this one was the worst of all others!

"What a poseur! Look at him!"

After a sketchy salutation to Rosanette, Delmar leaned against the mantelpiece and stood motionless, one hand on his heart, his left foot advanced, his eyes cast up toward heaven, his gilded laurel wreath over his hood, putting as much poetry as he could into his gaze, to fascinate the ladies. People were coming from all over the room to make a large circle around him.

La Vatnaz, however, when she had bestowed a prolonged embrace on Rosanette, came over to ask Hussonnet if he would look over the style of an educational book she wanted to publish: *A Bouquet for Young Ladies,* a collection of moral and literary pieces. The man of letters promised his help. She next asked if he could not promote her friend a little in one of the papers he wrote for, and even give him a part in one of his plays later on. Hussonnet was so startled by this that he forgot to take a glass of punch.

Arnoux had made it and, now, followed by the count's page carrying an empty tray, he was handing it round with some self-satisfaction.

When he reached Monsieur Oudry, Rosanette stopped him.

"We have some business, I think?"

He blushed a little, speaking to the old man:

"Our friend told me you would be kind enough . . ."

"Certainly, neighbor! At your service!"

And Monsieur Dambreuse's name was mentioned: they were speaking softly and Frédéric could only hear them indistinctly. He moved toward the other side of the fireplace where Rosanette and Delmar were chatting together.

The actor had a vulgar look about him, like stage scenery designed to be seen from a distance: coarse hands, large feet, and a heavy jaw. He denigrated the most celebrated actors, condescended to the poets, talked about "my voice," "my physique," "my talents," studding his discourse with words he liked but misunderstood such as "morbidezza," "analogous," and "homogeneity."

Rosanette listened to him with little nods of approbation. Her cheeks were bright with admiration beneath the rouge; and a moist look veiled her pale eyes, with their indefinable color. How could a man of that type charm her? Frédéric made an inward effort to despise him more than ever, perhaps in order to banish the kind of envy that he felt for him.

Mademoiselle Vatnaz was with Arnoux now and, though she was laughing very loudly, from time to time she glanced toward Rosanette; Monsieur Oudry never took his eyes off her.

Then Arnoux and La Vatnaz disappeared; the old man came up and spoke softly to Rosanette.

"All right, it's settled. Leave me alone!"

And she asked Frédéric to go and see if Monsieur Arnoux was in the kitchen.

A battalion of half-empty glasses covered the floor; and the casseroles, pots, turbot-kettle, and frying pan were all bubbling on the stove. Arnoux was issuing orders to the servants, addressing them in a familiar way, beating up the rémoulade, tasting the sauces, joking with the maid.

"Good," he said. "Tell her I'm ready to serve dinner."

The dancing had stopped, the women had just taken their seats, and the men were strolling about. In the middle of the room a curtain drawn across one of the windows was billowing in the wind; and the Sphinx, in spite of the comments from all sides, was exposing her perspiring arms to the draft. But where was Rosanette? Frédéric looked for her further afield, even in the boudoir and the bedroom. Some of the guests, to be by themselves or alone together, had sought refuge there. The gloom was full of whispers. There were little laughs, stifled by handkerchiefs, and fans fluttering over bosoms, slowly and softly, like the wing-beats of a wounded bird.

As he entered the conservatory, he saw Delmar lying flat on his stomach on a canvas sofa under the broad leaves of a caladium near the fountain; Rosanette was sitting beside him, her fingers twined in his hair, and they were gazing at each other. At the same moment, Arnoux came in from the far side, near the aviary. Delmar sprang up, then walked calmly out without looking round; he even stopped near the door and picked a hibiscus bloom, which he stuck into his buttonhole. Rosanette bowed her head. Frédéric, who could see her profile, noticed she was crying.

"Well! What's wrong with you?" said Arnoux.

She shrugged her shoulders without answering.

"Is it because of him?" he continued.

She put her arms round his neck and, kissing him on the forehead, said slowly:

"You know perfectly well I'll always love you, my fat friend. Let's not think about it anymore! Let's have supper!"

The dining room, whose walls were almost hidden by antique china plates, was lighted by a brass chandelier with forty candles; and this harsh light, falling from directly above, made the gigantic turbot at the center of the cloth surrounded by hors d'oeuvres and fruit seem even whiter than it was. There were plates of shellfish soup all around the edge of the table. The women sat down together with a rustle of fabrics, bunching up their skirts, sleeves, and sashes; the men stood in the corners. Pellerin and Monsieur Oudry were beside Rosanette; Arnoux opposite; Palazot and his mistress had just left.

"Right!" she said. "Sound the attack!"

And the Choir Boy, a facetious type, made a large sign of the cross and began the *Benedicite*.

The ladies were scandalized, especially the Fishwife, who had a daughter she was trying to bring up respectably. Arnoux also "didn't like that kind of thing," feeling that religion should be treated with respect.

A German clock struck two with the appearance of a cock, which provoked a great many jokes about cuckoos. This was followed by conversation on all sorts of subjects: puns, anecdotes, boasts, wagers, plausible lies, improbable assertions, a tumult of words that soon split up into separate conversations. The wines circulated, dish followed dish, the Doctor carved. People threw oranges and corks across the room; they left their places to chat to one another. Rosanette often turned toward Delmar, motionless behind her; Pellerin chattered away, Monsieur Oudry smiled, Mademoiselle Vatnaz ate almost the entire platter of crayfish on her own, and their shells crackled between her long teeth. The Angel, poised on the piano stool (her long wings made this the only possible place for her to sit), chewed placidly without a pause.

"What an appetite!" the astounded Choir Boy kept repeating. "What an appetite!"

The Sphinx was drinking brandy, screaming with the full force of her lungs and generally behaving like a lunatic. Suddenly her cheeks puffed out and, unable to keep back the blood choking her, she pressed her napkin to her lips, then threw it under the table.

Frédéric had seen.

"It's nothing."

And when he pressed her to go home and take care of herself, she replied slowly:

"Bah! What's the use? This is as good a way as any! Life's not such fun."

An icy sadness gripped him and he shuddered, as if he had caught a glimpse of entire worlds of misery and despair, a charcoal heater beside a trestle bed, and the corpses in the morgue dressed in leather aprons with cold water flowing from a tap onto their hair.

Hussonnet, meanwhile, crouched at the feet of the Female Savage, was braying in a hoarse voice, in imitation of the actor Grassot:

"Be not so cruel, O Celuta!* This little family party is delightful! Drown me in your charms, my loves! To wantonness! To wantonness!"

And he started kissing the women on their shoulders. They bridled, pricked by his moustache. Next he had the idea of breaking a plate over his head by rapping it gently. Others followed his example, fragments of china flew about like slates in a gale, and the Stevedore cried:

"Don't worry! It's all free! The manufacturer makes us a present of it!"

All eyes turned to Arnoux. He replied:

"Oh, I must beg to disagree, it's on the bill!" doubtless to give the impression that he was not, or was no longer, Rosanette's lover.

But two furious voices rang out:

"Imbecile!"

"Scoundrel!"

"At your service!"

"At yours!"

The Medieval Knight and the Russian Postilion were quarreling, the latter maintaining that armor did away with the need for courage and the former having taken it as an insult. He wanted to fight, everyone intervened, and the Captain tried to make himself heard above the tumult:

"Gentlemen, listen to me! Just one word! I have experience, gentlemen!"

Rosanette finally obtained silence by tapping her knife on a glass and, addressing first the Knight, who was still in his helmet, and then the Postilion, in a shaggy fur cap:

"Start by taking off your casserole! It makes me hot to look at it! And you, over there, your wolf's head! Damn it, will you obey me! Look at my epaulettes! I am your Field Marshal!"

They complied, and everyone applauded with shouts of:

"Vive la Maréchale! Vive la Maréchale!"

Then she took a bottle of champagne from the top of the stove and, lifting it high into the air, poured the wine into the glasses held up to her. The table was too broad to reach across so the guests, especially the women, stood on the rails of their chairs to lean toward her and for a moment there was a pyramidal group of headdresses, bare shoulders, outstretched arms, and slant-

*Celuta is the heroine of Chateaubriand's *Natchez*.

ing bodies—and the whole scene was sprayed with long jets of wine, for the Pierrot and Arnoux each let fly from bottles at opposite corners, spattering the upturned faces. The aviary door had been left ajar and the room was invaded by terrified little birds that flew around the chandelier, beat against the windowpanes and the furniture while some of them perched on the revelers' heads, like large flowers stuck in their hair.

The band had left. The piano from the hall was brought into the drawing room; La Vatnaz sat down to it and as the Choir Boy beat on a tambourine she broke into a frenzied quadrille, banging the keys like a horse pawing the ground and swaying to and fro to mark the rhythm. The Maréchale seized Frédéric, Hussonnet turned cartwheels, the Stevedore performed acrobatics like a clown, the Pierrot imitated an orangutan, and the Lady Savage, her arms outstretched, mimed the rocking of a boat. At last they all stopped, exhausted, and someone opened a window.

Daylight streamed in, with the cool morning air. There was an exclamation of surprise, then silence. The yellow candle flames wavered, cracking a drip-shield from time to time; the floor was strewn with ribbons, flowers, and pearls; the sofas were sticky with spots of punch and syrup; the hangings were soiled, the costumes crumpled and dusty; the women's braids hung down on their shoulders and the perspiration which had washed away their makeup revealed pale faces whose reddened eyelids blinked.

The Maréchale was as fresh as if she had just got out of her bath; her cheeks glowed and her eyes sparkled. She tossed her wig away and her hair fell around her like a fleece, hiding her whole costume except for the breeches—producing an effect both absurd and appealing.

The Sphinx, whose teeth were chattering with fever, needed a shawl. Rosanette ran into her bedroom to get one and the Sphinx followed, but she shut the door sharply in her face.

The Turk observed aloud that no one had seen Monsieur Oudry leave. Everybody was so tired that no comment was made on this malicious remark.

Then they wrapped themselves in cloaks and hoods as they waited for the carriages. Seven o'clock struck. The Angel was still in the dining room, sitting down to a mixture of sardines and butter, while beside her the

Fishwife was smoking cigarettes and giving her the benefit of her experience of life.

The cabs having finally arrived, the guests departed.
Hussonnet, who was Paris correspondent for a provincial
journal, had to read fifty-three papers before lunch; the
Lady Savage had a rehearsal at her theater, Pellerin a
model, the Choir Boy three assignations. But the Angel,
who was feeling the first pangs of indigestion, could not
move. The Medieval Baron carried her to the cab.

"Be careful of her wings!" cried the Stevedore from
the window.

On the landing, Mademoiselle Vatnaz said to Rosanette:

"Good-bye, my dear. A great success, your party."
Then, bending down, she whispered into her ear:

"Keep him!"

"Until better times," replied the Maréchale, turning slowly away.

Arnoux and Frédéric left together, as they had come.
The china dealer's expression was so somber that his companion thought he must be feeling ill.

"Me? Not a bit!"

He frowned and gnawed at his moustache. Frédéric
asked whether he was worried about his business.

"Not in the slightest!"

Then, suddenly, he said:

"You knew Old Oudry, didn't you?"

And added, with an expression of rancor:

"He's rich, the old scoundrel!"

Then Arnoux spoke of an important firing at his factory which was due to be completed today. He wanted
to see it. The train left in an hour. "But first I must
go home and kiss my wife."

"Oh, his wife!" thought Frédéric.

Then he went to bed with a blinding headache and
drank an entire carafe of water to quench his thirst.

He had acquired another thirst, a thirst for women,
luxury, and everything that life in Paris implies. He felt a
little giddy, like a man who had just disembarked from
a ship, and in the hallucination of his first sleep the
Fishwife's shoulders, the Stevedore's loins, the Polish
Woman's calves, and the Lady Savage's hair kept flicker-
ing before him. Then two great dark eyes which had
not been at the ball appeared and, light as butterflies,
brilliant as torches, they darted from place to place,
quivered, flew up to the ceiling, swooped down to his
mouth. Frédéric battled to recognize these eyes without suc-

cess. But already a dream was sweeping him away; it
seemed to him that he and Arnoux were both harnessed
to the pole of a cab and that the Maréchale, astride his
back, was raking his stomach with her golden spurs.

Chapter Two

Frédéric found himself a small town house at the corner of the Rue Rumfort and in one swoop he bought the brougham, the horse, the furniture, and two flower-stands from Arnoux to put on either side of his drawing room door. Beyond the drawing room lay a bedroom and another small room. It occurred to him to let Deslauriers have them. But then how would he receive *her,* his future mistress? The presence of a friend would be an obstacle. He tore down the partition to enlarge his drawing room and turned the small one into a smoking room.

He bought the works of his favorite poets, travel books, atlases, dictionaries, for he had endless projects. He hurried the workmen, haunted the shops, and, impatient to enjoy his purchases, bought everything without haggling.

When the bills came in, Frédéric realized he would soon have to pay out some forty thousand francs, not including the inheritance taxes which would amount to more than thirty-seven thousand. As his fortune was in land, he wrote to the notary at Le Havre asking him to sell part of it so that he could pay his debts and have some money at his disposal. Then, wishing to become acquainted finally with that vague, glittering, and indefinable thing called "society," he wrote a note to the Dambreuses asking if he might call on them. Madame replied that she expected him the following day.

It was her "at home" day. Carriages waited in the courtyard. Two footmen hurried forward under the awning, and a third, at the top of the staircase, walked before him.

He crossed an antechamber, a second room, then a great drawing room with tall windows whose monumental chimneypiece supported a spherical clock and two gigantic porcelain vases from which clusters of sconces bristled like golden bushes. The walls were hung with pictures in the style of Ribera, the heavy tapestry door-curtains hung in majestic folds; the armchairs, consoles, tables—all the furniture, in fact—was Empire and had something imposing about it, an aura of diplomacy. Frédéric smiled with pleasure in spite of himself.

At last he reached an oval room, paneled in rosewood, which was full of pretty, delicate furniture and lighted by a single window looking onto a garden. Madame Dambreuse was near the fire with a dozen people grouped around her. With a few amiable words she gestured to him to sit down, showing no surprise at not having seen him for so long.

They were praising the Abbé Coeur's eloquence when he came in. Then they deplored the immorality of servants, in connection with a theft committed by a valet; and then came a steady stream of gossip about various topics. Old Madame de Sommery had a cold, Mademoiselle de Turvisot was getting married, the Montcharrons wouldn't be back before the end of January, neither would the Bretancourts—people stayed in the country longer nowadays; and the poverty of the conversation was, as it were, underlined by the luxury of the surroundings. What was said was, however, less stupid than the way in which they talked, without purpose, continuity, or animation. Yet some of the guests were men of wide experience: a former minister, the priest of a large parish, two or three high government officials; they confined themselves to the most commonplace remarks. Some looked like worn-out dowagers, others resembled horse-dealers, and old men accompanied wives who could have passed for their granddaughters.

Madame Dambreuse treated them all graciously. She frowned with sorrow at the mention of an invalid, and if the conversation turned to balls or parties, she assumed an air of delight. She would soon be forced to do without these diversions, for she was going to take in an orphaned niece of her husband's, now at boarding school. Her self-sacrifice was extolled; such conduct befitted a true mother.

Frédéric watched her attentively. The pale skin of her face had a stretched look and her complexion was luster-less, like a preserved fruit. But her hair, which she wore in ringlets like an Englishwoman, was finer than

silk, her eyes were a brilliant blue, and all her movements were delicate. Sitting on a small sofa at the far
end of the room, she was stroking the red tassels of
a Japanese screen, probably to draw attention to her
hands. They were long, narrow hands, a little thin, with
fingers that turned up at the tips. She was dressed, like
a Puritan, in a gray watered-silk dress with a high neck.

Frédéric asked her if she would be going to la Fortelle
that year. Madame Dambreuse had no idea. He found this
easy to understand; she must be bored at Nogent. More
visitors arrived. There was a perpetual rustling of dresses
over the carpet; poised on the edges of their chairs, the
ladies tittered, made two or three remarks and left with
their daughters after five minutes. The conversation soon
became impossible to follow, and Frédéric was leaving
when Madame Dambreuse said:

"Every Wednesday, Monsieur Moreau, don't forget!"
compensating with a single sentence for any indifference
she had shown him.

He was pleased. Nevertheless, when he reached the
street he drew a deep breath and, feeling the need of a
less artificial atmosphere, recalled that he owed the Maréchale a visit.

The hall door was open. Two Havana lapdogs ran up to
him and a voice cried:

"Delphine! Delphine! Is that you, Félix?"

He stayed where he was, the two little dogs still
yapping around him, until Rosanette finally appeared,
wrapped in a sort of white muslin dressing gown trimmed
with lace, and with slippers on her bare feet.

"Oh, please excuse me, Monsieur! I took you for the
hairdresser. I'll be back in a moment!"

And he was left by himself in the dining room.

The blinds were closed. Frédéric was glancing round
the room, remembering the riotous scenes of the other
night, when he noticed a man's hat on the table. It was
an old felt, battered, greasy, filthy. Whose could it be?
Impudently displaying its lining, which had come un-
stitched, it seemed to say: "What do I care? I'm the
master!"

The Maréchale came in. She picked up the hat, opened
the door to the conservatory, threw it in, shut the door
(other doors opened and closed at the same moment),
and took Frédéric through the kitchen to her dressing room.

It was immediately apparent that this room was the
most constantly used of any in the house, its true spir-

itual center. The walls, armchairs, and an enormous, springy divan were covered in a chintz with a bold, leafy design; two large blue pottery bowls stood on a white marble table, and above it the glass shelves were covered with bottles, brushes, combs, makeup sticks, and boxes of powder; the fire was reflected in a tall cheval-glass; a cloth hung out of a bathtub and the air was filled with the scent of almond paste and benzoin.

"Sorry about the mess! I'm dining out this evening."

And, as she turned around, she almost crushed one of the little dogs. Frédéric pronounced them charming. She picked them both up and, holding their black muzzles up to his face, said:

"Come on, be nice, kiss the gentleman!"

A man dressed in a dirty overcoat with a fur collar entered abruptly.

"Félix, my boy," she said, "your little matter will be settled next Sunday, without fail."

The man started to do her hair. He gave her news of her friends: Madame de Rochegune, Madame de Saint-Florentin, Madame Lombard, all of them aristocrats just as they had been at the Dambreuses. Then he talked about the theater; a special performance was being given at the Ambigu that evening:

"Will you be there?"

"Gracious no! I'm staying at home."

Delphine appeared. She scolded her for having gone out without permission. The other swore that she had just got back from the market.

"Very well, bring your book! You'll excuse me, won't you?"

Rosanette read from the book in an undertone, commenting on every item. There was a mistake in the addition:

"Give me four sous!"

Delphine handed them over and, when she had sent her away:

"Dear God! How those people annoy me!"

This grumbling shocked Frédéric. It reminded him too vividly of what he had heard earlier, and seemed to establish an unpleasant kind of equality between the two houses.

Delphine, who had returned, came up to whisper in the Maréchale's ear:

"No! I don't want to!"

Delphine returned:

"She insists, Madame."

"What a nuisance! Throw her out!"

At that moment an old lady in black pushed open the door. Frédéric saw and heard nothing; Rosanette rushed into the bedroom to meet her.

When she reappeared her cheeks were flushed and she sank into one of the armchairs without speaking. A tear rolled down her cheek. Then she turned to the young man and said gently:

"What's your first name?"

"Frédéric."

"Ah, Federico! You don't mind my calling you that?"

And she gave him a coaxing, almost a loving look. Suddenly she exclaimed with pleasure at the sight of Mademoiselle Vatnaz.

The artistic lady had not a moment to lose, as she was due to preside over dinner at her boardinghouse at six o'clock on the dot and she was panting and exhausted. First she took a watch chain and a piece of paper out of her basket, then various other objects she had purchased.

"You know they've got some wonderful suede gloves in the Rue Joubert for thirty-six sous! Your dyer needs another week. I said we'd be back for the lace. Bugneaux has gotten his money on account. I think that's all! You owe me a hundred and eighty-five francs."

Rosanette went over to a drawer and took out ten napoléons. Neither of them had any change; Frédéric produced some.

"I'll pay you back," promised the Vatnaz, stuffing the fifteen francs into her bag. "But you're a bad man, I don't like you anymore! You didn't ask me to dance once the other night! —Oh, my dear, I've discovered the most divine case of stuffed hummingbirds in a little shop on the Quai Voltaire. If I were you I'd treat myself to them! Look! what do you think of this?"

And she displayed a short length of old pink silk which she had bought at a shop in the Temple to make into a medieval doublet for Delmar.

"He came today, didn't he?"

"No."

"That's odd!"

And, after a moment:

"Where are you off to this evening?"

"To Alphonsine's," said Rosanette. This was the third version of how she intended to spend the evening.

"What about the Old Man of the Mountain? Anything new?" continued Mademoiselle Vatnaz.

But Rosanette silenced her with a hasty wink and accompanied Frédéric as far as the hall to ask him if he would be seeing Arnoux soon.

"Well, tell him to come and visit me; not in front of his wife, of course!"

An umbrella leaned against the wall at the top of the steps, next to a pair of overshoes.

"La Vatnaz's rubbers," said Rosanette. "What a foot, hm? She's a strong girl, my little friend!"

And, in a melodramatic tone, rolling her "r":

"But not to be trrrusted!"

Emboldened by this confidence, Frédéric tried to kiss her neck. She said coldly:

"Oh, help yourself! It's free!"

He went out lightheartedly, convinced that the Maréchale would soon be his mistress. This desire awoke another and, in spite of the sort of rancor he felt for her, he was overcome by a longing to see Madame Arnoux.

Anyhow, he would have to pay them a visit to deliver Rosanette's message.

"But at this moment," he thought (it was striking six), "Arnoux is probably at home."

And he deferred his call to the following day.

She was sitting in the same position as on the first day, sewing a child's shirt. The little boy was playing with a collection of wooden animals at her feet, and Marthe was writing a little farther off.

He began by complimenting her on her children. She replied without a trace of exaggerated maternal imbecility.

The room had a tranquil air. Bright sunlight poured in through the windowpanes, the corners of the furniture gleamed, and a broad ray of sun coming through the window near which Madame Arnoux was sitting struck the kiss-curl at the nape of her neck and steeped her amber skin in liquid gold. Then he said:

"This young lady has grown up a lot in three years! Do you remember when you slept on my knees in the carriage, Mademoiselle?" Marthe could not remember. "Coming back from Saint-Cloud one evening?"

Madame Arnoux gave him a look of extraordinary sadness. Was it to forbid any allusion to their common memory?

The whites of her beautiful dark eyes shone as they

moved gently beneath their heavy lids, and there was an infinite kindness in the depth of her pupils. He was seized once again by an immense love for her, stronger than ever. The sight of her dazed him, but he shook it off. How was he to make an impression on her? By what means? After some effort Frédéric could think of nothing better than money. He started to talk about the weather, which was warmer than at Le Havre.

"You've been there?"

"Yes, on business . . . a family matter . . . an inheritance."

"I'm so glad," she replied, with an air of such genuine pleasure that he was as touched as if she had done him some great service.

Then she asked him what he was going to do; a man should occupy himself with something. He remembered his lie and said that he hoped to work for the Council of State with the aid of Monsieur Dambreuse, the deputy.

"Perhaps you know him?"

"Only by name."

Then, in a low voice:

"*He* took you to the ball the other day, didn't he?"

Frédéric said nothing.

"That is all I wanted to know. Thank you."

Then she asked him a few discreet questions about his family and his province. It was very nice of him not to have forgotten them when he had been in the country for such a long time.

"But . . . how could I?" he replied. "Did you think I would?"

Madame Arnoux stood up:

"I think that you have a sincere and lasting affection for us. Good-bye . . . until next time!"

And she held out her hand in a frank, manly way. Was not this an agreement, a promise? Frédéric was filled with the joy of life; he had to restrain himself from bursting into song; he felt expansive, ready for generosity and alms-giving. He looked around to see if there was anyone he could help. There were no beggars about, and his self-sacrificing impulse faded, for he was not the man to go seeking out the opportunity.

Then he remembered his friends. He thought first of Hussonnet, then of Pellerin. Dussardier's lowly position demanded his consideration; as for Cisy, he would be delighted to show off his wealth to him a little. So he wrote to the four of them, asking them to a housewarming party the following Sunday at eleven o'clock sharp, and he told Deslauriers to bring Sénécal.

The teacher had been dismissed from his third boarding school for his opposition to the presentation of prizes, a practice which he considered undermined the principle of equality. He was now working for a machine manufacturer and had not been living with Deslauriers for the last six months.

Their parting had not been a painful one. Toward the end of his stay, Sénécal had been inviting laborers into their rooms. All of them had been patriots, hard workers and excellent fellows, but the lawyer found their company tedious. Quite apart from this, certain of his friend's ideas, though excellent weapons in a fight, did not appeal to him. He kept quiet out of ambition, attempting to manipulate Sénécal by humoring him, for he was impatiently awaiting a great upheaval in which he expected to make his mark and find his place.

Sénécal's convictions were more disinterested. Every evening after work he returned to his attic and searched his books for justification of his dreams. He had annotated the *Contrat social.* He buried himself in the *Revue indépendante.** He knew Mably, Morelly, Fourier, Saint-Simon, Comte, Cabet, Louis Blanc, the entire cartload of socialist writers—those who demanded a life of barracks conformity for all mankind, those who wanted to entertain it in a brothel or chain it to a workbench —and, from a blend of all these theories, he had evolved his own concept of the virtuous democracy, a cross between a small farm and a spinning-mill, a sort of American Sparta, where the individual would exist solely to serve a State more omnipotent, absolute, infallible, and divine than a Grand Lama or a Nebuchadnezzar. He had no doubt that this ideal would soon be realized, and attacked everything he considered hostile to it with the logic of a mathematician and the righteousness of an inquisitor. Titles, medals, plumes, liveries especially, even too great a degree of fame outraged him—every day his studies, and his sufferings, spurred his fundamental hatred of any distinction or superiority whatsoever.

"What has this gentleman ever done for me that I should put myself out to be polite to him? If he wants to see me he can come to me!"

Deslauriers dragged him along.

*A left-wing review which appeared from 1841 to 1848.

They found their friend in his bedroom. Spring-blinds, double curtains, a Venetian looking-glass—nothing was lacking; Frédéric in a velvet jacket was lolling in an armchair smoking Turkish cigarettes.

Sénécal looked as gloomy as a teetotaler at an orgy. Deslauriers took in everything at a single glance, then, bowing low, said:

"My lord, I present my respects!"

Dussardier threw his arms round his neck.

"So you're rich now? That's wonderful, by George, wonderful!"

Cisy appeared with a crepe band around his hat. His grandmother's death had brought him a considerable fortune and his ambition was less to enjoy life than to distinguish himself from other people, to stand out from the crowd, in short to "be special." Those were his words for it.

It was now midday and everyone was yawning; Frédéric was waiting for someone. When he mentioned Arnoux, Pellerin made a face. He considered him a renegade since he had abandoned the arts.

"Let's forget about him. What do you think?"

They all agreed.

A servant in gaiters opened the door, disclosing the dining room with its high dado of oak picked out in gold and its two sideboards laden with china. The bottles of wine were warming on the stove, the blades of new knives glittered beside the oysters, the milky hue of the delicate glasses had a beguiling sweetness, and the table was hidden beneath its load of game, fruit, exotic dainties. All this careful preparation was lost on Sénécal.

He began by demanding ordinary bread (the harder the better), and this led to the murders at Buzançais and the food stortage.*

None of it would have happened if agriculture was better protected, if everything were not left to competition, to anarchy, to the deplorable maxim *"laissez faire, laissez passer"!* This was nothing but a feudal system based on money, and it was worse than the old kind! But let them beware! The masses would weary of it in the end and make the capitalists pay for all their misery,

---

*The food shortage of the winter of 1846-47 led to rioting in Indre during which several landowners were killed. The murderers were executed at Buzançais.

either by bloody decrees of death proscriptions or by looting their houses.

Frédéric had a momentary vision of a mob of bare-
armed men pouring into Madame Dambreuse's great drawing room, smashing the mirrors with their pikes.

Sénécal went on: when you took the inadequacy of
his wages into consideration, the workingman was worse
off than the helot, the Negro, or the pariah, above all
if he had children.

"Should he rid himself of them by suffocation, as prescribed by some English doctor whose name I have forgotten, a Malthusian?"

And, turning to Cisy:

"Are we to be reduced to following the advice of the
infamous Malthus?"

Cisy, who knew nothing of the infamy, or even of the
existence of Malthus, replied that even so a great deal
was being done to help the poor and that the upper
classes . . .

"Ah, the upper classes!" sneered the socialist. "To begin with there are no upper classes; nobility of heart is the
only thing that can make one man superior to another!
We are not asking for charity, you hear me! but for
equality and a just distribution of goods."

What he wanted was for the worker to have the opportunity to become a capitalist, as the private, a colonel.
Even the guilds in the old days, by limiting the number
of apprentices, at least prevented the creation of a glut
of workers and a feeling of brotherhood was sustained by
festivals and banners.

Hussonnet, as a poet, regretted the passing of the banners. So did Pellerin, a predilection he had acquired at the
café Dagneaux, listening to the conversations of some of
Fourier's disciples. He declared Fourier a great man.

"Oh, come on!" cried Deslauriers. "An old fool who
sees divine vengeance in the overthrow of empires! It's
like Saint-Simon and his church, with their hatred of the
French Revolution: a gang of frauds who'd like to res-
urrect Catholicism!"

Monsieur de Cisy, doubtless to clarify his ideas or perhaps to make a good impression, began gently:

"Then these two philosophers differ from Voltaire?"

"Voltaire! You can have him."

"What? I thought . . ."

"Oh, no! He had no feeling for the people!"

Then the conversation came down to the events of the

day: the Spanish marriages,* the embezzlements at Rochefort,† the new arrangements of Saint-Denis,‡ which would mean an increase in taxation. According to Sénécal they were paying enough already!

"And for what, my God! To build palatial monkey houses at the zoo, to have gaudy staff-officers strutting through our squares, and to keep up a gothic etiquette among the flunkeys at the Palace!"

"I saw in *la Mode*," said Cisy, "everyone wore really sumptuous costumes at the Tuileries ball on Saint Ferdinand's day."

"How puerile!" commented the socialist, shrugging his shoulders in disgust.

"And the Versailles museum!" cried Pellerin. "Let's talk about that! Those idiots shortened a Delacroix and enlarged a Gros. They've so restored, scraped, and generally messed up all the canvases at the Louvre that there may not be one of them left in ten years' time. As for the mistakes in the catalogue, some German has written an entire book about them. Foreigners think we're a joke!"

"Yes, we're the laughing stock of Europe," said Sénécal.

"It's because Art has been taken over by the Crown."

"As long as there is no universal suffrage . . ."

"Let me finish!" For the artist, who had been rejected at every Salon for the last twenty years, was furious with the authorities. "Why can't they leave us alone? I ask for nothing personally, but the Chamber of Deputies should enact a law protecting Art. A chair of aesthetics ought to be established whose holder, a man who combined theory and practice, might, I hope, succeed in educating the masses—it would be a good thing if you mentioned the idea in your paper, Hussonnet."

"Is the press free? Are we free?" cried Deslauriers passionately. "When I think that it is sometimes necessary to go through as many as twenty-eight steps just to keep a small boat on a river, I feel like going off to live with the cannibals. We are being devoured by the government! It controls everything, philosophy, law, the arts, the air we

*One of Louis-Philippe's sons, the Duc de Montpensier, married a daughter of the Queen of Spain in October, 1846.

†This refers to an administrative scandal at the arsenal at Rochefort.

‡A plan for the reorganization of the chapter of Saint-Denis had been adopted by the Chamber of Peers in 1847, but in 1848 had not yet been submitted to the Chamber of Deputies.

breathe; and France is gasping, exhausted, beneath the policeman's boot and the priest's cassock!"

The future Mirabeau continued to spew out his bile at some length. Finally he picked up his glass, rose to his feet, and with his eyes glowing and his hand on his hip, he cried:

"I drink to the complete destruction of the present system, of all that is known as Privilege, Monopoly, Control, Hierarchy, Authority, State!" and, raising his voice: "which I would like to break as I break this!" he dashed his beautiful wine glass onto the table, where it shattered into a thousand pieces.

They all applauded, especially Dussardier.

Any injustice moved him deeply. He worried about Barbès* and was the kind of man who would throw himself under the wheels of a carriage to help a fallen horse. His erudition was limited to two works, one entitled *Crimes of Kings* and the other *Mysteries of the Vatican*. He had listened to the lawyer in open-mouthed delight. Finally, unable to contain himself, he exclaimed:

"The thing I hold against Louis-Philippe is deserting the Poles!"†

"Just a moment!" said Hussonnet. "First of all, Poland does not exist; it was invented by Lafayette. The Poles, as a general rule, come from the Faubourg Saint-Marceau; all the real ones were drowned with Poniatowski."

In short, "he wasn't going to be taken in any longer," he'd "finished with all that!" It was like the sea-serpent, the revocation of the Edict of Nantes, and "that old fable about the Massacre of Saint-Bartholomew's!"

Sénécal, without defending the Poles, took up Hussonnet's final words. The Popes had been slandered; after all, they had defended the people; and he described the League as "the dawn of democracy, a great egalitarian movement against Protestant individualism."

Frédéric was a little startled by these ideas. Cisy was probably bored by them, for he turned the conversation to the *tableaux vivants* which were drawing large crowds at the Gymnase.

Sénécal found them deplorable. Shows like these corrupted the daughters of the proletariat, and they dis-

---

*Barbès was an ardent republican, frequently imprisoned for his opposition to Louis-Philippe.
†The Republican Party wanted France to go to the aid of the Poles, whose revolt against Russia in 1831 had been suppressed with extreme severity.

played such insolent luxury! For the same reason he approved of the Bavarian students who had insulted Lola Montes.* Like Rousseau, he valued a charcoal-burner's wife more highly than a king's mistress.

"That's just sour grapes!" replied Hussonnet disdainfully. And he undertook the defense of these ladies for the sake of Rosanette. Then, as he was speaking of her ball and of Arnoux's costume, Pellerin said:

"Is it true that he's pretty shaky financially?"

The art dealer had just emerged from a lawsuit over his land at Belleville, and he was now involved in a china-clay company in Lower Brittany with some other lightweights of the same ilk.

Dussardier knew more; his employer Monsieur Moussinot had made inquiries about Arnoux from the banker Oscar Lefebre, who knew he had renewed some bills and considered him far from sound.

Dessert was finished, and they moved into the drawing room, which was hung, like the Maréchale's, with yellow damask, and decorated in the style of Louis XVI.

Pellerin reproached Frédéric for not having chosen a neoclassical style; Sénécal struck matches on the hangings; Deslauriers made no comment. He made up for it in the library, which he described as girlish. Most contemporary writers were represented. It was impossible to discuss their works, as Hussonnet immediately broke into a string of personal anecdotes about them, criticizing their looks, their habits, their dress, praising some tenth-rate figures, denigrating those of real importance, and, of course, deploring modern decadence. Such and such a country ballad contained more poetry than all the lyrics of the nineteenth century; Balzac was overrated, Byron's reputation had been demolished, Hugo knew nothing about the theater, etc.

"But why," asked Sénécal, "don't I see anything by our worker-poets?"

And Monsieur de Cisy, who dabbled in literature, was astonished not to find some of "these new 'physiologies'" on Frédéric's table—*The Smoker's Physiology, The Fisherman's Physiology, The Toll-Keeper's Physiology*."

They succeeded in irritating Frédéric to such an extent that he felt like seizing them all by the scruffs of their necks and putting them out the door. "But that's stupid!"

*The King of Bavaria's mistress.

And, drawing Dussardier aside, he asked if he could be of any service to him.

The good fellow was touched. With his cashier's job he needed nothing.

Then Frédéric took Deslauriers to his bedroom and, taking two thousand francs from his desk, said:

"Here you are, old boy, take this! It's the rest of my old debts."

"But . . . what about the paper?" asked the lawyer. "You know quite well I've talked to Hussonnet about it."

And when Frédéric replied that "he was a little short at the moment," the other smiled bitterly.

After the liqueurs they drank beer, and after the beer, grog, and the pipes were filled time after time. At five o'clock they all finally left. They walked along together in silence till Dussardier remarked that Frédéric had been a perfect host. Everyone agreed.

Hussonnet observed that the lunch had been a little too rich. Sénécal criticized the frivolity of the interior decorations. Cisy agreed. It was entirely lacking in distinction.

Pellerin said, "I think he might at least have commissioned a picture from me."

Deslauriers fingered the banknotes in his trouser pocket and held his tongue.

Frédéric was left alone. He thought about his friends and it seemed to him that a great, shadowy chasm had opened between them. And yet he had held out his hand to them, and they had not responded to his open-hearted gesture.

He remembered what Pellerin and Dussardier had said about Arnoux. It was probably a fabrication, a slander. But why? And he had a vision of Madame Arnoux ruined, in tears, selling her furniture. The idea tormented him all night long; and the following day he went to see her.

Not knowing how to tell her what he had discovered, he asked casually if Arnoux still had his land at Belleville.

"Yes, it's still there."

"He's part of a clay company in Brittany now, I believe?"

"Yes, that's right."

"His factory is doing well, isn't it?"

"But . . . as far as I know."

And, as he hesitated:

"What is it? You are frightening me."

He told her of the bills Arnoux had renewed. She bowed her head and said:

"I feared as much."

Arnoux, in fact, in the hope of making a large profit, had refused to sell his land, had borrowed heavily on it, and, finding no buyers, had tried to make it good by building a factory. The expenses were more than he had anticipated. She knew no more; he evaded all her questions, declaring continually that "everything was going well."

Frédéric attempted to reassure her. It might be a purely temporary difficulty. In any case, if he found out anything more he would let her know.

"Oh yes, please do!" she said, joining her hands with a charming air of supplication.

So he could be of use to her. He was about to enter her heart and her existence.

Arnoux appeared.

"Oh, how nice of you, to come and take me out to dinner!"

Frédéric, startled, said nothing.

Arnoux talked about inconsequential matters, then warned his wife that he would be very late getting home, as he had an appointment with Monsieur Oudry.

"At his house?"

"Yes, of course. At his house."

As they went down the stairs he confessed that, as the Maréchale was free that evening, they were going on a spree to the Moulin-Rouge together; and feeling, as always, the need of a confidant, he made Frédéric accompany him to her door.

Instead of going in, he walked up and down on the sidewalk, watching the second-floor windows. All at once the curtains were drawn back.

"Ah, hurray, Old Oudry's left. Good night!"

So it was Old Oudry who was keeping her? Frédéric no longer knew what to think.

From that day on Arnoux was even friendlier than before; he invited him to dinner at his mistress', and soon Frédéric was a regular visitor at both houses.

Rosanette's amused him. People went round in the evening, after the club or the theater, to have a cup of tea and play a game of lotto; on Sundays there were charades. Rosanette, wilder than the others, was always full of amusing pranks, crawling around on all fours or rigging herself out in a cotton nightcap. She wore a leather

helmet to look out of the window at the passersby, she
smoked a Turkish pipe, and yodeled Tyrolean songs.
In the afternoons, when time lay heavy on her hands,
she would cut out the flowers from a piece of chintz
and stick them onto the windowpanes, daub her lapdogs
with rouge, burn scented pastilles, or tell her own fortune. Incapable of resisting an impulse, she would become infatuated with some trinket she had seen, would
lose sleep over it, rush off to buy it and then trade it
for another. She ruined dress fabrics, lost her jewels, threw
her money away with both hands, and would have sold her
shift for a stage box. She often asked Frédéric to explain
some word she had read but never listened to the answer, for she would have switched rapidly to another
idea, asking more and more questions. Her spasms of
gaiety would be succeeded by childish tantrums, or she
would sit on the floor in front of the fire, dreaming, her
head bowed and her knees locked in her hands, as
sluggish as a torpid snake. She would dress in front of
him, indifferent to his presence, slowly pulling on her
silk stockings, then splashing water over her face, bending
back from the waist like a shivering naiad; and her laughter, which showed her white teeth, the sparkle of her
eyes, her beauty, her gaiety, dazzled Frédéric and whipped
at his nerves.

He generally found Madame Arnoux teaching her little
son to read or standing behind Marthe's chair while she
played scales on the piano; when she was sewing it was a
great joy to be able sometimes to pick up her scissors. All
her movements had a tranquil, majestic quality; her little
hands seemed made for the distribution of alms and for
drying his tears; and her voice, naturally low, had intonations as caressing as the light touch of a breeze.

She did not go into ecstasies over literature, but her
simple, penetrating words showed an enchanting intelligence. She loved travel, the sound of wind in the woods,
and walking bareheaded in the rain. Frédéric learned all
this with delight, taking her confidences for the beginning
of her surrender.

The company of these two women made, as it were, two
strains of music in his life; one wild, gay, abandoned, the
other grave, almost religious; and, sounding at the same
time, they grew continually louder and, little by little, they
mingled; for if Madame Arnoux's finger merely brushed
against him, his desire of success immediately conjured up
the image of the other, since his chances were better with

her—and, when his heart happened to be touched while he was with Rosanette, he was at once reminded of his great love.

This confusion was caused by similarities between the two establishments. One of the chests that used to be at the Boulevard Montmartre now adorned Rosanette's dining room, the other Madame Arnoux's drawing room. The dinner service was the same in both houses, and even the same velvet smoking cap lay about on the chairs in both places; then there were a mass of small presents, screens, boxes, fans, which shuttled to and fro between wife and mistress, for Arnoux, without a trace of embarrassment, would often take back something he had given one of them to offer it to the other.

The Maréchale used to laugh at his odd ways with Frédéric. One Sunday, after dinner, she drew him behind the door and showed him a bag of cakes in Arnoux's overcoat pocket which he had just filched from the table, no doubt to take home as a present for his children. He used to play all kinds of tricks bordering on dishonesty. As far as he was concerned, cheating the city tax collector was a duty, he never paid for his seat at the theater, always traveled first class on a second-class ticket, and thought it an excellent joke that he had a habit of dropping a trouser button instead of a ten-sou piece into the attendant's box at the swimming baths; none of which prevented the Maréchale from loving him.

One day, however, when she was talking about him, she exclaimed:

"Oh! He gets on my nerves! I've had enough! Too bad, I'll find someone else!"

Frédéric remarked that he thought she had already found "someone else" and that his name was Oudry.

"Well?" said Rosanette. "What's wrong with that?"

And, in a tearful voice:

"And I ask him for so little, the beast, but he won't even let me have that! He just won't! As for promises, that's a different kettle of fish!"

He had even promised her a quarter of his profits from the clay pits he was always talking about; no profits had turned up, and neither had the cashmere shawl he had been tantalizing her with for the last six months.

Frédéric immediately thought of giving it to her as a present. Arnoux might take it as a lesson and be angry.

But still he was a good man, his wife said so herself. But mad as a hatter! Instead of bringing people home to dinner with him every night he was now taking them to restaurants. He had bought a lot of utterly useless junk: gold chains, clocks, household utensils. Madame Arnoux even showed Frédéric a great heap of kettles, foot-warmers, and samovars in the corridor. At last one day she admitted how worried she was: Arnoux had made her sign a bill made out to the order of Monsieur Dambreuse.

Frédéric, meanwhile, continued to work on his literary projects out of a vague feeling that he must keep faith with himself. He wanted to write a history of aesthetics, a result of his conversation with Pellerin; then, under the indirect influence of Deslauriers and Hussonnet, to dramatize different epochs of the French Revolution and compose a great play.

Often the image of one or the other of the two women would appear to him while he was working; he would struggle briefly against the desire to see her, then capitulate; and he was more depressed when he returned from seeing Madame Arnoux.

One morning he was nursing his melancholy by the fire when Deslauriers came in. Sénécal's inflammatory talk had disturbed his employer and, once again, he was destitute.

"What do you want me to do about it?" said Frédéric.

"Nothing! I know you have no money. But it wouldn't be much trouble for you to find him a position through either Monsieur Dambreuse or Arnoux."

Arnoux must need engineers in his factory. Frédéric had an inspiration. Sénécal could let him know when the husband was away, carry letters, help him on a thousand and one occasions that would arise in the future. Men would always do these things for each other. Anyhow, he would find ways to make use of him without his suspecting anything. Chance had offered him a helper; it was a good omen and he must seize the opportunity. Feigning nonchalance, he replied that it might be possible to arrange something and he would see what he could do.

He saw to it at once. Arnoux was taking a great deal of trouble over his factory. He was searching for the copper-red the Chinese had used but his colors evaporated in the firing process. To avoid cracks in his pottery, he mixed lime with his clay, but most of his pieces broke; when he painted on unbaked clay the enamel swelled up in bubbles; his large platters buckled, and, attributing these mishaps to the poor equipment of his factory, he was anxious to install different grinding-mills and dryers. Frédéric remembered some of this and he broached the subject by announcing that he had found him a very well qualified man, capable of discovering his much discussed red. Arnoux jumped up at this but, after hearing what Frédéric had to say, replied that he needed no one.

Frédéric praised Sénécal's prodigious knowledge; he was at once an engineer, a chemist, and a bookkeeper, being a first-rate mathematician.

The china manufacturer agreed to see him.

The two of them wrangled over wages. Frédéric intervened and succeeded, after a week, in getting them to conclude an agreement.

But since the factory was at Creil, Sénécal could be no help to him. This very simple reflection disheartened him as much as a more serious misfortune.

It occurred to him that the more distant Arnoux became from his wife, the greater were his own chances with her. Thus he set about pleading Rosanette's case; he pointed out to Arnoux how badly he had treated her, recounted the vague threats she had made a few days earlier, and even spoke of the cashmere shawl, mentioning that she had called him miserly.

Stung by the word (and feeling a bit worried besides), Arnoux took her the shawl but scolded her for having complained to Frédéric. When she said she had reminded him of his promise a hundred times he claimed that he had forgotten, busy as he was.

Frédéric went to see her the following day. Although it was two o'clock, the Maréchale was still in bed; Delmar was sitting at a little table beside her, finishing a slice of foie gras. She called across the room: "I've got it! I've got it!" Then, taking him by the ears, she kissed him on the forehead, overwhelmed him with thanks, even asked him to sit on her bed. Her beautiful, tender eyes sparkled, her moist mouth smiled, her two rounded arms emerged from her sleeveless nightdress, and from time to time he could feel the firm contours of her body through the batiste. Delmar, meanwhile, kept rolling his eyes and saying:

"But really, my dear, my dear girl!"

The same thing happened on subsequent occasions. As soon as Frédéric came in, she would stand on a cushion so that he could embrace her more easily, call him a darling, a sweetheart, put a flower in his buttonhole, straighten his cravat. These attentions were always exaggerated when Delmar was present.

Were they advances? Frédéric thought so. As for deceiving a friend, Arnoux wouldn't think twice about it if the situation were reversed. Besides, he felt he had a perfect right to behave badly with Arnoux's mistress, having always been a model of rectitude with his wife—for he believed that he had been that, or rather he would have liked to persuade himself into that interpretation, to justify his prodigious cowardice. He decided, however, that he was foolish and resolved to make an all-out attempt on the Maréchale.

So one afternoon, as she was bending over her commode, he approached her and made a gesture so eloquent and unmistakable that she straightened up, crimson in the face. He tried again at once, whereupon she dissolved into tears, saying that she was very unfortunate but that was no reason for despising her.

He repeated his attempts. She took another line, that of laughing at the whole thing. He thought it would be clever to reply in the same way. But he seemed too gay for her to believe in his sincerity; and their comradeship acted as a barrier to the expression of any serious emotion. Finally, one day she blurted out that she would not accept another woman's leavings.

"What other woman?"

"Oh, you know! Go find Madame Arnoux!"

For Frédéric often spoke of her; Arnoux had the same habit, and Rosanette was getting tired of always hearing that woman's praises, so this insinuation was a kind of vengeance.

Frédéric held a grudge against her because of it.

She was, moreover, beginning to get on his nerves. Sometimes she would pose as a woman of experience and talk cynically about love with a skeptical laugh that made him itch to slap her. A quarter of an hour later, it was the only thing in the world and, crossing her arms on her breast as if she were clasping someone to her, she would murmur: "Ah, yes, it's good, so good!" her eyes half-shut and ready to swoon with ecstasy. It was impossible to really know her—to discover, for instance, whether or not she loved Arnoux, for she made fun of him but also seemed jealous of him. It was the same thing with La Vatnaz, whom she would call a wretch one day and her best friend the next. Her whole person, down to the very twist of her chignon, exuded something hard to put into words, a kind of challenge—and he desired her above all for the pleasure of vanquishing and dominating her.

What could he do? For she often sent him packing without ceremony, poking her head around a door for a moment to whisper: "I'm busy; see you this evening!" or he would find her surrounded by a dozen people; and when they were alone you would have thought a wager had been laid against him, there were so many obstacles. He invited her to dinner but she always refused; once she accepted but did not turn up.

A Machiavellian scheme occurred to him.

Knowing from Dussardier of Pellerin's grumbles about him, he had the idea of commissioning a portrait of the Maréchale from the artist, a life-size portrait that would need many sittings; he would not miss one of them, and Pellerin's habitual unpunctuality would make tête-à-têtes easy. So he urged Rosanette to be painted so that she could present her likeness to her beloved Arnoux. She accepted, for she saw herself in the position of honor in the middle of the Grand Salon, with a crowd in front of her and the newspapers writing her up, which would "launch" her at once.

As for Pellerin, he seized on the proposition avidly. This portrait would be a masterpiece and make a great man of him.

He did a mental review of all the portraits by old masters he had seen and finally decided on a Titian, enhanced by ornaments in the manner of Veronese. This meant that he would execute his composition without any artificial shadows, in a direct light that would keep the flesh-tints to a single tone and make the accessories sparkle.

"How would it be," he thought, "if I did her in a pink silk dress with an Oriental burnoose? No, the burnoose would be vulgar! It might be better if she was dressed in glowing blue velvet against a gray background? Or I could even have her in a white lace collar with a black fan and a scarlet curtain behind her."

And through this kind of speculation his concept grew more elaborate every day and he marveled at it.

His heart beat faster when, accompanied by Frédéric, Rosanette arrived at his studio for the first sitting. He asked her to stand on a sort of platform in the middle of the room and, complaining of the light and full of regrets for his former studio, he made her first rest her elbow on a pedestal, then sit in an armchair, and, alternately standing back and approaching her to flick the folds of her dress into place, he gazed at her through narrowed eyes and briefly consulted Frédéric.

"No," he exclaimed, "I'll go back to my original idea. I shall paint you as a Venetian lady."

She would wear a flame-colored velvet dress with a belt of wrought gold, and her wide, ermine-lined sleeve would fall back to show her bare arm, resting on the bannister of a staircase rising behind her. To her left, a large column would soar to make an arc with architectural forms at the top of the canvas. Beneath them, indistinct masses of orange trees, so dark as to be almost black, against a blue sky streaked with white clouds. A silver dish on the tapestry-covered balustrade would hold a bunch of flowers, an amber rosary, a dagger, and an old casket of yellowing ivory overflowing with gold coins, some of which, lying scattered on the floor, would form a chain of bright splashes leading the eye to the tip of Rosanette's foot, for she would stand on the next to last step in a natural position and full in the light.

He went off to get a packing-case and put it on the platform to serve as the step; then he placed some props on the stool which did duty for the balustrade, his jacket, a shield, a tin of sardines, a bundle of quill pens, a knife; and, having thrown a dozen coins onto the floor in front of Rosanette, he made her take up her pose.

"Imagine that these things are treasures, magnificent gifts! The head a little to the right! Perfect! Stay like that! That majestic attitude suits your kind of beauty."

She was wearing a plaid dress with a big muff and trying not to laugh.

"For your hair—we'll thread a string of pearls through it. That always looks well with red hair."

The Maréchale protested that her hair was not red.

"Nonsense! The painter's red is different from the ordinary man's!"

He began to rough in the main outlines and his head was so full of the great artists of the Renaissance that he talked about them. For an hour he dreamed aloud over their magnificent lives, full of genius, glory, and splendor, crowded with triumphal entries into cities and torch-lit feasts with semi-nude women, beautiful as goddesses.

"You were made to live in those days! A woman of your caliber would have merited a nobleman!"

Rosanette thought his compliments very pretty. They decided on a day for the next sitting and Frédéric undertook to provide the accessories.

The heat of the stove had made her a little dizzy, so they went home on foot along the Rue du Bac and paused on the Pont Royal.

It was a beautiful day, clear and sharp. The sun was setting; and some of the windows on the Île de la Cité shone in the distance like panes of beaten gold, while behind them, on the right, the black towers of Nôtre-Dame were silhouetted against the blue sky, the horizon softly swathed in gray mists. There was a gust of wind; Rosanette declared that she was hungry and they went into the Pâtisserie Anglaise.

By the marble counter, covered with plates of little cakes under glass covers, young mothers stood eating with their children. Rosanette devoured two cream tarts. The powdered sugar made little moustaches at the corners of her mouth. From time to time she would draw a handkerchief from her muff to wipe it away; and her face, framed in its green silk hood, resembled a full-blown rose among its leaves.

They resumed their walk; on the rue de la Paix she stopped before a jeweler's window to look at a bracelet. Frédéric wanted to make her a present of it.

"No," she said, "keep your money."

He was wounded.

"Now what's wrong with my sweetie? Is he sad?"

And, with the renewal of the conversation, he began, as usual, to declare his love.

"You know perfectly well it's impossible!"

"Why?"

"Oh, because . . ."

They walked side by side, with Rosanette leaning on Frédéric's arm, and the flounces of her dress flapping against his legs. He remembered a winter twilight when Madame Arnoux had walked beside him in the same fashion over the same sidewalk, and the memory so absorbed him that he was no longer aware of Rosanette and did not give her another thought.

She looked vaguely in front of her, dragging a little on his arm like a lazy child. It was the time of day when everyone returned from the afternoon drive, and the carriages went past them at a fast trot over the dry road. She must have been thinking of Pellerin's compliments, for she heaved a sigh:

"Oh, some people have all the luck! I certainly was made for a rich man."

He replied brutally:

"Well, you've got one, haven't you?" for Monsieur Oudry was reputed to be a millionaire three times over.

She asked nothing better than to be rid of him.

"Who's stopping you?"

And he cracked a few bitter jokes at the expense of this bewigged old bourgeois, attempting to demonstrate that such a liaison was unworthy of her and she should break it off.

"Yes," replied the Maréchale, speaking as if to herself. "I suppose that's what I'll do in the end!"

Frédéric was charmed by her disinterestedness. She moved more slowly and he thought she must be tired, but she obstinately refused to take a carriage and she said good-bye to him at her front door, blowing him a kiss.

"What a shame! And to think that some idiots believe me to be rich!"

He was gloomy when he reached his house.

Hussonnet and Deslauriers were waiting for him.

The bohemian was sitting at the table drawing Turks' heads, and the lawyer, in dirty boots, was dozing on the sofa.

"Ah, at last," he exclaimed. "But what a grim look! Can you listen to me?"

He was losing his popularity as a crammer, for he stuffed his pupils with theories regarded unfavorably by the examiners. He had appeared in court two or three times and had lost, and each fresh disillusionment threw him back more forcibly onto his old dream—a paper where he could display himself, take his vengeance, pour out his bile and his ideas. Furthermore, he would win fortune and reputation. It was in this hope that he had made the bohemian his ally, for Hussonnet owned a paper.

At present he was printing it on pink paper; he invented stories, made up puzzles, tried to stir up controversies, and even (despite the unsuitable premises) tried to put on concerts! A year's subscription "entitles the buyer to an orchestra seat in one of the principal Paris theaters; moreover, the Management undertakes to provide foreigners with any information they may desire, artistic or otherwise." But the printer was threatening them, they owed three terms' rent to the landlord, there were all kinds of difficulties, and Hussonnet would have let *l'Art* die a natural death had it not been for the lawyer, who exhorted and encouraged him every day. He had brought him along to lend more weight to his proposals.

"We've come about the paper," he said.

"What, are you still thinking about that?" replied Frédéric absently.

"Of course I'm thinking about it!"

And he explained his plans once again. By means of reports on the Stock Exchange they would enter into relations with financiers and would thus obtain the indispensable hundred-thousand-francs security money. But if the paper was to be transformed into a political journal they must first have a large number of subscribers, and in order to get them they would have to meet certain expenses, so much to buy the newsprint, so much for the printers, so much for administrative expenses—in short, a sum of fifteen thousand francs.

"I have no money," said Frédéric.

"*We* certainly haven't!" said Deslauriers, folding his arms.

Frédéric, stung by this gesture, replied:

"Is that my fault? . . ."

"Oh, well said! Some people have wood in the fireplace, truffles on the table, a comfortable bed, a library, a carriage, everything that makes life agreeable. But if someone else is shivering with cold under the roof tiles, eating for twenty sous, working like a slave, and foundering in poverty, is that their fault?"

And he repeated: "Is that their fault?" with a Ciceronian irony reminiscent of the law courts. Frédéric tried to speak.

"But I quite understand. One has certain . . . aristocratic . . . needs; for doubtless, some woman . . ."

"Well, and what if there is? Am I not free . . ."

"Oh, completely free!"

And, after a moment's silence:

"Promises are so convenient!"

"Good Lord, I'm not breaking any promises!" said Frédéric.

The lawyer went on:

"Youngsters at school swear all kinds of things, to set up a phalange, imitate Balzac's *Treize!* Then when they see one another again, it's: 'good night, old pal, off with you now!' Because the one who could help the other keeps everything carefully for himself."

"What do you mean?"

"Yes, you haven't even introduced us to the Dambreuses!"

Frédéric looked at him; with his threadbare coat, his

dirty glasses, and his pale face, the lawyer looked so wretched that he could not prevent his lips from curving in a disdainful smile. Deslauriers noticed it and flushed.

He had already picked up his hat and was on his way out. The anxious Hussonnet attempted to soothe him with supplicating glances and, as Frédéric turned his back on him, he said:

"Come on, old fellow! Be my Maecenas! Protect the arts!"

With an abrupt gesture of resignation Frédéric took a sheet of paper, scribbled a few lines, and held it out to him. The bohemian's face lit up. Then, handing the letter to Deslauriers:

"Apologize, my lord!"

Their friend had written asking his notary to send him fifteen thousand francs as soon as possible.

"Ah, that's my old Frédéric there!" cried Deslauriers.

"You're a good man, on my honor!" added the bohemian. "You'll be numbered among the benefactors of the age!"

The lawyer resumed:

"You won't lose by it. It's an excellent speculation."

"I'd stake my head on it, damn it!" cried Hussonnet.

And he made so many stupid remarks and promised so many marvels (which he may have believed) that Frédéric didn't know whether the bohemian was laughing at the others or at himself.

That evening he received a letter from his mother. Although she teased him about it a little, she was really rather surprised that he had not yet become a minister. Then she talked about his health and told him that Monsieur Roque now visited her. "Since he has become a widower I have seen no obstacle to receiving him. Louise is much changed for the better." And, in a postscript: "You never mention your grand acquaintance, Monsieur Dambreuse: if I were in your shoes I should make use of him."

Why not? He had lost his intellectual ambitions and his fortune (he now realized) was insufficient; for, when he had paid his debts and handed over the agreed sum to the others, his income would be diminished by at least four thousand francs. Anyhow, he felt a need to break away from his present existence, to become attached to something. So the following day, when he was dining with Madame Arnoux, he remarked that his mother was nagging him to take up a profession.

"But I thought," she said, "that Monsieur Dambreuse

was going to arrange a position at the Council of State for you. That would suit you admirably!"

So it was her wish. He obeyed.

The banker was sitting in his office, as he had been the first time, and he signaled Frédéric to wait for a minute as a gentleman with his back to the door was discussing something important with him. It concerned coal mines and a merger to be arranged between different companies.

Portraits of General Foy and Louis-Philippe hung on either side of the mirror; the filing cabinets were stacked against the paneling as high as the ceiling, and there were six wicker chairs. Monsieur Dambreuse had no need of a more impressive setting for his business negotiations; it was like one of those dark kitchens where great feasts are prepared. The two enormous safes standing in the corners impressed Frédéric more than anything else. He wondered how many millions they might contain. The banker opened one and the iron door swung back, showing nothing but some blue paper notebooks.

At last the visitor passed in front of Frédéric. It was old man Oudry. They both blushed and bowed, which seemed to surprise Monsieur Dambreuse. For the rest, he was extremely gracious. Nothing could be easier than to recommend his young friend to the Keeper of the Seals. They would be only too happy to have him, and he put the finishing touch to his courtesies by inviting Frédéric to an evening party he was giving in a few days' time.

Frédéric was climbing into the brougham on his way to this affair when a note from the Maréchale arrived. By the light of the carriage lamps he read:

"My dear, I have taken your advice. I have just got rid of my encumbrance. From tomorrow evening, freedom! How's that for valor?"

Nothing more! But it was an invitation to fill the vacant place. He gave an exclamation, stuffed the note into his pocket, and set off.

Two mounted policemen were stationed in the street. A string of small lamps hung over the two carriage entrances, and the servants in the courtyard were shouting as they maneuvered the carriages up to the foot of the steps. Then, within the hall, the noise suddenly ceased.

The central well of the staircase was full of tall plants; the lamps with their porcelain globes shed a light that rippled on the walls like white watered satin. Frédéric mounted the stairs with a light heart. An usher announced

him; Monsieur Dambreuse held out his hand and Madame
Dambreuse appeared almost immediately.

She was in a mauve dress trimmed with lace, her hair
seemed to be arranged in even more ringlets than usual,
and she was not wearing a single jewel.

She complained of the infrequency of his visits and
made small talk for a few minutes. The guests were arriving; for greeting, some bent their bodies to one side,
others bowed low or merely nodded their heads; then a
married couple came in, and a family group, and they all
dispersed into the already crowded drawing room.

Under the central chandelier an enormous ottoman supported a flower-stand whose blooms curved down like
plumes, overhanging the heads of the seated women
around it. Others occupied the armchairs that formed two
straight lines broken at regular intervals by the long
window curtains in orange-red velvet and the tall doorways with their gilded lintels.

When seen from a distance, the crowd of men standing
about with their hats in their hands formed a solid black
mass, dotted here and there by the red ribbons in some of
their buttonholes, and made even more somber by the
monotonous whiteness of their cravats. Except for a few
adolescent youths with new whiskers, everyone seemed
bored; some dandies were rocking on their heels with a
sulky air. There were plenty of gray heads and wigs, an
occasional bald pate glistened, and on the withered
faces, either purple or very pale, could be seen the traces
of profound fatigue, for these men were mostly in business or politics. Monsieur Dambreuse had also invited
several scholars, some judges, and two or three celebrated doctors; and with humble mien he turned aside
compliments on his party, and allusions to his wealth.

There were footmen in gold lace everywhere. The great
candelabras, like bouquets of fire, shed their light over the
hangings and were reflected in the looking-glasses; and at
the far end of the dining room, which was decorated with
a jasmine-covered lattice, the sideboard looked like the
high altar of a cathedral or an exhibition of goldsmiths'
work, there were so many platters, dish covers, knives,
forks, and spoons in silver and silver-gilt, surrounded by
cut glass from which flashes of rainbow-hued light darted
over the food. The other three rooms were overflowing
with works of art; there were landscapes by old masters
on the walls, ivories and porcelains on the tables, curios
from China on the consoles, and lacquered screens stand-

ing before the windows; the fireplaces were filled with sheaves of camellias and music vibrated softly in the distance, like the humming of bees.

There were not many sets of quadrilles, and the dancers moved through them in a lethargic shuffle, as if fulfilling a duty. Frédéric overheard remarks like these:

"Were you at the last charity ball at the Hôtel Lambert, Mademoiselle?"

"No, Monsieur."

"It will be terribly hot in here later!"

"Oh yes, stifling!"

"Who composed this polka?"

"I'm afraid I don't know, Madame!"

And behind him three old dotards, standing in the embrasure of a window, were whispering obscenities to each other; others were discussing railways, free trade; a sportsman was telling a hunting story; a Legitimist was arguing with an Orléanist.

Wandering from group to group he found himself in the card room where, surrounded by serious-looking men, he recognized Martinon, "now attached to the Public Prosecutor's office in the capital."

His fleshy, wax-colored face fitted suitably into his beard and the beard itself was a work of art, so neatly trimmed were the black hairs; and, maintaining a happy medium between the elegance naturally aspired to by a man of his age and the dignity demanded by his profession, he stuck his thumbs into his armpits as dandies did, and then thrust his arm into the breast of his waistcoat in the style of the doctrinaires. Even though he wore highly polished patent-leather boots, he had shaved his temples to give himself an intellectual's high forehead.

After uttering a few chilly words, he turned back to his group. A landowner was saying:

"It's a class that dreams of social revolution."

"They are demanding the organization of labor!" broke in another. "Can you believe it?"

"What can you expect," said a third, "when you see Monsieur de Genoude hand in hand with *le Siècle*."*

"And the Conservatives are calling themselves Progressives! What are they trying to lead us into? A republic! As if such a thing were possible in France!"

*Monsieur de Genoude was one of the chiefs of the Legitimist party and the editor of the *Gazette de France*, while *le Siècle* was the mouthpiece of the constitutional left.

Everyone agreed that a republic was impossible in France.

"I still say," observed one gentleman in a loud voice, "that people spend too much time talking about the Revolution; there has been a tremendous amount written about it, histories, books . . ."

"Not to mention," said Martinon, "that there may be more serious subjects to study!"

An official complained of the scandalous state of the theater.

"This new play *la Reine Margot,* for example, really exceeds all bounds! What need was there to go on about the Valois? It all just shows the monarchy in an unfavorable light. It's like the press! Whatever people say about the September laws, they're not nearly severe enough! I should like to have court-martials to gag the journalists. At the slightest sign of insolence, hale them before a military tribunal! and that would do it!"

"Oh, careful, Monsieur, careful!" exclaimed a professor. "Don't attack the precious gains we made in eighteen thirty! Let's respect our liberties!"

"It would be better to decentralize, spread the surplus city population out over the countryside."

"But the towns are gangrenous!" cried a Catholic. "We must reaffirm Religion."

Martinon hastened to say:

"It certainly is a restraining influence!"

The whole problem came from the modern desire to rise above one's station in life, to enjoy luxuries.

"And yet," objected an industrialist, "luxury is good for business. That's why I approve of the Duc de Nemours' insistence on knee breeches at his evening parties."

"Monsieur Thiers went to one in trousers. You've heard his witticism on the subject?"

"Yes, delightful. But he's becoming a demagogue, and his speech on the separation of powers was partly to blame for the May twelfth uprising."

"Oh, nonsense!"

"Now, now!"

The circle was forced to make way for a servant carrying a tray, who was trying to get into the card room.

Under the green shades of the candles, the tables were covered with gold coins and rows of cards. Frédéric stopped at one of them, lost the fifteen napoléons he had in his pocket, turned on his heel, and found himself on the threshold of the boudoir where, as it happened, Madame Dambreuse was now sitting.

The room was full of women side by side on backless benches. Their long skirts ballooned out around them like waves from which their busts emerged; and their breasts were shown off by their low-cut bodices. Nearly all of them held bunches of violets. The matte tones of their gloves contrasted with the living whiteness of their arms; fringes and flowers hung down over their shoulders and sometimes, when they shuddered, the dress would seem on the point of falling off. But the provocativeness of their dress was tempered by the propriety of their faces; indeed, several of them had an almost animal placidity, and this group of semi-nude women evoked thoughts of the interior of a harem; a coarser comparison occurred to the young man. There were, in fact, beauties of every type: Englishwomen with keepsake-book profiles, an Italian whose black eyes smoldered like Vesuvius, three sisters from Normandy dressed in blue, fresh as apple blossoms in the spring, a tall redhead wearing amethysts —and the white sparkle of the sprays of diamonds trembling in their hair, the luminous patches of the jewels displayed on their breasts, and the soft glow of the pearls framing their faces mingled with the glitter of gold rings, the lace, the powder, the plumes, the vermillion of the small mouths and the pearly white teeth. The ceiling, swelling into a dome, gave the boudoir the shape of a basket; and a scented breeze stirred about the fluttering of the fans.

Frédéric, stationed behind them with his glass to his eye, decided that not all the shoulders were irreproachable; he thought of the Maréchale, which drove out his temptations, or else consoled him for them.

He inspected Madame Dambreuse, however, and found her charming, in spite of her rather wide mouth and her nostrils, which were a little too flared. But she had a grace all her own. Her curls had a kind of passionate languor about them, and her agate-colored forehead seemed to conceal a multitude of things and denote a masterful disposition.

She had placed her husband's niece, a rather ugly girl, next to her. From time to time, she would leave her seat to welcome a new arrival, and the murmur of female voices, growing louder, resembled the cackle of

They discussed the Tunisian ambassadors and their birds.

costumes. One lady had been to the latest reception at the
Academy; another talked about Molière's *Don Juan*, in a
new production at the Français. Madame Dambreuse,
with a meaningful glance at her niece, put a finger to her
lips, but a smile escaped her and gave the lie to her
austerity.

Suddenly Martinon appeared in the doorway opposite.
She rose. He offered her his arm. Frédéric, wishing to see
more of his gallantries, made his way through the gaming
tables and joined them in the drawing room. Madame
Dambreuse at once left her cavalier and struck up a
friendly conversation with him.

She understood why he did not dance or play cards.

"Youth is the time for sadness!" Then, taking in the
ball with a single glance:

"In any case, it's hardly amusing! For some people, at
any rate!"

And she stopped in front of the row of chairs, letting
fall an amiable word here and there, while old gentlemen
in spectacles came up to pay court to her. She introduced
Frédéric to some of them. Then Monsieur Dambreuse
touched him gently on the elbow and led him out onto the
terrace.

He had seen the Minister. It would not be an easy
matter. Before being taken on as an official of the Council
of State it was necessary to pass an examination. Frédéric,
filled with an inexplicable self-confidence, replied that he
knew the required subjects.

The financier was not surprised, after all that Monsieur
Roque had said in his praise.

At the sound of this name, little Louise, his home, his
bedroom rose again before Frédéric's eyes, and he remembered nights like this one when he had sat by his
window listening to the passing waggoners. The remem-
brance of his melancholy turned his thoughts to Madame
Arnoux and he fell silent, though he continued to stroll up
and down the terrace. The windows were long red panels
among the shadows, the sounds of the ball were growing
fainter, carriages were beginning to leave.

"But why," asked Monsieur Dambreuse, "are you so set
on the Council of State?"

And, speaking as a man of experience, he declared
that public office was a blind alley; he knew a good deal
on that score; business was a much better proposition.
Frédéric objected that it was difficult to get started in
business.

"Oh, nonsense! I'd teach you the ropes in no time!"

Was he offering to make him an associate in his business ventures? As if in a flash of lightning the young man saw an enormous fortune looming before him.

"Let's go in," said the banker. "You'll have supper with us, won't you?"

It was three o'clock and people were leaving. In the dining room a table had been laid for the closest friends of the family.

Monsieur Dambreuse noticed Martinon and, going over to his wife, said in a low voice:

"Did you ask him?"

She replied curtly:

"Yes, of course!"

The niece was not there. Everyone drank deep and laughed loudly and there were some broad jokes which shocked no one, since they were all feeling that elation that follows a prolonged period of constraint. Only Martinon remained grave; he thought it good form to refuse the champagne, but otherwise showed himself flexible and very polite; for when Monsieur Dambreuse, who had a narrow chest, complained of a feeling of oppression, he asked after his health several times, and then turned his bluish eyes toward Madame Dambreuse.

She challenged Frédéric to tell her which of the girls he had admired. He had noticed none of them and, moreover, preferred women of thirty.

"That may not be a bad idea!" she replied.

Then, as they were putting on their pelisses and overcoats, Monsieur Dambreuse said to him:

"Come and see me one of these mornings. We'll have a chat."

At the foot of the stairs, Martinon lighted a cigar, and his profile, as he puffed at it, was so coarse that his companion blurted out:

"My word, what a huge head you've got!"

"Well, a few girls have had theirs turned by it!" replied the young magistrate, with an air of mingled self-confidence and annoyance.

While Frédéric was getting ready for bed, he went over the whole evening in his mind. First of all his appearance (he had glanced at himself in the mirrors several times) had been irreproachable, from the cut of his coat to the knot of his shoelaces; he had spoken to important men, had had a close view of rich women. Monsieur Dambreuse had been kindness itself, and Madame

Dambreuse almost flirtatious. He weighed, one by one,
her slightest words, her glances, a thousand things which
were impossible to analyze but expressive nevertheless. It
would be a real feather in his cap to have a mistress like
that! And why not, after all! He was just as good as the
next man! Perhaps she was not really so unapproachable?
Then he remembered Martinon and went off to sleep with
a pitying smile for that fine fellow.

He was awakened by thoughts of the Maréchale; the
words "from tomorrow evening" in her note were obviously an invitation for this very day. He waited till nine
o'clock, then hastened round to see her.

Someone went up the staircase in front of him and shut
the door. He rang the bell. Delphine opened it and announced that Madame was not at home.

Frédéric insisted, implored. He had something very important to tell her, just one word. Finally, the persuasive
powers of a hundred-sou piece had their effect and the
maid left him alone in the hall.

Rosanette appeared. She was in her nightdress, her hair
loose around her shoulders, and, tossing her head, she
made from a distance a sweeping gesture with both her
arms to indicate that she could not receive him.

Frédéric went slowly down the stairs. This new caprice
topped them all. He was completely bewildered.

In front of the porter's lodge he was stopped by
Mademoiselle Vatnaz.

"Did she receive you?"

"No!"

"You were thrown out?"

"How did you know?"

"It's written all over you! But come on, let's get out
of here! I'm suffocating!"

And she led him out into the street. She was breathing
heavily, and he felt her thin arm trembling on his own.
Suddenly she burst out:

"Oh, the wretch!"

"Who do you mean?"

"But it's him! Delmar!"

This revelation humiliated Frédéric:

"Are you quite sure?"

"I tell you I followed him!" cried Mademoiselle Vatnaz.
"I saw him go in! So you see! Of course, I should have expected it; it was stupid of me to take him there in the first
place. And if you only knew! I took him in, I fed him, I
dressed him; and all I had to do to get him publicity in the

papers! I loved him like a mother!" Then, with a sneer: "Oh, but His Highness had to have a little luxury! He's taking a gamble, you can believe that! As for her! To think I knew her when she worked at sewing lingerie! If it hadn't been for me she'd have been in the gutter a score of times! But I'll push her there yet, you see if I don't! I'd like to see her die in the workhouse! I'll see that everyone finds out about her!"

And, like a torrent of dishwater carrying filth along with it, in her anger she poured out her rival's shameful secrets to Frédéric in a tumbling stream.

"She's slept with Jumillac, with Flacourt, with little Allard, with Bertinaux, with Saint-Valéry, the pock-marked one—no, it was the other! Oh, it doesn't matter, they're brothers! And when she was in a fix I always arranged everything, but what did I get for it? She's so tight-fisted! And then, of course, it was a kindness on my part even to speak to her! We do belong to different worlds, after all! Am I a whore? Do I sell my body? Quite apart from the fact that she's as stupid as an owl! She spells 'category' with a 'k'! In fact they'll suit each other very well; he's just the same type, in spite of calling himself an artist and thinking he's a genius. My God, if he had even ordinary common sense he'd never have done this! You don't leave a decent woman for a hussy! Oh, but what do I care—he was getting ugly! I detest him! If I met him now, you know what I'd do? I'd spit in his face!" She spat. "Yes, that's what I think of him now! And what about Arnoux? Isn't it revolting! He's forgiven her so many times! No one knows the sacrifices he's made! She should kiss his feet! He's so generous, so good!"

Frédéric enjoyed hearing Delmar abused. He had accepted Arnoux as her lover, but her present perfidy seemed to him abnormal and unfair, and, swept away by the old maid's emotion, he even felt a kind of tenderness for Arnoux. Suddenly he found himself in front of the latter's door; Mademoiselle Vatnaz, without his noticing, had led him down the Faubourg Poissonnière.

"Here we are," she said. "I can't go up. But there's nothing to stop you, is there?"

"But why should I?"

"To tell him everything, of course!"

As if awakening with a start from a nightmare, Frédéric understood the infamous action into which he was being pushed.

"Well?" she asked.

He looked up at the second story. Madame Arnoux's lamp was lighted. It was true that there was nothing to stop him going up.

"I'll wait for you here. Go on!"

This order completed the extinction of his sympathy for her, and he said:

"I'll be up there a long time. You'd better go home. I'll come round and see you tomorrow."

"No, no!" replied the Vatnaz, stamping her foot. "Take him there with you! Arrange for him to surprise them!"

"But Delmar will have left!"

She bowed her head:

"Yes, that may be true."

And she stood silently in the middle of the street, with the carriages passing on either side. Then, gazing at Frédéric with her wildcat's eyes:

"I can count on you, can't I? There's a real bond between us now! Go ahead. I'll see you tomorrow."

As Frédéric went along the corridor, he could hear two voices arguing. Madame Arnoux's said:

"Don't lie! I tell you, don't lie to me!"

He went in and they fell silent.

Arnoux was pacing up and down the room and Madame, very pale, was sitting in the little chair next to the fire, staring straight ahead. Frédéric made as if to leave. Arnoux, delighted by the arrival of an ally, seized him by the hand.

"But I'm afraid . . ." said Frédéric.

"Come on, stay!" whispered Arnoux into his ear. Madame went on:

"You must show indulgence, Monsieur Moreau! This is the kind of situation that sometimes occurs in a marriage."

"Only because someone else creates it," said Arnoux heartily. "Women's heads are always stuffed with fantasies about you! This one, for example, isn't at all bad. On the contrary! Well, she's spent the last hour pestering me with a lot of nonsense."

"It's true!" replied Madame Arnoux impatiently. "Because after all, you did buy it!"

"Me?"

"Yes, you! At the Persian shop!"

"The cashmere shawl!" thought Frédéric.

He felt guilty and frightened.

She added at once:

"It was last month, on a Saturday, the fourteenth."

"Ah! It so happens that I was at Creil on precisely that day! So you see!"

"Not at all! I know because we dined with the Bertins on the fourteenth."

"The fourteenth . . ." said Arnoux, casting his eyes up to heaven as if to remember a date.

"I can even tell you that the clerk who sold it to you had fair hair!"

"As if I'd remember the clerk!"

"Nevertheless he wrote the address at your dictation: eighteen, Rue de Laval."

"How do you know?" asked Arnoux, astounded.

She shrugged her shoulders:

"Oh, it's quite simple: I went there to have my own cashmere shawl repaired, and the department head told me they'd just sent a similar one to Madame Arnoux."

"Is it my fault if there is a Madame Arnoux on that street?"

"That's possible. But not a Jacques Arnoux," she replied.

Then he started to wander from the point, protesting his innocence. It was a mistake, a coincidence, one of those inexplicable things that happen sometimes. People should not be condemned on pure suspicion, vague evidence; and he cited the example of the unfortunate Lesurques.*

"Anyhow, I've told you you're making a mistake. Do you want me to give you my word?"

"Don't bother!"

"Why?"

She looked at him steadily, without a word; then she reached out, took down the silver casket from the mantelpiece, and held out an open bill to him.

Arnoux reddened to his ears and his agitated features grew puffy.

"Well?"

"But . . ." he replied slowly, "what does that prove?"

"Ah!" she said, with a singular intonation in which sorrow and irony were mingled. "Ah!"

Arnoux still held the bill and was turning it this way and that with his eyes fixed on it, as if he expected to find there the answer to some great problem.

"Oh yes, of course, I remember," he said at last. "It was

*Who had been wrongly found guilty and executed under the Directory.

an errand for someone—you must know about it, Frédéric, don't you?" Frédéric said nothing. "An errand I did for . . . for Old Oudry."

"And who was it intended for?"

"For his mistress!"

"For yours, you mean!" cried Madame Arnoux, springing to her feet.

"I swear . . ."

"Don't start that again! I know everything!"

"Oh, do you! So I'm being spied on!"

She replied coldly:

"Does that wound your sense of delicacy?"

"When people start getting emotional," went on Arnoux, searching for his hat, "and it is impossible to talk things over rationally! . . ."

Then, with a great sigh, he added:

"Never marry, my boy, take my advice!"

And he decamped, feeling the need of some fresh air.

A profound silence followed his departure, and everything in the apartment seemed stiller than before. The light from the oil lamp made a white circle on the ceiling while the shadows lay in the corners like layers of black gauze; they could hear the ticking of the clock and the crackle of the fire.

Madame Arnoux had just sat down again in the armchair on the other side of the fireplace. She bit her lips, shivering; she lifted her hands to her face, a sob escaped her, and she was crying.

He sat down in the little chair and, in the caressing voice one uses to an invalid, said:

"You must realize that I do not share . . ."

She did not reply. But, continuing her thoughts aloud, she said:

"I leave him free enough! There was no need for him to lie!"

"Certainly not," said Frédéric.

It was probably the result of his way of life, he had not given it much thought, and perhaps in more serious matters . . .

"What would you describe as a more serious matter?"

"Oh, nothing!"

Frédéric bowed, with a docile smile. Still, Arnoux had certain good qualities: he loved his children.

"He does his best to ruin them!"

That was a consequence of his easygoing temperament; he was, after all, a good-natured fellow.

She interrupted:

"But what do you mean by 'good-natured'?"

He went on defending him like this, with the vaguest excuses he could think of, and even while he pitied her, he rejoiced, exulting in his innermost heart. From a desire for vengeance or a need for affection, she would turn to him. His hopes, immeasurably increased, strengthened his love.

Never had she seemed so captivating to him, so profoundly beautiful. From time to time her chest would heave with a deep breath; her eyes, staring straight before her, seemed dilated by some inner vision, and her lips were parted as if to give passage to her soul. Occasionally she would press her handkerchief hard against her mouth; he would have liked to be that little scrap of cambric, all soaked with tears. In spite of himself, he glanced at the couch at the back of the alcove, imagining her head on the pillow, and he could visualize it so clearly that he had to restrain himself from seizing her in his arms. Calmed, inert, she shut her eyes. He approached and, bending over her, greedily examined her face. There was a sound of boots in the corridor; it was Arnoux. They heard him shut the door of his room. Frédéric, with a gesture, asked Madame Arnoux whether he should go to him.

She answered "Yes" in the same manner, and this mute exchange of thoughts was like a consent, the beginning of an adultery.

Arnoux was unfastening his coat, getting ready for bed.

"Well, how is she?"

"Better," said Frédéric. "She'll get over it."

But Arnoux was upset.

"You don't know her. Her nerves nowadays! . . . Damn fool clerk! You see what happens when you're too nice! If only I hadn't given Rosanette that blasted shawl!"

"Don't regret it! She couldn't be more grateful!"

"You think so?"

Frédéric had no doubt of it. The proof was that she had just given Old Oudry his marching orders.

"Oh, the poor darling!"

And, in the rush of his emotion, Arnoux wanted to hurry over to see her.

"It's not worth it! I've just come from her house. She's ill!"

"That's an additional reason!"

He scrambled back into his coat and had already

picked up his candle. Frédéric cursed himself for his stupidity and pointed out that he should, for decency's sake, stay with his wife that evening. He couldn't leave her alone; it would be too bad.

"Frankly, you'd be wrong to do it! There's no need to rush. You can go tomorrow. Come on! Stay for my sake."

Arnoux put down his candle and, embracing Frédéric, exclaimed:

"You really are a good fellow!"

Chapter Three

This was the beginning of a miserable existence for Frédéric. He became the parasite of the household.

If anyone was ill he called three times a day to ask after them, went to see the piano tuner, thought of a thousand little attentions. He endured, with every sign of contentment, Mademoiselle Marthe's sulks and the caresses of little Eugène, who always stroked his face with his dirty hands. He was present at dinners where the husband and wife sat opposite each other without exchanging a word, or else Arnoux would irritate his wife by making absurd remarks. After the meal, he would play with his son in the dining room, hiding behind the furniture and letting the child ride on his back while he crawled about on all fours, like Henry IV. Finally, he would go out and she would start immediately on her eternal subject of complaint: Arnoux.

It was not his misconduct which annoyed her. But her pride seemed to be wounded, and she let Frédéric see her repugnance for this man without delicacy, dignity, or honor.

"Or rather he is mad!" she would say.

Frédéric solicited her confidences adroitly. Soon he knew the whole story of her life.

Her parents were small shopkeepers at Chartres. One day Arnoux, sketching on the bank of the river (in those days he fancied himself a painter), had noticed her as she came out of church and had asked for her hand in marriage; her parents had had no hesitation, in view of his wealth. Moreover, he had been madly in love with her. She added:

"Heavens! He still loves me; in his way!"

They had spent their first months traveling in Italy.

Arnoux, despite his enthusiasm over landscapes and masterpieces, had spent his time complaining of the wine and organizing picnics with Englishmen to pass the time. A few pictures which he resold well had drawn him to dealing in paintings. Then he had become infatuated with the idea of a china factory. Now he was being tempted by other speculations and, as he became increasingly vulgar, he was falling into coarse and spendthrift habits. It was not so much his vices that offended her as his whole way of life. There was no possibility of change, and her unhappiness was irredeemable.

Frédéric declared that his life was a failure also.

But he was still very young. Why despair? And she gave him good advice: "Work! Marry!" He answered with bitter smiles; for, instead of divulging the true reason for his melancholy, he pretended to a different and more sublime one, taking on something of the accursed Anthony* —a style that was, as it happened, not completely foreign to his thoughts.

In certain men, the more strongly they desire something, the more difficult it is for them to act. They are hamstrung by a lack of self-confidence, terrified that they might offend. Besides, profound feelings are like chaste women; they are afraid of drawing attention and go through life with downcast eyes.

Although he knew Madame Arnoux better now (perhaps even for that very reason), he was more timid than ever. Every morning he vowed to be bold; but an invincible bashfulness overcame him and he could find no example to follow, since she was unlike all other women. He had dreamed of her so much that he had ended by placing her outside the human condition. Beside her he felt less important on this earth than the snippets of silk which fell from her scissors.

Then he would think of absurd, monstrous things, such as assaults at night with drugs and skeleton keys—anything seemed easier than to face her scorn.

Besides, the children, the two maids, the way the rooms were arranged, created insurmountable obstacles. So he resolved to have her to himself, and to go and live together far away, in some remote spot; he even deliberated as to which lake would be blue enough, which beach

---

*Anthony, the hero of the elder Dumas' play of that name, is an archetype of the doomed, melancholy Romantic hero as seen by the young men of the 1830's.

delightful enough, whether it should be in Spain, in Switzerland, or in the East; and, deliberately choosing the days when she seemed most irritated with Arnoux, he would tell her that she must escape from her present situation, find some way out, and that the only one he could see was a separation. But her love for her children would prevent her from ever going to such extremes. Such virtue increased his respect for her.

He spent his afternoons remembering his previous day's visit and looking forward to the one he would pay that evening. When he was not dining with them, he would post himself on the corner of the street about nine o'clock and, as soon as Arnoux had closed the outer door behind him, he would eagerly climb the stairs to the second floor and, with an innocent air, inquire of the maid if Monsieur were at home.

Then he would feign surprise at not finding him in.

Arnoux would often return unexpectedly. Then he would have to accompany him to a little café in the Rue Sainte-Anne, which was now a haunt of Regimbart's.

The Citizen would begin to giving vent to some new grievance against the Throne. Then they would chat, trading amicable insults, for the manufacturer took Regimbart for a first-rate thinker and, annoyed at the waste of such talent, would tease him about his laziness. The Citizen found Arnoux full of warmth and imagination but decidedly lacking in morals; so he treated him without the slightest indulgence, even refusing to dine at his apartment because "formality irritated him."

Sometimes, just as they were saying good night, Arnoux would suddenly feel hungry. He "had to have" an omelette or some baked apples and, as what he wanted was never to be found in the establishment, he would send out for it. They would wait. Regimbart did not leave, and ended up by grumpily accepting something to eat.

He was, however, a depressing companion, for he would spend hours sitting over the same half-empty glass. As Providence had not arranged the world according to his specifications, he was turning into a hypochondriac, no longer wanted to read the papers, and roared at the mere mention of England. Once, in connection with some poor service from a waiter, he exclaimed:

"Haven't we had enough insults from abroad!"

Apart from these moments of crisis he held his peace, meditating on "an infallible plan to sweep away the whole set-up."

While he was lost in his reflections, Arnoux, in a monotonous voice and with a rather glassy eye, would recount incredible anecdotes of which he was always the hero, thanks to his resourcefulness, and Frédéric (probably because of some hidden similarity between them) felt a certain attraction to him. He reproached himself for this weakness, feeling that, on the contrary, he ought to hate him. Arnoux would complain in Frédéric's presence of his wife's moods, her stubbornness, her unjust accusations. She was not like that in the old days.

"If I were in your shoes," said Frédéric, "I'd give her an allowance and live on my own."

Arnoux made no reply and, a moment later, would start singing her praises. She was good, devoted, intelligent, virtuous, and, turning to her physical qualities, he was prodigal in his revelations, like those heedless men who display their treasures in taverns.

He was thrown off his balance by a catastrophe.

He had joined a china-clay company as a member of the board of trustees. But, believing everything he was told, he had signed inaccurate reports and approved without verification the annual balance sheets which had been fraudulently drawn up by the manager. Now the company had collapsed and Arnoux, legally liable, had just been condemned, with the other trustees, to pay damages that lost him about thirty thousand francs, aggravated by the grounds on which the judgment had been given.

Frédéric read about this in a newspaper and hurried over to the Rue de Paradis.

He was received in Madame's room. It was breakfast-time, and a table near the fireplace was laden with bowls of coffee. There were slippers lying about on the carpet and clothes on the chairs. Arnoux, in a pair of drawers and a knitted jacket, had red eyes and his hair was standing on end; little Eugène was crying because of his mumps as he nibbled at his slice of bread and jam; his sister was eating peacefully and Madame Arnoux, a little paler than usual, was waiting on all three of them.

"Well," said Arnoux, with a heavy sigh, "so you know the news!" Frédéric made a gesture of sympathy, and he continued:

"That's the way it is! I am the victim of my trust in others!"

After this he fell silent and his depression was such that he pushed away his breakfast. Madame Arnoux lifted her eyes to heaven and shrugged her shoulders. He passed his hands over his forehead.

"After all, I am not guilty of anything. I have nothing to reproach myself with. It's a piece of bad luck but we'll come through all right! Oh well, it's no use crying over spilled milk!"

And he started munching a brioche, in obedience to his wife's entreaties.

That evening he wanted to dine alone with her in a private room at the Maison d'Or. Madame Arnoux could not understand this tender impulse, and even took offense at being treated like a light woman—treatment which, coming from Arnoux, was on the contrary a proof of affection. So, as he was bored, he went off to amuse himself at the Maréchale's.

Until now, people had overlooked his faults for the sake of his good nature. His lawsuit led to his being looked on as a man of shady reputation, and people avoided coming to his house.

Frédéric felt himself obliged, as a point of honor, to see more of them than ever. He took a box at the Italiens and invited them there every week. They were, however, at that stage of an ill-assorted marriage when the concessions each partner has made to the other give rise to an invincible lassitude that renders life intolerable. Madame Arnoux kept herself under tight control so as not to make scenes, Arnoux was sunk in gloom, and the sight of these two unfortunate creatures saddened Frédéric.

As Arnoux confided in him, she asked him to try and find out how his business affairs were going. But he was ashamed of himself for eating Arnoux's dinners while coveting his wife. He continued to do so, nevertheless, telling himself that he must protect her and that some chance might arise of being useful to her.

He had visited Monsieur Dambreuse a week after the ball and the financier had offered him twenty shares in his coal mines; Frédéric had not returned. Deslauriers wrote to him; he left his letters unanswered. Pellerin had asked him to come round to see the portrait; he kept refusing. He did accede, however, to the entreaties of Cisy, who was obsessed with the idea of making Rosanette's acquaintance.

She gave him a very friendly reception without, however, throwing her arms around his neck as she had in the old days. His companion was delighted to be in the house of a woman of easy virtue and, above all, to find himself chatting with an actor. Delmar was there.

A play in which he had taken the part of a peasant who lectures Louis XIV and prophesies the Revolution had made him so popular that the same role kept being manufactured for him, and his present function consisted in flouting monarchs from every country under the sun. As an English brewer he insulted Charles I, as a student from Salamanca cursed Philip II, or as a wounded father railed at La Pompadour; this last was the best of all! Little boys waited outside the stage door to see him, and his biography, which was on sale at intermission, depicted him as caring for his aged mother, reading the Bible, and helping the poor; in fact, as a kind of St. Vincent de Paul with a touch of Brutus and Mirabeau. They called him "Our Delmar." He had a mission—he was becoming the Messiah.

Rosanette had been fascinated by all this and she had got rid of Old Oudry without a second thought, as she was not avaricious.

Arnoux, who knew this quality in her, had taken advantage of it for a long time to keep her cheaply; the old man had come along and all three of them had been careful not to bring matters out into the open. Then, imagining that she had sent Oudry away purely for his sake, Arnoux had raised her allowance. But she kept making demands on him with a frequency which he found inexplicable, for she was living in a less expensive style; she had even sold the cashmere shawl, saying that she wanted to settle her old debts. He always gave her what she asked of him, for she bewitched and exploited him ruthlessly. The house was deluged with bills and writs. Frédéric felt that there must soon be a crisis.

One day he went to visit Madame Arnoux. She was out; Monsieur was working downstairs, in the shop.

Arnoux, in fact, amid his pots, was in the process of bamboozling a recently married young couple, bourgeois from the provinces. He spoke of turning and throwing, of mottling and glazing, and not wanting to look as if they did not understand, the pair nodded their heads in approbation and bought what they were offered.

When the customers had left, he told Frédéric about a minor altercation he had had with his wife that morning. To ward off any remarks about the amount of money he was spending, he had declared that the Maréchale was no longer his mistress.

"I even told her that she was yours!"

Frédéric was indignant, but reproaches might betray him; he stammered:

"But you shouldn't have done that, you really shouldn't!"

"Why, what's wrong with it?" said Arnoux. "There's no dishonor in passing for her lover, is there? I'm her lover and I'm proud of it! Wouldn't you be delighted to be in my shoes?"

Had she told him? Was this an insinuation? Frédéric hastened to reply:

"No! Of course not! On the contrary!"

"Well then?"

"Yes, you're right! It doesn't matter."

Arnoux went on:

"Why don't you come round to her place any longer?"

Frédéric promised to resume his visits.

"Oh, I was forgetting! Try . . . when you're talking about Rosanette . . . let something slip . . . I don't know what, but something will occur to you . . . some remark that will convince my wife that you're Rosanette's lover. I'm asking you as a favor, eh?"

The young man made no answer but an ambiguous grimace. This calumny would destroy his hopes. He went to see Madame Arnoux that very evening and swore that Arnoux's allegations were false.

"You're telling me the real truth?"

He seemed sincere and, after taking a deep breath, she said: "I believe you," with a beautiful smile. Then she bowed her head and, without looking at him, added:

"In any case, no one has any rights over you!"

So she had guessed nothing and must despise him, since she did not believe that he loved her enough to be faithful to her! Frédéric, forgetting his attempts on Rosanette, was outraged by her permissiveness.

Afterwards, she asked him to visit "that woman" from time to time so as to keep an eye on what was going on.

Arnoux came in and, five minutes later, wanted to drag him off to Rosanette's.

The situation was becoming intolerable.

His thoughts were turned in another direction by a letter from the lawyer to say he was sending on the fifteen thousand francs the next day and, to make up for his neglect of Deslauriers, he went round immediately to give him the good news.

The lawyer lived on the Rue des Trois-Maries on the

fifth floor, looking out onto a courtyard. The principal
decoration of his office, a cold little room with a tiled floor
and grayish wallpaper, was a gold medal, the trophy of
his doctorate, which hung in an ebony frame near the
looking-glass. A mahogany bookcase with glass doors contained almost a hundred volumes. The leather-topped desk
stood in the center of the room. There were four old
green velvet-covered armchairs in the corners and some
wood shavings blazed in the fireplace, where there was
always a fire laid, ready to be lit at the sound of the bell.
It was his consulting hour; the lawyer was wearing a white
cravat.

At the news of the fifteen thousand francs (which he
had doubtless given up expecting), he gave a chuckle of
pleasure.

"That's good, my friend, that's good, that's very good!"

He threw some wood on the fire, sat down again, and
immediately started to talk about the paper. The first
thing to do was to get rid of Hussonnet.

"That idiot gets on my nerves! As for representing any
one political opinion, to my mind the fairest and cleverest
thing to do is to remain neutral."

Frédéric looked surprised.

"But of course! The time has come to treat politics
scientifically. Those old fellows in the eighteenth century
started off in the right direction, but then Rousseau and
the other literary gentlemen brought in philanthropy and
poetry and all that stuff, much to the delight of the
Catholics; a natural alliance, anyhow, since the modern
reformers (I can prove it) all believe in Revelation. But,
if you have masses sung for Poland; if, in the place of the
God of the Dominicans, who was an executioner, you
worship the god of the Romantics, who is an upholsterer;
if, in fact, your conception of the Absolute is no larger
than your forefathers', the monarchy will creep in under
your republican forms and your red bonnet will never be
anything but a priest's calotte! The only differences will
be that solitary confinement will have replaced torture;
insult to religion, blasphemy; the Concert of Europe, the
Holy Alliance; and, in this wonderful system which is so
much admired, made up of debris from the reign of Louis
XIV and remnants of Voltairianism, covered with a lick
of Imperial paint and incorporating fragments of the
British constitution, you will find municipal councils trying
to score off the mayor, general councils their prefect, the
parliament the king, the press the authorities, and the

administration everyone! But there are good souls who go into ecstasies over the civil code, which was drawn up, whatever they may say, in a mean and tyrannical spirit; for the legislator, instead of doing his job, which is to codify tradition, has attempted to remodel society like a second Lycurgus! Why does the law restrict a father's rights to leave his property as he sees fit? Why does it restrict the compulsory sale of buildings? Why does it punish vagrancy as a crime when it shouldn't even be a misdemeanor? And there are other instances. I know them all! I am going to write a little work of fiction entitled *History of the Concept of Justice* which will be really funny! But I'm horribly thirsty. What about you?"

And he leaned out of the window and shouted to the concierge to go and fetch them some grog from the tavern.

"To sum up, I see three parties . . . no, three groups—none of which interests me: those who have, those who have had, and those who are trying to have. But they all agree on an idiotic adoration of Authority! Mably, for example, advocates that philosophers should be prevented from publishing their doctrines; Monsieur Wronski, the mathematician, has invented a language of his own in which he describes censorship as 'the critical repression of speculative spontaneity'; Father Enfantin gives his blessing to the Hapsburgs for 'having stretched a powerful hand across the Alps to restrain Italy'; Pierre Leroux wants us forced to listen to an orator, and Louis Blanc inclines toward a religion of the State, this nation of vassals has such a passion for being governed! But no form of government is legitimate, in spite of their eternal principles! For *principle* means *origin*, so you must always go back to a revolution, an act of violence, a transitory episode. Thus, the principle of our government is national sovereignty, under the form of parliamentary government, although this parliament would not agree! But why should the sovereignty of the people be more sacred than the divine right of kings? They are both fictitious! Away with metaphysics; we're had enough of ghosts! You don't need dogmas to keep the streets swept! They'll say that I'm overthrowing society! Well, and what's wrong with that? It's in a fine state at the moment, this society of yours!"

Frédéric could have found plenty of arguments to use against him, but seeing him so far from Sénécal's theories, he was full of indulgence. He contented himself with suggesting that the adoption of this kind of position for the paper would lead to their universal execration.

"On the contrary, as we shall have given every party proof that we hate its rivals, they will all rely on us. You must play your part as well, and write some transcendental criticism for us!"

They must attack all accepted ideas: the Academy, the École Normale, the Conservatoire, the Comédie-Française, everything that resembled an institution. By these means they would give a cohesive editorial policy to their Review. Then, when it was well established, it would suddenly become a daily paper; then they would start attacking individuals.

"And we shall be respected, you can be sure of that!"

Deslauriers was within an ace of attaining his old dream: the editorship of a newspaper; that is to say, the ineffable joy of giving orders to people, of chopping their articles up, of commissioning work and refusing it. His eyes sparkled behind his glasses. He was exhilarated and downed one drink after another without realizing what he was doing.

"You must give a dinner party once a week. It's indispensable, even if it takes half your income! Invitations will be sought after, it will be a meeting place for others, a lever for you, and, manipulating opinion from both the literary and the political angles, we shall hold a commanding position in Paris within six months, you see if we don't!"

Listening to him, Frédéric had a feeling of rejuvenation, like that of a man who, after a long confinement in his bedroom, is taken out into the fresh air. Deslauriers' enthusiasm won him over.

"Yes, you're right, I've been a lazy fool!"

"Hurray!" cried Deslauriers; "I've found my Frédéric again!"

And, holding his fist under his chin:

"Oh, how you've made me suffer! But what does it matter! I still love you!"

They were both standing and they gazed at one another, moved and near to embracing.

A woman's hat appeared in the hall doorway.

"What brings you here?" said Deslauriers.

It was Mademoiselle Clémence, his mistress.

She replied that she had happened to be passing the house and had been unable to resist her desire to see him;

she had brought some cakes, which she put down on the table, so that they could have a little snack together.

"Mind my papers!" snapped the lawyer. "And this makes the third time I've forbidden you to come here during my consulting hours."

She tried to embrace him.

"That's enough! Get out now! Vamoose!"

He pushed her away and she gave a great sob.

"Oh, you wear me out!"

"But I love you!"

"I don't want to be loved, I want to be obeyed!"

These harsh words dried Clémence's tears. She went over to the window and stood there, her forehead pressed against the glass. Her attitude and her silence irritated Deslauriers.

"When you're finished, you'll order your carriage, won't you!"

She turned round with a start.

"You're sending me away!"

"Exactly!"

She fixed her great blue eyes on him, presumably in a final appeal, then crossed the two ends of her tartan shawl, waited for another moment, and left.

"You should call her back," said Frédéric.

"Nonsense!"

And, as he had to go out, Deslauriers went into his kitchen, which he used as a dressing room. The remains of a meager lunch lay on the floor near a pair of boots, and a mattress and some bedclothes were rolled up in a corner.

"You can see from this," he remarked, "that I don't entertain many marquises! One can do without them easily enough, and the others too. The ones who don't cost anything take up your time, which is another form of money; well, I'm not a rich man! And they're all stupid, so stupid! Can you find anything to talk to a woman about?"

They separated at the corner of the Pont-Neuf.

"So it's agreed! You'll bring me the money tomorrow, as soon as you get it!"

"Agreed!" said Frédéric.

On awakening the following morning, he received through the post a bank draft for fifteen thousand francs.

This scrap of paper represented fifteen great bags of money, and he told himself that with a sum like that he could, in the first place, keep his carriage, which he would soon be forced to sell, for another three years, or he could buy two beautiful suits of chased armor he had seen on the Quai Voltaire, as well as a quantity of other things— paintings, books, and innumerable presents and bouquets for Madame Arnoux. In fact, anything would be better than to risk, or rather to lose, so much money in this paper! Deslauriers seemed arrogant to him; his cruelty the previous evening had chilled Frédéric's feelings toward him; and he was giving himself up to these regrets when he was astounded to see Arnoux—who came into the room and sat down heavily on the edge of the bed like a man overwhelmed by troubles.

"What's the matter?"

"I'm finished!"

That very day, in the office of Maître Beauminet, the lawyer on Rue Sainte-Anne, he had to hand over eighteen thousand francs which had been lent him by a certain Vanneroy.

"It is an inexplicable disaster! I gave him a mortgage, which should have pacified him! But he's threatened me with a writ if he's not paid this afternoon on the dot!"

"And then?"

"Then it's quite simple! He will expropriate my house. The first notice that goes up will ruin me, that's all! Oh, if only I could find someone to advance me that wretched eighteen thousand, he could take over Vanneroy's mortgage and I would be saved! You wouldn't have it by any chance?"

The draft for the money was still on the bedside table, next to a book. Frédéric picked up the volume and placed it on top of the piece of paper, replying:

"Good heavens, no, my good friend!"

But he hated to refuse Arnoux.

"Can't you think of anyone who would? . . ."

"No one! And to think that in a week I have some money coming in! There's about . . . fifty thousand francs due to me at the end of the month!"

"Can't you ask your debtors to advance their payments? . . ."

"A lot of use that would be!"

"But you must have some stocks, some securities?"

"Nothing!"

"But what is to be done?"

"That's what I ask myself," replied Arnoux.

He fell silent and began pacing up and down the room.

"It's not for myself, good heavens! But for my children, for my poor wife!"

Then, separating every word:

"Well . . . I shall be strong . . . I'll sell everything . . . and go off to seek my fortune . . . somewhere or other!"

"Impossible!" cried Frédéric.

Arnoux replied calmly:

"How do you think I can go on living in Paris now?"

There was a long silence.

Frédéric broke it to say:

"When could you repay this money?"

Not that he had it, of course! But there was nothing to stop him seeing his friends, taking some steps. And he rang for his servant to help him dress. Arnoux thanked him.

"It's eighteen thousand francs you need, isn't it?"

"Oh, I could manage with sixteen thousand! I should certainly get two thousand five hundred or three thousand for my silver, that is if Vanneroy gives me until tomorrow, and, I repeat, you can tell the lender—swear to him if you like—that in eight days, perhaps even in five or six, the money will be repaid. Anyhow, there's the mortgage as security. So there's no risk, you understand?"

Frédéric assured him that he understood and that he was setting out immediately.

He stayed at home, cursing Deslauriers, for he wanted to keep his word and yet oblige Arnoux.

"Suppose I asked Monsieur Dambreuse? But on what pretext could I ask him for money? On the contrary, I should be handing some over to him for the shares in his coal mines. Oh, he and his shares can go to hell! I don't owe him anything."

And Frédéric patted himself on the back for displaying such independence, as if he had refused to do something for Monsieur Dambreuse.

"Well," he said to himself next, "since I am losing money there—for with fifteen thousand francs I could have made a hundred thousand! That happens sometimes in the stock market—so, since I'm breaking my promise to him, can't I also— . . . Besides, what if Deslauriers does have to wait? No, no, that's wrong! Let's go!"

He looked at his watch.

"Oh, there's no hurry. The bank doesn't shut till five o'clock."

And, at half-past four when he had collected his money:

"There's no point in going round now, he'd be out. I'll go this evening!" Thus giving himself the opportunity to go back on his decision, for some trace of the sophisms that one has poured into one's conscience always remains; they leave an aftertaste, like a bad liqueur.

He went for a stroll along the boulevards and dined alone at a restaurant. Then, to take his mind off his problems, he dropped into the Vaudeville for one act. But his banknotes made him feel uneasy, as if he had stolen them. He would not have been sorry to have lost them.

On returning home, he found a letter containing these words:

> Is there any news?
> My wife joins me, dear friend, in the hope, etc.
> Yours,

And an initial.

"His wife! She is asking me for help!"

At that very moment Arnoux appeared to ask if he had found the urgently needed sum.

"Here you are," said Frédéric.

And, twenty-four hours later, he told Deslauriers:

"I haven't received anything."

Deslauriers returned on three successive days. He urged Frédéric to write to the lawyer. He even offered to go to Le Havre.

"No! It's useless! I'll go myself!"

At the end of the week, Frédéric timidly asked Arnoux for his fifteen thousand francs.

He was put off till the following day, then to the day after. Frédéric dared not venture out of the house unless it was pitch dark, fearing to be caught by Deslauriers.

One evening, someone bumped into him on the corner of the Madeleine. It was the lawyer.

"I'm on my way to get it," he said.

And Deslauriers accompanied him to the door of a house on the Faubourg Poissonnière.

"Wait for me!"

He waited. Finally, after forty-three minutes, Frédéric came out with Arnoux and signed to him to have patience a little longer. The china manufacturer and his companion went up the Rue Hauteville arm in arm and then took the Rue de Chabrol.

It was a dark night, with warm gusts of wind. Arnoux walked unhurriedly along, talking about the Commercial Arcades; a succession of covered passageways which were planned to lead from the Boulevard Saint-Denis to the Châtelet, a marvelous speculation in which he longed to take part. He paused from time to time to look through the shop windows at the young working-girls' faces, then continued his dissertation.

Frédéric could hear Deslauriers' footsteps behind him; they seemed like reproaches, each one a blow on his conscience. But he dared not ask Arnoux for the money, out of false pride and also because he feared it would be useless. Deslauriers drew nearer. He made up his mind.

Arnoux told him in a very offhand way that, as he had not been repaid what was owed to him, he could not at this moment return the fifteen thousand francs.

"I don't suppose you need them, do you?"

At this moment Deslauriers accosted Frédéric and, drawing him to one side, said:

"Be frank, have you got it? Yes or no?"

"All right, no!" said Frédéric. "I've lost it!"

"Ah! And how did you lose it?"

"Gambling!"

Deslauriers, without a word, made Frédéric a low bow and departed. Arnoux had made use of the opportunity to light a cigar in a tobacconist's shop. He rejoined Frédéric and asked him who the young man was.

"No one. A friend."

Then, three minutes later, in front of Rosanette's, Arnoux said:

"Do come up, she'd love to see you. What an unsociable creature you are nowadays."

The light from a street lamp opposite fell on his face and, with his cigar stuck between his white teeth and his happy expression, there was something intolerable about him.

"Oh, by the way, my lawyer visited yours this morning to transfer the mortgage. It was my wife who reminded me about it."

"A capable woman," replied Frédéric mechanically.

"She certainly is!"

And Arnoux started on his eulogy again. She had no equal for intelligence, affection, or thrift; and he added in a lower voice, rolling his eyes:

"And a body!"

"Good-bye!" said Frédéric.

Arnoux started:

"Why, what's wrong?"

And, his hand half-extended, he examined Frédéric, disconcerted by the anger in his face.

Frédéric replied curtly:

"Good-bye!"

And he went down the Rue de Bréda like a boulder down a mountain, furious with Arnoux, vowing never to see him again, or her either, heartbroken, disconsolate. Instead of the rupture he had been expecting, here, on the contrary, was Arnoux beginning to cherish his wife and, to cherish her completely, from the hair on her head to the depths of her soul. The man's vulgarity exasperated Frédéric. Did everything belong to him? He visualized him again on the courtesan's doorstep and the mortification of a breach added to his impotent rage. Moreover, Arnoux's honesty in offering securities for his money humiliated him; he would cheerfully have strangled him and, beneath his grief, like a fog seeping through his conscience, was the sense of his cowardice toward his friend. His tears choked him.

Deslauriers descended the Rue des Martyrs, swearing aloud in his indignation; for his plan, like a fallen obelisk, now seemed to him of an extraordinary grandeur. He thought of himself as the victim of a theft, as if he had suffered a grievous wrong. His friendship for Frédéric was dead, and he rejoiced at its demise; it was a compensation! Hatred of the rich flooded through him. He felt himself inclining toward Sénécal's opinions and vowed to support them.

Meanwhile, Arnoux, comfortably ensconced in an armchair before the fire, was sipping at a cup of tea, with the Maréchale on his knee.

Frédéric did not return to the Arnoux's house and, to take his mind off his disastrous passion, he adopted the first subject that came into his head and made up his mind to write a *History of the Renaissance*. Humanists, philosophers, and poets were piled higgledy-piggledy on his table; he went to the print room to look at the Marcantonio engravings; he tried to put his mind to Machiavelli. Gradually the serenity of the work soothed him. Plunging into other peoples' personalities he forgot his own, which is perhaps the only way to avoid suffering from it.

One day, as he was tranquilly making notes, the door opened and the servant announced Madame Arnoux.

It was indeed she! Alone? No, she was holding little Eugène's hand, and her maid, in a white apron, stood behind them. She sat down and, after a little cough, said:

"You haven't been to the house for a long time."

As Frédéric could think of no excuse she added:

"It is tactful of you!"

"Tactful?"

"Because of what you did for Arnoux!" she said.

Frédéric made a gesture signifying: "What do I care about him! I did it for you!"

She sent the child into the drawing room to play with the maid. They exchanged two or three remarks on their health, then fell silent.

She was wearing a brown silk dress, the color of Spanish wine, with a black velvet overcoat trimmed with sable; he wanted to stroke the fur and his lips were drawn to her long, glossy bandeaux. But something was troubling her and, turning her eyes to the door, she said:

"It's rather warm in here."

Frédéric divined the prudent motive of her glance.

"Excuse me! The door is ajar."

"Ah, so it is!"

And she smiled, as if to say: "I'm not afraid."

He at once asked her what had brought her.

"My husband," she replied with an effort, "asked me to come and see you, not daring to apply to you himself."'

"For what reason?"

"You know Monsieur Dambreuse, don't you?"

"Yes, a little."

"Oh, a little!"

And she fell silent.

"It doesn't matter. Finish what you were going to say."

Then she told him that two days previously, Arnoux had been unable to pay four bills for a thousand francs written to the banker's order which he had made her sign. She regretted having compromised her children's fortune. But anything was better than dishonor, and if Monsieur Dambreuse would stop the proceedings against them, he would certainly be paid soon, for she was going to sell a small house at Chartres which she owned.

"Poor woman!" murmured Frédéric. "I'll go! Count on me."

"Thank you!"

And she got up to leave.

"Oh, there's no need to hurry!"

She remained standing, examining the trophy of Mongolian arrows that hung from the ceiling, the library, the bindings of the books, all the writing materials; she picked up the bronze jar that held the pens; her heels rested on various places in the carpet. She had been to Frédéric's house several times, but always with Arnoux. They were alone now—alone in his own house. It was an extraordinary event, almost a stroke of fortune.

She asked to see his little garden; he offered her his arm to show her over his domain, thirty feet of open ground surrounded by houses, with shrubs in the corners and a flower bed in the middle.

It was early April. The lilac leaves were already green, there was a breath of freshness in the air, and small birds were twittering, their song alternating with the distant sound of a coachmaker's forge.

Frédéric went off to fetch the shovel from a set of fire irons, and while they walked side by side the child made sand castles on the path.

Madame Arnoux did not think that he would have much imagination when he grew up, but he was a sweet-natured child. His sister, on the contrary, had a natural coldness which sometimes hurt her.

"That will change," said Frédéric. "One must never despair."

She replied:

"One must never despair."

This mechanical repetition of his words struck him as a form of encouragement; he picked a rose, the only one in the garden.

"Do you remember . . . a certain bunch of roses, one evening, in the carriage?"

She blushed slightly and, with an expression of compassionate mockery, answered:

"Oh, I was very young!"

"And this one," continued Frédéric in a low voice, "will it share their fate?"

Twisting the stalk between her fingers like the thread on a spindle, she replied:

"No, I shall keep it."

She gestured to summon the maid, who picked up the boy in her arms; then, on the step of the door into the street, Madame Arnoux sniffed at the flower, bending her head toward her shoulder with a glance as tender as a kiss.

When he had regained his study he gazed at the armchair where she had sat and at all the objects she had touched. Something of her still lingered in the air around him. The caress of her presence persisted.

"So she really came!" he said to himself.

And he was engulfed in waves of infinite tenderness.

The next day he called on Monsieur Dambreuse at eleven o'clock. He was ushered into the dining room, where the banker was lunching opposite his wife. His niece was beside her, and on the other side sat the governess, an Englishwoman badly scarred by smallpox.

Monsieur Dambreuse invited his young friend to sit down with them and, when he refused, said:

"Well, what can I do for you? I'm waiting to hear."

With affected indifference, Frédéric declared that he had come to make a request on behalf of a certain Arnoux.

"Oh yes, the former picture dealer," said the banker, with a silent laugh that bared his gums. "Oudry used to act as his guarantor but there was a quarrel."

And he started to run through the letters and newspapers that lay beside his plate.

Two servants were waiting on the family, moving noiselessly over the parquet; and the height of the room, with its three tapestry door-hangings and two white marble fountains, the gleam of the dish-warmers, the arrangement of the hors d'oeuvres, and even the stiff folds of the napkins, all this luxurious comfort was contrasted in Frédéric's mind with another meal at Arnoux's. He did not dare interrupt Monsieur Dambreuse.

Madame noticed his embarrassment.

"Do you ever see our friend Martinon?"

"He's coming this evening," said the girl swiftly.

"Oh, are you sure?" replied her aunt, with an icy glance.

Then, as one of the footmen bent to whisper in her ear:

"Your dressmaker, my child! —Miss John!"

And the governess obediently disappeared with her pupil.

Monsieur Dambreuse, disturbed by the shifting chairs, asked what was going on.

"It's Madame Regimbart."

"Well, well, Regimbart! I know that name. I've come across his signature."

Finally, Frédéric got to the point of his visit. Arnoux deserved some consideration; he was even going to sell a house belonging to his wife, solely to pay off his debts.

"They say she's very pretty," said Madame Dambreuse.

And the banker added in a jovial tone:

"Are you an . . . intimate friend of theirs?"

Frédéric, without replying directly, said that he would be very obliged if Monsieur Dambreuse would consider . . .

"Well, as you want it, so be it! We'll wait. I still have some time for you. Shall we go down to my office?"

The meal was over; Madame Dambreuse bowed slightly, giving him a strange smile full of both politeness and irony. Frédéric had no time to think it over; as soon as they were alone, Monsieur Dambreuse said:

"You never came to pick up your shares."

And, without giving him a chance to excuse himself:

"Never mind. It is only right that you should know a little more about the business."

He offered him a cigarette and began.

The United French Coal Company had already been incorporated; they were only waiting for the official certificate. The mere fact of the merger would cut down the costs of administration and labor, and increase profits. Moreover, the company had thought of a new plan; they were going to give their employees an interest in the business. They would build houses for them, good clean homes; they would run a general store, selling them everything at cost price.

"And they'll be better off, Monsieur; that's true progress —a triumphant reply to the clamor of the republicans! On our board of directors (and he showed the prospectus) we have a peer of France, a learned member of the Institute, a retired general of engineers—all well-known names! A board like that will reassure timid investors and attract intelligent ones!"

The company would obtain orders from the government, then from the railways, the steamship companies, the ironworks, the gas companies, the kitchens of the middle classes.

"Thus we shall provide light and heat, and penetrate into even the humblest homes. But how, you are going to ask me, can we ensure our sales? Through tariffs, my dear sir, and we shall get them, leave it to us. For my part I'm quite frankly protectionist anyhow! The country must come first!"

He had been appointed a director but had not enough time to attend to certain details, the writing of reports among others.

"I get my authors mixed up; I've forgotten my Greek. I shall need someone who could . . . translate my ideas."

And, suddenly:

"Would you like to be that man, with the title of General Secretary?"

Frédéric did not know what to answer him.

"Well, why do you hesitate?"

His functions would be limited to writing a report for the stockholders every year. He would find himself in daily contact with the most important men in Paris. As the company's representative to the workers, he would naturally win their affection, which would permit him later on to become a member of the departmental council and then a deputy.

Frédéric's ears were buzzing. Why was he being shown such kindness? He stammered out his thanks.

But it would be a mistake, continued the banker, for him to be dependent on anyone. The best solution would be for him to buy some shares, "a wonderful investment in any case, since your capital guarantees your position and your position your capital."

"About how much should it amount to?" asked Frédéric.

"Good gracious, anything you like; from forty to sixty thousand francs I imagine."

This sum was so minute in Monsieur Dambreuse's eyes and his authority was so great that the young man immediately decided to sell a farm. He accepted. Monsieur Dambreuse would arrange a meeting in the near future to conclude their arrangements.

"So I can tell Jacques Arnoux? . . ."

"Anything you like! Poor chap! Anything you like!"

Frédéric wrote to the Arnoux's to tell them not to worry and sent the letter by his servant, who brought back the reply:

"Good!"

Surely his efforts deserved more than this. He awaited a visit, a letter at least. He received no visit. No letter arrived.

Was it an oversight on their part or were they neglecting him intentionally? Since Madame Arnoux had come once, what prevented her from returning? Was the sort of hint of avowal she had made to him no more than a maneuver dictated by self-interest? "Have they been using me? Is she an accomplice?" A sort of delicacy prevented him from visiting them, in spite of his desire to do so.

One morning (three weeks after their interview) Monsieur Dambreuse sent him a note saying that he was expecting him that very day, in an hour's time.

On the way, the idea of the Arnoux's again assailed him, and, unable to find a reason for their conduct, he was possessed by a sudden anguish, a sense of foreboding.

To rid himself of it he hailed a cab and had himself driven to the Rue Paradis.

Arnoux was away on a journey.

"And Madame?"

"In the country, at the factory!"

"When does Monsieur return?"

"Tomorrow, without fail!"

He would find her alone; it was his chance.

In his heart an imperious voice cried, "Go on, then!"

But what about Monsieur Dambreuse? "Well, it can't be helped! I'll say I was ill." He hurried to the station, then, once ensconced in a carriage, thought: "Perhaps I've done the wrong thing? Oh, nonsense, what does it matter!"

Green fields rolled away to the horizon on either side of the moving train; the buildings of the stations shone like stage scenery and the smoke from the engine, always blown to the same side, danced over the grass in fat, fleecy puffs for a few moments, then melted away.

Frédéric, alone on his seat, watched it for want of anything better to do, sunk in that languor which comes from the very excess of impatience. But some cranes and warehouses came into view. It was Creil.

The town stood on the side of two low hills—one bare, the other crowned with a wood—and with its church tower, its uneven houses, and its stone bridge it seemed to Frédéric to have something gay, unpretentious, and wholesome about it. A big barge was floating down the river which rippled in the wind, some hens were pecking in the straw at the foot of a wayside crucifix, a woman went past with a basket of wet laundry on her head.

He crossed the bridge and found himself on an island, with the ruins of an abbey to the right. A turning mill-wheel blocked the entire width of the second branch of the Oise, which was overhung by the factory. Frédéric was greatly surprised by the size of this building. His respect for Arnoux increased accordingly. A few yards farther on, he turned into an alley whose far end was barred by an iron gate.

He went in. The concierge called him back with a shout of:

"Have you got a pass?"

"What for?"

"To visit the factory."

Frédéric snapped that he had come to see Monsieur Arnoux.

"Who is Monsieur Arnoux?"

"He's the boss, the master, the owner, of course!"

"No, Monsieur, this factory belongs to Messieurs Leboeuf and Milliet!"

The woman must be joking. Some workers were arriving; he accosted two or three; they gave him the same answer.

Frédéric staggered out of the yard like a drunken man; he had such a bewildered expression that a shopkeeper who was smoking his pipe on the Pont de la Boucherie asked him if he was looking for something. This man knew Arnoux's factory. It was at Montataire.

Frédéric inquired about a carriage; they could only be found at the station. He returned there. A broken-down barouche, drawn by an old horse whose disintegrating harness dangled between the shafts, stood alone in front of the luggage office.

An urchin offered to find "old Pilon." He returned ten minutes later; old Pilon was having his lunch. Impatient, Frédéric set off. But the grade-crossing gates were closed and he had to wait till two trains had passed. Finally, he flung off through the countryside.

The monotonous green of the fields made it look like an immense billiard table. There were piles of iron slag on either side of the road, like heaps of pebbles. A cluster of factory chimneys smoked a little farther off. In front of him, a small turreted château stood on a round hill, next to the square church belfry. Beneath them long walls stretched crooked lines through the trees, and at the very foot sprawled the houses of the village.

They were only one story high, and the three steps leading up to their doors were made of unmortared blocks of stone. From time to time a grocer's bell could be heard. Heavy footsteps sank into the black mud and a fine rain was falling, hatching the pale sky with a thousand strokes.

Frédéric kept on down the middle of the highway; then, over the entrance to a road on his right, he noticed a large wooden arch bearing the word FAÏENCES in letters of gold.

It was not chance that had led Jacques Arnoux to select the neighbourhood of Creil; by placing his factory as near as possible to the other, which had a long-established reputation, he created a useful confusion in the mind of the general public.

The main building stood on the very edge of a river that crossed the meadow. The master's house, surrounded by a garden, was distinguished by its flight of steps deco-

rated with four urns bristling with cactus. There were
piles of white clay drying in open sheds; others lay out in
the open, and in the middle of the courtyard stood
Sénécal, with his everlasting blue overcoat lined with red.

The former teacher held out a cold hand.

"You've come to see the boss? He isn't here."

Frédéric, disconcerted, replied stupidly:

"I know." But, recovering himself at once, he went on:
"I've come on business that concerns Madame Arnoux.
Can she see me?"

"Oh, I haven't seen her for three days," replied Sénécal.

And he launched into a string of complaints. When he
had accepted the manufacturer's offer he had expected to
live in Paris, not buried out here in the country, away from
his friends and without newspapers. Never mind! He had
risen above that. But Arnoux seemed to pay no attention
to his merits. Moreover he was narrow-minded and old-
fashioned, impossibly ignorant! Instead of searching for
artistic improvements he would have done better to bring
in coal and gas heat. The boss was *going under;* Sénécal
emphasized the words. In short, his job displeased him
and he almost ordered Frédéric to put in a word for him
so that his wages would be raised.

"Don't worry!" said the other.

He met no one on the staircase. When he reached the
first floor, he stuck his head into an empty room—it was
the drawing room. He shouted as loudly as he could; there
was no answer. The cook and maid were probably both
out. Finally, he arrived at the second floor and pushed
open a door. Madame Arnoux was alone in front of a
wardrobe looking-glass. The belt of her half-open dressing
gown hung down over her hips. The half of her hair
streamed over her right shoulder in a black flood; her
arms were raised, one hand holding her chignon in place
while she drove a pin into it with the other. She gave a
cry and disappeared.

When she returned, she was fully dressed. Her figure,
her eyes, the rustle of her dress—everything about her
enchanted Frédéric, who had to restrain an impulse to
cover her with kisses.

"I'm sorry," she said, "but I couldn't . . ."

He was bold enough to interrupt her:

"Still . . . you looked very beautiful . . . just now!"

She probably found the compliment a little coarse, for
her cheeks reddened. He was afraid he might have offended her. She went on:

"What happy chance brings you here?"

He did not know what to answer and, after a little chuckle that gave him time to think, he said:

"If I told you, would you believe me?"

"Why shouldn't I?"

Frédéric related how, a few nights earlier, he had had a terrible dream.

"I dreamed that you were very ill, near death."

"Oh, neither my husband nor I are ever ill!"

"I dreamed only of you," he said.

She looked at him calmly:

"Dreams don't always come true."

Frédéric stammered, searched for words, and finally launched into a long dissertation on the affinity of souls. A force existed that could make two people aware of each other at a distance, inform them of each other's feelings, and draw them together.

She listened to him with bowed head, smiling her beautiful smile all the while. He watched her joyfully out of the corner of his eye and gave freer rein to his love in the guise of commonplaces. She offered to show him over the factory and, as she insisted, he agreed.

To interest him initially by showing him something entertaining, she started with a sort of museum that decorated the staircase. The specimens hanging on the walls or arranged on shelves bore testimony to Arnoux's efforts and his successive infatuations. After searching for the copper-red of the Chinese he had tried to produce majolica, faenza, Etruscan, and Oriental pottery, and had finally attempted some of the improvements of later eras. So the series contained large cases covered with mandarins, bowls of an iridescent bronze color, pots decorated with Arabic script, flagons in the style of the Renaissance, and large plates with two figures that looked as if they had been drawn in red chalk in an affected, wishy-washy style. He was now making signs and labels for wine; but his intelligence was neither great enough to attain to art nor mediocre enough to think of nothing but profits, so that he was ruining himself without pleasing anybody. They were both contemplating these things when Mademoiselle Marthe went past.

"Why, don't you recognize our guest?" said her mother.

"Yes indeed!" she replied, greeting him, while her clear and suspicious eyes, her virgin's eyes, seemed to murmur: "What are *you* doing here?" and she climbed the stairs, turning her head a little on her shoulder.

Madame Arnoux led Frédéric into the courtyard and then explained to him in a serious tone how the clays were ground, cleaned, and sifted.

"The most important part is the preparation of the pastes."

And she took him into a room full of vats where a vertical axle with horizontal arms was revolving. Frédéric was kicking himself for not having flatly refused her offer earlier.

"These are the drabblers," she said.

The word struck him as grotesque and almost unseemly in her mouth.

Broad belts ran from one end of the ceiling to the other, and wound around drums; and everything was in motion; ceaseless, mathematical, unnerving.

They left the room and passed close by a ruined shed where garden tools had formerly been stored.

"It is out of use now," said Madame Arnoux.

He replied in a trembling voice:

"It could serve as a shelter for happiness!"

The din of the steam-pump covered his words and they entered the roughing shop.

Seated at a narrow table, some men were placing lumps of clay on the revolving wheels in front of them; with their left hands they scooped out the inside, smoothing the surface with their right, and the vases took shape like blossoming flowers.

Madame Arnoux showed him the molds for the more difficult work.

In another room, they were decorating vases with fillets, grooves, and raised lines. On the floor above they were taking out the seams, and filling with plaster the little holes left by the preceding operations.

On the skylights, in the corners, in the middle of the corridors, everywhere, there were rows of pots.

Frédéric was beginning to be bored.

"Perhaps all this is tiring you?" asked Madame Arnoux.

Afraid that this might be the end of his visit, he affected, on the contrary, a great enthusiasm and even regretted not having gone into this industry.

She seemed surprised.

"Of course! I would have been able to be near you!"

He was trying to catch her eye, and Madame Arnoux, to avoid looking at him, picked up some little balls of paste which were lying on a table, the remains of unsuccessful repairs, flattened them into a cake and pressed her hand into it so as to leave a print.

"May I take it with me?" asked Frédéric.

"My goodness, what a child you are!"

He was about to reply when Sénécal came in.

As soon as he had crossed the threshold, the sub-manager noticed a breach of the rules. The workshops were supposed to be swept out every week; it was a Saturday and, as the workers had done nothing about it, Sénécal told them that they would have to stay for an extra hour. "That's your bad luck."

They bent over their work without a murmur, but their anger could be guessed from their hoarse breathing. In any case, they were difficult to control, having all been dismissed from the large factory. The republican ruled them harshly. A man of theories, he was only prepared to consider the masses and was pitiless to individuals.

Frédéric, embarrassed by his presence, asked Madame Arnoux in a low voice if there was any chance of seeing the ovens. They went down to the ground floor and she was in the middle of explaining the use of the cases when Sénécal, who had followed, pushed himself between them.

He continued the demonstration himself, expatiating on different types of fuel, insertion into the kilns, pyroscopes, hovel hearths, slips, glazes, and metals, with a profusion of chemical terms, chloride, sulphur, borax, carbonate, and the like. Frédéric understood nothing and kept turning to Madame Arnoux.

"You are not listening," she said. "Yet Monsieur Sénécal is very clear. He knows much more than I do about these matters."

The mathematician, flattered by this eulogy, offered to show them how the colors were applied. Frédéric gave Madame Arnoux an anxious glance of interrogation, but she remained impassive, wishing, no doubt, neither to be alone with him nor to leave him. He offered her his arm.

"No, thank you. The staircase is too narrow."

When they reached the next floor, Sénécal opened the door of a room full of women.

They were working with brushes, vials, shells, and glass plates. Along the cornice, against the wall, were rows of engraved blocks; scraps of paper fluttered in the air and a cast-iron stove exhaled a sickening heat mingled with the smell of turpentine.

Almost all of the work-women were poorly dressed. One of them, however, was wearing a Madras kerchief and long earrings. At once slender and plump, she had great black eyes and the fleshy lips of a Negro. Her ample breasts jutted out under her blouse, which was tied in at the waist by the belt of her skirt and, one elbow on the bench and the other arm dangling, she gazed dreamily out at the countryside. A bottle of wine and some cold meat lay beside her.

The regulations forbade eating in the workshops, a rule designed to safeguard the cleanliness of the work and the health of the workers.

Sénécal, out of a sense of duty or the desire to act like a despot, shouted from the other end of the room, pointing at a framed notice.

"Hey! You over there, the Bordelaise! Read me article nine out loud!"

"Well, what about it?"

"What about it, Mademoiselle? You'll pay a three-franc fine, that's what!"

She looked impudently into his face:

"So what? You think so? When he comes back, the boss will cancel your fine! I don't give a damn for you, little man!"

Sénécal, who was walking up and down the room with his hands clasped behind his back like an usher in a classroom, contented himself with a smile:

"Article thirteen, insubordination, ten francs!"

The Bordelaise went back to her work. Madame Arnoux said nothing, out of a sense of propriety, but she knitted her brows. Frédéric murmured:

"You are very hard for a democrat!"

The other replied in magisterial tones:

"Democracy is not the perversion of individualism. It is equality under the law, the division of labor, order!"

"You are forgetting humanity!" said Frédéric.

Madame Arnoux put her hand through his arm. Sénécal, perhaps offended by this tacit approbation, took himself off.

Frédéric felt an immense relief. He had been seeking an opportunity to declare his love since the morning; now it had arrived. Moreover, Madame Arnoux's spontaneous gesture seemed to him full of promise and he asked if he might go up to her room to warm his feet. But, once seated next to her, his difficulties began; he lacked a point of departure. Luckily, he thought of Sénécal.

"Nothing," he said, "could have been stupider than that punishment!"

Madame Arnoux replied:

"Severity is sometimes unavoidable!"

"How can you say that when you are so kind! But I forgot, you do sometimes like to make people suffer."

"I don't understand riddles, my friend."

And her stern gaze, even more than her words, brought him to a standstill. Frédéric was determined to continue. A volume of Musset happened to be lying on the bureau. He turned over the pages, then started to talk about love, its despairs and its ecstasies.

According to Madame Arnoux all of this was either criminal or artificial.

The young man was wounded by this denial and, to contest it, he cited as evidence the suicides one read about in the newspapers and extolled the great examples of love in literature—Phèdre, Dido, Romeo, Des Grieux. He was carried away by his own eloquence.

The fire on the hearth had gone out and the rain spattered against the windowpanes. Madame Arnoux sat motionless, her hands on the arms of her chair, the strings of her cap hanging down like the headbands of a sphinx, her pure profile a pale silhouette in the gloom.

He longed to throw himself on his knees before her. A creak came from the corridor; he did not dare.

Moreover, he was held back by a sort of religious awe. Her dress, blending with the shadows, seemed to him immense, infinite, impossible to lift and, for that precise reason, his desire redoubled. But the fear of doing too much or of not doing enough robbed him of all power of judgment.

"If I displease her," he thought, "let her send me away! If she wants me, let her encourage me!"

He said, with a sigh:

"So you do not admit that it is possible to love . . . a woman?"

Madame Arnoux replied:

"If she is single you marry her; if she belongs to another, you leave her alone."

"So happiness is unattainable!"

"No! But it is never to be found in lies, anxieties, and remorse!"

"What does that matter, if it brings sublime joy!"

"The price is too high."

He tried to attack her by using irony:

"So virtue is nothing but cowardice?"

"Let us say, rather, that it is foresight. Even for those

women who ignore the claims of duty or religion, ordinary
common sense should be enough. Egotism makes a solid
foundation for good behavior."

"How full of middle-class maxims you are!"

"But I have never pretended to be a great lady!"

At that moment the little boy ran in:

"Mamma, are you coming to dinner?"

"Yes, in a minute."

Frédéric stood up, and that moment Marthe appeared.
He could not make up his mind to leave and, with a
glance brimming with supplication, he said:

"These women you're talking about must be very hard-
hearted?"

"No! But deaf when it is necessary."

And she stood upright on the threshold of her room,
her two children at her side. He bowed without a word.
She silently acknowledged his salutation.

His first feeling was one of complete stupefaction. He
was crushed by this method of showing him the futility of
his hopes. He felt lost, like a man who has fallen into
an abyss and knows that he will not be rescued and that
his death is inevitable.

In spite of this, he started walking, but blindly, at
random; he stumbled over stones, he lost his way. A noise
of clogs sounded nearby; it was the workers coming out
of the foundry. At this he came to himself again.

The lights of the railway traced a line of fire on the
horizon. He arrived as a train was about to leave, let
himself be pushed into a carriage, and fell asleep.

An hour later, on the boulevards, the gaiety of Paris
in the evening suddenly removed his journeying to a past
that was already remote. He wanted to be strong, and
lightened his heart by denigrating Madame Arnoux, heaping her with insulting epithets:

"She's an idiot, a goose, a ninny! Forget her!"

On his return home, he found in his study an eight-
page letter on glossy blue paper initialled "R. A."

It began with friendly reproaches:

"What has become of you, my dear? I'm bored."

But the handwriting was so abominable that Frédéric
was about to throw the whole packet away, when he
noticed the postscript:

"I am counting on you to take me to the races
tomorrow."

What could this invitation mean? Was it another of the
Maréchale's tricks? But one does not make a fool of the

same man twice without reason and, his curiosity aroused, he reread the letter attentively.

Frédéric made out: "Misunderstanding . . . have taken the wrong turning . . . disillusionment . . . Poor children that we are! . . . Like two rivers flowing together again!" et cetera.

This style contrasted with the courtesan's normal language. What, then, could have changed?

He held the note for a long time. It smelt of iris and there was something in the shape of the letters and the irregular spacing of the lines that stirred him as a disordered dress would have done.

"Why shouldn't I go?" he finally said to himself. "But what if Madame Arnoux should hear of it? Oh, let her find out! So much the better! And let her be jealous! That will be my revenge!"

Chapter Four

The Maréchale was ready and waiting for him.

"It was nice of you to come," she said, gazing at him with her pretty eyes, at once tender and gay.

When she had tied the ribbons of her hood she sat down on the divan and remained silent.

"Shall we go?" said Frédéric.

"Oh no, not before one-thirty," as if she had set this limit to her uncertainty.

At last, the clock having struck:

"Well, *andiamo, caro mio!*"

And she bestowed a final pat on her hair and gave some instructions to Delphine.

"Will Madame be back for dinner?"

"Why should we? We'll dine together somewhere, the café Anglais or wherever you like!"

"All right!"

Her little dogs were yapping around her.

"We can take them with us, can't we?"

Frédéric carried them out to the carriage himself. It was a hired berlin with two post-horses and a postilion; he had put his own servant on the seat behind. The Maréchale seemed pleased with his attentions; then, as soon as she had taken her seat, she asked him if he had been to the Arnoux's lately.

"Not for a month," said Frédéric.

"I saw him the day before yesterday; in fact, he was supposed to come today. But he has all sorts of difficulties, another lawsuit and I don't know what else. What an odd man he is!"

"Yes, very odd!"

Frédéric added casually:

"By the way, are you still seeing—what was his name? That onetime singer—Delmar?"

She replied curtly:

"No, that's finished!"

So they had really broken off. Frédéric was encouraged.

They were going through the Bréda district at a walk; as it was Sunday the streets were deserted, and they could see the owners through the house windows. The carriage moved faster; the passersby turned at the sound of its wheels, the leather of the lowered hood glistened, the servant straightened his back, and the two little dogs sitting side by side looked like ermine muffs set down on the cushions. Frédéric let himself be lulled by the rocking of the braces. The Maréchale smilingly turned her head from side to side.

Her pearly straw hat was trimmed with black lace. The hood of her burnous fluttered in the wind behind her; and she shielded herself from the sun with a lilac satin parasol peaked at the top like a pagoda.

"What dear little fingers!" said Frédéric, gently taking her other hand, the left, which was adorned with a gold bracelet in the shape of a curb-chain. "Well, that's pretty; where did it come from?"

"Oh, I've had it for a long time," said the Maréchale.

The young man raised no objection to the hypocritical response. He preferred to "profit by the occasion." And, still holding her wrist, he pressed his lips to the space between the glove and the cuff.

"Stop it, someone will see us!"

"Nonsense! What does that matter!"

After the Place de la Concorde, they took the Quai de la Conférence and the Quai de Billy, where they noticed a cedar in one of the gardens. Rosanette thought the Lebanon was part of China; she laughed at her own ignorance and asked Frédéric to give her geography lessons. Then, leaving the Trocadéro to their right, they crossed the Pont d'Iéna, and finally drew up in the middle of the Champ de Mars, near some other carriages which were already lined up in the Hippodrome.

The grassy hillocks were covered with hoi polloi. There were spectators on the balcony of the École Militaire and the two pavilions outside the paddock, the two stands inside, and the third in front of the royal box were crowded with well-dressed people whose demeanor bore witness to their regard for this sport which was still something of a novelty. In those days, race-goers were drawn from a better class and their appearance was less vulgar; it was the era of trousers with straps, velvet collars, and white gloves. The women wore long, brilliantly colored dresses and, seated in tiers in the stands, they gave the effect of great banks of flowers, flecked with black here and there by the dark clothes of the men. But all eyes were turned on the famous Algerian, Bou-Maza,* who sat impassively between two staff officers in one of the private stands. The Jockey Club stand was occupied exclusively by serious-looking gentlemen.

The most enthusiastic spectators had taken their places down below, next to the track, which was protected by a double line of posts connected by ropes; in the enormous oval enclosed by the track, licorice-water vendors were shaking their rattles while the pedlars of race cards and cigars cried their wares. A vast hum rose from the crowd, policemen moved to and fro, and a bell rang from a post covered with numbers. Five horses appeared and everyone returned to the stands.

Meanwhile, heavy scrolls of cloud were skimming the tops of the elm trees opposite. Rosanette was afraid it was going to rain.

"I've got some umbrellas," said Frédéric, "and everything we need to enjoy ourselves!" he added, throwing back the top of the trunk, where there was a basket of provisions.

"Bravo! We understand one another!"

"And we're going to understand each other even better, aren't we?"

"It's possible!" she said, blushing.

The jockeys in their silk jackets were trying to get their mounts into line, using both hands to control them. Someone lowered a red flag and all five were off, bending forward over their horses' manes. To begin with, they stayed tightly bunched, but soon some began to trail and they divided into different groups; the jockey in the yellow jacket nearly fell in the middle of the first circuit; for a long time the race balanced between Filli and Tibi, then Tom Thumb took the lead, but Clubstick, who had been behind since the start, caught up and was first past the post, beating Sir Charles by two lengths. It was an upset;

---

*This Arab chieftain had been made a prisoner in 1847 during the Algerian war; he was honorably treated by the French government, who gave him a pension and permitted him to move about freely. He appeared at all social functions.

the spectators shouted and the wooden stands shook with their stamping.

"What fun we're having!" said the Maréchale. "I love you, my dear!"

Frédéric had no further doubts as to his good fortune; Rosanette's last words confirmed it.

A hundred yards away a lady appeared in a cab phaeton. She leaned out of the doorway, then quickly drew back; this happened several times. Frédéric could not distinguish her face but he was seized by the idea that it was Madame Arnoux. Yet that was impossible! Why should she have come? He got out of the carriage on the pretext of strolling round the paddock.

"You're not very gallant!" said Rosanette.

He took no notice and started forward. The phaeton swung round and made off at a trot.

At that very moment, Frédéric was buttonholed by Cisy:

"Hullo, old man! How are you? Hussonnet is over there! Do pay attention!"

Frédéric tried to free himself and follow the phaeton. The Maréchale signaled to him to rejoin her. Cisy saw her and was determined to greet her.

Since he had come out of mourning for his grandmother, he was doing his best to "live in style." Plaid waistcoat, short coat, large rosettes on his pumps, and admission ticket in his hatband—nothing, in fact, was lacking to complete what he himself called his "chic," the "chic" of an Anglomaniac and a musketeer. He began by complaining of the Champ de Mars, with its execrable turf, then spoke of the Chantilly races and the pranks that took place there, swore he could drink twelve glasses of champagne in the time that it took a clock to strike midnight, suggested a bet to the Maréchale, gently fondled her two lapdogs, and, leaning on the door with his elbow, continued to pour out a steady stream of fatuous remarks, sucking the knob of his cane with his legs straddled and his bottom stuck well out. Frédéric stood next to him, smoking and trying to discover what had become of the phaeton.

When the bell rang, Cisy took himself off, much to the joy of Rosanette, who said that she found him very boring.

Nothing in particular happened in the second race, nor in the third, except for a man who was carried off on a stretcher. The fourth, in which eight horses were competing for the Paris Cup, was more interesting.

The spectators in the stands had climbed onto the benches. The others, standing in their carriages, followed through their field glasses the maneuverings of the jockeys, who could be seen as red, yellow, white, and blue dots moving past the crowd that lined the entire circuit of the Hippodrome. From a distance, they did not seem to be going very fast; indeed, at the far end of the Champ de Mars they seemed to have slowed down and to be advancing only by a sort of sliding motion in which the horses' bellies touched the earth without any flexing of their outstretched legs. But, rapidly drawing nearer, they grew larger, they cut through the air as they passed, the ground shook, pebbles flew. The wind puffed out the jockeys' jackets and made them flutter like sails and they lashed their beasts with their whips to speed them past the finishing post. The numbers were taken down, another was hoisted and, to the sound of applause, the winner dragged himself as far as the paddock, covered with foam, stiff-legged, and with lowered head, while his rider clutched his sides as if he were dying in his stirrups.

The start of the final race was held up by a dispute. Bored, the crowd began to circulate. Groups of men stood about chatting in front of the stands. The conversation was becoming coarse; some of the ladies were leaving, scandalized by the courtesans' presence.

There were also celebrities from the dance halls, and boulevard actresses—and it was not the most beautiful among them who received the greatest homage. Old Georgine Aubert, whom a vaudeville comedian had called "the Louis XI of prostitution," horribly painted and now and then laughing with a cackle that sounded like a snarl, lay stretched out in her long barouche under a sable tippet as if it were midwinter. Madame de Remoussot, whose lawsuit had made her famous, was holding court on the box of a break in the company of some Americans; and Thérèse Bachelu, who resembled a gothic virgin, filled with her twelve furbelows the interior of a carriage whose apron had been replaced by a flowerstand filled with roses. The Maréchale was jealous of these celebrities; to attract attention she began to gesture in an exaggerated manner and talked very loudly.

Some of the gentlemen recognized her and waved. She responded, telling Frédéric their names. They were all counts, viscounts, dukes, and marquises, and he held his head higher, for a certain respect for his good fortune lurked in every eye.

Cisy, surrounded by a circle of older men, seemed equally happy. They were smiling above their cravats as if they were making fun of him; finally, they shook hands with the oldest and advanced toward the Maréchale.

She was eating a slice of foie gras with an affected gluttony, and Frédéric was dutifully imitating her, a bottle of wine on his knees.

The phaeton reappeared; it was Madame Arnoux. She grew extraordinarily pale.

"Give me some champagne!" said Rosanette.

And, holding her full glass as high as she could reach, she cried:

"Hey, you over there! All you respectable women, my protector's wife, hey!"

Those around her burst out laughing and the phaeton disappeared. Frédéric tugged at her dress; he was about to fly into a rage. But Cisy was there, in the same attitude as earlier, and, with an overweening self-confidence, he asked Rosanette to dine with him that same evening.

"Impossible!" she replied. "We are going to the café Anglais together."

Frédéric remained silent, as if he had heard nothing, and Cisy went off with a disappointed air.

While Cisy, standing next to the right-hand door, had been talking to the Maréchale, Hussonnet had come up on the left and, picking up the reference to the café Anglais, remarked:

"That's a good spot. Suppose we drop in for a bite there, eh?"

"Whatever you say," replied Frédéric, slumped in the corner of the berlin, as he watched the phaeton disappear over the horizon, feeling that something irreparable had just happened and that he had lost the love of his life. And there, next to him, was the other one, joyous and simple. But weary, full of contradictory desires, and no longer even sure of what he wanted, he was filled with a boundless melancholy, a longing for death.

A loud sound of footsteps and voices made him raise his head, some street urchins, clambering over the ropes around the course, had come to look at the stands; everyone was leaving. A few drops of rain fell. The crush of carriages grew worse. Hussonnet had disappeared.

"Well, that's just as well!" said Frédéric.

"You would rather we were alone?" replied the Maréchale, laying her hand on his.

At that moment, a magnificent landau, glittering with brass and steel, passed in front of them. It was drawn by four horses, with two jockeys in velvet jackets with gold fringes riding as postilions. Madame Dambreuse sat next to her husband, Martinon on the seat opposite, and all three seemed startled.

"They recognized me!" said Frédéric to himself.

Rosanette wanted to stop, so as to have a better view of the procession of vehicles. Madame Arnoux might reappear. He cried to the postilion:

"Go on, go on! Keep moving!"

And the berlin set off toward the Champs Elysées, amid a throng of carriages, barouches, britzskas, wurts, tandems, tilburies, dog-carts, leather curtained vans filled with workmen in a holiday mood, and one-horse carriages carefully driven by the father of the family himself. There were victorias crammed with passengers where some young man, seated on the others' feet, dangled his legs outside; slumbering dowagers trundled past in large broughams with cloth-covered seats; or a magnificent highstepper swept past, drawing a chaise as simple and as elegant as a dandy's black coat. Meanwhile, the downpour grew heavier. Umbrellas, parasols, and raincoats were brought out and people shouted to each other from a distance: "Hullo! —How goes it? —Yes! —No! —See you soon!" and the faces flickered past with the speed of images cast by a magic lantern. Frédéric and Rosanette sat in silence, the sight of so many wheels ceaselessly turning beside them producing a kind of stupor.

At times the congestion was such that the files of carriages would all stop at once in several lines. Then they waited side by side and engaged in a mutual inspection. Indifferent glances fell on the crowd, from doors decorated with coats of arms; envious eyes glared from the depths of cabs; a haughty bearing was greeted with disparaging smiles; gaping mouths betrayed an idiotic admiration; and here and there some pedestrians, strolling in the middle of the road, would jump back to avoid a horseman galloping between the carriages to make his way out. Then everything began to move again, the coachmen gave their teams their heads and lowered their long whips, the lively horses shook their curb-chains, scattering foam around them, and their croups and the damp harnesses steamed in the watery mist. The rays of the setting sun passed through the Arc de Triomphe and a swathe of reddish light, as high as a man, glittered on the wheel hubs, the door handle, the tips of the poles, and the rings on the saddles, while on both sides of the great avenue—like a river whose waves were manes, clothes, and human heads—the trees, glistening with rain, stood like two green walls. Above them the sky, turning blue again in places, seemed as soft as satin.

At this moment, Frédéric remembered those already distant days when he had yearned for the ineffable joy of riding in one of these carriages, beside one of these women. Now that joy was his and he was none the happier for it.

The rain had stopped. Those who had sought refuge between the columns of the Garde-Meubles were leaving. The strollers in the Rue Royale turned back toward the boulevard. A row of idlers lined the steps in front of the Ministry of Foreign Affairs.

As they drew level with the Chinese Baths, the berlin slackened its pace because of holes in the roadway. A man in a brown overcoat was walking along the edge of the sidewalk. A jet of mud spurted out from under the springs and splashed across his back. The man swung round, furious. Frédéric paled; it was Deslauriers.

He dismissed the carriage at the door of the café Anglais. Rosanette went in ahead of him while he paid the postilion.

He found her chatting with a man on the staircase. Frédéric took her arm. But a second gentleman stopped her in the middle of the corridor.

"Go on!" she said. "I'll be with you in a moment!"

And he entered the private room alone. Through the two open windows, he could see people in the windows of the house opposite. Large puddles rippled on the drying asphalt and a magnolia scented the room from the edge of the balcony. The fragrance and the coolness calmed his nerves; he slumped onto the red divan beneath the looking-glass.

The Maréchale returned and, kissing him on the forehead, remarked:

"Poor dear, you're feeling sad?"

"Maybe!" he replied.

"You're not the only one, you know!" which meant, "Let's forget it and enjoy ourselves!" And she placed a flower petal between her lips and held it out for him to nibble. The gesture was full of grace and an almost lascivious gentleness and it touched Frédéric.

"Why do you hurt me?" he asked, thinking of Madame Arnoux.

"Me, hurt you?"

And, standing before him, she looked at him through half-shut eyes, her hands on his shoulders.

All his rectitude, all his bitterness, vanished in a bottomless cowardice. He replied:

"Because you won't love me!" drawing her onto his knees.

She did not resist; he put both arms around her waist and the crackling of her silk dress inflamed him.

"Where are they?" said Hussonnet's voice in the corridor.

The Maréchale got up abruptly and went to stand at the other end of the room, turning her back to the door.

She asked for oysters and they sat down at the table.

Hussonnet was not amusing. As a result of writing every day on a great variety of subjects, reading vast quantities of newspapers, hearing endless discussions and turning out paradoxes to dazzle his audience, he had ended by losing his grasp of reality, blinding himself with his own spluttering fireworks. The difficulties of a life which had once been lighthearted but had now become hard kept him in a state of perpetual agitation; and his literary impotence, which he would not admit even to himself made him surly and sarcastic. Apropos of a new ballet called *Ozaï*, he made a sally against dancing as an art, and from dancing he went on to the Opéra; then to the Italian opera, which had now been replaced by a troupe of Spaniards, "as if we hadn't had a surfeit of the Castilles!" This grated on Frédéric, with his romantic love of Spain and, to change the conversation, he asked about the Collège de France, from which Edgar Quinet and Mickiewicz* had just been dismissed. But Hussonnet, who was an admirer of Monsieur de Maistre, declared himself in favor of Authority and Spiritualism. This, however, did not prevent him from doubting the best-proven facts,

---

*Quinet had been professor of Mediterranean Languages and Literature at the Collège de France since 1842; his chair was taken from him in 1846 in consequence of his attacks on the Catholic Church, particularly on the Jesuits. Adam Mickiewicz, the celebrated Polish patriot, occupied a chair of Slavonic Languages and Literature at the Collège which was abolished in 1846 because of the republican demonstrations that his teaching provoked.

denying the lessons of history, and calling into question the most obvious matters, to the point of crying out, at a passing mention of geometry: "What a farce geometry is!" His whole conversation was larded with imitations of actors; Sainville was his favorite model.

Frédéric was bored by this nonsense. He made a movement of impatience and accidentally kicked one of the little dogs under the table.

They both began barking in an odious manner.

"You should have them taken home!" he snapped.

Rosanette would not entrust them to anyone.

Then he turned to the bohemian:

"Come on, Hussonnet, put yourself out a little!"

"Oh yes! That would be sweet of you!"

Hussonnet went off without waiting to be begged.

How could he be recompensed for his obliging behavior? Frédéric gave the matter no thought. He was even beginning to enjoy their tête-à-tête when a waiter came in.

"Someone is asking for you, Madame."

"What, again?"

"Still, I must see who it is!" said Rosanette.

He thirsted after her, needed her. This disappearance struck him as a breach of the rules governing this sort of situation, almost an obscenity. What was she up to? Wasn't it enough to have insulted Madame Arnoux? Not that he cared about her! Now he hated all women, and his tears choked him, for his love had been slighted and his lust tricked.

The Maréchale returned, bringing Cisy with her.

"I invited this gentleman to join us; that's all right, isn't it?"

"Yes, of course, certainly!" And with the smile of a man on the rack, Frédéric waved him to a seat.

The Maréchale began to run through the menu, stopping at the dishes with odd-sounding names:

"Suppose we had a turban of rabbits à la Richelieu and a pudding à la d'Orléans?"

"Oh, no d'Orléans!" cried Cisy, who was a legitimist and believed he was making a joke.

"Would you rather have a turbot à la Chambord?" she replied.

Frédéric was offended by this politeness.

The Maréchale decided on a simple tournedos, crayfish, truffles, a pineapple salad, and some vanilla ices.

"After that, we'll see. Let's get started. Oh, I was forgetting! Waiter, bring me a sausage! Without garlic!"

And she addressed the waiter as "young man," tapped on her glass with her knife, and flicked pellets of bread up to the ceiling. She wanted to drink some burgundy right away.

"You never start with burgundy," said Frédéric.

According to the viscount this was sometimes done.

"Oh no, never!"

"Ah yes, I assure you!"

"There! You see!"

And her look signified: *"He's* a rich man; pay attention to him!"

All this while the door was continually opening, the waiters chattered, and in the next room someone played a waltz on an abominable piano. Then, after a conversation about the races, they went on to discuss the art of horsemanship. Of the two rival systems, Cisy was defending Baucher's and Frédéric that of the Comte d'Aure when Rosanette shrugged her shoulders:

"Oh, that's enough! He knows more about it than you do!"

She was sitting with one elbow on the table, biting into a pomegranate; the flames of the candles in front of her trembled in the draft and their white light imbued her skin with pearly tones, tinting her eyelids with rose and making her eyeballs shine; the red of the fruit mingled with the purple of her lips, her fine nostrils quivered, and there was something insolent, intoxicated, and abandoned about her that exasperated Frédéric and, at the same time, stirred wild desires in his heart.

Then, in a calm voice, she asked who owned the big landau with the servants in maroon livery.

"The Countess Dambreuse," replied Cisy.

"They're very rich, aren't they?"

"Yes, very rich, though Madame Dambreuse's inheritance—she was plain Mademoiselle Boutron, a prefect's daughter—was no better than ordinary."

Her husband, on the other hand, would inherit from several people; Cisy enumerated them. As a regular visitor to the Dambreuses he knew all about them.

Frédéric deliberately attempted to offend Cisy by stubbornly contradicting him. He maintained that Madame Dambreuse had been a de Boutron and attested to her nobility.

"I don't care about that, but I'd love to have her carriage!" said the Maréchale, leaning back in her armchair.

And the sleeve of her dress slipped up a little, uncovering a bracelet with three opals on her left wrist.

Frédéric noticed it:

"But what's . . ."

And they all three looked at each other and flushed.

The door was pushed open discreetly and a hat-brim appeared, followed by Hussonnet's profile.

"Sorry if I'm disturbing you lovebirds!"

Then he stopped, astounded at the sight of Cisy and the fact that he had taken his place.

Another plate was brought and, as Hussonnet was very hungry, he seized fistfuls of food at random from among the remains of the dinner, meat from one plate, fruit from the basket, holding his glass in one hand and helping himself with the other, all the while talking of his errand. The two lapdogs had been returned; there was nothing new at the house. He claimed to have found the cook with a soldier; a story he had invented purely for effect.

The Maréchale unhooked her hood from the peg. Frédéric threw himself on the bell and shouted to the waiter while he was still some distance away:

"A carriage!"

"Mine is here!" said the viscount.

"But, Monsieur!"

"Nevertheless, Monsieur!"

And they glared into each other's eyes, both pale and with trembling hands.

Finally, the Maréchale took Cisy's arm and, pointing to the bohemian who was still eating, said:

"Do take care of him! He's choking himself. I don't want his devotion to my dogs to kill him!"

The door closed behind them.

"Well?" said Hussonnet.

"Well what?"

"I thought . . ."

"What did you think?"

"Aren't you . . . ?" He completed his phrase with a gesture.

"Oh no! Not on your life!"

Hussonnet pressed no further.

He had had an object in asking himself to dinner. As his paper, which had changed its title from *L'Art* to *Le Flambard* with the epigraph "Stand to your guns!" was far from prosperous, he wanted to turn it into a weekly magazine on his own, without Deslauriers' help. He brought the old project up again and expounded his new plan.

Probably not understanding what he was being told, Frédéric responded vaguely. Hussonnet took a fistful of cigars from the table and disappeared with a "Good night, old man."

Frédéric asked for the bill. It was a long one and the waiter was waiting for his money, a napkin over his arm, when one of his fellows, a pallid individual who resembled Martinon, came up and said:

"Excuse me, but the cashier forgot to add in the cab."

"What cab?"

"The one that the gentleman took just now for the little dogs."

And the waiter's face grew longer, as if he were sorry for the poor young man. Frédéric wanted to slap him. He gave him as tip the twenty francs he received in change from the bill.

"Thank you, my lord!" said the man with the napkin, bowing low.

Frédéric spent the following day nursing his anger and humiliation. He reproached himself for not having struck Cisy. As for the Maréchale, he swore he would never see her again; there were plenty of others just as beautiful and, since one must have money to own that kind of woman, he would play the stock market with the price he had received for his farm. He would be rich and would crush the Maréchale and everyone else beneath the weight of his luxury. When evening arrived, he was surprised to realize that he had not given a thought to Madame Arnoux.

"So much the better! What's the use?"

Two days later, Pellerin came round to visit him at eight in the morning. He began by admiring his furniture and flattering him. Then he said abruptly:

"Weren't you at the races on Sunday?"

"Alas, yes!"

The artist then started inveighing against the anatomy of English horses, praising the horses painted by Géricault and the horses on the Parthénon. "Rosanette was with you?" And he launched into an adroit eulogy of her charms.

Frédéric's coldness disconcerted him. He could not think how to bring the conversation round to the portrait.

His first intention had been to create a Titian. But little by little he had been seduced by his model's varied coloring and he had worked boldly, piling paint on paint and light on light. At first, Rosanette was enchanted; then her meetings with Delmar had interrupted the sittings and given Pellerin plenty of time to be dazzled by his work. Later, when his admiration had died down, he started to wonder if the painting did not lack grandeur. He had been to see the Titians again, recognized the distance between them and his own work, and understood his mistake. He had begun to repaint his outlines, simplifying them. Then he had blurred them, in an attempt to blend the tones of the head and those of the background, and the face had taken on a greater consistency and the shadows a new vigor; everything seemed more solid. At last the Maréchale returned. She had been so bold as to raise objections; naturally the artist had persevered but, after furiously denouncing her stupidity, he had admitted to himself that she might be right. Then a period of doubts began, conflicting thoughts that led to indigestion, fever, and self-disgust. He had plucked up enough courage to retouch the portrait, but his heart was not in it and he felt that his work was bad.

Now he merely complained of having been refused at the Salon and then reproached Frédéric with not having come to see the Maréchale's portrait.

"I don't give a damn for the Maréchale!"

Emboldened by this remark he went on:

"Would you believe it, that idiot doesn't want to have anything more to do with it."

He omitted to mention that he had asked her for a thousand écus. The Maréchale took very little interest in who paid for the portrait and, preferring to wheedle money out of Arnoux for more urgent matters, she had not even mentioned it to him.

"Well, what about Arnoux?" asked Frédéric.

She had sent Pellerin to see him. The former picture dealer had no use for the portrait.

"He maintains that it belongs to Rosanette."

"That's right, it's hers."

"What! But it was she who referred me to you!" cried Pellerin.

If he had believed in the excellence of his work, he might not have thought of exploiting it. But a fee (and a large fee) would be a defense against criticism and a reassurance to himself. Frédéric, to get rid of him, made a courteous inquiry as to the price. The exorbitance of the sum infuriated him and he replied:

"No! Oh no!"

"But you're her lover and you're the one who commissioned it in the first place!"

"I beg your pardon, I was the intermediary!"

"But I can't be left with it on my hands!"

The artist flew into a rage.

"I never realized you were so avaricious!"

"Nor I that you were a miser! Good day!"

He had just left when Sénécal arrived.

Frédéric, in his disturbed state, felt a twinge of anxiety.

"What is it?"

Sénécal told his tale.

"On Saturday, at about nine o'clock, Madame Arnoux received a letter summoning her to Paris; it so happened that there was no one there to go to Creil for a carriage, so she asked me to go myself. I refused, as it was not part of my job. She left, and returned on Sunday evening. Yesterday morning, Arnoux visited the factory. The Bordelaise complained. I don't know what passed between them, but he cancelled her punishment in front of everyone. We exchanged a few heated words. To cut a long story short, he sacked me, and here I am!"

Then, slowly, with a pause between every word:

"Well, I have no regrets! I did my duty. That doesn't alter the fact that you were the cause of the whole business!"

"What!" cried Frédéric, fearing that Sénécal had guessed his secret.

Sénécal had guessed nothing, for he resumed:

"I mean that if it hadn't been for you I might have found something better."

Frédéric felt a kind of remorse.

"What can I do for you now?"

Sénécal asked for some sort of employment, a position.

"It's easy for you, you know so many people. Monsieur Dambreuse among others, if what Deslauriers tells me is true."

This reminder of Deslauriers was unpleasant. He was not anxious to go back to the Dambreuses after their encounter at the Champ de Mars.

"I'm not a close enough friend to recommend anyone for employment."

The democrat endured this refusal stoically and, after a moment's silence:

"I'm sure that the Bordelaise and your Madame Arnoux are responsible for the whole thing."

What little goodwill Frédéric still bore toward Sénécal vanished at the sound of that *your*. His sense of delicacy, however, prompted him to reach for the key of his desk.

Sénécal forestalled him:

"No, thank you."

Then, forgetting his troubles, he started talking about affairs of state; the quantities of crosses of honor distributed on the king's birthday, a change in the cabinet, the Drouillard and Bénier affairs,* scandals of the day; then he inveighed against the bourgeois and predicted a revolution.

A Japanese kris† hanging on the wall caught his eye. He took it down, tried the grip, then threw it on the sofa with an air of disgust.

"Well, good-bye! I've got to get to Nôtre-Dame de Lorette."

"Oh, why?"

"They're holding Godefroy Cavaignac's‡ anniversary service there today. There was a man who died in harness! But it's not all over yet . . . who knows?"

And Sénécal held out his hand stoutly.

"We may never see each other again! Good-bye!"

This twice-repeated good-bye, his frown when he looked at the dagger, his resignation, and above all his solemnity gave Frédéric some thought, but he soon forgot about it.

That same week, his lawyer in Le Havre sent him the money from the sale of his farm, one hundred and seventy-four thousand francs. He divided it in two, investing one part in government bonds and taking the second to a stockbroker to gamble with on the exchange.

He ate in the fashionable restaurants, went to the theater regularly, and was doing his best to keep busy when he received a letter from Hussonnet with a lively description of the manner in which the Maréchale had sent Cisy on his way the day after the races. Frédéric was glad to hear this; it did not occur to him to wonder why the bohemian had let him know.

It so happened that he ran into Cisy three days later.

---

*Drouillard, a Parisian banker, was found guilty in 1847 of bribery during an election. Bénier, a government official, had been accused of embezzlement.

†A kris is, of course, Malayan, not Japanese.

‡Godefroy Cavaignac, an ardent republican who had been imprisoned after the risings in April, 1834, was idolized by the people whose demands and hopes he incarnated. He died in 1845.

The nobleman put a good face on it, and even asked him to dine the following Wednesday.

The morning of that day, Frédéric received an official notification that, by the terms of a court order, Monsieur Charles-Jean-Baptiste Oudry had become the owner of a property situated at Belleville belonging to Monsieur Jacques Arnoux and that he was ready to pay the price of two hundred twenty-three thousand francs. But the same document showed that, as the sum of the mortgages on the building came to more than the purchase price, Frédéric's claim was completely nullified.

The whole trouble came from the registration of the mortgage not having been renewed at the right time. Arnoux had undertaken to see to this and had then forgotten about it. Frédéric was furious with him; then, when his anger had passed, he said to himself:

"Oh well . . . what of it? If it can save him, well and good! I won't die of it. Forget it!"

But, turning over the papers on his desk, he came across Hussonnet's letter and noticed the postscript, which he had overlooked the first time. The bohemian asked him for five thousand francs, no more and no less, to get the transformation of the paper under way.

"Oh! How that man annoys me!"

And he refused point-blank, in a curt note. After which he changed his clothes to go to the Maison-d'Or.

Cisy introduced him to his guests, beginning with the most respectable, a stout man with white hair.

"The Marquis Gilbert des Aulnays, my godfather."

The next was Monsieur Anselme de Forchambeaux, a fair, delicate-looking young man who was already going bald. Then Cisy pointed to a plain-mannered man of forty or so: "My cousin, Joseph Boffreu; and here is my former tutor, Monsieur Vezou," a figure halfway between a waggoner and a seminarian, with heavy whiskers and a long frock coat, which fastened at the bottom with a single button and was arranged over his chest like a shawl.

Cisy was waiting for one other person, Baron de Comaing, "who may or may not be coming." He kept darting in and out of the room and seemed uneasy; finally, at eight o'clock, they went into a dining room, which was magnificently lit and far too big for the number of guests. Cisy had chosen it on purpose, out of a desire for ostentation.

A silver-gilt centerpiece, full of flowers and fruit, occupied the middle of the table, which was covered with

silver platters in the old French style; they were surrounded by a border of pickle bowls full of seasonings
and spices; pitchers of iced vin rosé stood at regular intervals, and five glasses of different sizes were ranged before
each plate, with ingenious implements whose purposes
could only be guessed at. For the first course alone, there
was a sturgeon's jowl moistened with champagne, a York
ham cooked in Tokay, thrushes *au gratin*, roasted quail, a
vol-au-vent Béchamel, a sauté of red-legged partridges,
and at either end of this spread a dish of potato straws
mixed with truffles. The room, which was hung with red
damask, was lit by a chandelier and some candelabras.
Four servants in black liveries stood behind the morocco-
leather chairs. At the sight of this magnificence, the guests
broke into exclamations of admiration, especially the tutor.

"Upon my word, our host has done us proud! This is
superb!"

"This?" said the Viscount de Cisy. "Oh, come now!"

And, as soon as he had taken his first spoonful, he
remarked:

"Well, des Aulnays old man, have you been to the
Palais-Royal to see *Père et Portier?*"*

"You know I haven't got time for that kind of thing!"
replied the marquis.

His mornings were devoted to a course in arboriculture,
his evenings to the Agricultural Club, and all his afternoons to visiting factories where they made agricultural
implements. Living in Saintonge nine months of the year,
he took advantage of his visits to the capital to inform
himself, and his wide-brimmed hat, which lay on one of
the side tables, was full of brochures.

But Cisy, noticing that Monsieur Forchambeaux was
refusing the wine, exclaimed:

"Come on now, drink up, dammit! You're not being
very dashing, considering it's your last meal as a bache-
lor!"

At these words everyone bowed and congratulated him.

"And the young lady," said the tutor, "is charming,
I'm sure?"

"Of course!" cried Cisy, "but still he's making a mistake! Marriage is so stupid!"

"You're being flippant, my boy!" replied Monsieur des

*A comedy in two acts by Ancelot and Bourgeois.

Aulnays, as his eyes filled with tears at the memory of his dead wife.

And Forchambeaux, tittering, repeated several times: "You'll come to it yourself, you'll come to it!"

Cisy protested. He preferred to amuse himself, "to be Regency." He wanted to learn *savate* so that he could visit the thieves' kitchens of the Cité like Prince Rudolphe in the *Mystères de Paris;* and he pulled a cutty pipe out of his pocket, spoke harshly to the servants, drank to excess and critized all the dishes to impress his guests. He even sent the truffles back to the kitchen, and the tutor, who had found them delectable, said hypocritically:

"They can't match your grandmother's *oeufs à la neige!*"

Then he went back to his conversation with his neighbor, the agronomist, who maintained that country life had many advantages, not the least of which was the possibility of bringing up one's daughters with simple tastes. The tutor applauded his views and fawned on him, believing him to have some influence with his own former pupil, whose steward he secretly desired to become.

When he arrived, Frédéric had been full of ill will toward Cisy but the latter's stupidity had disarmed him. Now his gestures, his face, his whole person reminded him of the dinner at the café Anglais, and irritated him more and more; and he willingly lent an ear to the unkind remarks muttered by his Cousin Joseph, a good fellow with no money, a lover of hunting and a speculator on the stock exchange. By way of a joke Cisy called him a "swindler" several times; then suddenly he exclaimed:

"Ah, the Baron!"

And in came a stalwart fellow of thirty or so, with a rather coarse face, supple limbs, his hat cocked over one ear and a flower in his buttonhole. This was the viscount's ideal. He was overjoyed at his arrival, and, excited by his presence, even attempted a pun. He remarked, as they passed around a *coq de bruyère:*

"Here is the best of La Bruyère's characters!"

Then he bombarded Monsieur de Comaing with questions about various people unknown to the rest of the company, and suddenly, as if the idea had just struck him, inquired:

"By the way, did you remember me?"

The other shrugged his shoulders:

"Can't be done, my child! You're not old enough."

Cisy had asked him to put him up for membership in

his club. But the baron, probably to salve his host's wounded pride, continued:

"Oh, I forgot! My congratulations on your bet!"

"What bet?"

"The one you made at the races, to spend that very evening with the lady."

Frédéric felt as if struck by a whip, but Cisy's unnerved expression calmed him.

The Maréchale had, in fact, repented of her action the following morning when Arnoux, her prime lover, her man, had come in that same day. They had both given the viscount to understand that he was in the way and unceremoniously thrown him out.

He pretended not to have heard the baron, who added:

"How is good old Rosie anyhow? Are her legs as pretty as ever?" proving, by this remark, that he knew her intimately.

Frédéric was annoyed by this revelation.

"It's nothing to blush about," went on the baron. "She's a good catch!"

"Ah, not as good as all that!"

"Oh?"

"Goodness, yes! To begin with, I don't see anything extraordinary about her; and besides you can collect that kind by the handful, after all . . . she's for sale!"

"Not to everyone!" said Frédéric harshly.

"He thinks he's different from the others!" retorted Cisy. "What a joke!" And a ripple of laughter went round the table.

Frédéric felt as if the thudding of his heart would suffocate him. He tossed off two glasses of water, one after the other.

But the baron had pleasant memories of Rosanette.

"Is she still with a man called Arnoux?"

"I wouldn't know," said Cisy. "I never met the man!"

In spite of this, he volunteered that he was some kind of scoundrel.

"Wait a minute!" cried Frédéric.

"But it's well known. He was taken to court!"

"It's not true!"

Frédéric undertook Arnoux's defense. He guaranteed his honesty, came to believe in it himself, made up facts and figures. The viscount, spiteful and tipsy besides, stuck so obstinately to his claims, that Frédéric inquired gravely:

"Are you trying to offend me, Monsieur?"

And the pupils of his eyes, as he looked at Cisy, glowed like the tip of his cigar.

"Oh, far from it! I'll even admit that there's one excellent thing about him—his wife!"

"Do you know her?"

"Hell, everyone knows Sophie Arnoux!"

"What did you say?"

Cisy, who had risen to his feet, repeated, stammeringly: "Everyone knows her!"

"Shut up! She's not the kind of woman you go about with!"

"I pride myself on that!"

Frédéric threw his plate at Cisy's face. It flew across the table like a bolt of lightning, knocked over two bottles, demolished a bowl, broke in three against the centerpiece, and struck the viscount in the stomach.

Everyone sprang up to restrain him. He struggled, shouting, in a kind of frenzy. Monsieur des Aulnays kept repeating:

"Calm yourself! Now, now! My dear boy!"

"But this is disgraceful!" cried the tutor.

Forchambeaux was trembling, livid as the plums; Joseph was howling with laughter; the waiters were mopping up the wine and collecting the wreckage on the floor, and the baron went over to close the window, for the fracas could have been heard in the street, despite the noise of the traffic.

As everyone had been talking at once at the moment when the plate was hurled, it was impossible to determine the offense—whether it was because of Arnoux, Madame Arnoux, Rosanette, or someone else. What was clear was the unspeakable brutality of Frédéric's conduct, for which he refused to express the slightest regret.

Monsieur des Aulnays, Cousin Joseph, the tutor, Forchambeaux himself, all tried to bring him around. The baron, meanwhile, was comforting Cisy, who had given way to a nervous collapse and was in tears. Frédéric, on the contrary, grew more and more infuriated and they would have been there all night if the baron, to close the matter, had not said:

"The viscount's seconds will call on you tomorrow, Monsieur!"

"At what time?"

"At noon, if that is convenient for you?"

"Perfectly, Monsieur."

Once outside, Frédéric drew a deep breath. He had

been keeping his emotions under tight control for too long. Now, at last, he had given them free rein, and he felt a kind of virile pride, a superabundance of his innermost strength which intoxicated him. He needed two seconds. Regimbart was the first to occur to him, and he set off at once for a coffeehouse in the Rue Saint-Denis. The shutters were closed but a light shone through the pane of glass over the door. It opened and he went in, stooping low under the awning.

A candle on the edge of the counter lit up the deserted room. All the stools had been piled onto the tables with their legs in the air. The proprietor and his wife, with their waiter, were having supper in the corner by the kitchen; Regimbart, his hat on his head, was sharing their meal and, indeed, cramping the waiter, who was forced to turn slightly to one side with each mouthful. After giving him a brief account of the incident Frédéric asked Regimbart for his assistance. The Citizen said nothing at first; he rolled his eyes reflectively, walked about the room several times, and finally answered:

"Yes, with pleasure!"

And his wrinkles smoothed in a murderous smile when he learned that Frédéric's adversary was a nobleman.

"We'll teach him a lesson, don't worry about that! First . . . with swords . . ."

"But," objected Frédéric, "perhaps I haven't the right . . ."

"I tell you, you must choose swords!" replied the Citizen sharply. "Do you know how to use one?"

"A little."

"A little! That's what they all say! And they have this passion for fencing! Fencing lessons are no earthly use! Now listen to me: keep away from him, swing in circular sweeps around yourself, and give ground, give ground! It's entirely legitimate! Tire him out! Then lunge at him boldly! And above all no feinting, no strokes à la Fougère. No! Just plain one-two and disengage. Like this, see? With a twist of the wrist, as if you were turning a key in a lock. Lend me your cane, Père Vauthier—oh, this will do."

And he seized the rod used to ignite the gas, rounded his left arm, bent his right, and started lunging at the partition. He darted about, stamping his feet and even pretending to encounter difficulties, repeatedly crying: "You see what I mean? You follow me?" and his enormous shadow, with its hat which seemed to touch the ceiling, danced across the wall. From time to time, the coffeehouse keeper would say: "Bravo! Well done!" His wife was equally caught up in admiration, despite her trembling. Théodore, a former soldier, was rooted to the spot with amazement, being in any case a fanatical admirer of Monsieur Regimbart.

Early the next day, Frédéric hurried around to the shop where Dussardier worked. After a series of rooms, all full of bolts of cloth arranged on shelves or spread over the tables, with shawls displayed on wooden stands among them, he found Dussardier in a kind of barred cage surrounded by registers, where he was standing up at a desk writing. The good fellow abandoned his work immediately.

The seconds arrived before noon. Frédéric believed that it would not be good form for him to be present at the meeting.

The baron and Monsieur Joseph declared that they would be contented with the most perfunctory apology. But Regimbart, one of whose principles it was never to give way on anything, and who was determined to defend Arnoux's honor (Frédéric had not mentioned any other cause of the quarrel), demanded that the viscount should apologize. Monsieur de Comaing was outraged by this presumption. The Citizen refused to accede. As all conciliation was now impossible, the duel would take place.

Other difficulties arose, for the choice of weapons by rights belonged to Cisy as the offended party. But Regimbart insisted that he had become the aggressor by sending the challenge. His seconds maintained that, whatever he might say, a blow was the worst insult imaginable. Regimbart started splitting hairs, declaring that throwing a plate at someone was not the same as striking him. Finally, they decided to submit their dispute to the adjudication of the army; and the four seconds set off to consult the officers at one of the barracks.

They stopped at the barracks on the Quai d'Orsay and Monsieur de Comaing buttonholed two captains and laid the matter before them.

The captains couldn't make head or tail of the exposition, confused as it was by Regimbart's interpolations, and they advised the gentlemen to draw up a written statement, upon which they would base their decision. At this the four withdrew to a café and even, in the interests of discretion, designated Cisy by an "H" and Frédéric by a "K." Then they returned to the barracks.

Finally they reappeared and declared that the choice of arms obviously lay with Monsieur "H." They all went back to Cisy's house and Regimbart and Dussardier waited outside on the sidewalk.

On hearing the result of the morning's activities, the viscount was so upset that he made his seconds repeat their account several times; and when Monsieur de Comaing came to Regimbart's demands Cisy murmured: "But still . . ." not being far, himself, from complying. Then he sank into an armchair and declared that he would not fight.

"Eh? What did you say?" said the baron.

Then Cisy abandoned himself to a confused flood of words. He wanted to fight with blunderbusses, at point-blank range, with a single pistol:

"Or we could put some arsenic in a glass and draw lots for it. That's sometimes done, I've read about it!"

The baron, who was not a naturally tolerant man, snapped:

"They're waiting for your answer. This is indecent. Well, what's your choice? Swords?"

The viscount nodded his head and the meeting was fixed for the next day, at the Porte Maillot, at exactly seven o'clock.

Dussardier had to go back to the shop, so Regimbart went to let Frédéric know what had been going on. He had been left without news all day and his impatience had grown intolerable.

"So much the better!" he exclaimed.

The Citizen was pleased with this attitude.

"They tried to make us apologize, would you believe it? It would have been nothing, just one word! But I soon set them straight! And I was right, wasn't I?"

"Of course," said Frédéric, thinking that he should have chosen a different second.

As soon as he was alone he said to himself several times aloud: "I'm going to fight. Well, I'm going to fight. How extraordinary!" He was pacing up and down the room and, as he passed the mirror, he noticed he was pale.

"Could I be frightened?"

And he felt a pang of agony at the thought that he might be afraid on the dueling ground.

"After all, I might be killed. That's how my father died. Yes, I shall be killed!"

Suddenly, he had a vision of his mother in a black

dress; his head filled with incoherent images. His own cowardice exasperated him and he was flooded with a surge of furious courage, a lust for blood. He would not have flinched from a battalion. When this fever subsided, he felt himself, to his delight, to be unshakable. For distraction he went to the Opéra, where they were giving a ballet. He listened to the music, ogled the dancers, and tossed off a glass of punch during the intermission. But when he returned home, the sight of his furniture and his study, in which he might be standing for the last time, brought on a momentary weakness.

He went down into the garden. The sky was full of stars; he gazed at them. The idea of fighting for a woman's sake ennobled him, increasing his stature in his own eyes. Then he went calmly to bed.

Cisy's reaction was quite different. After the baron's departure, Joseph had tried to cheer him up and, when the viscount remained sunk in melancholy, he said:

"Well, old man, if you'd prefer to drop the whole thing, I'll go and tell them so."

Cisy was not brave enough to reply: "Go on, then," but he held a grudge against his cousin for not having performed this service on his own without asking him.

He hoped that Frédéric would die of a stroke during the night, or that a riot would break out and there would be enough barricades the next day to close all the approaches to the Bois de Boulogne, or that something would happen to prevent one of the seconds from turning up, for without all the seconds the duel could not take place. He longed to escape on an express train to anywhere at all. He regretted his ignorance of medicine—he might have dosed himself with something harmless that would make people believe that he was dead. He reached the point of wishing he could fall seriously ill.

In search of advice and comfort, he sent for Monsieur des Aulnays. The excellent man had returned to Saintonge, having received word of the illness of one of his daughters. To Cisy this seemed like an evil omen. Happily Monsieur Vezou, his tutor, called and he opened his heart to him:

"What can I do? My God, what can I do?"

"In your place, Monsieur de Comte, I should hire a tough from Les Halles to give him a beating."

"He'd still know who was behind it," replied Cisy.

From time to time he gave a groan, then he asked:

"But is it legal to fight a duel?"

"It's a relic of barbarism! Nothing can be done about it."

The tutor was obliging enough to ask himself to dinner. His pupil ate nothing and, after the meal, felt the need of some fresh air.

They passed a church and Cisy suggested:

"Suppose we went in . . . just to look around?"

Monsieur Vezou asked nothing better and even offered him some holy water.

It was May, the month dedicated to Mary; the altar was covered with flowers, the choir sang, the organ thundered. But Cisy found prayer impossible; all this religious pomp turned his thoughts to funerals and he seemed to hear the strains of the *De profundis*.

"Let's go. I'm not feeling well!"

They spent the whole night playing cards. The viscount did his utmost to lose, as an insurance against bad luck, and Monsieur Vezou profited by it. Finally, in the early morning, the exhausted Cisy slumped over the card table in a sleep that brought nothing but bad dreams.

If, however, courage lies in dominating one's weakness, then the viscount was a brave man, for at the sight of his seconds coming to fetch him, he pulled himself together with all his strength, his vanity prompting the realization that to flinch now would be the end of him. Monsieur de Comaing complimented him on how well he was looking.

But on the way to the Bois de Boulogne the heat of the morning and the swaying of the cab unnerved him. His energy flagged and he could no longer even tell where they were.

The baron took a certain pleasure in adding to his terror, by talking about the "corpse" and how it could best be smuggled back into town. Joseph joined in; they both thought the whole affair ridiculous and were sure that it would be settled.

Cisy was sitting with his head sunk on his chest; he lifted it slowly and remarked on the absence of a doctor.

"It's pointless to have one," replied the baron.

"Then there's no danger?"

Joseph responded gravely:

"Let's hope not!"

And no one in the carriage said another word.

They arrived at the Porte Maillot at ten past seven. Frédéric and his seconds were waiting for them, all three dressed in black. Instead of a cravat, Regimbart was wearing a horsehair collar like a soldier, and he carried a

sort of elongated violin case, made especially for this kind
of venture. They greeted one another coldly. Then they all
moved into the Bois de Boulogne along the Madrid road
in search of a suitable place.

Regimbart turned to Frédéric, who was walking between him and Dussardier, and said:

"Well, what are we going to do about the funk you're
in? If you need anything, just ask. I understand! Fear is
natural to man."

Then, in a low voice:

"Stop smoking now. It's weakening!"

Frédéric threw away his cigar, which was making him
uncomfortable, and continued to advance with a firm step.
The viscount followed, leaning on the arms of his seconds.

Few people crossed their path. The sky was blue, and
occasionally they heard a rabbit bounding away. At a turn
in the path, a woman in a Madras kerchief was talking to
a man in a smock; and in the main avenue, some servants
in linen jackets were exercising their horses under the
chestnuts. Cisy remembered the happy days when, astride
his chestnut mare, his monocle in his eye, he rode beside
the doors of the barouches; these memories increased his
anguish, he burned with an intolerable thirst, the buzz of
the flies mingled with the throbbing of his arteries, his
feet sank into the sand, and it seemed to him that he had
been walking for an eternity.

The seconds scrutinized the park on either side as they
walked along. They discussed whether to go to the Crois
Catelan or beneath the walls of the Bagatelle. Finally,
they turned off to the right, and stopped in a kind of
quincunx among some pine trees.

A spot was picked where neither side had any advantage from the ground. The two adversaries' places were
marked. Then Regimbart opened his case. It was lined
with quilted red hide and contained four elegant swords,
with grooved blades and hilts decorated in filigree. A ray
of light pierced the screen of leaves and fell on them; to
Cisy they seemed to glow like silver vipers in a sea of
blood.

The Citizen demonstrated that they were all the same
length; then took the third one for himself, so as to be
able to separate the combatants if the need arose. Monsieur de Comaing held a cane. Silence fell. They gazed at
each other. There was a trace of fear or cruelty in every
face.

Frédéric had discarded his frock coat and waistcoat.

Joseph helped Cisy to follow his example; on the removal of his cravat a religious medal which he wore around his neck was revealed. Regimbart smiled pityingly.

Then Monsieur de Comaing (so as to give Frédéric another moment or two for reflection) tried to raise some minor quibbles. He claimed the right to wear a glove and to seize the adversary's sword with the left hand. Finally the baron said to Frédéric:

"Everything depends on you, Monsieur. There is never any dishonor in admitting one's faults."

Dussardier nodded his approval. The Citizen cried indignantly:

"Do you think we're here for a picnic, dammit? On guard!"

The principals were standing facing each other, their seconds on either side. He gave the signal:

"Go!"

Cisy grew fearfully pale. The tip of his sword trembled like a riding crop. His head lolled back, his arms flopped to either side, and he fell on his back in a dead faint. Joseph propped him up and held a bottle of smelling-salts under his nose, shaking him vigorously. The viscount reopened his eyes, then suddenly leaped on his sword like a madman. Frédéric had held onto his weapon and was waiting for him, his eye steady and his guard high.

From the direction of the road came the sound of a galloping horse and a voice crying: "Stop, stop!" The hood of a cab came crashing through the branches with a man leaning out of the window waving a handkerchief and still shouting: "Stop! Stop!"

Monsieur de Comaing, under the impression that the police were intervening, lifted his cane:

"That's enough. The viscount is bleeding!"

"Me?" said Cisy.

Sure enough he had grazed his left thumb when he fainted.

"But he did it when he fell," objected the Citizen.

The baron pretended not to hear.

Arnoux had jumped down from the cab.

"I've arrived too late—no! Thank God!"

And he hugged Frédéric tightly, feeling him all over and covering his face with kisses.

"I know why you did it! You were defending your old friend! That was noble, really noble! I'll never forget it! How good you are! Oh, my dear boy!"

And he gazed at Frédéric, the tears running down his

face, which was wreathed in smiles of happiness. The baron turned to Joseph:

"I feel that we are intruding on this little family re-union! It's settled, I think, gentlemen—Viscount, put your arm in a sling; here, take my scarf." Then, with an imperious gesture: "Come along now! No hard feelings! That's the rule!"

The two adversaries shook hands limply. The viscount, Monsieur de Comaing, and Joseph disappeared in one direction, while Frédéric and his friends went off in the other.

The restaurant de Madrid was not far away, and Arnoux suggested having a glass of beer there.

"We could even have lunch," said Regimbart.

But Dussardier had no time, so they confined themselves to a snack in the garden. They were all in the grip of that exhilaration that follows a happy ending, though the Citizen was annoyed that the duel had been interrupted just as it was about to get under way.

Arnoux had heard about it from a certain Compain, a friend of Regimbart's, and had hastened to intervene in a surge of affection for Frédéric—believing, moreover, that he was the cause of the quarrel. He begged Frédéric to tell him more about it. Frédéric, moved by the evidence of Arnoux's feeling for him, scrupled to add to his illusions.

"Please!" he said. "Let's not mention it again."

Arnoux thought this reserve very well bred. Then, in his usual volatile style, he turned to another topic:

"Well, Citizen, what's new?"

And they started to discuss bills and due dates. For greater ease they even went off to whisper together at another table.

Frédéric overheard:

"You'll buy some shares for me— Yes, but you, of course . . . —Finally clinched it for three hundred! —A nice commission, I must say!" In short, it was clear that Arnoux and the Citizen were involved in a good many shady deals together.

Frédéric thought of asking for his fifteen thousand francs, but Arnoux's recent conduct forbade reproaches, even the gentlest. Anyhow, he was tired. It was not a suitable place. He put it off to another day.

Arnoux, seated in the shade of a privet bush, was smoking with a jovial air. He looked round at the doors of the private rooms, all of which opened onto the garden, and remarked that he had often come here in the old days.

"Not alone, I am sure?" said the Citizen.

"Good lord!"

"What a scoundrel you are! And you a married man!"

"Well, what about you!" replied Arnoux, and added, with an indulgent smile:

"I'd even bet that rascal has a room somewhere where he entertains little girls!"

By simply raising his eyebrows, the Citizen admitted as much. Then the two gentlemen expatiated their preferences: Arnoux's taste now ran to young working girls, while Regimbart detested "phonies" and prized matter-of-factness above all. The conclusion, drawn by the pottery-maker, was that women should not be taken seriously.

"Nevertheless, he loves his wife!" reflected Frédéric, on his way home, and he concluded Arnoux was dishonest. He was angry with him because of the duel as if it had been for him that he had just risked his life.

But he was grateful to Dussardier for his devotion; the clerk, at his urging, was soon visiting him every day.

Frédéric lent him books: Thiers, Dulaure, Barante, Lamartine's *Les Girondins*. The good fellow listened to him with devout attention and accepted his opinions like those of a master.

One evening he arrived in a panic.

That morning on the boulevard, a man running full tilt had bumped into him, and, having recognized him as a friend of Sénécal's, had blurted out:

"They've just arrested him—I'm on the run."

It was quite true. Dussardier had spent the day making inquiries. Sénécal was under lock and key, accused of attempting a political crime.

Born at Lyons, the son of a foreman, he had been taught by a former disciple of Chalier's, and had joined the Société des Familles, a sort of socialist club, on his arrival in Paris. His activities were known, and the police kept an eye on him. He had fought in the May, 1839, uprising and had laid low thereafter. But he grew steadily more fanatical, a passionate supporter of Alibaud, the would-be assassin of Louis-Philippe, confusing his own grievances against society with those of the people against the monarchy, and he awoke every morning hoping for a revolution which would transform the world in the space of two weeks or a month. Finally, disgusted by the spinelessness of his fellows, infuriated by the obstacles in the way of his dreams, and despairing of his country, he had joined the incendiary bomb plot as a chemist and had been caught in the act of taking some gunpowder to be tested at Montmartre, in a supreme attempt to establish the Republic.

Dussardier was no less eager for the victory of republicanism, which he believed would lead to freedom and universal happiness. One day when he was fifteen years old, in front of a grocer's shop in the rue Transnonain,* he had seen some soldiers with bloody bayonets and hair on the butts of their guns; he had loathed the government ever since as the very incarnation of injustice. He was inclined to confuse murderers and policemen; in his eyes an informer was the equivalent of a parricide. He naïvely attributed all the evil in the world to Authority and hated it with an undying hatred that filled his whole being and refined his sensibility. Sénécal's invective had dazzled him. It made no difference to him whether or not he was guilty, nor how odious the plot had been. Once he had become the victim of Authority, it was one's duty to help him.

"The Peers will certainly convict him! Then they'll take him away in a Black Maria, like a criminal condemned to the galleys, and shut him up in Mont-Saint-Michel, where the government kills them! Austen went mad! Steuben committed suicide! When they transferred Barbès to a dungeon they dragged him by his legs and his hair! They trampled on him, and his head bounced from step to step the whole length of the staircase. It's abominable! The villains!"

His sobs of anger choked him and he prowled the room as if in the grip of some agonizing pain.

"Still, we've got to do something! Let's think! I don't know! Suppose we tried to rescue him? While they're taking him to the Luxembourg we could ambush the convoy in the passage! A dozen determined men can do anything!"

And Frédéric trembled at the fire in his eyes.

Sénécal seemed to him a greater man than he had realized. He recalled his sufferings, his austere life; with-

*A famous incident, which took place during the riots in April, 1834. Someone fired on the soldiers from a window of 12, Rue Transnonain (now the Rue Beaubourg), and the latter massacred every soul in the building. The memory Flaubert attributes to Dussardier is inspired by Daumier's famous lithograph of the scene.

out Dussardier's enthusiasm for him, he still felt the admiration inspired by any man who sacrifices himself for an ideal. He felt that if he had helped him Sénécal would not have come to this, and the two friends racked their brains for some way of saving him.

It was impossible for them to get to him.

Frédéric searched the newspapers for any mention of his fate and for three weeks he haunted the reading rooms.

One day he came across several issues of *Flambard*. The leading article was invariably consecrated to the destruction of some well-known man. Then came the society news and the gossip. Then there were jokes about the Odéon, Carpentras, pisciculture and, when there were any, men under sentence of death. The disappearance of a liner provided a subject for pleasantries through a whole year. The third column was devoted to a survey of the arts where, disguised as anecdotes or as advice, you could find tailors' advertisements, accounts of parties, announcements of sales, and book reviews; a volume of verse rubbing shoulders with a pair of boots. The only part worth anything was the criticism of the little theaters, where two or three directors were furiously attacked and the interests of Art were involved in speaking of the scenery at the Funambules or an actress at the Délassements.

Frédéric was just going to throw the sheet aside when his eye caught an article entitled: "A Pullet between three Cocks." It was the story of his duel, told in a lively, vulgar style. He recognized himself without difficulty, for he was designated by the pun: "A young man from the college of Sens who hasn't any." He was represented as a poor little provincial, an inconsequential booby trying to make his way among the gentry. As for the viscount, he came off the hero of the tale, first at the supper where he forced his way in, then in the wager, since he had carried off the lady, and finally on the dueling ground, where he had acquitted himself as a gentleman should. Frédéric's courage was not precisely denied, but the writer let it be understood that an intermediary, the "protector" himself, had arrived just in time. The whole thing ended with the question, heavy with treacherous implications: "Why are they so fond of each other? Who can tell! And, as Don Basilio says, who the devil is deceiving whom here?"

There could be no doubt that this was Hussonnet's revenge on Frédéric for having refused him the five thousand francs.

What could he do? If he tried to have it out with him the bohemian would protest his innocence and nothing would be gained. It would be best to swallow the insult in silence. After all, nobody read *Flambard*.

As he left the reading room, he noticed a crowd in front of a picture-dealer's window. They were looking at the portrait of a woman under which, in black letters, appeared the inscription: Mademoiselle Rose-Annette Bron, the property of Monsieur Frédéric Moreau, of Nogent."

It was certainly she—or a reasonable likeness—painted full face, with her breasts uncovered, her hair loose, and a red velvet purse in her hands, while a peacock behind her pushed his beak over her shoulder, covering the wall with his great fan of feathers.

Pellerin had arranged this exhibition to compel Frédéric to pay up, for he was convinced that he was famous and that the whole of Paris would rise to his defense.

Was it a plot? Had the painter and the journalist planned their attacks together?

His duel had been no help. He was becoming ridiculous and everyone was laughing at him.

Three days later, at the end of June, the North Railway shares rose by fifteen francs and, as he had bought two thousand a month earlier, he found that he had made thirty thousand francs. This piece of good luck gave him back his confidence. He told himself that he needed no one, that all his troubles came from his hesitations and timidity. He should have been blunt with the Maréchale from the start, refused Hussonnet's request the first time he had mentioned it, avoided compromising himself with Pellerin; and, to show that he had nothing to be ashamed of, he went round to the Dambreuses on one of her regular "at home" evenings.

In the middle of the hall Martinon, who had arrived at the same time, turned to him and said:

"What, you come here, do you?"

He seemed surprised, even provoked, to see him.

"Why not?"

And, still trying to think of a reason for this reception, Frédéric advanced into the drawing room.

It was dim, despite the lamps in the corners, for the three wide-open windows formed three broad parallel oblongs of darkness. The spaces between, under the pictures, were filled with flowerstands as high as a man's head; a silver teapot and samovar were reflected in a mirror at the far end of the room. There was a discreet murmur of voices, and the men's pumps squeaked as they moved over the carpet.

He made out some black evening coats, then a round table lit by a big, shaded lamp, seven or eight women in summer dresses and, at the far end of the room, Madame Dambreuse, seated in a rocking chair. Puffs of muslin showed through the slashed sleeves of her lilac taffeta dress, the soft tone of the stuff complemented the shade of her hair, and she sat leaning slightly backwards, the toe of her shoe resting on a cushion—as unruffled as a delicate work of art or a highly cultivated flower.

Monsieur Dambreuse and an old man with white hair were walking up and down the length of the room. Some people, sitting on the edge of the small sofas which were scattered here and there, were chatting to each other; the others stood in a circle in the middle of the room.

They were talking about votes, amendments, counter-amendments, Monsieur Grandin's speech and Monsieur Benoist's reply. The Third Party was certainly going too far! The Center Left should be more mindful of its origins! The Minister had had some hard knocks. Nevertheless, it was reassuring that no one could think of anyone to take his place. In short, the situation was completely analogous to 1834.

As all this bored Frédéric, he went over to the ladies. Martinon was standing near them, his hat under his arm, his face in three-quarter profile, and so impeccably dressed that he looked like a piece of Sèvres porcelain. He picked up a *Revue des Deux-Mondes,* which was lying on the table between an *Imitation of Christ* and an *Annuaire de Gotha,* and criticized a famous poet for the benefit of the company, then remarked that he was attending Saint-François' lectures, complained of his throat—swallowing a lozenge every now and then— meanwhile holding forth on music and chatting lightly. Mademoiselle Cécile, Monsieur Dambreuse's niece, who was embroidering a pair of cuffs, glanced at him surreptitiously out of her pale blue eyes; and Miss John, the flat-nosed governess, had abandoned her tapestry; both seemed to be saying to themselves: "How handsome he is!"

Madame Dambreuse turned toward him.

"Give me my fan, will you? It's on that table over there. No, not that one, the other!"

She rose to her feet and, as he came back, they met face to face in the middle of the drawing room; she said something sharply, a rebuke, to judge by the haughty expression on her face; Martinon tried to smile, then he went off to join a group of substantial-looking men. Madame Dambreuse resumed her former position and, leaning over the arm of her chair, said to Frédéric:

"The day before yesterday I saw someone who mentioned you: Monsieur de Cisy. You know him, don't you?"

"Yes . . . a little."

Suddenly Madame Dambreuse exclaimed:

"Duchess! Oh, how delightful!"

And she went as far as the door to meet a litle old lady who was wearing a light brown taffeta dress and a guipure lace cap wtih long strings. Daughter of a companion-in-exile of the Count d'Artois and widow of a marshal of the Empire who had been created a peer of France in 1830, she had ties with both the new court and the old, and possessed great influence. The men who were standing talking drew to one side, then resumed their discussion.

It had now turned to pauperism, all the descriptions of which, according to these gentlemen, had been much exaggerated.

"Nevertheless," objected Martinon, "poverty exists, there's no denying it! But the remedy does not lie in the hands of either science or government. It is a matter purely for the individual. When the lower orders choose to rid themselves of their vices, they will free themselves from their wants. If the people were more moral they would be less poor!"

According to Monsieur Dambreuse nothing worthwhile could be accomplished without a superabundance of capital. Thus it followed that the only possible path was to entrust, "as has incidently been proposed by the Saint-Simonians to give the devil his due" (heavens, they did have some good in them!) "to entrust, I say, the cause of progress to those who can add to the national wealth." Gradually the talk came round to the great industrial concerns, railways, and coal mines. Monsieur Dambreuse said softly to Frédéric:

"You never came by to discuss our business."

Frédéric pleaded illness but, feeling that the excuse would not hold water, added:

"Anyhow, I needed my capital."

"To buy a carriage?" asked Madame Dambreuse, who was going past with a cup of tea in her hand; and she considered him for a moment, her head a little on one side.

She thought that he was Rosanette's lover; the allusion was quite clear. It seemed to Frédéric that all the women were looking at him from across the room and whispering together. To find out what they thought he rejoined them.

On the other side of the table, Martinon was standing with Mademoiselle Cécile turning the pages of an album. It contained lithographs of Spanish costumes and he read the captions out loud: "Sevillian woman. —Valencian gardener. —Andalusian picador"; and once he looked down to the foot of the page and continued in the same breath:

"Published by Jacques Arnoux. —One of your friends, eh?"

"Yes," replied Frédéric, stung by his manner. Madame Dambreuse resumed:

"That's right, you came round one morning . . . about . . . a house, I believe? Yes, a house belonging to his wife." (This implied: "She is your mistress.")

He blushed to the roots of his hair; and Monsieur Dambreuse, who came up at that moment, added:

"You seemed to take a great interest in them."

These last words completed Frédéric's discomfiture. His consternation, which he felt must be obvious, would confirm people's suspicions. Then Monsieur Dambreuse drew closer to him and said in a grave voice:

"I assume that you have no business dealings with him?"

He protested, shaking his head repeatedly, without understanding the banker's intention which was to give him a warning.

He wanted to leave, but feared it would seem cowardly. A servant removed the tea tray; Madame Dambreuse was talking to a diplomat in a blue coat; two of the girls had their heads together over a ring; the others, sitting in a semicircle on the armchairs, turned their white faces framed in blonde or black hair gently from side to side; in short, no one was paying any attention to him. Frédéric turned on his heel and, by a series of long zigzags, had almost reached the door when he passed near a side-table on which he noticed a newspaper folded in two and thrust between a Chinese vase and the paneling. He pulled it out a little and read the words: *Le Flambard*.

Who could have brought it? Cisy! It could obviously be no one else. Anyhow, what did that matter! They would believe the article, perhaps they all believed it already. Why was he being hounded? An ironic silence enfolded him; he felt as if he were lost in a desert. Martinon raised his voice:

"Speaking of Arnoux, I saw the name of one of his employees, Sénécal, among the accused in the incendiary bomb affair. Is that our friend?"

"It is," said Frédéric.

Martinon repeated in a very loud voice:

"What, our Sénécal! our Sénécal!"

At this, he was bombarded with questions on the conspiracy; surely his position with the public prosecutor's office must mean that he had some information?

He confessed that he had not. Moreover, he hardly knew the man, having met him only two or three times, but he felt there was no question, he was quite clearly a dangerous rascal. Indignant, Frédéric cried:

"Absolutely not! He's a very worthy man!"

"But Monsieur," said a landowner, "a conspirator cannot be a worthy man!"

Most of the men in the room had served in at least four governments and would have betrayed France, or the human race, in order to protect their property, to avoid any discomfort or difficulty, or simply out of pure baseness, an instinctive worship of power. They all declared political crimes to be inexcusable. Those which sprang from poverty were much easier to condone. And they didn't fail to bring up the eternal example of the father of a family stealing the eternal loaf of bread from the eternal bakery.

One government official even exclaimed:

"As far as I am concerned, Monsieur, if I found that my own brother was part of a conspiracy I would denounce him!"

Frédéric invoked the right to resist and, recalling some arguments of Deslauriers', he cited Desolmes, Blackstone, the Bill of Rights in England, and Article Two of the Constitution of 1791. It was by virtue of that right that Napoléon had been dethroned; it had been recognized in 1830 and inscribed at the head of the Charter.

"Moreover, when a sovereign fails to fulfill his contract it is only just that he should be overthrown."

"But that's appalling!" exclaimed a prefect's wife.

All the others remained silent, vaguely frightened, as if

they had heard the whistle of bullets. Madame Dambreuse rocked in her chair and smiled as she listened.

An industrialist, a one-time carbonaro,* undertook to prove to him that the d'Orléans were a fine family; of course there were some abuses . . .

"Well, then?"

"But one should not talk about them, my dear sir! If you only knew how bad all this noisy opposition is for business!"

"I don't give a damn for business!" replied Frédéric.

The corruption of these old men exasperated him and, carried away by that bravery which sometimes transforms the most timid of men, he attacked the businessmen, the deputies, the government, the king; took the Arabs' side, said a great many foolish things. Some of the bystanders encouraged him ironically: "That's right! Keep it up!" while others murmured: "Good lord, what a fanatic!" Finally, he thought it proper to leave; and as he was going Monsieur Dambreuse said, in allusion to the job as secretary:

"Nothing has been decided yet. But hurry!"

And Madame Dambreuse added:

"We will be seeing you again soon, I hope?"

Frédéric took their farewells as a final mockery. He was determined never to return to this house, to see no more of all these people. He believed that he had offended them, not realizing the unfathomable depths of society's indifference. The attitude of the women aroused his particular indignation. Not one of them had supported him by so much as a glance. He was angry with them for not having been moved by his eloquence. As for Madame Dambreuse, there was a mixture of languor and dryness about her that prevented him from putting her into any definite category. Did she have a lover? Who was he? Was it the diplomat or someone else? Could it be Martinon? Impossible! Nevertheless, he felt a kind of jealousy toward him, and toward her an inexplicable ill will.

Dussardier had come round that evening as usual, and was waiting for him. Frédéric's heart was full; he unburdened it, and his troubles saddened the good-hearted clerk, vague and difficult to understand though they were. He even lamented of his sense of isolation. After some

---

*The Carbonari was a revolutionary secret society which started in Italy and intrigued against the government under the Restoration. Many of its members later supported the regime of Louis-Philippe, and even some of the king's ministers were Carbonari.

hesitation, Dussardier suggested they go to see Deslauriers.

At the mention of his name, Frédéric was seized by an intense yearning to see him again. His intellectual solitude was profound, and Dussardier's company was not enough. He told him to arrange matters as he thought best.

Since their break, Deslauriers too had felt a gap in his life. He had no trouble in accepting their friendly advances.

They embraced and set to talking of neutral matters.

Deslauriers' reserve touched Frédéric, and, as a kind of reparation, the following day he told him the story of his loss of fifteen thousand francs, without saying that these francs had originally been intended for him. The lawyer, however, did not doubt it. This misadventure justified his prejudices against Arnoux and completely dispelled his grudge against Frédéric; he did not mention the old promise again.

Frédéric, misled by his silence, believed he had forgotten it. Some days later, he asked Deslauriers if there was not some means of regaining his money.

It would be possible to dispute the previous mortgages, bring suit against Arnoux on grounds of fraud, or take proceedings against the wife at her house.

"No! No! Not against her!" cried Frédéric and, in response to the ex-clerk's persistent questioning, he admitted the truth. Deslauriers was convinced that he was not telling him the whole story, probably out of delicacy . . . He was wounded by this failure of intimacy.

Their friendship, nevertheless, was as close as ever, and they took so much pleasure in being together that even Dussardier's presence was an intrusion. On the pretext of having appointments, they contrived little by little to rid themselves of him. There are certain men whose only function in life is to serve as intermediaries; one crosses them like bridges and continues on the other side.

Frédéric hid nothing from his old friend. He told him about the business of the coal mines and Monsieur Dambreuse's proposal. The lawyer became thoughtful:

"That's odd! They need someone who knows a good deal of law for that position!"

"But you could help me," replied Frédéric.

"Yes . . . well . . . yes, of course!"

That same week he showed him a letter from his mother.

Madame Moreau reproached herself for having misjudged Monsieur Roque, who had given her a satisfactory explanation of his conduct. She went on to speak of his fortune and of the possibility of a marriage with Louise later on.

"That might not be such a bad idea!" said Deslauriers.

Frédéric rejected it out of hand; anyhow, Roque was an old swindler. This, in the lawyer's opinion, was completely irrelevant.

At the end of July there was an inexplicable slump in Northern Railway shares. Frédéric had not sold his holdings; he lost sixty thousand francs at one blow. His income was markedly diminished; he would have either to cut back his spending, find a position, or make a good marriage.

At this point, Deslauriers reminded him of Mademoiselle Roque. There was nothing to stop him going to take a look at the situation for himself. Frédéric was rather tired; provincial life and being at home with his mother would be restful. He decided to go.

The sight of the streets of Nogent, as he drove through them in the moonlight, conjured up old memories; and he felt a sort of anguish, like someone returning from a long journey.

At his mother's house he found all the usual visitors of the old days: Messieurs Gamblin, Heudras, and Chambrion, the Lebrun family, the Misses Auger. In addition, there was Old Roque and, seated opposite Madame Moreau at a card table, Mademoiselle Louise. She had become a woman. She rose with a cry. Everyone was in a flutter. She stood immobile and the light from the four silver candlesticks on the table increased her pallor. When she started to play again, her hand trembled. Frédéric, whose self-esteem had been damaged, was inordinately flattered by this display of emotion; "You at any rate will love me!" he said to himself and, in revenge for the mortifications he had suffered in the capital, he started to play the Parisian, the social lion, giving news of the theater, recounting anecdotes about society which he had culled from the scandal-sheets—in short, dazzling his fellow townsmen.

The next day Madame Moreau expatiated on Louise's virtues, then enumerated the woods and farms that would eventually be hers. Monsieur Roque's fortune was a large one.

He had acquired it in making investments for Monsieur Dambreuse, for he lent money to people who could offer good mortgage guarantees, which made it possible for

him to charge higher interest or commissions. Thanks to
his unremitting surveillance, there was never any risk to
the capital. Moreover, Old Roque never hesitated to fore-
close; then he would buy the mortgaged property at a low
price, and seeing his investments pay off in this way,
Monsieur Dambreuse felt that his business affairs were in
good hands.

But this extralegal manipulation put him in his steward's power. He could refuse him nothing. It was at his
request that he had taken such an interest in Frédéric.

Old Roque, in fact, nurtured a particular ambition in
the depths of his soul. He wanted his daughter to be a
countess and Frédéric was the only young man through
whom he could attain this goal without risking her happiness.

Monsieur Dambreuse would use his influence to have
his ancestor's title revived for Frédéric, since Madame
Moreau was the daughter of the Count de Fouvens and
was, moreover, related to the oldest families in Champagne, the Lavernades, and d'Étrignys. As for the Mo-
reaus, a gothic inscription near the Villeneuve-l'Arche-
vêque mills mentioned a Jacob Moreau who had rebuilt
them in 1596, and the tomb of his son, Pierre Moreau,
who had been Louis XIV's Master of the Horse, was in
the chapel of St. Nicholas.

These noble connections fascinated Monsieur Roque,
whose father had been a servant. Even if Frédéric did not
attain a count's coronet, he would have other consolations,
for the young man might become a deputy when Monsieur
Dambreuse was raised to the peerage, and then help him
in his business and obtain supplies and concessions for
him. Monsieur Roque liked him personally. And, finally,
he wanted him as his son-in-law because he had been
enamored of the idea for a long time and it became
increasingly attractive.

He was now a regular churchgoer; and he had won
over Madame Moreau, mainly by playing on her hopes of
the title. She had, however, refrained from giving him a
definite answer.

So it happened that eight days later, without any promise having been made, Frédéric was regarded as Mademoiselle Louise's "intended," and Old Roque, who had few
scruples, left them alone together from time to time.

Chapter Five

Deslauriers had taken the copy of the deed of subrogation from Frédéric's house, together with a properly made power of attorney giving him full authority to act, but when he had climbed the five flights of stairs and sat alone in his leather armchair in the middle of his dreary office, the sight of the stamped paper disgusted him.

He was tired of these things, and of restaurants where the bill came to thirty-two sous, of traveling by bus, of his poverty, and of his exertions. He picked up a handful of papers; next to them lay others, prospectuses for the coal company, with the list of mines and the details of their capacity. Frédéric had left him all this so that he could give an opinion on it.

An idea occurred to him: why not go to Monsieur Dambreuse and ask for the job as secretary himself? The position would certainly require the purchase of some shares. He realized the scheme was a foolish one, and said to himself:

"No, that would be wrong!"

Next, he tried to think of some means of recovering the fifteen thousand francs. A sum like that meant nothing to Frédéric! If only *he* had had it, what a lever it would have made! And the onetime clerk grew indignant that the other's fortune was so large.

"And he uses it in such a paltry way. He's selfish. Ah, what do I care for his fifteen thousand francs?"

Why had he lent them? For Madame Arnoux's sake. She was his mistress, Deslauriers was certain of it. "There's one more example of what you can do with money!" And a surge of spiteful thoughts swept through him.

Then he considered Frédéric's appearance. This had al-

ways charmed Deslauriers in an almost feminine way; and
soon he was admiring his friend for a success of which he
knew himself to be incapable.

Still, wasn't determination the most important ingredi-
ent in any enterprise? And if, with its help, any obstacle
could be overcome . . .

"Oh, that would be something!"

But he was ashamed of this treachery and then, a
minute later:

"Nonsense! Am I scared?"

He had heard so much about Madame Arnoux that she
had ended by making an extraordinarily vivid impression
on his imagination. The persistence of Frédéric's love for
her irritated him like a riddle. His own rather theatrical
austerity now bored him. Besides, the society woman (for
so he imagined her to be) dazzled the lawyer as the
symbol and epitome of a host of unknown pleasures. A
poor man, he coveted luxury in its most obvious guise.

"After all, even if he does get angry, what do I care?
He's treated me too badly for me to have any scruples! I
have no reason to believe that she's his mistress! He's
denied it to me! So I'm free to do what I like!"

From then on, the desire to put his plan to the test
never left him. It was a trial of strength which he longed for
—and so overpowering was the impulse that one day, on
the spur of the moment, he polished his own boots, bought
some white gloves, and set off, taking Frédéric's place
and almost imagining himself to be Frédéric through a
strange intellectual process that was a blend of vengeance
and sympathy, imitation and audacity.

He had himself announced as "Doctor Deslauriers."

Madame Arnoux was surprised, not having sent for a
doctor.

"Oh, I'm so sorry! I'm a doctor of law. I've come on
behalf of Monsieur Moreau."

The name seemed to disturb her.

"Good!" thought the ex-clerk, "since she yielded to him
she will accept me!" fortifying himself with the commonly
accepted notion that it is easier to supplant a lover than
a husband.

He had had the pleasure of meeting her once, at the
Palais; he even mentioned the date. Madame Arnoux was
astonished at such a memory. He went on, in honeyed
tones:

"Your business affairs were already . . . somewhat
difficult!"

She made no reply, so it must be the truth.

He started talking about this and that, her apartment, the factory; then, seeing some medallions around the mirror:

"Ah, family portraits I suppose?"

He noticed one of an old woman, Madame Arnoux's mother.

"She looks like a fine woman. A southern face."

And, to the objection that she came from Chartres:

"Chartres! A beautiful town."

And he praised its cathedral and its pâtés. Then, returning to the portrait, he found points of resemblance with Madame Arnoux and flattered her indirectly. She did not take offense. He grew more confident and said that he had known Arnoux for a long time.

"He's a good fellow, but always getting himself into problematic situations! This mortgage, for instance—it's difficult to imagine a more blundering . . ."

"Yes, I know," she answered, with a shrug of the shoulders.

This involuntary evidence of her contempt encouraged Deslauriers to venture further:

"This china-clay business of his—you may not know about it, but it nearly turned out very badly and even his reputation . . ."

He was halted by a frown.

Falling back on generalities, he spoke pityingly of those poor women whose husbands wasted their fortunes . . .

"But it's all his, Monsieur; I have nothing!"

Never mind! One never knew . . . A man of experience might be useful. He offered his devoted services, and vaunted his own merits as he gazed into her face through his glittering spectacles.

She was in a state of vague torpor but suddenly roused herself and said:

"Please, let's get down to business!"

He showed her the dossier.

"This is Frédéric's power of attorney. With a paper like this, in the hands of an officer of the court who would make out a writ—nothing simpler. In twenty-four hours . . ." (She remained impassive; he changed his tactics.) "As far as I'm concerned, I can't understand why he wants to recoup this money; after all, he hasn't the slightest need of it."

"What! Monsieur Moreau has been good enough to . . ."

"Oh, I agree!"

And Deslauriers launched into a eulogy of Frédéric, then, very gently, began to denigrate him, describing him as forgetful, selfish, and miserly.

"I thought he was your friend, Monsieur?"

"That doesn't prevent me from seeing his faults. For instance, he has very . . . little feeling for . . . how shall I put it . . . affection . . ."

Madame Arnoux was turning the pages of the thick notebook. She interrupted him to ask the meaning of a word.

He leaned over her shoulder, so close to her that he brushed against her cheek. She blushed; her blush inflamed Deslauriers and he kissed her hand voraciously.

"What are you doing, Monsieur?"

And, upright against the wall, she held him motionless with the angry glare of her large, dark eyes.

"Listen to me! I love you!"

She burst into laughter, shrill, desperate, hideous laughter. Deslauriers was so furious that he felt like strangling her. He controlled himself, and, with the air of a captive begging for mercy, said:

"You are wrong! I wouldn't do what he . . ."

"Whom are you talking about?"

"Frédéric!"

"I've already told you, I'm not concerned about Monsieur Moreau!"

"Oh, I apologize, I apologize!"

Then, in a biting voice, dragging out his words:

"I did believe you took enough interest in him to learn with pleasure . . ."

She turned deathly pale. The former clerk added:

"He is going to be married."

"He is!"

"In a month at the latest, to Mademoiselle Roque, the daughter of Monsieur Dambreuse's steward. He is at Nogent solely for that reason."

Her hand went to her heart, as if at the shock of a heavy blow, but she rang the bell immediately afterwards. Deslauriers did not wait to be thrown out. When she turned around, he had vanished.

Madame Arnoux felt near to suffocation. She went over to the window for a breath of air.

On the far side of the road a workman in shirtsleeves was nailing down a packing case. Some cabs went by. She closed the window and sat down again. The tall houses on either side cut off the sun, and the apartment was filled with the cold light of day. Her children were out; everything around her was still. She felt utterly deserted.

"He is going to be married! Can it be true!"

And a fit of nervous trembling shook her.

"Why am I doing this? Do I love him?"

Then, suddenly:

"Yes, I love him! I love him!"

It seemed to her that she was sinking into some deep pit. The clock struck three. She listened to the dying vibrations. And she remained on the edge of her armchair, gazing fixedly before her, a smile frozen on her lips.

At that same moment of that same afternoon, Frédéric and Mademoiselle Louise were strolling in Monsieur Roque's garden at the tip of the island. Old Catherine was watching them from a distance; they walked side by side and Frédéric was saying:

"Do you remember when I used to take you into the country?"

"How good you were to me!" she replied. "You helped me make sand-pies and fill my watering can, and you pushed me on my swing!"

"What's become of all your dolls, who were named for queens or marchionesses?"

"Goodness, I've no idea!"

"And Moricaud, your little dog?"

"He drowned, poor darling."

"And the *Don Quixote* whose illustrations we colored together?"

"I still have it."

He reminded her of the day of her first communion and how sweet she looked at vespers with her white veil and her big candle, while all the girls filed round the choir and the bells rang.

These memories presumably held no charm for Mademoiselle Roque; she could think of no answer and, a moment later, said:

"You're wicked! You didn't write me your news, not even once!"

Frédéric protested that he had a great deal of work.

"Well, what do you do?"

The question embarrassed him; then he replied that he was studying politics.

"Oh!"

And without inquiring any further, she continued:

"That keeps you busy; but I . . ."

And she told him of her arid existence, with no one to

see, devoid of any kind of pleasure or distraction. She wanted to ride.

"The curate insists it isn't proper for a young girl; how stupid propriety is! They used to let me do anything I wanted; now, nothing!"

"Still, your father loves you!"

"Yes, but . . ."

And she sighed, as if to say: "That is not enough to make me happy!"

There was a silence. They heard nothing but the crunch of the sand beneath their feet and the murmur of the waterfall. The Seine divides into two branches above Nogent and the one that drives the mills disgorges its overflow at this point, to rejoin the natural course of the river lower down. Coming from the bridges, to the right on the opposite bank, rises a grassy mound topped by a white house. To the left, lines of poplars stretch away across the meadow; and the view ahead is bounded by a curve of the river, which lies as still as a mirror with large insects skating over its tranquil water. Tufts of reeds and rushes form an uneven border, and there are plants of all sorts, covered with tight, round, golden blossoms, trailing clusters of yellow flowers, shooting up amethyst spikes and throwing out random green shoots. There was a little cove carpeted with water-lilies, and a row of old willows with spring-traps concealed beneath them was the garden's only protection on this side of the island.

Inside, four walls with a slate coping enclosed the vegetable garden, where the fresh-plowed squares of earth made slabs of brown. The cloches over the melon plants shone in a row on their narrow bed, and artichokes, beans, spinach, carrots, and tomatoes gave way to one another as far as an asparagus bed, that looked like a little forest of feathers.

Under the Directory, all this land had been what was called "a folly." The trees had grown enormously since those days. The arbors were a tangle of clematis, the paths were covered with moss, and brambles tumbled everywhere. There were chunks of statues, crumbling away under the grass. Walking, one's feet caught in iron wires, the wreckage of some decoration. The pavilion had disappeared, except for two ground-floor rooms with strips of blue paper on the walls. There was an Italian trellis in front of them, with brick pillars and wooden latticework that supported a vine.

They passed beneath it, and, as the light fell through

the ragged openings in the green canopy, Frédéric talked to Louise beside him, and watched the shadows of the leaves falling on her face.

In the chignon of her red hair she wore a pin tipped with a glass imitation emerald; and her bad taste was so naïve that, despite her mourning, she was wearing straw slippers trimmed with pink satin, vulgar curios she had doubtless bought at some fair.

He noticed them and complimented her sardonically.

"Don't make fun of me!" she replied.

Then, looking him up and down, from his gray felt hat to his silk socks:

"How elegant you are!"

Then she asked him to recommend some books. He mentioned several and she exclaimed:

"How much you know!"

While still a little girl she had been smitten by one of those childish loves that combine the purity of religion with the violence of hunger. He had been her playmate, her brother, her master; he had diverted her mind, stirred her heart and, without intending it, had created in her deepest self a latent and unending intoxication. Then he had left her at a moment of tragedy, with her mother hardly dead, and the two sorrows had merged in her mind. In his absence, she had idealized her memories of him; he returned with a kind of halo and ingenuously she gave herself up to the pleasure of seeing him.

For the first time in his life, Frédéric felt himself to be loved; and this novel pleasure, which was no more than an agreeable sensation, produced a kind of inner satisfaction; so that he spread his arms and threw back his head.

At that moment a large cloud drifted across the sky.

"It's moving toward Paris," said Louise; "you'd like to follow it, wouldn't you?"

"Me? Why?"

"Who knows?"

And, searching his face with a piercing gaze:

"Perhaps you have some . . ." (she hesitated, looking for a word) "attachment there."

"Oh, I have no attachments!"

"Are you sure?"

"Yes, Mademoiselle, quite sure!"

In less than a year an extraordinary transformation had taken place in this girl. Frédéric was astonished. After a minute's silence, he added:

"We should use each other's Christian names, as we used to; what do you think?"

"No."

"Why?"

"Because!"

He insisted. She replied, bowing her head:

"I daren't!"

They had reached the end of the garden and were standing on the bank of the Livon. Frédéric started skipping stones like a boy. She ordered him to sit down. He obeyed and, looking at the waterfall, remarked:

"It's like Niagara!"

He went on to speak of distant lands and great journeys. She was delighted by the idea of travel. Nothing would have frightened her, neither storms nor lions.

Sitting side by side they scooped up handfuls of the sand in front of them, then let it run through their fingers as they talked—and the warm wind from the fields brought them gusts of lavender mingled with the smell of tar from a barge on the far side of the sluice. The sun shone on the cascade; the greenish blocks that formed the little wall over which the water flowed seemed to be veiled by a strip of eternally unrolling silver gauze. At its foot, a long bar of foam spurted rhythmically upwards. Then came a stretch of whorls and eddies, a hundred conflicting currents that ended by merging into a single limpid sheet.

Louise murmured that she envied the existence of the fishes.

"It must be so wonderful to roll about there, feeling caressed all over."

And she shivered, with a movement of sensual ecstasy. But a voice cried:

"Where are you?"

"Your maid is calling you," said Frédéric.

"All right! All right!"

Louise made no move to return.

"She'll be angry," he went on.

"That doesn't worry me! Anyhow . . ." Mademoiselle Roque made a gesture signifying that she could handle her.

She got up, nevertheless, then complained of a headache. And, as they passed in front of an enormous shed full of faggots of brushwood, she suggested:

"Suppose we went in under there, inside the *égaud?*"

He pretended not to understand the dialect word, and

even teased her about her accent. Little by little the corners of her mouth tightened, she bit her lips and moved away, sulking.

Frédéric caught up with her, swearing that he had not meant to hurt her feelings and that he was very fond of her.

"Are you really?" she cried, looking at him with a smile that lit up her whole freckled face.

He could not resist the candor of her emotion nor the freshness of her youth and went on:

"Why should I lie to you? . . . you don't believe me? . . . eh?" putting his left arm round her waist.

She gave a cry as soft as the coo of a dove, her head fell back, and she grew faint; he supported her. And all his honorable scruples were unnecessary; confronted by this virgin who offered herself to him, he was suddenly afraid. Afterwards, he gently helped her while she took a few steps. His tender talk had ceased and, determined to speak only of neutral things, he discussed people in Nogent society.

Suddenly she pushed him away and said, in a bitter voice:

"You wouldn't have the courage to take me away!"

He stood still, looking completely thunderstruck. She burst into sobs and, burying her head in his chest, said:

"How can I live without you!"

He tried to calm her. She put her hands on his shoulders to see his face better and, lifting to his her green eyes, in whose moist gaze there was something almost ferocious, she said:

"Do you want to be my husband?"

"But . . ." replied Frédéric, searching for a response, "probably . . . I would ask for nothing better."

At that moment Monsieur Roque's cap appeared behind a lilac bush.

He carried off his "young friend" for two days on a little trip round his properties in the neighborhood; when Frédéric returned he found three letters waiting for him.

The first was a note from Monsieur Dambreuse asking him to dinner the previous Tuesday. What could have caused this politeness? Had they forgiven him for his outburst?

The second was from Rosanette. She thanked him for having risked his life for her; at first Frédéric didn't understand what she was trying to say, but finally, after many circumlocutions, she implored him, invoking their friendship, trusting in his considerateness, on her knees, as she said, because of the urgency of her need, and as one would beg for bread, a little help in the shape of five hundred francs. He immediately decided to provide them.

The third letter, from Deslauriers, dealt with the subrogation and was long and obscure. The lawyer had done nothing as yet. He urged him not to disturb himself: "There is no point in your returning!"; and he stressed this point with a strange insistence.

Frédéric fell into a maze of conjectures and wanted to return to Paris; he rebelled at this attempt to dictate what he should do.

Moreover, he was beginning to feel homesick for the boulevards, and then his mother was pressing him so hard, Monsieur Roque buzzed around him so assiduously, and Mademoiselle Louise loved him so devotedly that he could stay no longer without declaring himself. He needed an opportunity to think things over; he would weigh things more clearly from a distance.

Frédéric invented some tale as a reason for his departure and left, telling everyone—and believing himself—that he would soon be back.

Chapter Six

His return to Paris gave him no pleasure; it was an evening at the end of August; the boulevard seemed empty, the passersby had scowls on their faces, here and there smoke rose from a boiler full of asphalt, in many of the houses the blinds were pulled right down. He reached his house; there was dust on the hangings and, dining alone, Frédéric had a strange feeling of desertion; his thoughts turned to Mademoiselle Roque.

The idea of marrying no longer seemed outlandish. They would travel, they would go to Italy, to the Orient! He saw her standing on a hillock contemplating a landscape or leaning on his arm in a Florentine gallery, pausing before the pictures. What a delight it would be to see this good little soul blossoming under the influence of the splendors of Art and Nature! Once removed from her environment, she would very soon make a charming companion. And, Monsieur Roque's fortune was tempting. But, this kind of consideration repelled him as a weakness or a degradation.

However, he was completely resolved to change his way of life, no matter what the cost; that is, no longer to waste his heart in fruitless love affairs; and he even hesitated to perform the errand Louise had given him. It was to buy for her from Jacques Arnoux two large polychrome statuettes of Negroes, like the ones at the Troyes prefecture. She knew the manufacturer's cipher and did not want them from anyone else. Frédéric was afraid that, if he went back to *their* house, he would again be ensnared in his old love.

These reflections took up his entire evening, and he was on the point of going to bed when a woman came in.

"It's me," said Mademoiselle Vatnaz with a laugh. "Rosanette asked me to come."

So they were friends again?

"Good heavens, yes! I don't bear grudges, you know. Besides, the poor girl . . . But that's too long a story."

In short, the Maréchale wanted to see him, she was waiting for an answer, her letter having been forwarded from Paris to Nogent. Mademoiselle Vatnaz had no idea of its contents. Then Frédéric asked how things were with the Maréchale.

She was now with a very rich man, a Russian, Prince Tzernoukoff, who had seen her at the races at the Champ de Mars the previous summer.

"She has three carriages, a saddle horse, liveries, an English-style groom, a house in the country, a box at the Italiens, masses of other things. So you see, my dear."

And, as if she herself had profited from this change of fortune, La Vatnaz seemed gayer, the picture of happiness. She took off her gloves and examined the furniture and knickknacks in the bedroom. She priced them correctly, like a dealer in secondhand goods. He should have consulted her so as to get them more cheaply, and she congratulated him on his good taste:

"It's pretty, very well done. No one else has such good ideas!"

Then, noticing a door at the side of the alcove:

"That's where you let your young women out, is it?"

And she took him amicably by the chin. He shivered at the touch of her long hands, skinny and gentle at the same time. She had a lace ruffle round her wrists, and the bodice of her green dress was trimmed with braid like a hussar's tunic. The brim of her black tulle hat turned down over her face, hiding a little of her forehead; her eyes gleamed beneath it; a whiff of patchouli escaped from her hair; the lamp, standing on a table, illuminated her face from below like footlights, throwing her jaw into relief—and suddenly, in the presence of this ugly woman whose body moved like a panther's, Frédéric felt an enormous lust, a desire for animal sensuality.

Pulling three squares of paper out of her wallet, she said in an unctuous voice, "You're going to buy these from me!"

They were three tickets for a benefit performance for Delmar.

"What! Him?"

"Certainly!"

Without further explanation, Mademoiselle Vatnaz added that she adored him more than ever. In her estimation, the actor was definitely to be classed as one of the "glories of the times." In fact, he represented not such and such a character on the stage, but the very spirit of France and of the people! He had "a humanitarian soul"; he understood "the priesthood of the Artist!" Frédéric, to escape these eulogies, gave her the money for the three seats.

"There's no point in your mentioning this at Rosanette's! —Good heavens, how late it is! I must leave you. Oh, I forgot to give you the address: it's Fourteen, Rue Grange-Batelière."

And, on the threshold:

"Good-bye, heart-breaker!"

"Whose heart?" thought Frédéric. "What an odd creature she is!"

And he remembered that one day when Dussardier was talking about her, he had said: "Oh, she's nothing special!" as if alluding to something rather dishonorable in her past.

The next day he paid a call on the Maréchale. She was living in a new house, with awnings that jutted out over the street. On each landing there was a mirror hanging on the wall and a rustic flower-stand in front of the windows; the stairs were carpeted with canvas and, when one came in from the street, the brightness of the staircase was refreshing.

The door was opened by a servant, a footman in a red waistcoat. A woman and two men, probably tradesmen, were waiting on the padded bench in the hall, as if they were in a minister's antechamber. To the left, through the half-open door to the dining room, he could see empty bottles on the sideboards and napkins draped over the backs of the chairs; it was flanked by a verandah, whose gold-colored posts supported a climbing rose bush. In the courtyard beneath, two servants with bare arms were polishing a landau. Their voices rose into the hall, accompanied by the intermittent sound of a curry-comb being struck against a stone.

The footman returned. "Madame will see Monsieur"; and he took him across a second hall, and then through a large drawing room hung with gold damask; looped in the corners were satin ropes that met in the middle of the ceiling and seemed to continue in the serpentine arms of

the chandelier. There must have been a party the previous
night. The tables were still flecked with cigar ash.

Finally, he entered a kind of boudoir dimly lit by
stained-glass windows. The spaces above the doors were
decorated with fretwork trefoils; three purple mats
formed a divan behind a balustrade, with the tube of a
platinum hookah trailing across it. Instead of a mirror
above the fireplace there was a pyramid of shelves bearing
a whole collection of curiosities: old silver watches, Bohemian vases, jeweled clasps, jade buttons, enamels, grotesque ivory figurines from China, and a little Byzantine
virgin with a silver-gilt cope; and all this blended in a soft
golden haze, with the bluish color of the carpet, the pearly
gleam from the stools, and the tawny tone of the walls,
which were covered with brown leather. On pedestals in
the corners stood bronze vases containing bunches of flowers whose scent hung heavy on the air.

Rosanette appeared, dressed in a pink satin jacket,
white cashmere trousers, a necklace made of piastres, and
a red skullcap wreathed in jasmine.

Frédéric gave a start of surprise, then said that he had
brought "the thing you mentioned" and presented her
with a bank note.

She looked at him in astonishment and, as he was still
holding the note and didn't know where to put it down,
he exclaimed:

"Well, take it!"

She snatched it, then threw it on the divan and said:
"It's very kind of you."

She needed it to make a payment on a piece of land at
Bellevue, which she was buying in yearly installments.
This offhandedness hurt Frédéric. Otherwise, so much the
better. This would be his revenge for the past.

"Sit down," she said. "Here, nearer me." And, in a
grave tone: "First of all I have to thank you, my dear,
for having risked your life."

"Oh, it was nothing!"

"What do you mean? It was very noble of you!"

And the Maréchale was embarrassingly grateful, for
clearly she was under the impression that he had fought
solely to defend Arnoux—since the latter believed this to
be the truth and must have yielded to the temptation to
tell her.

"Perhaps she's laughing at me" thought Frédéric.

There was nothing to keep him here and he got up,
pleading an appointment:

"Oh no, do stay!"

He sat down again and complimented her on her clothes.

She replied dejectedly:

"It's the prince who likes me this way! And I have to smoke gadgets like that," she added, pointing to the hookah. "Suppose we tried it? Would you like to?"

A light was brought in, but the tombac pipe was difficult to kindle and she started stamping with impatience. Then she became languid and lay immobile on the divan, a cushion under her arm and her body slightly twisted, with one knee bent and the other leg straight. The long red morocco-leather serpent lay in loops on the ~)or and encircled her arm. She put the amber mouthpiece to her lips and gazed at Frédéric, blinking from time to time, through the scrolls of smoke which enveloped her. The water gurgled as her chest rose and fell, and she occasionally murmured:

"Poor darling! Poor dear!"

He tried to find an agreeable subject of conversation, and remembered La Vatnaz.

He remarked that she seemed to him to be very elegantly turned out.

"Certainly" replied the Maréchale. "She's lucky to have me, I can tell you!"

And so difficult was conversation between them that she said nothing more.

Both of them felt some constraint, some inhibition. Actually Rosanette believed herself to be the cause of the duel, and it flattered her vanity. Then she had been amazed when he had not hurried round to be rewarded for his action and, to force him to come back, she had invented this need for five hundred francs. But why on earth was Frédéric not demanding a little tenderness as a reward? She marveled at his delicacy and, on a sudden impulse, said:

"Wouldn't you like to come to the seaside with us?"

"What do you mean, *us?*"

"Me and my boyfriend; I'll pass you off as my cousin, the way they do in the old plays."

"Thank you very much!"

"Well, then, you could take a place near ours."

The idea of hiding from a rich man humiliated him.

"No! It's impossible."

"Whatever you say!"

Rosanette turned away, a tear in the corner of her eye.

Frédéric noticed it and, to show his interest in her, said how happy he was to see her in an excellent position at last.

She shrugged her shoulders. What was troubling her? Could it be that she was not loved?

"Oh, people always love me!"

She added, "What matters is *how* they do it."

Complaining that she was "dying of heat," the Maréchale undid her jacket and, with nothing round her torso but her silk chemise, she leaned her head on his shoulder, with the provocative air of a slave-girl.

The possibility of the viscount, Monsieur de Comaing, or anyone else coming in would never have occurred to a less self-conscious man. But Frédéric had been fooled too often by these very glances to risk another humiliation.

She wanted to know what had been happening to him and how he had been amusing himself; she even asked about his business affairs and offered to lend him money if he needed it. Frédéric could stand it no longer, and picked up his hat.

"Well, my sweet, have a good time at the seaside. Goodbye!"

She opened her eyes wide then, in a dry voice, said, "Good-bye!"

He went back through the yellow drawing room and the second hall. On the table, between a bowl full of visiting cards and an inkstand, stood a chased silver casket. It was the one that belonged to Madame Arnoux! He was filled with tenderness and, at the same time, with outrage, as though at a sacrilege. He wanted to touch it, to open it, but he was afraid someone would notice him and he left the house.

Frédéric was virtuous. He did not go back to the Arnoux's.

He sent his servant to buy the two Negroes, having given him all the necessary instructions, and the packing case left for Nogent that very evening. The next day, as he was going to visit Deslauriers, he suddenly came face to face with Madame Arnoux at the corner of the Rue Vivienne and the boulevard.

Their first impulse was to draw back; then the same smile came to both their lips and they went up to each other. For a moment neither of them spoke.

She stood in the full sunlight and her oval face, her long eyelashes, her black, lace shawl molding the shape of her shoulders, her shot-silk dress, the bunch of violets at the corner of her hood—everything seemed to him to have an extraordinary splendor about it. An immense sweetness flowed from her beautiful eyes and, stammering out the first words that came into his head, he asked:

"How's Arnoux?"

"Well, thank you!"

"And your children?"

"They are very well!"

"Ah! . . . Ah! . . . What lovely weather we're having."

"Wonderful, isn't it."

"Are you doing your shopping?"

"Yes."

And, with a slow inclination of her head:

"Good-bye!"

She had not held out her hand, had not said one affectionate word, had not even invited him to come around and see her. What did it matter! He would not have exchanged this meeting for the most beautiful of adventures, and he pondered its sweetness as he continued on his way.

Deslauriers was surprised to see him and concealed his vexation—for he still, obstinately, treasured some hopes about Madame Arnoux, and he had written telling Frédéric to stay at Nogent to afford himself a clear field for his maneuvers.

He did, however, say that he had been to visit her in order to find out if their marriage contract stipulated community property, for in that case one could have proceeded against the wife: "and she looked very odd when I told her about your marriage."

"Well! What a fabrication!"

"It was necessary, to show that you needed your capital. A woman who didn't care for you would not have had the near-stroke she did."

"Really?" cried Frédéric.

"Oh ho, my lad, you're giving yourself away! Why not be frank?"

An immense cowardice overcame Madame Arnoux's suitor.

"No . . . I assure you . . . On my word of honor!"

These half-hearted denials completely convinced Deslauriers that his theory was correct. He complimented Frédéric and asked for "details." Frédéric did not give him any, and even resisted the temptation to invent them.

As for the mortgage, he told him to do nothing, to

wait. Deslauriers maintained he was wrong, and even remonstrated quite harshly with him.

In other respects, he was more gloomy, malevolent,
and irascible than ever. In a year's time, if his luck
hadn't changed, he would embark for America or blow
his brains out. In fact, he was so furious with the whole
world and so absolute in his radicalism that Frédéric
could not help saying:

"You've become another Sénécal!"

At this, Deslauriers told him that the ex-schoolmaster
had been released from Sainte-Pélagie, presumably because the preliminary investigation had not turned up
enough evidence to bring him to trial.

Overjoyed by this deliverance, Dussardier wanted to
"throw a punch party" for him and begged Frédéric to
join them, but not without warning him that he would
find himself in the same room as Hussonnet, who had
been very kind to Sénécal.

The *Flambard* had, in fact, established a business office,
whose prospectus proclaimed it to be a: "Wine-growers'
Bureau—Advertising Agency—Debt-collecting and Information Service, etc." But the bohemian was afraid that
his business affairs would harm his literary reputation and
he had taken on the mathematician to keep the accounts.
It was not much of a position, but without it Sénécal
would have died of hunger. Frédéric did not want to
hurt the worthy clerk's feelings; he accepted his invitation.

Three days before the party, Dussardier himself had
polished the red tile floor of his attic, beaten the armchair, and dusted the mantelpiece where an alabaster
clock stood under a glass bell between a stalactite and a
coconut. As his two candlesticks and his taper-stand were
inadequate for the occasion, he had borrowed two more
from the concierge; and these five lights burned on the
bureau, which was covered with three napkins so that
some macaroons, some biscuits, a brioche, and twelve
bottles of beer could be more fittingly displayed. Opposite
it, against the yellow-papered wall, stood a small mahog-
ony bookcase which contained Lachambeaudie's *Fables*,
the *Mystères de Paris*, Norvins' *Napoléon*—and, in the
middle of the alcove, smiling out of a rosewood frame,
the face of Béranger!*

The guests, apart from Deslauriers and Sénécal, were a

---

*Pierre Jean de Béranger (1780-1857) was a lyric poet and close
friend of Lucien Bonaparte. His strongly republican verse was
immensely popular at this period.

recently qualified pharmacist, who lacked the capital to set up in his profession; a young man from Dussardier's firm; a traveler in wines; an architect; and a gentleman who worked for an insurance company. Regimbart had been unable to come. There was some regret at his absence.

They welcomed Frédéric in a very friendly fashion, for Dussardier had told them about his outburst at the Dambreuses. Sénécal merely offered his hand with a dignified air.

He was standing in front of the fireplace. The others sat with their pipes in their mouths listening to him discourse on universal suffrage, the result of which would be the triumph of democracy and the application of the principles of the Gospels. Besides, the moment was approaching; the Reform Banquets* in the provinces were growing more numerous and Piedmont, Naples, Tuscany . . .†

"It's true," said Deslauriers, cutting him short. "It can't last for much longer!"

And he started to outline the situation.

We had sacrificed Holland to induce England to recognize Louis-Philippe, and then the celebrated English alliance had been scuttled by the Spanish marriages! In Switzerland, Monsieur Guizot, in the wake of the Austrians, was upholding the treaties of 1815. Prussia, with its Customs Union, would be troublesome in the future. The eastern question was hanging fire.

"Russia is not to be trusted merely because the Grand Duke Constantin sends presents to Monsieur d'Aumale. As for domestic affairs, blindness and stupidity are unprecedented! Even their majority was shaky. Everywhere you look in fact, as someone said, there's nothing, nothing, nothing! And," continued the lawyer, putting his hands on his hips, "confronted with this shameful situation they say that they are satisfied."

This allusion to a famous vote provoked a round of applause. Dussardier uncorked a bottle of beer; the foam splashed onto the curtains, but he took no notice; he filled pipes, cut the brioche, and handed it around, went downstairs several times to see what had happened to the punch. His guests soon became excited, since Authority infuriated all of them in the same way. Their violent exas-

*See note page 36. These propaganda banquets were particularly numerous from July to December, 1847.

†At the end of 1847 and beginning of 1848 there was great political unrest in these states, and the liberals had made some gains.

peration was caused simply by hatred of injustice, and they mingled the stupidest complaints with their legitimate grievances.

The pharmacist was decrying the deplorable state of the navy. The insurance broker could not tolerate Marshall Soult's two sentries. Deslauriers denounced the Jesuits, who had just installed themselves openly at Lille. Sénécal hated Monsieur Cousin much worse, for by teaching people to discover the truth by the use of reason, eclecticism developed self-concern, and destroyed solidarity. The traveler in wines, who understood very little of these matters, remarked aloud that there were a lot of scandals he had not yet mentioned:

"The royal carriage on the Northern Railway is going to cost eighty thousand francs! Who's going to pay for it?"

"Yes, who's going to pay for it?" repeated the clerk, as angry as if the money had been taken out of his own pocket.

Then there were recriminations against the stock exchange sharks and the corruption of the bureaucracy. According to Sénécal, one should go higher up and lay the primary blame on the princes, who were reviving the manners and morals of the Regency.

"Did you hear that recently some friends of the Duc de Montpensier, on their way back from Vincennes and probably drunk, disturbed the workers in the Faubourg Saint-Antoine with their singing?"

"People even shouted: 'Down with the robbers!'" said the pharmacist. "I was there. I shouted."

"And a good thing too! The Teste-Cubières* case has finally aroused the masses."

"I was saddened by that case," said Dussardier, "because it dishonored an old soldier."

"Do you know," Sénécal continued, "that at the Duchesse de Praslin's† house they found . . ."

But the door was kicked open and in came Hussonnet.

"Good evening, my lords!" he said, sitting down on the bed.

No allusion was made to his article, which he regretted writing in any case, as the Maréchale had berated him soundly on account of it.

---

*Teste, the Minister of Public Works, and General Cubières, the Minister of War, were found guilty of corruption in 1847.
†The Duchesse de Choiseul-Praslin was murdered by her husband on August 18, 1847; her husband committed suicide before he could be brought to trial.

He had just come from the Théâtre Dumas, where he had seen *Le Chevalier de Maison-Rouge* which he found "a bore."

This verdict astounded the democrats, for the play's implications, or rather its setting, followed their own prejudices. They protested. To conclude the argument, Sénécal asked if the play was helpful to the cause of democracy.

"Yes . . . maybe, but the style . . ."

"Well, then it's a good play! What does the style matter? It's the ideas that count!"

And, without giving Frédéric a chance to speak, he went on:

"As I was saying, the Praslin affair . . ."

Hussonnet interrupted him:

"Oh, that's an old story. I'm bored to death with it!"

"You're not the only one!" replied Deslauriers. "It's been responsible for the seizure of a mere five papers! Listen to this!"

He pulled out his notebook and read:

"Since the establishment of this best of republics, one thousand two hundred and twenty-nine press trials have taken place, resulting in writers being sentenced to three thousand one hundred and forty-one years in jail, with the trifling sum of seven million one hundred and ten thousand five hundred francs in fines. Charming, isn't it?"

They all sniggered bitterly. Frédéric, as excited as the others, chimed in:

"*Le Démocratie Pacifique* has been prosecuted because of its serial, a novel entitled *Women's Share*.

"Well, that's great!" said Hussonnet. "Are they going to forbid us our share of women!"

"But what is not forbidden nowadays?" cried Deslauriers. "Smoking in the Luxembourg is forbidden, singing the hymn to Pius IX* is forbidden!"

"And they've forbidden the printers to hold their banquet!" pronounced a rumbling voice.

It came from the architect, hidden in the shadows of the alcove and silent until this moment. He added that the previous week someone named Mullet had been sentenced for having insulted the king.

"They'll fry that mullet!" said Hussonnet.

This joke struck Sénécal as such poor taste that he

*Pius IX had made certain reforms in the Papal States which had brought him popularity with the republicans.

rebuked Hussonnet for defending "the juggler from City Hall,* the friend of the traitor Dumouriez."

"Me? On the contrary!"

He found Louis-Philippe full of hackneyed sentiment and cracker-barrel philosophy, a shopkeeper in a cotton nightcap! And, placing his hand on his heart, the bohemian declaimed the sacred formulas:

"It is with ever-renewed pleasure . . . The Polish nation shall not perish . . . We shall continue our mighty labors . . . Give me some money for my little family . . ." Everyone laughed uproariously, and pronounced him a great wit, and their joy increased at the sight of the punch bowl which a coffeehouse keeper carried into the room.

The combined flames of the candles and the alcohol soon warmed up the attic; and the glow from its window shone out across the courtyard, lighting up the edge of a roof, whose chimney pot stood silhouetted in black against the night sky. They all talked at once, very loudly; they had taken off their frock coats; they bumped into furniture and clinked their glasses together. Hussonnet cried, "Bring up the great ladies so that it's more like the Tour de Nesle,† Rembrandt, and local color, by Jove!"

And the pharmacist, endlessly stirring the punch, sang out, full-throated:

> I've two white oxen in my barn
> Two strong white . . .

Sénécal clapped his hand over his mouth; he could not bear a rowdy scene; and the other lodgers appeared at their windows, surprised at the unaccustomed noise from Dussardier's room.

Their good-natured host was happy and said it reminded him of their gatherings at the Quai Napoléon in the old days, although there were several faces missing, "Pellerin, for instance . . ."

"We can do without *him*," responded Frédéric.

And Deslauriers asked after Martinon.

"What's become of that interesting gentleman?"

---

*An allusion to a political caricature which depicted Louis-Philippe as a conjurer making three balls labeled Liberty, Revolution, and July Fourteenth disappear.

†An allusion to a famous 13th-century scandal when the daughter-in-laws of King Philip IV were discovered meeting their lovers in this tower.

Immediately Frédéric, giving free rein to the ill will he felt toward him, launched into an attack on his intelligence, his character, his sham elegance, everything about him. He was a perfect specimen of a peasant who had made good. The new aristocracy of the bourgeois was no match for the earlier one of the noblemen. He upheld this thesis and the democrats applauded it—as if he were a member of the latter group and they rubbed elbows with the former. They were all enchanted with him. The pharmacist even compared him to Monsieur d'Alton-Shée, who had taken up the cause of the people in spite of being a peer of France.

It was time to leave. They separated with warm handshakes; out of affection, Dussardier saw Frédéric and Deslauriers home. As soon as they reached the street, the lawyer grew pensive, and after a moment's silence he said:

"So you've got a great grudge against Pellerin, have you?"

Frédéric did not conceal his rancor.

But still, the painter had removed the famous picture from the shop window. It was wrong to quarrel over trifles. What was the point of making an enemy?

"He gave way to a bad-tempered impulse; it's excusable in a man without a penny to his name. Of course *you* can't be expected to understand that!"

And, after Deslauriers had turned in at his own front door, Dussardier did not leave Frédéric in peace; he even urged him to buy the portrait. The fact was that Pellerin, despairing of forcing Frédéric's hand, had enlisted their aid so that he would take the picture.

Later, Deslauriers came back to the subject insistently. He maintained that the artist's claims were reasonable.

"I'm sure that for, say, five hundred francs . . ."

"Oh, let him have them! Here you are!" said Frédéric.

The picture was brought around that very evening. It struck him as being even more abominable than he had thought at first glance. The half-tones and the shadows had been retouched so many times that they were leaden, and they seemed even darker in comparison with the highlights that still shone here and there, clashing with the whole.

Frédéric avenged himself for having bought it by criticizing it bitterly. Deslauriers took his word for it and was pleased with what he had accomplished, for his ambition was still to form a band of men whose chief he would be;

there are certain people who enjoy forcing their friends to do things they dislike.

Frédéric, meanwhile, had not been back to the Dambreuses'. He had not enough capital. There would be endless explanations, and he couldn't make up his mind. Perhaps he was doing the right thing? Nothing was certain nowadays, the coal business no more than anything else; he should give up this kind of society; and, finally, Deslauriers dissuaded him from taking part in the enterprise. Hatred was turning the latter into a man of principle and, besides, he preferred Frédéric to remain a mediocrity. In this state he was still his equal and their friendship was more intimate.

The figures ordered for Louise had turned out badly. Her father wrote to him, giving the most precise explanation of the problem and ending his letter with a joking, "Hoping that you won't have to work like a black!"

There was no way for Frédéric to avoid going back to the Arnoux's. He went up to the shop but there was no one there. As the business was foundering, the staff was imitating their master's own negligence.

He walked the length of the long shelves loaded with crockery which filled the room from end to end; then, having reached the counter at the far end, he trod more heavily, so that someone would hear him.

The door-curtain was lifted and Madame Arnoux appeared.

"What, it's you! You here!"

"Yes," she stammered, a little taken aback. "I was looking for . . ."

He caught sight of her handkerchief near the desk and realized that she had come down to her husband's office to find out how matters were going, probably to investigate something which had been troubling her.

"But . . . perhaps you need something?" she asked.

"Nothing really, Madame."

"These clerks are intolerable. They are never here!"

They should not be blamed for that. On the contrary, he was glad of the chance to see her.

She gave him an ironic glance.

"Well, what about this marriage?"

"What marriage?"

"Yours!"

"Me? Never!"

She made a gesture of denial.

"But what if it were true? One falls back on mediocrity in despair of having one's best dreams come true."

"Not all your dreams, however, were so . . . upright."

"What do you mean?"

"When you turn up at the races with . . . certain people!"

He cursed the Maréchale, then remembered something:

"But it was you yourself who asked me to see her, at one time, for Arnoux's sake!"

Tossing her head she replied:

"And you took advantage of that to amuse yourself!"

"Good gracious, can't we forget all this nonsense!"

"That's only fitting, since you're going to be married!"

And she bit her lips to hold back a sigh.

"How many times do I have to tell you it isn't true?" he cried. "Can you believe that I, with my intellectual needs and my habits, am going to bury myself in the provinces and pass my time playing cards, overseeing builders, and walking around in wooden clogs! What would be the point of it? You've been told that she's rich, haven't you? What do I care about money! Is it likely that, after longing for the perfection of beauty, tenderness, enchantment —for a kind of paradise in human form—when I found this ideal at last, when the sight of it blinds me to everything else . . ."

And, taking her head in his hands, he started kissing her on the eyelids, repeating:

"No! No! No! I shall never marry! Never! Never!"

She accepted his caresses, transfixed by surprise and ecstasy.

The door from the shop onto the staircase slammed shut. She jumped and stayed with her hand held out, as if ordering him to keep silent. The sound of footsteps drew nearer; then someone outside said:

"Is Madame there?"

"Come in!"

Madame Arnoux had her elbow on the counter and was tranquilly twirling a pen between her fingers when the bookkeeper opened the door-curtains.

"Good day to you, Madame. The service will be ready, won't it? I can count on it?"

She made no reply, but this silent complicity set her face flaming with all the blushes of an adulterous wife.

Frédéric returned the following day and, to follow up his advantage, immediately and without preamble launched into a justification of his presence at the Champ de Mars. It was sheer chance that he had been with that woman. Even admitting that she was pretty (which was not true), how could she hold his attention, even for a moment, since he was in love with another!

"You know all about it, I've told you!"

Madame Arnoux bowed her head.

"I am sorry that you told me."

"Why?"

"The most elementary laws of propriety now demand that I should not see you again!"

He protested the innocence of his love. The past should be his warranty for the future; he had vowed to himself that he would not disturb her in any way nor deafen her with his laments.

"But yesterday my heart overflowed."

"We must never think of that episode again, my friend!"

Still, what would be the harm in two poor creatures mingling their sorrow?

"For you are no happier than I am! Oh, I know you, you have no one to answer your need for affection, for devotion! I will do anything you want! I won't offend you —I swear I won't!"

And he fell to his knees involuntarily, sinking beneath an inner weight which had grown too heavy to bear.

"Get up!" she said. "I order you to do so!"

And she declared imperiously that if he did not obey her he would never see her again.

"I defy you to do that!" replied Frédéric. "What is the purpose of my existence? Others strive for riches, for fame, for power! But I have no profession, you are my sole occupation, my entire fortune, the goal, the center of my existence and my thoughts. I can no more live without you than without the air I breathe! Can't you feel the aspiration of my soul soaring toward yours, and that they must mingle, and that I am dying of it?"

Madame Arnoux started to tremble in all her limbs.

"Go, I implore you, go!"

He was stopped by the agitation in her face. Then he took a step toward her. But she recoiled, clasping her hands:

"Leave me! In heaven's name! In God's!"

And Frédéric loved her so much that he went out.

He was soon furious at himself, felt he was an idiot, and, twenty-four hours later, he returned.

Madame was not in. He stood on the landing, dizzy with anger and indignation. Arnoux appeared and told him that his wife had left that very morning to set up house in a little country cottage they had rented at Auteuil, no longer having the one at Saint-Cloud.

"It's another of her whims! However, since it suits her! And me as well, what's more! So much the better! Shall we have dinner together this evening?"

Frédéric pleaded an urgent engagement, then hastened to Auteuil.

Madame Arnoux gave a cry of joy. At this all his rancor vanished.

He did not speak of his love. He even exaggerated his reserve in order to inspire more confidence in her and, when he asked if he might come back, she replied: "But of course," offering him her hand which she withdrew almost at once.

From then on Frédéric increased the number of his visits. He would promise the cabbie a large tip. But often the horse's lagging would make him so impatient that he would get down; then, breathless, he would clamber into an omnibus; and how disdainfully he examined the faces of the other passengers, who were not on their way to see her!

He could recognize her house from a distance by an enormous honeysuckle that covered the planks of the roof on one side; it was a sort of Swiss chalet, painted red with a balcony running around the outside. There were three old chestnut trees in the garden, and in the middle, on a mound, a thatched roofshade on a tree trunk. Under the slates on the walls, a large vine had come loose from its supports and hung down in places like a rotted cable. The bell at the iron gate, a bit stiff to pull, gave a prolonged peal, and it was always some time before anyone came. Each time he felt a pang of agony, a nameless apprehension.

Then he would hear the maid's slippers flapping over the sand, or Madame Arnoux herself would appear. One day he arrived when her back was turned to the gate and she was crouching in the grass, searching for violets.

She had been forced by her daughter's dispositon to educate her at a convent. The little boy spent his afternoons at school. Arnoux had long lunches at the Palais-Royal with Regimbart and his friend Compain. There was no intruder to surprise them.

It was quite understood that they could not belong to each other. This convenant kept them from danger, and made it easier for them to pour out their hearts.

She told him about her life in the old days, at her
mother's house in Chartres; her devoutness at twelve,
which was succeeded by a passion for music, when she
sang till nightfall in her little room, with its view of the
ramparts. He told her of his melancholy periods at college, and how a woman's face shone in his poetic heavens
so that when he saw her for the first time he had recognized her.

Normally, these conversations encompassed only the
years during which they had known each other. He reminded her of insignificant details, the color of her dress
at such and such a time, who had come in on a certain
day, what she had said on another occasion; and she replied, marveling, "Yes, I remember!"

Their tastes and opinions were identical. Often which-
ever of them was listening would cry, "So do I!"

And the other in his turn would chime in, "So do I!"

Then their interminable laments against Fate:

"Why were the heavens against us! If we had met . . ."

"Oh! If I had been younger!" she sighed.

"No! If I had been a little older."

And they imagined a life of nothing but love, fecund
enough to fill the vastest solitude, exceeding all joys, defy-
ing all sorrows, whose hours would have melted away in
a perpetual exchange of confidences and which would
have become something shining and lofty, like the shim-
mering of the stars.

They usually sat outside, at the top of the steps; the
summits of the trees, yellowed by autumn, stretched away
before them in a series of uneven hummocks to the edge
of the pale sky; or they would go to the far end of the
avenue where there was a summerhouse furnished only
with a sofa upholstered in gray cloth. The mirror was
spotted with black, the walls exuded a musty odor—and
they would sit there enraptured, talking of themselves, of
others, of anything under the sun. Sometimes the sun's
rays, coming through the Venetian blinds, stretched like
the strings of a lyre from ceiling to floor, and specks of
dust danced in the luminous bars. She amused herself by
breaking them with her hand. Frédéric would catch it
gently and contemplate the interlacing veins, the grain of
her skin, the shape of her fingers. To him, each of her
fingers seemed more than a thing, almost a person.

She gave him her gloves and, the following week, her
handkerchief. She called him "Frédéric" and he called her
"Marie," adoring this name which, he said, had been

created especially to be sighed in ecstasy and seemed enveloped in clouds of incense and strewn with roses.

After a time, they used to settle in advance the days when he would visit her and, going out as if by chance, she would meet him on his way.

She did nothing to encourage his love, lost in that carefree mood which is a characteristic of great happiness. During the whole period she wore a brown silk morning dress trimmed with matching velvet, whose loose cut suited her languid attitudes and serious face. She had, besides, arrived at the August of a woman's life, a period at once of reflection and of tenderness, when the beginning of maturity lends a deeper ardor to the eye, when strength of emotion is mingled with experience of life and when, at the culmination of its blossoming, the whole being overflows with a wealth of harmonious beauty. Never had she been sweeter nor more indulgent. Sure that she would not falter, she gave herself up to a feeling that seemed to her a right she had earned by her sorrows. Besides, it was so good and so strange! There was a vast gulf between the vulgarity of Arnoux and Frédéric's adoration!

He was fearful of losing by a word all that he believed he had won, telling himself that a lost opportunity might recur but one could never unsay a stupid remark. He wanted her to give herself, not to take her. The assurance of her love delighted him as a foretaste of possession; and then the charm of her presence troubled his heart more than his senses. It was a vague beatitude, so intoxicating that he forgot even the possibility of an absolute happiness. Away from her he was devoured by furious lusts.

Soon their conversations were broken up by long intervals of silence. Sometimes a kind of sexual modesty made them blush when they were together. All the precautions they took to hide their love made it more evident; the stronger it grew the more reserved they became. Living a lie in this way made their sensibility more acute. The scent of wet leaves caused them an exquisite pleasure; they suffered when the wind blew from the east, were the prey of groundless irritations and ominous presentiments; the sound of footsteps, the cracking of the woodwork terrified them as if they were guilty; they felt that they were being pushed toward an abyss; a stormy atmosphere enveloped them; and when Frédéric blurted out some words of complaint, she would accuse herself:

"Yes, I'm behaving badly! I'm a coquette! You mustn't come anymore."

Then he would repeat the same vows—which she always heard with pleasure.

Her return to Paris and the Christmas season interrupted their meetings a little. When he returned there was a new boldness in his manner. She kept leaving the room to give orders and, despite his pleas, received all the dull people who came to see her. Then the talk would turn to Léotade, Monsieur Guizot, the Pope, the insurrection at Palermo, and the banquet in the Twelfth Arrondissement,* which was causing some anxiety.

Frédéric relieved his feelings by abusing the Authorities for, like Deslauriers, he hoped for an upheaval that would change everything, so embittered was he now. For her part, Madame Arnoux had become gloomy. Her husband, lavishly extravagant, was keeping a working girl from the factory, the one they called La Bordelaise. Madame Arnoux herself told Frédéric about it. He tried to use it as an argument: "Since she was being betrayed . . ."

"Oh, that doesn't bother me anymore!" she declared.

This avowal seemed to him to set the final seal on their intimacy. Did Arnoux mistrust them?

"No, not now."

And she told him how one evening he had left them alone together and had then returned and listened on the other side of the door. As they had been speaking of indifferent matters, he had lived from that time on in complete security on their account.

"And he's right, isn't he?" said Frédéric bitterly.

"Yes, of course!"

She would have been wiser not to make such a remark.

One day she was not at home at the time when he usually came. This struck him as a kind of betrayal.

Then he became angry at always seeing the flowers he brought stuck into a glass of water.

"Where would you like me to put them?"

"Well, not there! Though they'd be even colder next to your heart!"

Some time later he reproached her with having been to the Italiens the previous evening without telling him in advance. Others had seen her, admired her, perhaps loved her; Frédéric clung to his suspicions purely to have some-

*Léotade was a friar who had been sentenced to life imprisonment for the murder of a young girl; the insurrection at Palermo against the King of Naples took place in January, 1848; and the Reformist Banquet in the Twelfth Arrondissement (which corresponded to what is now the Sixth) had been forbidden by the police.

thing to quarrel with her about and torment her with; for he was beginning to hate her, and the least she could do was to share his sufferings!

One afternoon, toward the middle of February, he found her in a state of great agitation. Eugène was complaining of a sore throat. The doctor however had said it was nothing serious, a bad cold or the flu. Frédéric was startled by the child's dazed look. Still, he reassured his mother, citing several children of that age who had recently suffered from similar diseases and who had quickly recovered.

"Really?"

"Yes, I'm certain of it."

"Oh, how good you are!"

And she took his hand. He clasped it in his own.

"Let go."

"But why? I'm only consoling you . . . You think I'm useful for that sort of thing but you doubt me . . . when I speak about my love!"

"I don't doubt you, my poor dear!"

"Why this mistrust, as if I were some kind of depraved . . ."

"Oh! No . . ."

"If I only had some proof!"

"Proof?"

"One that you would give to anybody, that you have already accorded to me."

And he reminded her that they had once gone out together in the twilight of a foggy winter evening. All that was so far away now! What, then, was stopping her from letting herself be seen on his arm in public, without fear on her part or ulterior design on his, there being no one around to worry them?

"So be it!" she said, making up her mind with a courage which at first stupefied Frédéric.

But he replied briskly:

"Shall I meet you at the corner of the Rue Tronchet and the Rue de la Ferme?"

"Good heavens, my dear . . ." stammered Madame Arnoux.

Without giving her time for reflection he added:

"On Tuesday, then?"

"Tuesday?"

"Yes, between two and three o'clock!"

"I'll be there!"

And she turned away her face at a sudden twinge of shame. Frédéric kissed the back of her neck.

"Oh! You mustn't do that," she said. "You'll make me repent."

He drew away, fearing the normal fickleness of women. Then, in the doorway, he murmured gently, as if he were speaking of something that was quite settled:

"Till Tuesday!"

She lowered her eyes discreetly, with an air of resignation.

Frédéric had a plan.

He hoped that, thanks to the sun or the rain, he would be able to get her to pause in a doorway, and that once in the doorway she would enter the house. The difficulty was to discover a suitable one.

So he started looking and, toward the middle of the Rue Tronchet, he saw from a distance a notice: *Furnished Rooms.*

The servant, understanding what he wanted, immediately showed him a bedroom and dressing room on the mezzanine with two entrances. Frédéric took them for a month and paid in advance.

Then he went to three different shops to get the rarest perfume, he bought a piece of machine-made lace to replace the dreadful red cotton counterpane, he chose a pair of blue satin bedroom slippers; and only the fear of seeming vulgar limited his purchases. He brought them back, and with greater devoutness than if he were decking an altar of repose, he moved the furniture around, draped the curtains himself, put some heather in the fireplace and some violets on the chest of drawers; he would have liked to pave the entire room with gold. "It is tomorrow," he said to himself, "yes, tomorrow! I'm not dreaming," and he felt his heart beating hard with delirious hope, then, when everything was ready, he carried off the key in his pocket, as if the happiness which was sleeping there might escape.

A letter from his mother was waiting for him at home.

"Why have you been absent for so long? Your behavior is beginning to seem ridiculous. I can understand to some degree why you might at first have hesitated to commit yourself to this union; think it over, though!"

And she stated the matter precisely: forty-five thousand livres a year. Moreover, people were "talking" and Monsieur Roque expected a definite answer. As for the young lady, her position was really embarrassing. "She loves you very much."

Frédéric tossed the letter aside without finishing it and opened another, a note from Deslauriers:

> Old Man,
> The pear* is ripe. In accordance with your promise, we are counting on you. We're meeting at dawn tomorrow, Place de Panthéon. Come to the café Soufflot. I must speak to you before the demonstration.

"Yes, yes, I know all about their demonstrations. Thanks, but I have something better to do."

And the following day, Frédéric had left home by eleven. He wanted to give a final check to the preparations and then, who knows, she might happen to be early? As he came out of the Rue Tronchet, he heard a great clamor coming from behind the Madeleine; he went forward and saw, at the end of the square on the left, a group of bourgeois and workers.

A manifesto published in the newspapers had, in fact, summoned all the subscribers to the Reformist Banquet to this spot. Almost immediately the ministry had posted a notice forbidding the meeting. The previous evening the parliamentary opposition had given up the project, but the patriots did not know of their leaders' decision, and had come to the meeting place, followed by a large number of spectators. A students' deputation had just been to Odilon Barrot's house. They were now at the ministry of foreign affairs, and no one knew whether or not the Banquet would take place, the government would carry out its threats, the National Guards would arrive. They were as angry with the deputies as they were with the authorities. The crowd was growing from minute to minute and suddenly the strains of the "Marseillaise" rang out.

It was the column of students arriving. They were marching slowly, two by two, in good order. They looked angry, their hands were empty, and from time to time they all cried out:

"Long live Reform! Down with Guizot!"

Frédéric's friends were certainly there. They would spot him and drag him along with them. He quickly took cover in the Rue de l'Arcade.

When the students had marched around the Madeleine

---

*Louis-Philippe had been nicknamed "the Pear" because of the shape of his head.

twice they went down toward the Place de la Concorde. It was full of people, and from a distance the tightly packed crowd looked like a field of black corn swaying to and fro.

At that moment, some troops were forming in battle order to the left of the church.

The groups of people held their ground, however. To put an end to the whole thing, some plainclothes policemen seized the most active figures in the crowd and roughly dragged them off to the police station. Frédéric held his peace, despite his indignation; he might have been arrested with the others, and then he would have missed Madame Arnoux.

Shortly afterwards the helmets of the municipal guard came into view. They were striking out around them with the flats of their sabers. A horse fell, people ran to help it, and, as soon as the rider was back in the saddle, everyone fled.

Then there was a great silence. The fine rain that had dampened the asphalt was falling no longer. The clouds were moving off, swept away by a gentle breeze from the west.

Frédéric began to walk up and down the Rue Tronchet, looking before and behind him as he did so.

It finally struck two.

"Ah! Now's the time!" he said to himself, "she's leaving her house, she's coming"; and, a moment later: "She would have had enough time to get here." Until three o'clock he attempted to keep calm. "No, she's not late; try to be patient!"

For want of anything better to do, he examined the few shops: a bookshop, a saddler's, a shop where they sold mourning items. Soon he knew the titles of all the works, all the sets of harness, all the fabrics. The shopkeepers, who saw him continually passing and repassing, were surprised at first, then frightened, and they put up their shutters.

Probably she had been delayed by something and was suffering too. But what rapture they would share in a little while! For she was coming, that was certain! "She did promise me!" Meanwhile an intolerable anguish was rising in him.

On an absurd impulse, he went back to the lodging house, as if she could have been there. At that very moment she might be coming up the street. He hurried out. No one! And he went back to patrolling the sidewalk.

He examined the cracks between the paving stones, the spouts of the gutters, the lampposts, the numbers above the doors. The most unimportant objects became his companions, or rather ironic spectators; and the regular façades of the houses seemed to him pitiless. His cold feet were hurting him. He felt himself dissolving with despair. The reverberation of his steps jarred his brain.

When he saw by his watch that it was four o'clock, he felt a sort of dizziness, a pang of fear. He tried to recite poetry to himself, to do mental arithmetic, to invent a story. It was impossible! He was obsessed by the image of Madame Arnoux, and he longed to run to meet her. But which way should he go not to miss her?

He accosted a messenger, slipped five francs into his hand, and told him to go to Jacques Arnoux's house in the Rue Paradis and ask the porter "if Madame Arnoux was in." Then he took up his position at the corner of the Rue de la Ferme and the Rue Tronchet so as to be able to see simultaneously in both directions. In the distance, on the boulevard, vague masses of people were moving about. Sometimes he could pick out a dragoon's cockade or a woman's hat, and he strained his eyes to see who it was. A ragged child, who was exhibiting a marmot in a box, smiled at him and asked for money.

The man in the velvet jacket returned. "The porter had not seen her go out." What could be keeping her? If she was ill the man would have said so. Could it be a visitor? But nothing was easier than to be "not at home." He struck his brow:

"Oh, what an idiot I am! It's the riot!" This natural explanation comforted him. Then, suddenly: "But her district is quiet!" And he was assailed by a terrible apprehension: "Suppose she isn't coming? Suppose her promise was no more than a way of getting rid of me? No, no!" No doubt she was being prevented from coming by something extraordinary, one of those events that baffle the most careful planning. In that case she would have written. And he sent the boy from the lodging house round to his home in the Rue Rumfort to see if there was any letter.

No letter had been delivered. This absence of news reassured him.

He searched for omens in the number of coins in a handful picked up by chance, in the faces of the passers-by, in the color of the horses; and, when the augury was unfavorable, he tried hard not to believe in it. In his fits of fury against Madame Arnoux he insulted her under his breath. Then came spells of weakness, when he felt ready to faint, followed by sudden revivals of hope. She was about to appear. She was there, behind his back. He turned round: nothing! Once he saw a woman, about thirty feet away, who was the same size as she and wearing a similar dress. He went up to her; it was a stranger! Five o'clock came, half past five, six o'clock! They were lighting the gas. Madame Arnoux had not come.

She had dreamed, the previous night, that she had been on the sidewalk of the Rue Tronchet for a long time. She was waiting there for something vague that was nevertheless important and, without knowing why, she was frightened of being noticed. But a nasty little dog had taken a dislike to her and was biting at the hem of her dress. He kept obstinately coming back and barked louder and louder. Madame Arnoux woke up. The dog's yelping continued. She listened. It was coming from her son's room. It was the child himself who was coughing. His hands were burning, his face was red, and his voice was peculiarly hoarse. The obstruction of his breathing seemed to grow worse by the minute. Until daybreak she remained bent over his bed, watching him.

At eight o'clock, the drum of the National Guard warned Monsieur Arnoux that his comrades were waiting for him. He dressed quickly and went off, promising to call right away on their doctor, Monsieur Colot. At ten o'clock, Monsieur Colot not having arrived, Madame Arnoux sent round her maid. The doctor was away, and the young man who was replacing him was out on his rounds.

Eugène lay on the bolster with his head to one side, constantly knitting his brows and dilating his nostrils; his poor little face was whiter than the sheets, and each time he inhaled a whistling sound came from his larynx, growing ever more short, dry, and almost metallic. His cough resembled the noise made by those barbarous devices that produce the barking of toy dogs.

Madame Arnoux was filled with terror. She threw herself on the bells and called for help, crying:

"A doctor, a doctor!"

Ten minutes later an old gentleman in a white cravat with neatly trimmed gray whiskers arrived. He asked a great many questions about the young patient's habits, age, and constitution; then he examined his throat, put his ear to his back, and wrote out a prescription. There was something odious about the calm of this old fogey. He might have been at an embalming. She wanted to strike him. He said he would come back in the evening.

Soon the horrible fits of coughing began again. From time to time, the child would suddenly start up. The muscles of his chest would shake with convulsive movements, and when he inhaled his stomach drew in as if he were panting for breath after running. Then he would collapse onto the bed, his head thrown back and his mouth wide open. With infinite precautions Madame Arnoux tried to get him to swallow the contents of the bottles, some ipecac and a cough medicine. But he pushed away the spoon, sobbing feebly. He seemed to be gasping out his words.

Occasionally she reread the prescription. The formula frightened her. Perhaps the pharmacist had made a mistake! Her helplessness made her desperate. Monsieur Colot's apprentice arrived.

He was an unassuming young man, new to his profession, who did not hide his feelings. At first, he could not decide on anything, frightened of committing himself; finally, he prescribed the application of pieces of ice. It took a long time to find any ice. The bladder containing the pieces burst. They had to change the boy's nightshirt. All this disturbance brought on another and more terrible attack.

The child started to rip at the cloths wrapped around his throat, as if he were trying to pull away the obstacle that was suffocating him, and he scraped at the wall and clutched the curtains of his bed, searching for some support for his breathing. His face was bluish now and his whole body, drenched in a cold sweat, seemed to grow thinner. In his terror he fastened his haggard eyes on his mother. He threw his arms around her neck, holding on desperately, and, holding back her sobs, she stammered out endearments:

"Yes, my love, my angel, my treasure!"

Then came moments of calm.

She went to look for some toys, a puppet, a collection of pictures, and spread them out on his bed to distract him. She even tried to sing.

She began a song that she used to croon to him in the old days when she rocked him and dressed him on that same little tapestry chair. But he shuddered through the whole length of his body, like a wave whipped by the wind, and his eyeballs started from his head. She thought

he was about to die and turned away her head so as not
to see.

A moment later, she felt strong enough to look again.
He was still alive. The hours went by, heavy, dismal, interminable, full of affliction; she no longer noticed the
passage of time except as it was reflected by the progress
of his agony. The spasms in his chest wrenched him forward as if they would break him to pieces; finally he
vomited something strange which looked like a tube of
parchment. What could it be? She imagined that he had
thrown up a piece of his bowels. But he was breathing
deeply and regularly. This apparent well-being frightened
her more than anything else; she was standing petrified,
her arms hanging down and her eyes fixed, when Monsieur Colot arrived. The child, he said, was out of danger.

At first she didn't understand, and she made him repeat
the phrase. Perhaps it was one of those consoling remarks
doctors always make? Monsieur Colot went off with a
tranquil air. She felt as if the cords cutting her heart had
been untied.

"Out of danger! Can it be true!"

Suddenly, clearly and inexorably, she was confronted
with the image of Frédéric. It was a warning from Providence. But the good Lord, in his mercy, had not wished
to punish her completely! What an expiation there would
be later, if she persevered in this love! Perhaps her son
would be insulted because of her, and Madame Arnoux
saw him as a young man, wounded in a duel and brought
back dying on a stretcher. She threw herself down beside
the little chair and, sending up her soul with all her
strength, she offered up as a holocaust the sacrifice of her
first love, her only weakness.

Frédéric had gone home. He stayed slumped in an armchair without even the strength to curse her. He fell into
a kind of slumber and, through his nightmares, he heard
the sound of falling rain, believing that he was still in the
same place on the sidewalk.

The next day, in a final moment of cowardice, he sent
another messenger round to Madame Arnoux's.

Whether the Savoyard did not deliver the message, or
whether she had too much to say to be able to explain
herself in a couple of words, he brought back the same
response. It was too insolent! He was filled with the fury
of wounded pride. He vowed he would no longer feel even
a twinge of desire and, like a leaf before the blast of a
hurricane, his passion disappeared. He was left with a

feeling of relief, a stoical happiness, then a craving for violent action, and he set off at random through the streets.

Men from the outlying districts passed him armed with guns and old swords; some of them were wearing red caps, and they were all singing the "Marseillaise" or the "Girondins." Here and there a National Guard was hurrying to his local town hall. There were drums beating in the distance and fighting at the Porte Saint-Martin. Something gay and warlike was in the air. Frédéric went on walking. The bustle of the great city exhilarated him.

When he reached Frascati's, he caught sight of the Maréchale's windows; a mad juvenile idea occurred to him. He crossed the boulevard.

The courtyard gate had been closed and Delphine, the maid, was writing "Arms already handed in" on it with a piece of charcoal; she said excitedly:

"Oh, Madame is in a terrible state! She dismissed her groom for insulting her this morning. She thinks there will be looting everywhere! She's dying of fright! And especially with Monsieur gone!"

"What Monsieur?"

"The prince!"

Frédéric went into the boudoir. The Maréchale appeared in her petticoat, her hair down her back, frantic.

"Oh, thank you! You've come to save me! This is the second time! And *you* never ask for payment."

"Forgive me!" said Frédéric, seizing her waist in both his hands.

"What? What are you doing?" stammered the Maréchale, surprised and pleased by this approach.

"I'm following the fashion," he answered. "I'm reforming."

She let herself be pushed back onto the divan and continued to laugh under his kisses.

They spent the afternoon watching the people in the street from their window. Then he took her to the Trois-Frères-Provençaux for dinner. The meal was long and carefully chosen. They returned on foot, for lack of a carriage.

The mood of Paris had been transformed by the news of a change of government. People were strolling about, everyone was merry, and the lanterns at every floor of the buildings made it as light as day. The soldiers were slowly going back to their barracks, weary and sad-looking. They were greeted with cries of: "Long live the

Regulars!" They went on their way without replying. The officers of the National Guard, on the other hand, brandished their swords, red-faced with enthusiasm, and shouted: "Long live Reform!" and the word "reform" made the two lovers laugh each time they heard it. Frédéric cracked jokes and was very gay.

They reached the boulevards through the Rue Duphot. The houses were hung with Venetian lanterns that formed garlands of light. Beneath them a great swarm of people were jostling about; here and there, the white gleam of a bayonet stood out against the gloom. A great uproar began. It was impossible for them to return directly, the crowd was too tightly packed; and they were turning into the Rue Caumartin when suddenly behind them there was a crackling noise, like the sound of an immense piece of silk being torn. It was the fusillade of the Boulevard des Capucines.

"Ah, they're knocking off a few bourgeois!" remarked Frédéric calmly, for there are times when the least cruel of men is so detached from his fellows that he could see the entire human race perish without batting an eyelid.

The Maréchale's teeth were chattering as she hung on his arm. She declared that she was incapable of going another step. So, in a refinement of hatred, the better to violate Madame Arnoux in his heart, he took her to the lodging house in the Rue Tronchet and the room he had prepared for the other.

The flowers had not yet withered. The lace was spread out over the bed. He took the little slippers out of the cupboard. Rosanette appreciated the delicacy of these attentions.

Toward one o'clock, she was awakened by distant rumblings and she saw that he was sobbing, his head buried in the pillow.

"What's wrong, my darling?"

"I'm too happy," said Frédéric. "I've wanted you for such a long time!"

PART THREE

Chapter One

The sound of shots roused him abruptly from his sleep and, in spite of Rosanette's entreaties, Frédéric insisted on going out to see what was happening. He made his way down the Champs-Élysées, from where the firing had come. At the corner of the Rue Saint-Honoré, he met some workers shouting:

"No! Not that way! To the Palais-Royal!"

Frédéric followed them. The railings around the Church of the Assumption had been torn down. Farther on, he noticed three paving stones in the middle of the roadway, probably the beginnings of a barricade, then some fragments of broken bottles and coils of wire intended to obstruct the cavalry. Suddenly a tall, pale young man dashed out of an alley. His black hair hung down to his shoulders, and he wore a kind of jersey with colored dots on it. He was holding a long military musket and ran on tiptoe in his sandals, lithe as a tiger but with the air of a sleepwalker. From time to time an explosion sounded.

The previous evening, the sight of a wagon containing five corpses picked up among those on the Boulevard des Capucines had changed the people's mood; and while the messengers came and went at the Tuileries, while Monsieur Molé, who was forming a new cabinet, did not return, while Monsieur Thiers tried to construct another, and while the king shuffled and hesitated then gave Bugeaud overall command only to prevent him from using it, the insurrection, as if directed by a single brain, became formidably well-organized. Speakers harangued the mob with frenetic eloquence from the street corners;

in the churches others rang the tocsin as hard as they could; lead was being melted down, cartridges manufactured; the trees lining the boulevards, the urinals, benches, railings, and street lamps, everything had been torn up and overturned. In the morning, Paris was covered with barricades. Resistance did not last very long; the National Guard intervened everywhere, and to such effect that by eight o'clock the people, by force or by consent, had taken possession of five barracks and almost all the local town halls and major strategic points. Without a direct attack, the monarchy was rapidly disintegrating of its own accord, and now the guard-post at Château-d'Eau was being attacked to set free fifty prisoners, who were not there.

Frédéric was forced to halt at the entrance to the square. It was filled with groups of armed men. Companies of regular troops occupied the Rue Saint-Thomas and the Rue Fromanteau. The Rue de Valois was blocked by an enormous barricade. The cloud of smoke hanging over it parted, men ran across the top, waving their arms, then they disappeared and the firing started again. The guard-post returned the fire, though no one could be seen inside; its windows were protected by oak shutters pierced with loopholes, and the building, with its two stories and two wings, its fountain on the first floor and its little door in the middle, began to show white flecks where the bullets struck. Its flight of three steps remained empty.

Next to Frédéric, a man in a Greek cap, with a cartridge pouch over his woolen jacket, was arguing with a woman in a Madras kerchief. She was begging him to come home.

"Leave me alone!" replied the husband. "You can look after the lodge perfectly well on your own. Citizen, I ask you, is it fair? I've done my duty every time, in eighteen-thirty, in 'thirty-two, in 'thirty-four, in 'thirty-nine! They are fighting today! I must fight! Go away!"

And she ended by giving way to his remonstrances and to those of a National Guardsman near them, a man of about forty, whose kindly face was adorned with a fringe of blond beard. He was loading his weapon and firing while he talked to Frédéric, as calm in the midst of the riot as a gardener in his plot. A boy in a shopkeeper's apron coaxed him to hand over some percussion caps so that he could use his weapon, a beautiful sporting carbine which had been given him by "a gentleman."

"Take a handful from my back pouch," said the man, "and get out of here! You'll get yourself killed!"

The drums beat the charge. Piercing cries and triumphant cheers sounded. The crowd swayed to and fro in constant eddies. Frédéric did not move; he was trapped between two dense masses and, in any case, fascinated and enjoying himself immensely. The wounded falling to the ground and the dead lying stretched out did not look like real dead and wounded. He felt as if he were watching a play.

Above the swell of the crowd, an old man dressed in black could be seen sitting on a white horse with a velvet saddle. In one hand he held a green branch, in the other a piece of paper, and he was waving them stubbornly. Finally, giving up hope of making himself heard, he withdrew.

The infantry had disappeared and only the municipal guards remained to defend the post. A wave of dauntless men swept up the steps; they fell, others followed them; and the quivering door resounded beneath the strokes of their iron bars; the municipal guards would not surrender. But a barouche stuffed with hay and burning like a giant torch was dragged against the walls. Wood, straw, and a barrel of brandy were quickly brought. The fire rose all along the stone wall; the whole building began to smoke like a volcano; and at the top, large flames burst through the balustrade around the terrace with a harsh roar. The first floor of the Palais-Royal was lined with National Guardsmen. Guns were firing from all the windows around the square; bullets whistled through the air; and the water of the shattered fountain mingled with blood, to form pools on the ground. People slipped on clothes, shakos, and weapons in the mud; Frédéric felt something soft underfoot; it was the hand of a sergeant in a gray topcoat who lay with his face in the gutter. New groups of workers kept arriving, pushing those who were fighting toward the guardhouse. The liquor shops were open; from time to time, people would go in to smoke a pipe and drink a glass of beer, then return to the struggle. A lost dog was howling. This raised a laugh.

Frédéric staggered under the impact of a man who fell against his shoulder, the breath rattling in his throat and a bullet in his back. This shot, which might have been aimed at him, enraged Frédéric; and he was plunging forward when he was stopped by a National Guardsman:

"It's pointless. The king has just left. If you don't believe me, go and see for yourself.!"

This calmed Frédéric. The Place du Carrousel looked quiet enough. The Hôtel de Nantes still stood in solitary state; the houses behind, the dome of the Louvre opposite, the long wooden gallery to the right, and the vacant land which stretched unevenly away to the open-air stalls seemed bathed in the gray air and distant noises blended into the fog—while at the other end of the square the harsh daylight falling through a chink in the clouds onto the façade of the Tuileries outlined all its windows with white. A dead horse was stretched out near the Arc de Triomphe. Groups of five or six people talked together behind the railings. The doors of the palace were open, and the servants on the threshold were letting people come in.

Cups of coffee were being handed out in a small room on the ground floor. Some of the sightseers sat down at the table, joking; others remained standing, among them a cab driver. He grabbed a jar full of powdered sugar, looked nervously to left and right, then started eating voraciously, burying his nose in its neck. At the foot of the great staircase, a man was writing his name in a book. Frédéric recognized his back:

"Well, if it isn't Hussonnet!"

"In person," replied the bohemian. "I am introducing myself to the court. This is fun, isn't it?"

"Suppose we go upstairs?"

And they went up to the marshals' gallery. All the portraits of these worthies were intact except for Bugeaud's, which had a hole in the stomach. They had been painted leaning on their swords, in front of gun carriages, and in impressive poses that seemed incongruous in the present circumstances. The hands of the large clock marked twenty past one.

Suddenly the "Marseillaise" rang out. Hussonnet and Frédéric leaned over the banisters. It was the mob. It rushed up the staircase in a dizzying flood of bare heads, helmets, red caps, bayonets, and shoulders, so impetuously that people disappeared into the swarming mass that still swept upwards, like a river forced back in its course by a spring tide, with a long roar, driven by an irresistible impulse. When it reached the top of the stairs, the mob spread out and the singing stopped.

Now the only sounds were the trampling of innumerable shoes and the ripples of talk. The crowd's mood was inoffensive, and they contented themselves with staring. But occasionally, in the crush, an elbow would go through a pane of glass, or a vase or statuette would roll off a table to the floor. The paneling cracked under the pressure. All the faces were red, and sweat streamed down them in large drops. Hussonnet remarked:

"Heroes don't smell too good!"

"How infuriating you are!" replied Frédéric.

And, carried along willy-nilly, they entered a room with a red velvet canopy stretched across the ceiling. On the throne beneath it sat a member of the proletariat with a black beard, his shirt half-open, as jolly and stupid as a clown. Others climbed onto the platform to sit in his place.

"What a myth!" said Hussonnet. This, then, is the sovereign people!"

Someone picked up the throne, holding it above his head, and it was passed from hand to hand, rocking as it went, the entire length of the room.

"Good Lord! See how she rolls! The ship of state is tossing on a stormy sea! It's doing the can-can! It's doing the can-can!"

It had reached one of the windows and was thrown out, to the sound of boos.

"Poor old thing!" said Hussonnet, as he watched it fall into the garden, where it was snatched up to be taken to the Bastille and then burned.

At this there was a frenzied outburst of joy, as if a future of boundless happiness had appeared in place of the throne; and the mob, less from a desire for vengeance than from a wish to assert the fact that they were in possession, broke and tore mirrors, and curtains, chandeliers, sconces, tables, chairs, stools, all the furniture, even sketchbooks and embroidery baskets. Since they had gained the victory, they had a right to amuse themselves, hadn't they? The rabble decked themselves mockingly in laces and cashmeres. Gold fringes were tied around smock sleeves, ostrich-feather hats adorned the heads of blacksmiths, sashes of the Legion of Honor became belts for prostitutes. Everyone followed his own whim; some danced, others drank. In the queen's bedroom, a woman was greasing her hair with pomade; behind a screen, two gamblers were playing cards; Hussonnet pointed out a man who was smoking his clay pipe leaning on the balcony; and the delirious racket continued unceasingly, augmented by the sounds of breaking china and of the fragments of crystal that tinkled as they fell like the notes of a harmonica.

Then the fury of the mob became more sinister. Driven by an obscene curiosity they rummaged in all the cupboards and corners, opened all the drawers. Criminals who had served their time in the galleys thrust their arms into the princesses' beds, and rolled about on them as a consolation for having been unable to rape them. Evil-faced men wandered about looking for something to steal, but the crowd was too thick. Peering through the doorways into the suites of rooms, nothing could be seen but the dark mass of people framed by the gilded walls under a cloud of dust. Everyone was panting for breath, the heat was becoming more and more stifling; the two friends went out, afraid that they might be smothered.

In the hall, a streetwalker was standing on a pile of clothes, posed as a statue of Liberty—immobile, wide-eyed, horrifying.

They were not three paces from the door when an advancing platoon of municipal guards in overcoats, taking off their police caps and thus uncovering their rather bald heads, bowed very low to the mob. At this show of respect, the ragged victors drew themselves up proudly. Hussonnet and Frédéric were no more immune than the others to a certain feeling of gratification.

Filled with ardor, they returned to the Palais-Royal. In the Rue Fromanteau, soldiers' corpses were piled up on some straw. They walked past impassively, and were even proud to feel that they were showing no emotion.

The palace was overflowing with people. There were seven bonfires burning in the inner court. Pianos, chests of drawers, and clocks flew out of windows. Fire engines were pumping jets of water as high as the roofs. Some roughnecks were trying to cut through the hoses with their swords. Frédéric urged a student at the Polytechnic to intervene. The polytechnician did not understand and, moreover, seemed to be almost an imbecile. Finding itself master of the wine cellars, the mob was giving itself up to a hideous orgy all around in the two arcades. Wine ran in streams, feet were wet with it, and the riff-raff were drinking the dregs and staggering about shouting.

"Let's get out of here," said Hussonnet. "These people disgust me."

All along the Orléans gallery wounded men lay on mattresses on the ground, covered with purple curtains;

and the wives of the local shopkeepers were bringing them soup and bandages.

"I don't care!" said Frédéric. "I still think the people are sublime."

The great hall was filled with a struggling mass of furious men trying to reach the upper stories to complete the destruction, and National Guardsmen on the steps were striving to keep them back. The most daring of these was a bareheaded rifleman, his hair bristling and his buff-leather coat in tatters. His shirt bulged out between his trousers and his jacket, and he was fighting furiously amid the other guards. Hussonnet, who had excellent eyesight, recognized him from a distance as Arnoux.

Then they went into the Tuileries garden for a breath of fresh air. They sat down on a bench and closed their eyes for a few minutes, so dazed that they had no strength to speak. The people walking past were accosting each other. The Duchess d'Orléans had been appointed regent; it was all over; and they were experiencing that sense of well-being which follows a rapid resolution to a dangerous situation, when servants appeared at every garret window of the palace, tearing up their liveries. They threw them into the garden as a sign of abjuration. The mob hooted at them. They withdrew.

Frédéric and Hussonnet were distracted from this scene by a tall young man who was walking quickly through the trees, a gun on his shoulder. His red jacket was held at the waist by a cartridge belt, and he had a handkerchief tied around his forehead under his cap. He turned his head. It was Dussardier and, throwing himself into their arms, he exclaimed:

"Oh, what a joyful day!" so breathless from delight and fatigue that he was unable to say more.

He had been on his feet for the last forty-eight hours. He had worked on the barricades in the Latin Quarter, had fought in the Rue Rambuteau, had saved three dragoons, had entered the Tuileries with Dunoyer's column; and since then had been to the Chamber of Deputies and then to the Hôtel de Ville.

"I've just come from there. Everything is going well! The people have triumphed! The middle classes and the workers are embracing each other! Oh, if only you knew all I've seen! What wonderful people! How glorious it all is!"

And, without noticing that they were unarmed:

"I was sure I'd find you here! It was tough for a few minutes, but it doesn't matter!"

A drop of blood trickled down his cheek and he answered their questions with:

"Oh, it's nothing! A scratch from a bayonet!"

"But you must have it tended!"

"Nonsense, I'm as strong as an ox. What does it matter? The Republic has been proclaimed! Now we'll all be happy! Some journalists who were talking just now in front of me said we would go on to liberate Poland and Italy! No more kings. Do you understand! The whole world free! The whole world free!"

And, circling the horizon with a single glance, he threw open his arms in a gesture of triumph. But a long line of men were running along the terrace beside the water.

"Oh, good Lord, I forgot! The forts are still occupied. I must go there! Good-bye!"

He turned back, brandishing his gun, to cry: "Long live the Republic!"

Great clouds of black smoke were gushing from the chimneys of the palace, carrying sparks with them. The bells in the distance sounded like frightened bleating. To the right and the left, all around them, the victors were letting off their guns. Frédéric, although no warrior, felt his Gallic blood quickening. He was caught up by the magnetism of the enthusiastic crowds. He sniffed voluptuously at the stormy air, sharp with the smell of powder; and at the same time he was quivering from the emanations of an immense love, of a supreme and universal tenderness, as if the heart of all humanity were beating within his chest.

"Perhaps," Hussonnet said with a yawn, "this might be the moment to undertake the education of the masses!"

Frédéric went with him to his press agency in the Place de la Bourse and there set down a lyrical account of the events for the Troyes paper—a real masterpiece, which he signed. Then they dined together in a tavern. Hussonnet was in a thoughtful mood; the eccentricities of the Revolution were greater than his own.

After coffee, when they went over to the Hôtel de Ville to hear the latest news, his normal urchin humor was uppermost again. He scaled the barricades like a mountain goat and replied to the sentries' challenges with patriotic jests.

They heard the provisional government proclaimed by

torchlight. Finally, at midnight, Frédéric returned home, completely exhausted.

"Well," he said to his servant, who was undressing him, "are you pleased?"

"Yes, of course, Monsieur! But the thing I dislike is the mob all marching in step!"

When he woke up the next morning, Frédéric thought of Deslauriers. He hurried round to his apartment. The lawyer had just left, for he had been appointed a provincial commissioner. The previous evening he had managed to see Ledru-Rollin and, by pestering him in the name of the law schools, had wrested a job and a mission from him. Whatever happened, according to the porter, he would be writing the following week to give his address.

After this, Frédéric went off to see the Maréchale. She received him frostily, for she held his desertion against him; but her rancor was dispelled by his repeated assurances of peace. Everything was calm now, there was no need to be frightened; he embraced her and she declared herself in favor of the Republic—a stand already adopted by the Lord Archbishop of Paris and about to be espoused with a remarkably rapid flowering of zeal by the Bench, the Council of State, the Institut, the Marshals of France, Changarnier, Monsieur de Falloux, all the Bonapartists, all the Legitimists, and a considerable proportion of the Orléanists.

The fall of the monarchy had been so swift that, once the middle classes had recovered from their first stupefaction, they felt a kind of astonishment at still being alive. The summary execution of a few thieves, who were shot without a trial, seemed an entirely just procedure. For a month, Lamartine's remark about the red flag: "which has only gone round the Champ de Mars, whereas the tricolor has gone round the world," was repeated constantly, and everyone fell into line behind the flag, each party seeing only one of the three colors—its own—and resolving to tear off the other two as soon as it got the upper hand.

With business at a standstill, worry and curiosity drove everyone out into the streets. People dressed in a careless way that blurred the distinctions between classes, hatreds were concealed and hopes blossomed, the crowd was in good humor. Pride at having won their rights shone from every face. People had a carnival gaiety about them, the easy mood of a bivouac prevailed; Paris during those first days was the most delightful place.

Frédéric gave the Maréchale his arm, and they strolled about the streets together. She was amused by the rosettes in every buttonhole, the flags hanging from all the windows, the multicolored posters plastered over the walls, and now and then she would throw some money for the wounded into a box which had been placed on a chair in the middle of the street. Then she would stop at caricatures showing Louis-Philippe as a pastry cook, a mountebank, a dog, or a leech. But Caussidière's men,* with their swords and their sashes, frightened her a little. Sometimes they came across a Tree of Liberty being planted. Ecclesiastics took part in the ceremonies, blessing the Republic, escorted by attendants in gold lace, and the people were very pleased. The commonest sight was that of a delegation from something or other on its way to make some demand at the Hôtel de Ville—for all the trades and industries expected the government to put an absolute end to all their problems. Some of them, it is true, had gone to see the government in order to advise or congratulate it, or simply to pay a little visit and see how the machine worked.

One day, toward the middle of March, when he was crossing the Pont d'Arcole on an errand for Rosanette in the Latin Quarter, Frédéric saw a column of men with bizarre hats and long beards coming toward him. At their head, beating a drum, marched a Negro who had once been an artist's model; and their banner, which unfurled in the breeze to show the inscription: PAINTERS, was carried by none other than Pellerin.

He signaled Frédéric to wait for him, then reappeared after five minutes, having time to kill, for at the moment the government was receiving the stone-cutters. He and his colleagues meant to ask for the creation of an art forum, a kind of stock exchange, where aesthetic interests would be discussed; this pooling of their genius by all the artists would result in the production of sublime works of art. Paris would soon be covered with gigantic monuments; he would decorate them; he had even started a figure of the Republic. One of his fellows came to fetch him, for the delegation from the poultry industry was hot on their heels.

*Caussidière, a former political prisoner, had been made chief of police after the Revolution. He organized a police force made up of men who had fought in the February uprising.

"What a farce!" grumbled a voice in the crowd. "All this nonsense! Nothing important!"

It was Regimbart. He did not greet Frédéric but took advantage of the opportunity to pour out his bitterness.

The Citizen spent his days wandering round the streets pulling at his moustache, rolling his eyes, hearing and repeating gloomy pieces of news; and he had only two stock interjections: "Be careful, we're being outflanked!" and "But dammit, they're filching the Republic!" He was dissatisfied with everything, and especially with the fact that we had not taken back our natural frontiers. The mere mention of Lamartine's name made him shrug his shoulders. He didn't think that Ledru-Rollin* was "adequate to the task in hand," spoke of Dupont (from the Eure) as an old fogey, Albert as an idiot, Louis Blanc as a utopian, Blanqui as an extremely dangerous man, and, when Frédéric asked him what should have been done he replied, seizing his arm in a crushing grip:

"Take the Rhine, I tell you, take the Rhine, damn it!" Then he denounced the reactionaries.

They were beginning to come into the open. The sack of the castles of Neuilly and Suresne, the burning of Batignolles, the troubles in Lyons, all the excesses and all the grievances were being exaggerated at the moment, and to them were added Ledru-Rollin's circular,† the forced issuing of bank notes, the drop of government stock to sixty francs, and finally, the height of iniquity, the last straw, the supreme horror, the forty-five centime tax!‡ And, to cap it all, there was still socialism! Although these theories were just about as novel as "Hunt the Thimble" and the discussions of them during the past forty years would have filled entire libraries, they still threw the bourgeois into as great a panic as a hail of meteorites would have done. Indignation sprang from

*Alexandre Auguste Ledru-Rollin (1807-1874) was a member of the Chamber of Deputies and a prominent supporter of the Reform Banquets, who became Minister of the Interior in Lamartine's government after the overthrow of Louis-Philippe. He sided with the workers during the insurrection in June, 1848, was a candidate for president in December of that year but was defeated by Louis-Napoléon. He attempted to overthrow the government in 1849, and after failing fled to England. He remained in exile until the fall of the Second Empire.

†Ledru-Rollin's circular recommended republican candidates in the elections for the Constituent Assembly.

‡The tax rate was raised by forty-five centimes for every hundred francs, a very unpopular measure.

that hatred that is provoked by every new idea simply because it is an idea, an abhorrence that gives it prestige eventually and which always makes for the inferiority of its enemies, no matter how mediocre the idea itself may be.

Now Property was raised in men's eyes to the level of Religion and became confused with God. The attacks made on it seemed sacrilegious, almost cannibalistic. In spite of the most humane laws that had ever been enacted, the specter of '93 reappeared, and the knife of the guillotine vibrated in every syllable of the word "Republic"—which in no way prevented the government being despised for its weakness. France, realizing that she was without a master, started crying with fright like a blind man deprived of his stick, or a child who has lost his nurse.

No man in France was more terrified than Monsieur Dambreuse. The new situation threatened his fortune but, even more important, it contradicted his experience. Such a good system, such a wise king! Could it be possible! The world was coming to an end! The very next day he dismissed three servants, sold his horses, bought a soft hat to wear in the street, and even thought of growing his beard. He stayed at home, prostrate, bitterly reading only those papers most hostile to his own ideas, and became so gloomy that the jokes about Flocon's pipe* couldn't even make him smile.

As a supporter of the previous government, he dreaded the vengeance of the mob on his estates in Champagne. When Frédéric's lucubration fell into his hands, he imagined that his young friend was a person of considerable influence who, if he could not help him, could at least defend him; so that one morning Monsieur Dambreuse turned up at Frédéric's house accompanied by Martinon.

The only object of this visit, according to the banker, was to spend a few minutes with his host and have a chat. Taking them by and large, he rejoiced at the turn of events and he gladly adopted "our sublime device: *Liberty, Equality, Fraternity,* having always been a republican at heart." If he had voted with the government under the former regime, it had been simply in order to hasten its inevitable downfall. He even inveighed against Monsieur Guizot, "who, let's face it, has got us into a fine

---

*Flocon, former editor of *La Reforme*, was Minister of Commerce in the provisional government, and his pipe, which never left his mouth, made him a favorite with the cartoonists.

mess!" Lamartine, on the other hand, had elicited his admiration by showing himself "magnificent, upon my word, when he said of the red flag . . ."

"Yes, I know," said Frédéric.

After this, he declared his sympathy for the workers. "For, after all, we are all workers to a greater or lesser degree!" and he carried his impartiality as far as admitting that Proudhon argued logically, "oh, good lord, very logically!" Then, with the detachment of a superior intellect, he spoke of the exhibition where he had seen Pellerin's picture. He thought it was original and well executed.

Martinon supported everything he said with approving remarks; he too felt that one should "come out openly on the side of the Republic," and he spoke of his father as a laborer, and took on the role of the peasant, the man of the people. The conversation soon turned to the elections for the National Assembly and to the candidates in the Fortelle district. The opposition candidate had no chance.

"You should take his place!" said Monsieur Dambreuse. Frédéric demurred.

"Well, why not?" He would have the extremist vote because of his personal opinions and the conservative on account of his family. "And," said the banker, smiling, "perhaps also thanks, in some small measure, to my own influence."

Frédéric objected that he had no idea how to go about it. Nothing could be easier; all he had to do was to arrange to be recommended to the Aube patriots by one of the Paris clubs. It was a matter of setting out not a profession of faith, the sort of thing one saw every day, but a serious exposition of his principles.

"Bring it to me; I know what goes down well in the district! And, I repeat, you could render great service to the country, to all of us, to myself."

In times like these, we must all help each other and, if Frédéric needed something, for himself or for his friends . . .

"Oh, no, thank you very much!"

"On the understanding that you'd do the same thing for me, of course!"

The banker was certainly a good fellow. Frédéric could not help thinking over what he advised and soon he was seized by a kind of dizzying intoxication.

The great figures of the convention passed before his

eyes. It seemed to him that a wondrous day was about to dawn. Rome, Vienna, and Berlin were in a state of insurrection, the Austrians had been chased out of Venice, the whole of Europe was in turmoil. Now was the time to throw oneself into the movement, to add to its momentum, perhaps; and then he was attracted by the uniform which it was said the deputies would wear. Already he saw himself in a waistcoat with lapels, and a tricolor sash; and this itch, this hallucination, became so strong that he confided in Dussardier.

The good fellow's fervor had not diminished.

"Yes, of course! Do stand!"

Nevertheless, Frédéric consulted Deslauriers. The bull-headed opposition, which was hampering the commissioner in his province, had made him more liberal than ever. He replied by return mail with violent exhortations.

But still Frédéric needed the approval of a greater number; and he confided his project to Rosanette one day in the presence of Mademoiselle Vatnaz.

La Vatnaz was one of those Parisian spinsters who, every evening, when they have given their lessons or tried to sell their little drawings or place their pathetic manuscripts, go home with mud on their petticoats, cook their dinners, eat them alone and then, with their feet on a brazier, by the light of a dirty lamp, dream of a love affair, a family, a home, a fortune, all that they lack. Thus, like many others, she had welcomed the Revolution as the coming of vengeance and poured out an unrestrained socialist propaganda.

According to La Vatnaz, the emancipation of the proletariat was only possible with the emancipation of women. She wanted all employments opened to them, investigation into the paternity of illegitimate children, a new legal code, the abolition or at least "a more intelligent regulation" of marriage. Every Frenchwoman would be obliged to marry a Frenchman or to look after an old man. Nurses and midwives would be salaried State officials, there would be a jury to examine works of art produced by women, special publishers for women, a polytechnic school for women, a National Guard for women, everything for women! And, since the government disregarded their rights, they should beat force with force. Ten thousand female citizens with serviceable muskets would make the Hôtel de Ville shake in its shoes!

Frédéric's candidacy seemed likely to benefit her ideas.

She encouraged him, with talk of future glory. Rosanette was delighted at the idea of a man of hers speaking in the Chamber.

"And then, who knows. They may give you a good position."

Frédéric, prey to every weakness, was caught up by the universal madness. He wrote a speech and took it round for Monsieur Dambreuse to see.

As the great gate clanged shut he caught a glimpse of a woman holding back the curtain of one of the windows. He did not have enough time to recognize her. In the hall, he was brought up short by a picture, Pellerin's picture, standing, temporarily no doubt, on a chair.

It represented the Republic, or Progress, or Civilization, in the guise of Jesus Christ driving a locomotive through a virgin forest. After a moment of contemplation, Frédéric exclaimed:

"What an outrage!"

"Isn't it?" said Monsieur Dambreuse, who had come in at that moment and imagined that Frédéric was referring not to the painting but to the doctrine glorified by the picture. Martinon arrived simultaneously, and they went into the study, where Frédéric was taking the paper from his pocket when Mademoiselle Cécile suddenly entered and said with an ingenuous air:

"Is my aunt here?"

"You know perfectly well she isn't," replied the banker. "But never mind! Make yourself at home, Mademoiselle."

"Oh, no, thank you. I'm going."

She had hardly left when Martinon made a pretense of searching for his handkerchief.

"I've left it in my overcoat. Excuse me!"

"Of course!" said Monsieur Dambreuse.

He was obviously not duped by this maneuver, and even seemed to approve of it. Why? But Martinon soon reappeared, and Frédéric launched into his speech. From the second page, which referred to the preponderance of financial interests as something shameful, the banker grimaced. Then, moving on to reforms, Frédéric demanded the freedom of trade.

"What? But allow me . . ."

Frédéric did not hear him and went on. He called for a tax on incomes, graduated taxation, a European federation, the education of the masses, and massive subsidies for the arts.

"If the state were to provide men like Delacroix or

Hugo with incomes of a hundred thousand francs, where would be the harm?"

The whole thing finished with some advice to the upper classes.

"And you, oh rich men, keep nothing back! Give! Give!"

He stopped but remained standing. His seated audience of two did not speak. Martinon's eyes were round with amazement and Monsieur Dambreuse was very pale. Finally, hiding his emotion under a bitter smile, the latter said:

"Your speech is perfect!" And he praised its form highly so as not to have to give his opinion of its contents.

This virulence on the part of an inoffensive young man frightened him, particularly as a symptom. Martinon tried to reassure him. In a short time, the Conservative Party would be sure to take its revenge; the provisional government's commissioners had already been thrown out of several towns; elections were not due until April 23rd, there was plenty of time. In short, Monsieur Dambreuse himself must stand as a candidate in the Aube; and from then on Martinon never left him, becoming his secretary and surrounding him with filial attentions.

Frédéric arrived at Rosanette's very pleased with himself. Delmar was there and told him that he would "definitely" be standing as a candidate in the Seine elections. In a poster addressed to "the People," in which he spoke to them familiarly, the actor boasted that "he" was able to understand them and that, for their salvation, he had had himself "crucified by Art," so that he was their incarnation, their ideal. He did, in fact, believe himself to have an enormous influence over the masses, to the point where later on, in a government office, he proposed to pacify a riot singlehanded and, when asked what methods he would use, replied:

"Don't worry! I will show them my face!"

Frédéric, wanting to spite him, told him of his own candidacy. The actor, as soon as he heard that it was in the provinces that his future colleague meant to run, offered to help him and to introduce him to the various clubs.

They visited all or nearly all of them: the red and the blue, the frenzied and the tranquil, the puritanical, the bohemian, the mystical, and the drunken, clubs that decreed the death of kings, and clubs that decried cheating grocers; and everywhere they went tenants were cursing landlords, the smock was denouncing the frock coat, and the rich were conspiring against the poor. Some people wanted indemnities for their sufferings at the hands of the police, others were begging for money to develop inventions, or there were plans for phalansteries,* schemes for regional fairs, systems for the general happiness. Here and there, like a flash of intelligence amid these clouds of stupidity, there would be an impassioned address, as sudden as a thunderclap, a legal principle articulated in an oath and the bloom of eloquence on the lips of some lout with a sword belt across his bare chest. Sometimes, too, a gentleman would appear, an aristocrat with humble ways, and the talk of a laborer, who had left his hands unwashed so that they would look calloused. Some patriot would spot him, the hard-liners would abuse him, and he would leave with rage in his heart. It was a requirement to show common sense by continually denigrating lawyers and using as often as possible such phrases as: "add one's stone to the building—social problem—workshop."

Delmar never missed a chance to take the floor and, when he could think of nothing further to say, he fell back on posing with one hand on his hip and the other thrust into his waistcoat, abruptly turning his head to show his profile to best advantage. Then there would be an outburst of applause, provided by Mademoiselle Vatnaz at the back of the room.

Despite the poor quality of the speeches, Frédéric did not dare expose himself. All these people seemed to him too uneducated or too hostile.

But Dussardier made inquiries and informed him that there was a club in the Rue Saint-Jacques, called "Le Club de l'Intelligence." A name like that augured well, Anyhow, he would bring his friends there.

He brought those whom he had invited to his punch party: the bookkeeper, the traveler in wines, the architect; even Pellerin had come, while Hussonnet might turn up later; and Regimbart was standing on the sidewalk in front of the door with two companions, one of whom was his faithful Compain, a rather thick-set man, pockmarked and red-eyed, and the other an apeish dark man,

*In Fourier's scheme for the reorganization of society, a phalanstery was a building or set of buildings occupied by a phalanx or socialist community numbering about 1,800 persons.

an extremely hairy fellow whom he knew only as a "patriot from Barcelona."

They went down a passageway and were shown into a large room, probably intended as a carpenter's workshop, whose newly built walls still smelled of plaster. Four lamps hanging in a row shed a harsh light. A desk with a bell stood on a platform at the far end, below it was a table that served as a speaker's rostrum and, on either side, two lower tables for the secretaries. The audience which filled the benches was made up of old daubers, assistant schoolmasters, and unpublished writers. Along these lines of greasy-collared overcoats there appeared from time to time a woman's bonnet or a workman's overall. The back of the room, in fact, was full of workers, who had probably come out of idle curiosity or had been brought in by some of the speakers to provide them with applause.

Frédéric took care to place himself between Dussardier and Regimbart, who had hardly sat down before he folded his hands on his cane, leaned his chin on his hands, and closed his eyes, while Delmar dominated the meeting from the other end of the room.

Sénécal appeared at the chairman's desk.

Dussardier had thought that this surprise would please Frédéric. It vexed him.

The crowd showed great deference to its chairman. He was among those who, on February 25th, had demanded the immediate organization of work;* the next day, at the Prado, he had advocated an attack on the Hôtel de Ville; and as at that time everyone patterned himself on some model—one copying Saint-Just, another Danton, another Marat—Sénécal did his best to resemble Blanqui, who in his turn was imitating Robespierre. His black gloves and his cropped hair gave him a severe look that suited him very well.

He opened the session by the declaration of the rights of man and the rights of the citizen, the usual act of faith. Then a loud voice intoned Béranger's *Souvenirs du Peuple*.

Other voices cried:

"No, no, not that!"

The patriots at the back of the room started to shout: "The Cap, The Cap!"

*On February 25, 1848, the workers presented a petition demanding a guaranteed right to work and a minimum wage for a working man and his family in case of sickness or inability to work.

And they chanted in chorus a popular poem of the day:

> Doff your hats before my cap,
> On your knees to the worker!

At a word from the chairman, the audience fell silent. One of the secretaries proceeded with the reading of letters.

"Some young men announce that they will burn a copy of the *Assemblée Nationale* every evening in front of the Panthéon, and they urge all patriots to follow their example."

"Bravo! Adopted!" cried the crowd.

"Citizen Jean-Jacques Langreneux, printer, Rue Dauphine, wants a monument to the martyrs of Thermidor to be erected."

"Michel-Évariste-Népomucène Vincent, ex-professor, expresses the hope that European democracy will adopt a common language. A dead language could be used, a modernized Latin for instance."

"No, not Latin!" cried the architect.

"Why not?" a schoolmaster responded.

And the two men started an argument which others joined, each one trying to dazzle the audience with their remarks, which soon grew so tiresome that many people left.

But a little old man wearing green spectacles under an immensely high forehead asked to take the floor for an urgent communication.

It was a memorandum on the tax assessments. He reeled off endless strings of figures. At first the audience showed its impatience by murmurs and conversations; he took no notice. Then there were whistles and cries of "knock it off!" Sénécal rebuked them; the speaker went on like a machine. They had to take him by the elbow to stop him. The old man looked as if he had just awakened from a dream and, pushing up his glasses, said calmly:

"I apologize, citizens, I apologize! I'll step down! Please forgive me!"

This failure disconcerted Frédéric. He had his speech in his pocket, but an improvised address would have served him better.

At last the chairman announced that they would take up the important business of the evening, the question of

elections. They would not argue about the main lists of
republican candidates; nevertheless the "Club de l'Intelligence" had the same right as any other club to prepare
a list of its own "if it doesn't offend the pashas of the
Hôtel de Ville," and citizens who sought the people's
mandate could state their qualifications.

"Go on!" said Dussardier.

A man in a soutane, with frizzy hair and a petulant
face, had already raised his hand. He sputtered out a
declaration that his name was Ducretot and he was a
priest and agronomist, author of a work entitled "On
Fertilizers." He was sent off to join a horticultural circle.

Then a patriot in a workman's smock climbed up onto
the platform. This man was a plebeian, with broad shoulders, a plump, very gentle face, and long black hair.
He glanced around the assembly in an almost voluptuous
style, threw back his head and finally, spreading out his
arms, said:

"You have rejected Ducretot, oh my brothers! and you
have done well. But it is not for want of religion, for we
are all religious."

Many of his audience sat open-mouthed, looking like
catechumens, in ecstatic poses.

"Nor was it because he is a priest, for we too are
priests! The worker is a priest, as was the founder of
socialism, the Master of us all, Jesus Christ!"

The time had come to inaugurate the Kingdom of God!
The gospels led straight to '89. The abolition of slavery
would be followed by the abolition of the proletariat.
The age of hatred was past, the age of love was about to
begin.

"Christianity is the keystone and the foundation of the
new order . . ."

"Are you pulling our legs?" shouted the traveler in
wines. "Who's slapped this sniveling priest on us?"

This interruption shocked the assembly. Most of the
audience jumped onto the benches, shaking their fists and
howling: "Atheist! Aristocrat! Scum!" while the chairman's bell rang ceaselessly and the cries of "Order!
Order!" grew louder. But the intrepid salesman, who was,
moreover, bolstered by three "coffees" he had drunk
before coming, stood his ground in the midst of the
crowd.

"What, me! An aristocrat? What tripe!"

When he was finally given a hearing, he declared that
there would never be any real peace as long as there were

priests around and, since there had been talk of saving money earlier, a good way of doing it would be to abolish the churches, the sacred ciboriums and, finally, all forms of worship.

Someone objected that he was carrying things to extremes.

"Yes! I *am* going to extremes! But when a ship is caught in a storm . . ."

Without waiting for the end of the comparison another interrupted:

"I agree! But that would be to demolish everything at one blow, like a mason who can't distinguish . . ."

"You're insulting masons!" shouted a citizen whose clothes were covered with plaster; and, obstinately convinced that he had been provoked, he spewed out a stream of insults, tried to fight, and clung so stubbornly to his bench that three men were none too many to throw him out.

Meanwhile the workman was still standing at the rostrum. The two secretaries told him he must step down. He protested at the injustice which was being done to him.

"You can't prevent me from crying: eternal love to our beloved France! and eternal love to the Republic!"

"Citizens!" said Compain. "Citizens!"

And when, by dint of repeating, "Citizens!" he had obtained comparative silence, he leaned his red, stumplike hands on the speaker's table, bent forward and, blinking, said:

"In my opinion we should give a greater importance to the calf's head."

Everyone stopped talking, thinking that they must have misheard.

"Yes, the calf's head!"

Laughter burst simultaneously from three hundred throats. The ceiling trembled. Compain recoiled before all these faces convulsed with hilarity, then, in tones of fury, he resumed:

"What! Don't you know about the calf's head?"

This touched off a paroxysm of delirious laughter. People held their sides. Some of them even rolled on the ground under the benches. Compain, unable to stand it any longer, took refuge next to Regimbart and tried to drag him away.

"No, I shall stay till the end!" replied the Citizen.

At these words Frédéric made up his mind; and, look-

ing round for his friends to support him, he noticed
Pellerin up in front at the rostrum. The artist treated the
crowd with disdain.

"I would like to know where the candidate of Art is to
be found in all this? I have painted a picture . . ."

"Pictures are no use to us!" a thin man with red
patches on his cheeks said brutally.

Pellerin protested that he was being interrupted.

But in a tragic voice, the other went on:

"Should not the government have already passed a
decree abolishing prostitution and poverty?"

And, these words having immediately gained him the
favourable attention of the audience, he went on to rail
against the corruption of the cities.

"Shame and infamy! We should grab the bourgeois as
they come out of the Maison d'Or and spit in their faces!
If at least the government didn't encourage dissipation!
But the city tax collectors act so indecently toward our
daughters and sisters . . ."

A distant voice put in:

"What a riot!"

"Throw him out!"

"They make us pay for their debauchery! Like these
enormous salaries for actors . . ."

"Let me speak!" cried Delmar.

He jumped onto the rostrum, pushed everyone aside,
struck his pose and, declaring that he had nothing but
contempt for such empty accusations, expatiated on the
civilizing mission of the actor. Since the theater was the
medium of national education he voted for its reform and,
to start off with, there should be no more managers, no
more privileges!"

"No! No privileges of any kind!"

The actor's performance had excited the audience and
there was a sudden flurry of subversive motions:

"No more academies! Down with the Institut!"

"No more missions!"

"No more baccalauréat!"

"Down with university degrees!"

"Let us retain them," said Sénécal, "but let them be
conferred by universal suffrage, by the people, the only
true judges!"

Anyhow, this was not the most important matter. The
first thing to be done was to level down the rich. And he
pictured them gorging themselves with crime under their
gilded ceilings while the poor, writhing with hunger in

their garrets, practiced all the virtues. The applause became so loud that he paused. For a few moments he stood, his eyes closed and his head thrown back, as if rocking on the waves of the anger he had aroused.

Then he started speaking again, dogmatically, using phrases as imperious as laws. The State should take over the bank and the insurance companies. Legacies would be abolished. A public fund would be set up for the workers. There were many other measures which would be required in the future. These were enough for the moment and, reverting to the elections, he said:

"We need righteous citizens, entirely new men! Will anyone come forward?"

Frédéric stood up. There was a buzz of approval from his friends. But Sénécal, imitating the expression of a Fouquier-Tinville, started to interrogate him about his surname, first name, antecedents, life and morals.

Frédéric replied briefly, biting his lips. Sénécal asked if anyone objected to this candidacy.

"No! No!"

But Sénécal had some. Everyone leaned forward and stretched their ears. The would-be candidate had not handed over a certain sum promised for the foundation of a democratic enterprise, a paper. Moreover, on the 22nd of February, although he had been given adequate warning, he had failed to show up at the meeting point, in the Place du Panthéon.

"I swear that he was at the Tuileries!" cried Dussardier.

"Can you swear to having seen him at the Panthéon?"

Dussardier hung his head. Frédéric was silent; shocked, his friends looked at him uneasily.

"Can you at least call on one patriot to vouch for your principles?" continued Sénécal.

"I will!" said Dussardier.

"Oh, that's not enough! Someone else!"

Frédéric turned toward Pellerin. The artist's reply was a spate of gestures signifying:

"They've turned me down, dammit! What do you want me to do?"

Then Frédéric jogged Regimbart's elbow.

"Yes, you're right, it's time. I'll go up!"

And Regimbart stepped onto the platform; then, pointing to the Spaniard who had followed him, said:

"Allow me, citizens, to present to you a patriot from Barcelona!"

The patriot made a deep bow, rolled his silvery eyes like a robot and, with his hand on his heart, declared in Spanish:

*"Ciudadanos! Mucho aprecio el honor que me dispen-
sáis, y si grande es vuestra bondad mayor es vuestro
atención.**

"I demand a hearing!" cried Frédéric.

*"Desde que se proclamó la constitucion de Cadiz, ese
pacto fundemental de las libertades españolas, hasta la
ultima revolución, neustra patria cuenta numerosos y
heroicos martires."*†

Frédéric again tried to make himself heard:

"But citizens . . ."

The Spaniard continued:

*"El martes proximo tendrá lugar en la iglesia de la
Magdelena un servicio funebre."*‡

"But it's absurd. Nobody understands him!"

This observation exasperated the crowd.

"Throw him out! Throw him out!"

"Who? Me?" asked Frédéric.

"Yes!" said Sénécal majestically. "Leave!"

He got up to go and the voice of the Iberian pursued him:

*"Y todos los españoles descarian ver alli reunidas las
deputaciones de los clubs y de la milicia nacional. Une
oración funebre en honor de la libertad española y del
mundo entero, sera prononciado por un miembro del clero
de Paris en la sala Bonne-Nouvelle. Honor al pueblo
frances, que llamaría yo el primero pueblo del mundo,
sino fuese ciudadano de otra nación!"*§

"Aristo!" yelped a guttersnipe, shaking his fist at Frédéric, who rushed out into the courtyard in a state of indignation.

He upbraided himself for his devotion to the Republic,

*"Citizens! I much appreciate the honor you are doing me and I hope that your attention will equal your kindness."

†"From the time of the proclamation of the Constitution of Cadiz, that fundamental document of Spanish freedom, up to the last revolution, there have been many heroic Spanish martyrs."

‡"On next Tuesday a memorial service will be held in the Madeleine."

§"And all Spaniards hope to see there delegations from the clubs and from the National Guard. A funeral oration in honor of liberty in Spain and in the entire world will be given by a member of the Paris clergy, in the Bonne-Nouvelle room. Honor to the French people, whom I would call the greatest people in the world were I not a citizen of another country!"

without thinking that the accusations which had been brought against him were, after all, justified. What a disastrous idea this candidacy had turned out to be! But what jackasses, what cretins! He compared himself to these men and soothed his wounded pride with the thought of their stupidity.

Then he felt a desire to see Rosanette. After so much ugliness and pomposity, her sweet presence would be a refreshment. She knew that he had been going to present himself to a club that evening, but when he came in she didn't ask him a single question.

She was sitting beside the fire unpicking the lining of a dress. He was surprised to see her doing this kind of work.

"Well! What are you doing?"

"You can see," she said sharply. "I'm patching my clothes together! And it's because of your Republic!"

"Why *my* Republic?"

"Do you think it's mine?"

And she started blaming him for everything that had happened in France for the last two months, accusing him of having caused the Revolution, of being the reason why everyone was ruined, why the rich were leaving Paris, and why she would later die in the poorhouse.

"It doesn't matter to you, you and your private income! Although at the rate things are going you won't have that much longer."

"That's possible," said Frédéric, "the most dedicated ones are never appreciated, and if it weren't for your own conscience the louts you have to associate with would disgust you with the whole idea of self-sacrifice!"

Rosanette looked at him through narrowed eyes.

"Eh? What? What self-sacrifice? Monsieur didn't have much success it seems! All the better! That will teach you to give patriotic donations! Oh, don't deny it! I know you gave them three hundred francs; after all you have to pay for her keep don't you, your Republic! All right, go play with her, my boy!"

Under this avalanche of idiocy, Frédéric's other disappointment was lost in a more painful disillusionment.

He had retreated to the far end of the room. She followed him.

"Look, just think it over for a moment! A country is like a household, there must be a master; otherwise everyone takes their cut of the housekeeping money. In the first place, everyone knows that Ledru-Rollin is loaded with

debts! As for Lamartine, how do you expect a poet to
understand politics? Oh, it's all very well for you to shake
your head and think that you're cleverer than the rest of
us, it's still the truth! But you always quibble about everything, no one else can get a word in edgewise! Look at
Fournier-Fontaine, for example, the one with the Saint-
Roch shops: do you know how much he lost? Eight hundred thousand francs! And Gomer, the carrier across the
street, another republican. He broke the pincers over his
wife's head and he's drunk so much absinthe that they're
going to shut him up in an asylum. That's what they're
all like, your republicans! A cut-rate republic! Oh, yes,
you've got something to boast about!"

Frédéric went off. The woman's stupidity, suddenly revealed in this vulgar language, disgusted him. He even
felt his patriotism reviving a little.

Rosanette's temper continued to deteriorate. Mademoiselle Vatnaz's enthusiasm irritated her. Believing that she
had a mission, La Vatnaz adored haranguing and cate-
chising, and, being cleverer than her friend about these
things, would overwhelm her with arguments.

One day she arrived furious with Hussonnet, who had
just presumed to make some loose jokes at the women's
club. Rosanette approved of this behavior and even declared that she would put on men's clothes herself, to go
and tell those women off and give them a whipping. Frédéric came in at that moment and Rosanette appealed to
him:

"You'd come with me, wouldn't you?"

And, despite his presence, they went on squabbling,
one taking the viewpoint of the housewife and the other
that of the philosopher.

According to Rosanette, women had been created solely for love or for bringing up children and running
a house.

In Mademoiselle Vatnaz' view, women should have
their place in the State. In former times the women of the
Gauls made laws and so did the Anglo-Saxons, and the
wives of the Hurons belonged to the tribal council. The
work of civilization was common to both men and women.
Every woman should contribute to it, so that at last selfishness would be replaced by brotherhood, individualism
by association, and small-holding by collective farming.

"So you're an expert on agriculture now, are you?"

"Why not? Anyhow, I'm talking about humanity, and
its future!"

"You'd better take care of your own!"

"That's my business!"

They were getting angry. Frédéric intervened. The Vatnaz, growing more and more excited, even went so far as to uphold communism.

"It's so stupid!" said Rosanette. "How could it ever work?"

Her opponent cited the Essenes, the Moravian Brethren, the Jesuits in Paraguay, the Pingon family near Thiers in the Auvergne; and she was gesticulating so freely that her watch chain got caught on a little gold sheep hanging in her bundle of charms.

Rosanette suddenly grew extraordinarily pale.

Mademoiselle Vatnaz went on untangling her trinket.

"You needn't take so much trouble," said Rosanette; "now I know all about your political opinions!"

"What?" said the Vatnaz, blushing like a virgin.

"Oh, you understand what I mean!"

Frédéric was at a loss. It was obvious that something more important and more intimate than socialism had come up between them.

"Well, what of it?" replied the Vatnaz, drawing herself up boldly. "It's a loan, my dear, debt for debt!"

"I'm not denying mine, dammit! For a few thousand francs, that's a likely story! I borrow at least; I don't steal from anyone!"

Mademoiselle Vatnaz forced a laugh.

"Oh, I'd put my hand in the fire on that!"

"Be careful! It's dry enough to burn!"

The older woman stuck out her right hand toward Rosanette and, holding it up just in front of her, said:

"But some of your friends find it suits them!"

"Andalusians, perhaps? To use as castanets?"

"Whore!"

The Maréchale bowed low:

"No one could be more ravishing!"

Mademoiselle Vatnaz made no reply. Beads of sweat stood on her temples. Her eyes were fixed on the carpet. She was panting for breath. Finally she went out of the door and, slamming it behind her, said:

"Good-night! You'll be hearing from me!"

"I look forward to it!" said Rosanette.

Her self-control had exhausted her. She fell onto the divan trembling, stammering out insults, shedding tears. Was it the Vatnaz' threat that was worrying her? No, she couldn't care less about that! Well, perhaps the other owed her some money? No, it was the gold sheep, a present; and, in the midst of her tears, Delmar's name escaped her. So she loved that ham!

"Then why did she accept me?" wondered Frédéric. "How did he get back into the picture? Why doesn't she get rid of me? What does the whole thing mean?"

Rosanette's little sobs continued. She was still on the divan, lying on one side, her right cheek resting on her hands—and she seemed so delicate, so self-conscious and so sad that he went over and kissed her gently on her forehead.

Then she assured him of her love for him; the prince had just left, they would be free. But, for the moment, she was . . . having difficulties. "You saw for yourself the other day, when I was using my old linings." No more carriages for the moment! And that was not all; the upholsterer was threatening to take back the furniture in the bedroom and the large drawing room. She didn't know what to do.

Frédéric had an impulse to reply: "Don't worry, I'll pay!" But the lady might be lying. He had learned from experience. He limited himself to consoling words.

Rosanette's fears were not empty; she did have to send back the furniture and give up the beautiful apartment in the Rue Drouot. She took another, on the Boulevard Poissonnière, on the fourth floor. There were enough knickknacks from her former boudoir to make the three rooms look elegant. There were Chinese blinds, an awning on the terrace, and a card table which still looked new, and pink silk poufs in the drawing room. Frédéric had contributed liberally to these acquisitions; he felt the gratification of a young husband who at last has a house and a wife of his own; and he enjoyed himself so much in the apartment that he slept there almost every night.

One morning, as he was coming out of the vestibule, he saw the shako of a National Guardsman who was climbing the stairs and had already reached the third floor. Where could he be going? Frédéric waited. The man continued upwards, his head slightly bent; then he raised his eyes. It was Arnoux. The situation was clear. They blushed at the same moment, gripped by the same embarrassment.

Arnoux was the first to find a way out.

"She's better, I hope?" he said, as if Rosanette had been sick and he had come round to inquire after her.

Frédéric made the most of this opening.

"Yes, certainly. At least so her maid told me," attempting to imply that he had not been admitted.

Then they stood face to face, each unsure of what to do and observing the other. It was a question of which of them would stay. Once again it was Arnoux who found the solution.

"Oh well, I'll come back later! Where are you going? I'll keep you company!"

And when they reached the street, he chattered away as naturally as ever. Probably he was not a jealous man, or perhaps he was too good-natured to be angry.

Anyhow, he was preoccupied with the state of the country. Nowadays he was never out of uniform. He had taken part in the defense of the offices of *La Presse* on March 29th. When the chamber of deputies had been invaded he had been conspicuous by his courage; and he had attended the banquet in honor of the National Guard of Amiens.*

Hussonnet, who was always on duty with him, used Arnoux's flask and his cigars more than anyone else but, irreverent by nature, amused himself by contradicting him, disparaging the ungrammatical style of the decrees, the conferences at the Luxembourg, the Vesuvians,† the Tyroleans, everything, down to the Chariot of Agriculture, which was drawn by horses instead of oxen and escorted by a bevy of unattractive girls. Arnoux, on the other hand, defended the authorities and dreamed of the fusion of all the parties. Meanwhile, his business affairs had taken a turn for the worse. This appeared to worry him very little.

Frédéric's liaison with the Maréchale did not distress him, for this discovery justified him (in his own eyes) in cutting off the allowance which he had begun paying her again after the prince's departure. He pleaded financial problems, loudly bewailed his lot, and Rosanette was gen-

*The offices of *La Presse* were attacked by a crowd of republican demonstrators after the publication of an article by Émile de Girardin inquiring what the government would do if the Assembly did not proclaim the Republic. The Chamber of Deputies was occupied on May 15, 1848, by rioters demonstrating for the dissolution of the Assembly, who were dispersed by the National Guard.

†The conferences at the Luxembourg, presided over by Louis Blanc, dealt with the organization of labor. The Vesuvians were women of dubious morals who had founded a club, "Club de la Légion des Vésuviennes," ostensibly to promote the cause of women's rights.

erous. From then on Monsieur Arnoux considered himself her real lover, which raised him in his own esteem and made him feel much younger. Never suspecting that Frédéric was not paying the Maréchale, he imagined that he was "playing a good joke" on his young friend and was even prepared to keep it secret and to leave the field to him when they met.

This system of sharing hurt Frédéric's feelings, and his rival's courtesies seemed to him a joke that had gone on long enough. But to quarrel would be to cut off any chance of returning to Madame Arnoux; and then, seeing her husband was his only way of getting news of her. The china-merchant, either out of habit or through malice, often referred to her in his conversation and even asked Frédéric why he did not come around to see her anymore.

Frédéric, having exhausted all his excuses, assured him that he had been to the house several times without finding her at home. Arnoux believed him, for he often marveled in front of his wife over their friend's absence, and she always responded that she had been out when he called, so that, rather than contradicting, the two lies corroborated each other.

The young man's meekness and the pleasure of duping him made Arnoux cherish him more than ever. He carried familiarity to its farthest limits, not because he despised Frédéric but because he trusted him. One day he wrote to tell him that he had to go to the provinces for twenty-four hours on urgent business and begged him to stand guard in his place. Frédéric dared not refuse and reported for duty at the guard-post near the Carrousel.

He had to put up with the company of the National Guardsmen. Except for a metal-refiner, a jocular fellow who drank an enormous amount, they all seemed to him as stupid as their cartridge pouches. Their main topic of conversation was the replacement of their buff-leather equipment with sword belts. Others railed against the national workshops.* One would say: "What are things coming to?" The person addressed would widen his eyes, as if he had reached the edge of an abyss, and reply: "What

---

*These had been organized, by a decree on February 27, 1848, for the benefit of unemployed workers, who received a wage of two francs a day. Apart from costing the State fifteen hundred thousand francs a day, these workshops were a center of violent socialist agitation, which frightened the middle classes and paralyzed commerce.

are things coming to?" at which some bolder spirit would cry: "It can't go on like this! We must put a stop to it!" As the same conversations were repeated all day long, Frédéric was bored to death.

He was greatly surprised when Arnoux appeared at eleven o'clock, explaining immediately that he had come to relieve him, for his business was completed.

There had never been any business. It was a trick of Arnoux's to get Rosanette to himself for twenty-four hours. But the gallant Arnoux had overestimated himself, and in his exhaustion remorse had overtaken him so he had come to thank Frédéric and take him out to dinner.

"Many thanks, but I'm not hungry! All I want is my bed!"

"All the more reason for eating together in a while! How spineless you are! No one goes home at this hour! It's too late, it would be dangerous!"

Frédéric gave in once again. No one had expected to see Arnoux; and his brothers-in-arms made a great fuss over him, especially the refiner. Everybody liked him, and he was such a good-humored man that he even regretted Hussonnet's absence. But he had to close his eyes just for a moment.

"Sit beside me," he said to Frédéric as he lay down on the camp bed without taking off his equipment. Fearing an alert he even kept his musket with him, against the regulations; and, babbling a few words: "My dearest! My little angel!" he lost no time dropping off to sleep.

The talking stopped and, little by little, complete silence descended on the post. Frédéric, who was being eaten alive by fleas, looked around him. Half-way up the yellow-painted wall was a long shelf, where the knapsacks formed a row of little humps; underneath, the lead-colored muskets stood side by side, and the air was filled with the sound of snores from the National Guardsmen, their stomachs dimly visible in the darkness. An empty bottle and some plates stood on the stove. Three straw-bottomed chairs were drawn up to the table, where a card game had been spread out. A drum lay in the middle of the bench, its shoulder strap dangling. The warm breeze from the open door made the lamp smoke. Arnoux was sleeping with his arms stretched out and, as his musket was resting at a slight angle, with its butt on the floor, the muzzle was under his armpit. Frédéric noticed this and was alarmed.

"But no, I'm wrong, there's nothing to be afraid of!
But suppose he died . . ."

And immediately his head was filled with an endless
succession of pictures. He saw himself with Her, at night,
in a post-chaise; then beside a river on a summer evening
and in the lamplight at home, in their own house. He even
dwelt upon domestic details and household arrangements,
contemplating and handling his happiness already—and all
that was needed to bring it about was for the hammer of
the musket to be cocked! He could push it with the tip of
his toe, the gun would go off, it would be an accident,
nothing more!

Frédéric elaborated on this idea, like a dramatist writing a play. Suddenly it seemed to him that it was about
to be enacted, that he was going to play his part, that he
wanted to; at this he was filled with terror. But in the
midst of this agony he experienced a certain pleasure and
he buried himself more and more deeply in it, feeling with
dismay his scruples melting away; in the frenzy of his
reverie the rest of the world disappeared and he was only
conscious of himself because of an unbearable tightness
in his chest.

"Shall we have some white wine?" said the refiner, who
had just woken up.

Arnoux jumped to his feet and, having disposed of the
white wine, wanted to take over Frédéric's sentry duty.

Afterwards, he took him to dinner at Parly's, in the Rue
de Chartres, and as he needed to build himself up, he
ordered two meat dishes, a lobster, a rum omelette, a
salad, and so on, washing it all down with an 1819
Sauterne and a '42 Romanée, not to mention champagne
with the dessert, and liqueurs.

Frédéric made no effort to stop him. He was uncomfortable, as if Arnoux could have seen the trace of his
thoughts on his face.

Arnoux put both his elbows on the table and, leaning
forward and gazing unwaveringly into Frédéric's face, he
confided his schemes to him.

He would like to take a lease on all the Northern Railway's embankments and plant them with potatoes, or to
organize a gigantic parade along the boulevards featuring
"celebrities of the day." He would rent out all the windows which, at an average of three francs, would bring
in a pretty penny. In short, he dreamed of cornering some
market to make his fortune in a single stroke. He had his
principles, however; he disapproved of excesses and mis-

conduct, spoke of his "poor father," and, so he said, examined his conscience every evening before offering up his soul to God.

"What about a little curaçao, eh?"

"Whatever you say."

As for the Republic, things would work themselves out; all things considered, he was the happiest man on earth and, forgetting himself, he vaunted Rosanette's qualities, even comparing her with his wife. They were in quite a different class! It was impossible to imagine more beautiful thighs!

"Your health!"

Frédéric drank. Out of politeness, he had drunk a little too much; besides, the bright sunlight made him dizzy and, when they retraced their steps up the Rue Vivienne, their epaulets rubbed together in brotherly fashion.

When he got home Frédéric slept till seven, then went to the Maréchale's. She had gone out with someone. With Arnoux, perhaps? Not knowing what to do, he walked on along the boulevard but there were so many people at the Porte Saint-Martin that he could go no farther.

Conditions had thrown a sizable number of workers onto their own resources and they gathered there every evening, probably to take stock of themselves and wait for some signal. In spite of the law against public assemblies, these "Clubs of Despair" were growing at a frightening pace; and many middle-class persons visited them daily, out of bravado or because it was the fashion.

Suddenly three paces away Frédéric caught sight of Monsieur Dambreuse accompanied by Martinon. He looked away, for he bore a grudge against Monsieur Dambreuse, who had got himself elected to the Assembly. But the capitalist stopped him.

"A word with you if you please, sir! I owe you an explanation."

"I haven't asked for one."

"Please, listen to me."

He was completely blameless. He had been begged, almost compelled, to act as he did. Martinon immediately confirmed this; a deputation of people from Nogent had arrived at his house.

"Moreover, I considered myself free to accept, since . . ."

A surge of people on the sidewalk forced Monsieur Dambreuse to draw back. A moment later he reappeared, saying to Martinon:

"You really did me a good turn. You won't regret it . . ."

The three of them stood with their backs to the wall of a shop to converse more easily.

From time to time shouts of: "Long live Napoléon! Long live Barbès! Down with Marie!"* rang out. Everyone in the enormous crowd was talking at the top of his voice; and all the voices, reverberating from the houses, made a sound like the perpetual lapping of the waves in a harbor. Occasionally they would fall silent and then the "Marseillaise" would ring out.

Under the porte-cochères mysterious looking men were offering sword-sticks for sale. Occasionally, two men would pass each other, wink, and make off hastily. The sidewalks were filled with groups of idlers; a dense throng occupied the street. Whole groups of policemen disappeared into the crowd as soon as they emerged from the side alleys. There were little red flags here and there, which looked like flames; high on their boxes, coachmen waved their arms, then turned back. All this commotion made a most entertaining spectacle.

"How Mademoiselle Cécile would have enjoyed all this!" said Martinon.

"As you well know, my wife doesn't like my niece to accompany us," replied Monsieur Dambreuse with a smile.

He was almost unrecognizable. For the last three months he had been shouting: "Long live the Republic!" and he had even voted for the banishment of the Orléans family. But these concessions had to end. He had become enraged to the point of carrying a blackjack in his pocket.

Martinon had one too. Since appointments to the judiciary were no longer for life, he had left the public prosecutor's office; and in consequence his attitude was even more violent than Monsieur Dambreuse's.

The banker particularly hated Lamartine (for his support of Ledru-Rollin) and he also detested Pierre Leroux, Proudhon, Considérant, Lemennais, all the wild men, all the socialists.

"For, after all, what do they want? The tax on meat is abolished, and debtor's prison too; a plan for a mortgage

*Louis-Napoléon, afterwards Napoleon III, had returned to Paris from London after the revolution in February, made overtures to the provisional government which were rejected, and gone back to London leaving behind numerous partisans who were working on his behalf. Marie was the deputy who had introduced the law against illegal assemblies and was, therefore, extremely unpopular.

bank is under discussion right now, and only the other day it was a national bank! And five million francs budgeted for the workers! But mercifully that's all over, thanks to Monsieur de Falloux.* Let them take themselves off! Good riddance!"

Indeed, having no idea how to provide food for the hundred and thirty million men in the national workshops, the Minister of Public Works had that very day signed a decree suggesting that all citizens between the ages of eighteen and twenty should either enlist as soldiers or leave for the provinces to work on the land.

This alternative aroused the people's indignation and convinced them that an attempt was being made to destroy the Republic. The thought of life away from the capital saddened them as though they were being sent into exile; they imagined themselves dying of fever in primitive lands. Many of them, moreover, were accustomed to skilled work, and to them agricultural labor seemed a degradation; in short it was a trap, a mockery, an express denial of every promise that had been made to them. If they resisted, force would be used against them; they were fully aware of it and were taking measures to forestall it.

Toward nine o'clock the crowds which had gathered at the Bastille and the Châtelet surged out onto the boulevard. From the Porte Saint-Denis to the Porte Saint-Martin, there was nothing but a swarming mass of men, a single block of deep blue, almost black. All the men one caught sight of had burning eyes, pale complexions, and faces drawn with hunger and frenzied by injustice. Meanwhile the clouds were piling up; the stormy sky had the same effect on the mob as a charge of electricity and it swirled about undecidedly, swaying like the sea. In its depths one could sense an incalculable strength, an elemental energy. Then everyone started chanting "Lights! Lights!"† Several windows remained dark; their panes were shattered by stones. Monsieur Dambreuse thought it prudent to leave. The two young men saw him home.

He foresaw great disasters. The mob might invade the

---

*Monsieur de Falloux, the head of a committee appointed by the government to investigate the national workshops, had recommended their immediate dissolution.

†Ever since the Restoration it had been customary for mobs in Paris to raise this cry, at which all householders were meant to show their solidarity with the demonstrators by putting lights in their windows.

Chamber again, and in this connection he told them how
he would have been killed on May 15th, had it not been
for the bravery of a National Guardsman.

"But he's a friend of yours—I was forgetting. Your
friend the porcelain manufacturer, Jacques Arnoux!" He
had been suffocating in the midst of the rioters when the
gallant citizen had picked him up bodily and carried him
out of the crowd. Since then, a sort of bond had grown
up between them.

"We must all have dinner together one of these days
and, since you see him frequently, do tell him I'm very
fond of him. He's an excellent fellow and I think he's
been greatly slandered; an amusing rascal too! My regards
once again, and a very good evening to you!"

After leaving Monsieur Dambreuse, Frédéric went back
to the Maréchale's and told her with great gravity that
she must choose between himself and Arnoux. She replied gently that she didn't understand "that kind of gossip," was not in love with Arnoux and, in fact, didn't care
for him in the least. Frédéric was eager to leave Paris.
She humored his whim and they left for Fontainebleau
the following day.

The hotel at which they stayed differed from the others
in having a fountain splashing in the middle of its courtyard. The doors of the bedrooms opened onto a gallery,
as they do in monasteries. Theirs was large, well furnished, hung with chintz and, thanks to the scarcity of
travelers, quiet. Prosperous citizens with time on their
hands strolled along in front of the houses, and in the
evenings children played prisoner's base in the street under their windows; and this tranquillity, coming after the
tumult of Paris, surprised and soothed them.

Early in the morning, they set off to visit the palace.
As they stepped through the gate they could see the entire
front of the building, the five towers with their pointed
roofs and the horseshoe-shaped staircase at the far side
of the courtyard, which was flanked on either side by two
blocks of lower buildings. The lichens on the paving stones
blended in the distance with the tawny hue of the bricks
and the whole palace, rust-colored like an old suit of
armor, had an air of regal impassivity, a sort of grandeur
at once martial and melancholy.

Finally, a servant appeared, carrying a bunch of keys.
First he showed them the queen's apartments, then the
Pope's oratory, the François I gallery, the little mahogany
table on which the Emperor had signed his abdication

and, in one of the rooms into which the old Galérie des Cerfs had been divided, the spot where Christina had had Monaldeschi assassinated. Rosanette listened attentively then, turning to Frédéric, remarked:

"She did it out of jealousy, I suppose. Watch out!"

After this they went through the Council Chamber, the Guard Room, the Throne Room, Louis XIII's salon. A pale light came from the high, uncurtained windows, a thin film of dust dulled the window catches, and the bronze feet of the console tables, the armchairs, were all hidden under coarse sheets; there were Louis XV hunting scenes above the doors, and here and there hung tapestries representing the gods of Olympus, Psyche, or Alexander's battles.

Whenever she passed a looking-glass Rosanette would pause for a moment and smooth her hair.

After going through the Turret Court and the Chapel of Saint-Saturnin, they reached the banqueting hall.

They were dazzled by the splendor of the ceiling, divided into octagonal panels embossed with gold and silver, carved more beautifully than any jewel, and by the vast quantity of paintings that covered the walls from the enormous fireplace, with the arms of France surrounded by crescent moons and quivers, to the minstrels' gallery at the far end stretching the whole width of the room. The ten colonnaded windows were wide open; the sunlight made the paintings glisten; the blue sky extended the ultramarine of the arches into infinity; and, from the depths of the woods whose misty treetops filled the horizon, there seemed to come an echo of the mort sounded on ivory horns, and of those mythological pageants in which princesses and lords disguised as nymphs and wood-gods were brought together under the leafy branches— an age of uncomplicated science, violent passions, and sumptuous art, when men strove to transform the world into a dream of the Gardens of the Hesperides and when king's mistresses seemed like stars. The most beautiful of these renowned ladies had had herself painted, to the right, in the guise of Diana the Huntress and even as Diana of the Underworld, no doubt to denote the reach of her power even beyond the gates of death. All these symbols confirmed her glory; and in this room something of her still lingered, the murmur of a voice, a distant radiance.

Frédéric was seized by an indescribable feeling of retrospective lust. To distract his desire he gazed tenderly at

Rosanette, asking her if she would not have liked to be that woman.

"What woman?"

"Diane de Poitiers!"

He repeated:

"Diane de Poitiers, the mistress of Henri II."

She gave a little "Ah!" That was all.

Her silence made it obvious that she knew and understood nothing, so that out of politeness he said:

"Perhaps you're bored?"

"No, no, on the contrary!"

And, raising her chin and glancing vaguely around her, Rosanette remarked:

"It brings back memories!"

However, her face betrayed that she was making an effort and intended to show respect and, as this grave expression made her prettier than ever, Frédéric forgave her.

She was more amused by the carp pond, where she spent a quarter of an hour throwing pieces of bread into the water so that she could watch the fish jumping for them.

Frédéric had sat down next to her, under the lime trees. He thought of all the people who had moved within these walls, Charles V, the Valois, Henri IV, Peter the Great, Jean-Jacques Rousseau and "the beautiful women who wept in the stage boxes,"* Voltaire, Napoléon, Pius VII, Louis-Philippe; he felt beset and jostled by the tumultuous dead, and his head was filled with such a profusion of images that he was dazed, even though it pleased him.

Eventually they went down into the flower garden.

It is an enormous rectangle displaying to a single glance its broad yellow paths, squares of turf, box edgings, pyramid-shaped yews, low shrubs, and narrow flowerbeds where sparsely sown flowers make splashes of color against the gray earth. At the far end of the garden lies a park whose entire length is divided by a long canal.

There is a peculiar melancholy about royal residences, probably stemming from their size too great for their few inhabitants, their silence which is surprising after so many fanfares, and their unchanging luxury, whose age under-

---

*A reference to Rousseau's *Confessions*, where he describes the first performance of his operetta "Le Devin du Village" at Fontainebleau. Rousseau sat in a box surrounded by ladies of the court, who wept at the more pathetic moments.

lines the transience of dynasties, the eternal vanity of all things; and this exhalation of the centuries, numbing and funereal as the scent of a mummy, has its effect on even the most ingenuous mind. Rosanette yawned immoderately. They went back to the hotel.

After they had lunched, an open carriage was brought around. They left Fontainebleau by way of a large circle where several roads converged, then proceeded at a walk up a sandy road through a coppice of small pine trees. The trees became larger and now and then the coachman would say: "There are the Siamese Twins, the Pharamond, the King's Nosegay . . ." omitting none of the famous beauty spots, sometimes even stopping so that his passengers could admire them.

They entered the Forest of Franchard. The carriage slid forward over the turf like a sleigh; unseen pigeons cooed; suddenly a waiter appeared and they got out of the carriage at a fenced garden full of little round tables. Then, leaving the walls of a ruined abbey to their left, they walked across some large rocks and soon reached the bottom of the gorge.

One side of it was a jumble of sandstone slabs and juniper bushes while the other, almost bare, sloped down to the hollow of the valley, where a path made a pale line through the purple of the heather; and in the distance rose the crest of a hill like a flattened cone, with a telegraph tower behind it.

Half an hour later, they stepped out of the carriage again, this time to climb the heights of Aspremont.

The path zigzagged among the squat pines beneath the sharp-edged rocks; there is something muffled, rather silent and meditative about this whole part of the forest. It makes one think of the hermits, companions of the great deer with fiery crosses between their horns, who welcomed with paternal smiles the good kings of France who knelt before their grottos. The warm air was filled with the smell of resin and the roots on the ground were interwoven like veins. Rosanette, stumbling over them, lost heart and felt like weeping.

But when they reached the summit she recovered her spirits on finding, under a roof thatched with branches, a sort of tavern where they sold wood-carvings. She drank a bottle of lemonade, bought herself a walking-stick made out of holly and, without a glance at the view from the plateau, disappeared into the Brigands' Cave in the wake of a small boy carrying a torch.

Their carriage was waiting for them at Bas-Bréau.

A painter in a blue smock was working under an oak tree, with his paint box on his knees. He lifted his head and watched them as they passed.

Halfway down the Chailly slope, a sudden cloudburst forced them to put up the hood. The rain stopped almost at once, and the paving stones of the roadway were shining in the sun when they came back to the town.

Some travelers who had just arrived told them that a dreadful battle was drenching Paris in blood. Rosanette and her lover were not surprised. Then everyone left, the hotel was peaceful again, the gas was extinguished, and they fell asleep to the murmur of the fountain in the courtyard.

The next day they went to see the Wolf's Gorge, the Fairies' Pond, the Long Rock, the Marlotte; the day after, they set off again without any definite objective, leaving the route to their coachman, without asking where they were, and often even neglecting famous beauty spots.

They were so comfortable in their old landau, which was as low as a sofa and upholstered in a faded, striped fabric! Ditches full of brushwood unrolled before their eyes in a gentle, continuous movement. White sunbeams cut like arrows through the tall ferns; sometimes a disused road appeared right in front of them, with occasional ragged plants growing out of it. In the middle of the crossroads signposts stretched out their four arms; elsewhere, stakes leaned over like dead trees, and little crooked paths, disappearing under the leaves, roused a yearning to follow them; immediately, the horse would turn in that direction and they would sink into the mud; farther on, moss grew on the edges of deep ruts.

They felt as if they were far from human existence, completely isolated. Then, suddenly, they would pass a gamekeeper with his gun or a group of ragged women with long faggots on their backs.

When the carriage stopped, the silence was complete; all that could be heard was the breathing of the horse between the shafts and the repeated notes of a barely audible bird call.

In some places, the light struck the fringes of the wood, leaving its depths in shadow; in others, it would be dimmed to a sort of twilight in the foreground, while shining with a white clarity in the violet-misted distance. At midday the sun beat down onto the broad expanse of verdure, spattering it with light, hanging silver drops on

the tips of the branches, striping the turf with trails of
emeralds, splashing the drifts of dead leaves with gold;
looking upwards one could see the sky between the tops
of the trees. Some of them were immensely tall and had
the look of patriarchs and emperors, or leaned together,
so that their long trunks formed arcades fit for a
triumphal procession; others grew obliquely and resembled
columns about to fall.

This throng of thick vertical lines would open out a
little and then immense billows of green undulated away
to the bottom of the valleys where they met the ridges of
other hills, over straw-colored plains, which finally disappeared in an indefinite pale haze.

Standing side by side on some piece of high ground
they sniffed at the wind, and felt their hearts swelling with
the pride of a free life, an overflowing vitality, an un-
reasoning joy.

The different kinds of trees offered an ever-varying
spectacle. The beeches, with their pale, smooth bark, in-
terwove their leafy crowns; the glaucous boughs of the
ash trees curved softly downward; bronze hollys bristled
among the young hornbeams; then came a row of slender
birches, bent over in elegiac attitudes; and pines, symmetrical as organ pipes, which seemed to sing as they
swayed unceasingly. There were enormous rugged oak
trees, which stretched writhing from the ground, clasping
one another and, standing firmly on their torsolike
trunks, threw out their naked arms in gestures of despair
and wild menace, like a group of Titans immobilized in
their anger. A heavier atmosphere, a feverish languor,
hovered over the ponds that spread their sheets of water
among thickets of thorns; the lichens along their banks,
where the wolves come down to drink, were the color of
sulphur, burned as if by the footsteps of a witch; and the
continual croaking of the frogs echoed the cries of the
wheeling crows. Afterwards they crossed monotonous
clearings, with an occasional sapling standing where it had
been left when the rest were cut down. The sound of iron
on stone rang out, the blows falling thick and fast; it was
a group of quarrymen working among the rocks. These
rocks became more and more numerous, until in the end
they filled the entire landscape; cube-shaped, like houses,
or flat as tiles, propping each other up, overhanging one
another, jumbled together like the unrecognizable and
monstrous ruins of some vanished city. But the very fury
of their chaos made one think rather of volcanos, of

floods, of gigantic, unknown cataclysms. Frédéric said that
they had been there since the beginning of the world and
would stay so to the end; Rosanette turned away her
head, remarking that "it would drive her mad," and went
off to pick heather. Its little purple flowers grew closely together, in uneven patches, and the earth trickled down
from beneath, the plants fringing with black the mica-
sparkling sand.

One day they climbed halfway up an enormous sand
dune. Its untrodden surface was marked with symmetrical
undulations; here and there, like promontories on the bed
of a dried-up ocean, rose rocks bearing a vague resemblance to animals, tortoises poking out their heads, seals
slithering forward, hippopotamuses, and bears. No one.
Not a sound. The sands shone dazzlingly in the sun—and
suddenly, in that quivering light, the beasts seemed to
move. They turned back quickly, fleeing their vertigo, almost afraid.

They took on the gravity of the forest; and they spent
hours of silence when, abandoning themselves to the rocking of the springs, they sat as if stupefied in a state of calm
intoxication. With his arm round her waist, he listened to
her chatter while the birds twittered, and even took in
with the same glance the black grapes on her hood and
the berries on the juniper bushes, the folds of her veil,
and the scrolls of the clouds; and, when he leaned toward
her, the fresh scent of her skin mingled with the all-
encompassing smell of the woods. Everything interested
them; they showed one another, as if they had been
curiosities, strands of gossamer hanging on the bushes,
holes full of water in the middle of stones, a squirrel in
the branches, two butterflies chasing each other or, under
the trees some twenty yards away a doe calmly walking
past with a gentle and noble air, her fawn at her side.
Rosanette would have liked to run after them to give it a
hug.

She was very frightened once when a man suddenly appeared in front of her and showed her three vipers in a
box. She threw herself into Frédéric's arms and he was
happy to feel that she was weak and that he was strong
enough to protect her.

That evening they had dinner in an inn beside the Seine.
Their table was next to the window; Rosanette sat opposite him and he gazed at her white, delicately molded little
nose, her pouting lips, her bright eyes, her curly chestnut
hair, her pretty oval face. Her natural-colored silk dress

clung to her rather sloping shoulders while her hands, emerging from their simple cuffs, cut up her food, poured out wine, and moved over the tablecloth. They dined off a chicken, with its wings and legs sticking out, an eel stew served in an earthenware pot, harsh wine, hard bread, and chipped knives. All this added to their enjoyment, to their illusions. They almost believed themselves to be traveling in Italy, on their honeymoon.

Before leaving they went for a walk along the riverside.

The sky was a soft blue, rounded like a dome, and supported at the horizon by the notched line of the woods. Before them, on the far side of the meadows, stood the tower of a village church; and farther away, to the left, the roof of a house made a splash of red on the river, whose entire, sinuous length seemed to be motionless. The reeds bent over, however, and the water pushed against the poles stuck in the banks to serve as anchors for nets, and made them tremble slightly; there were two or three old rowboats and a wicker eel-pot. Near the inn, a girl in a straw hat was drawing water from a well; and each time the bucket came up, Frédéric listened to the creaking of the chain with an inexpressible joy.

He had no doubt that his present happiness would continue till the end of his life, it seemed so natural, inherent in his life and in this woman. His need made him speak tenderly to her. She responded by loving words, little touches on the shoulder, and in sweet ways whose unexpectedness charmed him. He found a completely new beauty in her, which may have been no more than the reflection of their surroundings, unless it was that their secret potentialities had brought her into flower.

When they rested in the countryside he would lie down with his head on her knees, in the shade of her parasol; or, sprawled on their stomachs in the middle of the grass, they looked into one another's eyes, thirsting for each other, a thirst they were always quenching and then lying silent with half-shut eyes.

Sometimes they would hear the roll of a distant drum. It was the alarm, which was being beaten in the villages to call people to the defense of Paris.

"Oh yes, the riots!" Frédéric would say, in tones of pitying disdain; all this agitation seemed petty to him, compared to their love and eternal nature.

They talked of anything and everything, of things they knew thoroughly, of people who did not interest them, of

a thousand and one foolish trifles. She told him about her
maid and her hairdresser. One day she forgot herself and
let slip her age: twenty-nine; she was getting old.

Several times, without meaning to, she mentioned details of her earlier life. She had been "a young lady in a
shop," had visited England and begun studying to be an
actress, but all these were isolated facts and he was unable
to reconstruct the whole picture. She told him more one
day when they were sitting under a plane tree beside a
meadow. Below them, on the edge of the road, a cow was
grazing, watched by a little girl, her feet bare in the dust.
As soon as she noticed them she came to ask for charity
and, holding up her ragged petticoat with one hand, she
scratched her black hair, which surrounded her head like
a seventeenth-century peruke, with the other. Her brown
face was lit up by a pair of splendid eyes.

"She'll be a beauty later," said Frédéric.

"She's in luck if she hasn't got a mother!" replied
Rosanette.

"Eh? What?"

"Oh yes, if it hadn't been for my mother . . ."

And she started talking about her childhood. Her parents had been silk-weavers in the Croix-Rousse district of
Lyons. She had acted as her father's apprentice. Although
the poor man worked to the point of exhaustion, his wife
used to curse him and sold everything to buy drink.
Rosanette could still see their room, with the looms along
the wall by the windows, the stockpot on the stove, the
bed painted to look like mahogany, the cupboard opposite
it, and the dark loft where she had slept until she was
fifteen. In the end a gentleman had come, a fat man with
a face the color of boxwood, and pious mannerisms,
dressed in black. He had a talk with her mother, with the
result that, three days later . . . Rosanette paused and,
with a shameless, bitter look, concluded:

"It was done!"

Then, in response to Frédéric's gesture:

"As he was married, and was afraid of being discovered
if it had happened at his house, I was taken to a private
room in a restaurant. I'd been told that I would be happy,
that I'd be given a fine present.

"The first thing that struck me when I came in at the
door was a silver candelabrum on a table set with two
places. It was reflected in a mirror on the ceiling, and the
blue silk covering the walls made the entire room look
like a sleeping alcove. I was thunderstruck. You can imag-

ine, a poor creature who'd never seen anything! In spite of being dazzled I was scared. I wanted to leave. But I stayed.

"The only seat was a divan next to the table. It gave softly under me, the heating vent under the carpet puffed warm air at me; and I sat there without touching anything. The waiter, who was standing, tried to get me to eat. He poured out a large glass of wine for me immediately; my head swam and I wanted to open the window but he said: 'No, mademoiselle, that's not allowed.' Then he left me by myself. The table was covered with a mass of things I had never seen before. Nothing looked good to me. So I fell back on a pot of jam and I went on waiting. I didn't know what was keeping him. It was very late, midnight at least, and I was exhausted; pushing back one of the cushions to have more room to stretch out, I found a sort of album under my hand, a portfolio; it was full of obscene pictures . . . I was asleep on top of it when he came in."

She bowed her head and remained pensive for a while.

The leaves murmured around them, a tall foxglove waved above a tangle of plants, the sunlight flowed over the turf like a wave; and at short intervals the silence was broken by sounds from the grazing cow which they could no longer see.

Rosanette was gazing fixedly at a spot on the ground a yard away, her nostrils quivering, absorbed in her thoughts. Frédéric took her hand.

"How you have suffered, my poor darling!"

"Yes," she replied, "more than you know! . . . To the point of wanting to put an end to it all; they fished me out again."

"What?"

"Oh, don't let's think about it anymore! I love you, I'm happy! Kiss me!" And she picked off, one by one, the sprigs of thistle that clung to the hem of her dress.

Frédéric was thinking above all of what she had left unsaid. How had she managed to escape from her poverty? To which of her lovers did she owe her education? What kind of life had she led up to the day when he had met her for the first time? Her last words precluded questions. He asked her only how she had met Arnoux.

"Through La Vatnaz."

"Wasn't it you I saw once at the Palais-Royal with both of them?"

He gave the exact date. Rosanette made an effort.

"Yes, that's right! . . . I wasn't very gay in those days!"

But Arnoux had been nice to her. Frédéric didn't doubt it; nevertheless their friend was an odd man, full of faults; he took care to remind her of them. She agreed.

"Never mind! I'm still fond of the old villain in spite of it all!"

"Even now?" asked Frédéric.

She started to blush, half laughing, half angry.

"Oh no! That's ancient history. I'm not hiding anything from you. Even if it were true, it's different with him! What's more, I don't think you're very kind to your victim."

"My victim?"

Rosanette took him by the chin.

"Of course!"

And, lisping like a children's nurse:

"We haven't always been a good boy! Went sleepy-byes with his wife!"

"Me! Never!"

Rosanette smiled. He was hurt by her smile, which he took for a proof of indifference. But she went on gently, with one of those looks that beg for a lie!

"Quite sure?"

"Of course!"

And Frédéric gave his word of honor that he had never even thought of Madame Arnoux, being too much in love with someone else.

"With who, then?"

"Why, with you, my beauty!"

"Oh, don't make fun of me! You're being very irritating!"

He thought it prudent to invent a story of a love affair. He gave circumstantial details. The woman in question had, in any case, made him very unhappy.

"You certainly do have bad luck!" said Rosanette.

"Oh, I don't know!" hoping she would take this to mean he had had several successful affairs, so that she would have a better opinion of him. In the same way Rosanette did not mention all her lovers, so that he should hold her in greater esteem. For, even in the most intimate confidences, there are always reservations, out of false pride, delicacy, or pity. We discover precipices or swamps in ourselves or in the other person which stop us from going farther; moreover we feel that we shall be misunderstood; it is difficult to express anything exactly. It is because of this that complete unions are so rare.

The poor Maréchale had never known a better one. When she gazed at Frédéric her eyes often filled with tears, then she would lift them to heaven or toward the horizon, as if she had seen some great dawn, a prospect of unbounded happiness. Finally, one day, she admitted that she would like to have a mass said: "to bring good fortune to our love."

Then why had she resisted him for so long? She didn't know herself. He questioned her about it several times and she replied, clasping him in her arms:

"It was because I was frightened of loving you too much, darling!"

On Sunday morning, Frédéric read Dussardier's name on a list of the wounded in a newspaper. He gave an exclamation and, showing the paper to Rosanette, declared that he must leave immediately.

"But why?"

"To see him and take care of him, of course!"

"You're not going to leave me here alone, I suppose?"

"Come with me."

"No thank you, I've no intention of getting mixed up in that kind of brawl!"

"Well, I can't . . ."

"Fiddlesticks! As if there weren't enough nurses in the hospitals! Anyhow, what's it got to do with you? Every man for himself, that's what I say!"

Frédéric was outraged by her selfishness and reproached himself for not being in Paris with the others. There was something mean and bourgeois about such indifference to the sufferings of one's country. His love suddenly weighed on him like a crime. They both sulked for an hour.

Then she begged him to wait, not to take any risks. "Suppose you were killed!"

"I'd only have done my duty!"

Rosanette jumped up. To begin with, his duty was to love her. He must be tired of her, that was it! It was flying in the face of common sense! Good God, what an idea!

Frédéric rang for the bill. But it was not easy to get back to Paris. The Leloir coach had just left, the Lecomte berlins were not running, the Bourbonnais stagecoach passed through late at night and might be full; no one could tell. After he had wasted a good deal of time on these inquiries, the idea of taking a post-chaise occurred to him. The postmaster refused to let him have any horses, as Frédéric had no passport. In the end, he hired a barouche (the same one they had driven round the forest in) and they drew up in front of the Hôtel du Commerce, at Melun, about five o'clock.

The marketplace was covered with stacks of arms. The prefect had forbidden the National Guards to go on into Paris. Those who came from other departments wanted to continue their march. People were shouting. The inn was in a tumult.

Rosanette, frightened, declared that she would go no farther and again begged him to remain with her. The innkeeper and his wife supported her. A worthy fellow who was having his dinner joined in, maintaining that the battle would soon be over; anyhow, a man must do his duty. At this the Maréchale's sobs redoubled. Frédéric was exasperated. He gave her his purse, kissed her quickly, and disappeared.

When he arrived at the Corbeil station, he was told that the rebels had cut the rails in several places, and the coachman refused to take him any farther; his horses, he said, were "played out."

Through his connections, however, Frédéric managed to get a broken-down gig which, for sixty francs excluding the tip, consented to take him as far as the barrière d'Italie. But a hundred yards from the toll gate the driver made him get down and turned back. Frédéric was walking along the road when a sentry suddenly barred his way with his bayonet. Four men seized him, shouting:

"Here's one of them! Look out! Search him! Thief! Scum!"

And he was so stunned that he let himself be dragged to the post at the toll gate, right in the middle of the crossroads where the Gobelins and Hôpital boulevards and Godefroy and Mouffetard streets met.

At the ends of the four streets were four barricades, formed of enormous heaps of paving stones; torches crackled here and there; in spite of the clouds of dust he was able to make out some line-infantrymen and National Guards, all with black faces, disheveled and haggard. They had just taken the position, and had shot several men; they were still angry. Frédéric said that he had come from Fontainebleau to help a wounded friend who lived in the Rue Bellefond; no one was willing to believe him at first; they examined his hands and even sniffed at his ears to see if he smelt of powder.

However, by dint of repeating the same thing over and over, he was finally able to convince a captain, who ordered two fusiliers to escort him to the post at the Jardin des Plantes.

They set off down the Boulevard de l'Hôpital. There was a strong wind blowing. This revived him.

Next they turned down the Rue du Marché-aux-Chevaux. The Jardin des Plantes formed a great black mass on their right; while on the left the entire front of the Pitié hospital glowed as if it was on fire, with every window lighted and shadows moving rapidly across the panes.

Frédéric's two escorts left and another soldier accompanied him as far as the Polytechnic School.

The Rue Saint-Victor was in total darkness, without a single gas lamp or a light in any of the windows. Every ten minutes there would be a shout of:

"Sentries! Attention!"

And this cry, ringing out in the silence, echoed on like the reverberations of a stone falling into an abyss.

From time to time they would hear the sound of heavy footsteps drawing nearer. This would be a patrol of at least a hundred men; whispers and vague metallic chinkings came from the confused mass; it receded with a rhythmic, swaying motion, and melted into the darkness.

In the center of each crossroad a dragoon sat on his horse, immobile. Occasionally, a messenger would gallop past and then silence would fall again. In the distance, heavy guns were moving across the paving stones with a hollow and awesome rumble; and these sounds, so different from the sounds of ordinary life, gripped the heart. They even seemed to swell the silence, which was profound and absolute—a black silence. Men in white smocks came up to the soldiers, said a word or two to them and vanished like ghosts.

The post at the Polytechnic was overflowing with people. The doorway was obstructed by women who wanted to see their husbands or their sons. They were being sent on to the Panthéon, which had been transformed into a depository for corpses—and no one would pay any attention to Frédéric. He persisted, swearing that his friend Dussardier was waiting for him, dying. Finally he was given a corporal to take him to the top of the Rue Saint-Jacques, to the town hall of the Twelfth Arrondissement.

The Place du Panthéon was full of soldiers lying on straw. Dawn was breaking. The bivouac fires were going out.

This part of the city had been badly scarred by the insurrection. The surface of every street was pockmarked from one end to the other. There were still omnibuses, gas pipes, and cart-wheels on the ruins of the barricades; there were little black patches here and there which could only be blood. The houses had been riddled with shell fire, and their woodwork showed where the plaster had flaked off. Blinds hung like rags from a single nail. Stairs had crumbled away, doors opened onto a void. One could see into rooms whose wallpaper hung in shreds; occasionally some fragile object had survived. Frédéric noticed a clock, a parrot's perch, some prints.

When he entered the town hall, the National Guardsmen were engaged in endless discussion of the deaths of Bréa and Négrier, of the deputy Charbonnel, and of the Archbishop of Paris.* There were rumors that the Duc d'Aumale had landed at Boulogne, that Barbès had escaped from Vincennes, that artillery was arriving from Bourges, and that help from the provinces was pouring in. Toward three o'clock someone brought good news: representatives of the rebels were meeting with the president of the Assembly.

At this there was general rejoicing and as he had still twelve francs in his pocket, Frédéric sent out for a dozen bottles of wine, hoping that this would hasten his release. Suddenly they thought they heard the sound of a fusillade. The toasts stopped and all eyes turned suspiciously on the stranger; he might be Henri V!

To rid themselves of any responsibility for him, they took Frédéric to the town hall of the Twelfth Arrondissement, which he was not allowed to leave until nine o'clock in the morning.

He ran as far as the Quai Voltaire. At an open window an old man in shirt sleeves was weeping, his eyes raised to the heavens. The Seine flowed past peacefully, the sky was blue and birds were singing in the trees in the Tuileries.

Frédéric was crossing the Place du Carrousel when a litter was carried past. The soldiers at the post immediately presented arms and the officer, his hand to his shako, said: "Honor to the dead heroes!" This phrase had become almost obligatory; those who pronounced it always

---

*Generals Bréa and Négrier and the deputy Charbonnel were killed by the rebels in different parts of Paris on June 25. The Archbishop of Paris was accidentally shot while attempting to arrange a cease-fire on the same day.

seemed moved by a solemn emotion. The litter was escorted by a group of furious men crying:

"We shall avenge you! We shall avenge you!"

Carriages moved along the boulevard and women were sitting in the doorways making dressings. But the revolt was almost over; a proclamation of Cavaignac's, just posted, announced its defeat. A platoon of Mobile Guards appeared at the top of the Rue Vivienne. At this the bourgeois shouted with enthusiasm; they waved their hats, applauded, danced, tried to embrace them, offered them drinks—and the ladies threw down flowers from the balconies.

Finally, at ten o'clock, just as the cannon boomed out for the attack on the Faubourg Saint-Antoine, Frédéric arrived at Dussardier's. He found him in his garret, stretched out on his back, fast asleep. A woman tiptoed out of the neighboring room; it was Mademoiselle Vatnaz.

She drew Frédéric aside and told him how Dussardier had been wounded.

On Saturday, from the top of a barricade in the Rue Lafayette, a boy wrapped in a tricolor flag had shouted to the National Guards: "Are you going to fire on your brothers?" As they advanced Dussardier had thrown down his musket, swept the others aside, leapt onto the barricade and, felling the rebel with a kick, had snatched the flag from him. They had found him under the debris, his thigh pierced by a copper slug. They had had to open up the wound and remove the bullet. Mademoiselle Vatnaz had arrived that same evening and had not left him since.

She prepared his dressings skillfully, helped him to drink, anticipated his slightest wish, moved about the room as quietly as a mouse, and gazed tenderly at her patient.

Frédéric came every morning for two weeks; one day he was speaking of La Vatnaz's devotion when Dussardier shrugged his shoulders:

"Oh, no! She's doing it for reasons of her own."

"Do you think so?"

"I'm sure of it!" he replied, without vouchsafing any further explanation.

She loaded him with attentions, to the point of bringing him the newspapers that praised his heroic deed. These tributes seemed to disturb him, and to Frédéric he revealed the scruples that troubled his conscience.

Perhaps he ought to have been fighting on the other

side, with the workers; for, after all, they had been promised all kinds of things which had come to nothing. Their conquerors detested the Republic; and in any case, they had been treated so cruelly! They had been in the wrong, of course, but not completely, and the honest fellow was tortured by the idea that he might have fought against a just cause.

Sénécal, who was imprisoned in the Tuileries under the riverside terrace, suffered none of these agonies.

There were nine hundred men there, thrown helter-skelter in the filth, black with powder and clotted blood, shaking with fever, screaming with fury; and those who died were left among the others. Sometimes, at the sound of a sudden explosion, they would imagine that they were all about to be shot; then they would hurl themselves against the walls and afterwards sink back into their places, so stupefied by suffering that it seemed to them they were living in a nightmare, a dreadful hallucination. The lamp that hung from the vaulted ceiling looked like a splash of blood; and tiny green and yellow flames flickered here and there, produced by the vapors in the cellar. For fear of an epidemic, a commission was appointed to investigate. Before he had taken more than a few steps down the staircase, the chairman fled, appalled by the reek of excrement and corpses. Whenever the prisoners approached a ventilation hole, the National Guardsmen who were on duty—to prevent them from shaking the bars loose—thrust their bayonets at random into the mass.

Most of the National Guardsmen were pitiless. Those who had not fought in the streets hoped to distinguish themselves now. In a panic, they were taking their revenge at once against the newspapers, the clubs, the demonstrations, the doctrines, against everything that had infuriated them during the last three months; and, despite their victory, equality (as if to rebuke its defenders and taunt its enemies) emerged triumphant—an equality of brutish beasts, a common level of bloodstained savagery. For the fanaticism of the rich was as great as the frenzy of the poor, the aristocracy was a prey to the same madness as the rabble, and the cotton nightcap proved as hideous as the revolutionary bonnet. The mind of the nation was unbalanced, as it is after great natural upheavals. Certain intelligent men stayed fools for life because of it.

Old Roque had become very brave, almost foolhardy.

He had arrived in Paris on the 26th with the Nogentais and, instead of going home with the rest of them, he had joined the detachment of National Guard who were stationed in the Tuileries; he was very happy when he was given sentry duty at the terrace by the water. There, at least, he had the criminals under his own control! He was delighted by their defeat, their abject condition, and could not keep from haranguing them.

One of the prisoners, an adolescent with long, fair hair, pressed his face against the bars to ask for bread. Monsieur Roque ordered him to be still. But the young man repeated in a heartbreaking voice:

"Bread!"

"Do you think I've got any?"

Other prisoners appeared at the grating, with bristling beards and burning eyes, all jostling and screaming:

"Bread!"

Old Roque was enraged at seeing his authority flouted. To frighten them he leveled his musket at them; and the young man, borne up to the ceiling by the throng who were stifling him, flung back his head and shouted again:

"Bread!"

"Here's your bread!" cried Old Roque, and pulled the trigger.

There was a tremendous howl, then nothing. There was still something white on the edge of the grille.*

Monsieur Roque thereupon went home; he owned a house in the Rue Saint-Martin, where he kept a small apartment for himself, and the damage inflicted on the street-front of the building during the riot had played no small part in infuriating him. Now that he saw it again he felt he had exaggerated the harm done. His recent action appeased him, as if he had been compensated. His daughter herself opened the door to him. She told him that she had been worried by his long absence; she thought he had had an accident or been wounded.

Old Roque was touched by this proof of daughterly devotion, but he expressed surprise that she should have come without Catherine. "I've just sent her on an errand," replied Louise.

And she inquired about his health, and one thing and

---

*This episode is based on a true incident. A drunken National Guardsman let off his musket by accident and the others, believing that the prisoners were in revolt, fired blindly into the crowd, killing or wounding two hundred people.

another; then, offhandedly, asked if he had happened to
run into Frédéric.

"No, I haven't seen a sign of him."

She had made the journey purely for the young man's
sake. There were steps in the corridor. She murmured:
"Oh, excuse me!" and vanished.

Catherine had not found Frédéric. He had been away
for several days and his close friend, Monsieur Deslauriers, lived in the country now.

Louise reappeared, trembling from head to foot and
unable to speak. She leaned on the furniture for support.

"What's wrong? What's happened to you?" cried her
father.

She made a sign to say it was nothing and, with a great
effort, pulled herself together.

Soup was sent in from the restaurant across the way.
But Old Roque had suffered too violent an emotional
upheaval. He "couldn't get it down," and during the
dessert he had a sort of fainting spell. A doctor was
hastily sent for; he prescribed a potion. Once in bed,
Monsieur Roque demanded as many blankets as possible,
to make him sweat. He sighed and groaned:

"Thank you, my dear Catherine! —Louise, give your
poor father a kiss, my chick! Oh, these revolutions!"

And, as his daughter scolded him for having made himself ill worrying over her, he replied:

"Yes, you're right! But I can't help myself! I'm too
tender-hearted!"

Chapter Two

Madame Dambreuse was seated in her boudoir between her niece and Miss John, listening to Monsieur Roque's tales of his military hardships.

She was biting her lips and seemed to be in pain.

"Oh, it's nothing, it will pass!" she said.

And she added graciously:

"One of your acquaintances, Monsieur Moreau, is coming to dinner."

Louise started.

"Otherwise, only a few intimate friends, Alfred de Cisy among others."

And she praised his manners, his appearance and, above all, his character.

Madame Dambreuse was lying less than she imagined: the viscount was thinking of marriage. He had mentioned it to Martinon, adding that he was sure that he could make himself agreeable to Mademoiselle Cécile and that her relatives would accept him.

To risk such a disclosure he must have heard something favorable about the dowry. Now, Martinon suspected that Cécile was Monsieur Dambreuse's natural daughter; and it would probably have been a wise move to chance asking for her hand himself. Such audacity had its risks, however, and Martinon had till now been careful to avoid any commitment; besides, he could not think how to rid himself of the aunt. Cisy's confidences had decided him and he had made his proposal to the banker who, seeing no objection, had just told Madame Dambreuse about it.

Cisy came in. She rose and said:

"You've been neglecting us . . ." adding, in English, "Cécile, shake hands!"

Frédéric came in at that moment.

"Ah, we've finally caught up with you!" cried Old Roque. "I've been to your house with Louise three times this week!"

Frédéric had been carefully avoiding them. He declared that he spent every day at the bedside of a wounded friend. Moreover, he had been very busy for a long time, and he tried to think of a convincing story. Luckily, the guests were arriving: first Monsieur Paul de Grémonville, the diplomat whom he had seen for a moment at the ball; then Fumichon, the industrialist whose conservative zeal had shocked him one evening; they were followed by the old Duchess de Montreuil-Nantua.

But two voices rose in the hall:

"I'm absolutely certain," said one.

"My dear lady! My dear lady! Compose yourself!" replied the other.

It was Monsieur de Nonancourt, an old dandy, who looked as if he had been mummified in cold cream, and Madame de Larsillois, the wife of one of Louis-Philippe's prefects. She was trembling like a leaf, for she had just heard a barrel organ play a polka that was used as a signal by the insurgents. Many members of the middle class had similar fancies; they believed that men in the catacombs were plotting to blow up the Faubourg Saint-Germain; they heard noises in cellars and saw suspicious activities through windows.

Everyone, however, exerted themselves to calm down Madame de Larsillois. Order was restored. There was nothing to fear any longer. "Cavaignac has saved us!" As if the insurrection had not produced horrors enough, people exaggerated them. There had been no less than twenty-three thousand convicts on the side of the socialists!

They believed implicitly in the stories of poisoned food, of Mobile Guards sandwiched between two planks and sawn in half, of banner legends calling for looting and arson.

"And something else too!" added the former prefect's wife.

"Oh, my dear!" said Madame Dambreuse prudishly, with a meaningful glance at the three unmarried girls.

Monsieur Dambreuse came out of his office with Martinon. His wife turned her head away and replied to Pellerin's greetings as he came toward her. The artist was looking at the walls, a worried expression on his face. Monsieur Dambreuse drew him to one side and explained that he had, for the present, been forced to hide his canvas glorifying the revolution.

"Of course!" said Pellerin, whose defeat at the "Club de l'Intelligence" had modified his opinions. The banker murmured courteously that he would commission further works from him.

"But excuse me . . . Ah, my dear fellow! How nice to see you!"

Monsieur and Madame Arnoux stood before Frédéric. He had a moment of giddiness. Rosanette, with her admiration for the soldiers, had been irritating him all afternoon; and he felt his old love reviving.

The butler came in to announce that dinner was ready. Madame Dambreuse signaled with a glance to the viscount to take Cécile's arm, hissed "Wretch!" to Martinon, and everyone moved into the dining room.

In the center of the table, under the green leaves of a pineapple, lay a dolphin, its head pointing toward a haunch of venison and its tail touching a dish heaped with crayfish. Figs, enormous cherries, pears, and grapes (the early fruits from the Paris orchards) were piled in pyramids in antique Dresden baskets; here and there a vase of flowers stood among the shining silver. The white silk blinds had been pulled down over the windows, and they suffused the room with soft light; it was cooled by two fountains containing pieces of ice, and the meal was served by tall footmen in knee breeches. All this seemed even better by contrast with the anxiety of the preceding days. Once more the guests were enjoying the things they had been afraid of losing, and Nonancourt voiced the general sentiment by exclaiming:

"Ah! Let us hope the republicans will allow us to eat dinner!"

"In spite of their fraternity!" added Monsieur Roque wittily.

These two guests of honor were on either side of Madame Dambreuse, her husband sat opposite her with Madame de Larsillois, who was next to the diplomat on one side of him and the old duchess, elbow to elbow with Fumichon, on the other. Then came the painter, the pottery manufacturer, Mademoiselle Louise, and—thanks to Martinon, who had preempted his place in order to sit by Cécile—Frédéric found himself beside Madame Arnoux. She was wearing a black wool chiffon dress, with a

gold bracelet round her wrist and, as on the first occasion
when he had dined at her house, there was something red
in her hair: a spray of fuchsia entwined in her chignon.
He could not prevent himself from saying:

"It's a long time since we've seen each other!"

"Ah!" she replied coldly.

He continued, in a gentle voice that mitigated the
impertinence of his question:

"Have you ever thought of me?"

"Why should I think of you?"

This wounded Frédéric:

"You may be right, after all."

But, repentant at once, he swore he had spent not a
single day without being ravaged by memories of her.

"I don't believe a word of it, Monsieur."

"But you know that I love you!"

Madame Arnoux made no reply.

"You know that I love you."

She remained silent.

"All right, go to the devil!" said Frédéric to himself.
And, raising his eyes, he caught sight of Mademoiselle
Roque at the other end of the table.

She had imagined it would be smart to dress entirely
in green, a color which clashed abominably with her red
hair. Her belt buckle was too high, her collar dwarfed
her neck, and this lack of elegance had certainly contributed to Frédéric's initial coolness. She was watching
him from a distance with curiosity; and though Arnoux,
her neighbor, lavished flattery on her he could hardly get
three words out of her. Finally he gave up the idea of
pleasing, and turned his attention to the general conversation. Now the topic was the pineapple purées they
served at the Luxembourg.

Louis Blanc, according to Fumichon, owned a hotel
in the Rue Saint-Dominique and refused to let rooms to
workers.

"What I find amusing," said Nonancourt, "is Ledru-
Rollin hunting in the royal parks!"

"He owes twenty thousand francs to a jeweler," added
Cisy; "and they even say . . ."

Madame Dambreuse stopped him.

"How disagreeable, all this excitement over politics!
A young man like you, shame on you! You ought to be
paying attention to your neighbor!"

Next, the more serious-minded guests attacked the
newspapers.

Arnoux undertook their defense; Frédéric joined in, maintaining that they were business enterprises like any others. Their writers were usually fools or fakes; he claimed to know them inside out and deflated his friend's generous attitude with sarcasms. Madame Arnoux did not realize that he was avenging himself on her.

Meanwhile, the viscount was racking his brains in the hope of conquering Mademoiselle Cécile. First, he displayed his artistic tastes, criticizing the shape of the decanters and the engraving on the knives. Then he talked about his horses, his tailor, and his shirtmaker. Finally, he touched on religion and found a way of letting her know that he fulfilled all his duties in that direction.

Martinon did better. He gazed steadily at his neighbor and, in monotonous tones, praised her birdlike profile, her insipid blonde hair, her stubby hands. The ugly girl glowed at this shower of compliments.

It was impossible to hear a word as everyone talked his loudest. Monsieur Roque wanted France to be governed with an "iron hand." Nonancourt even expressed regret that the death penalty had been abolished for political crimes. All those scoundrels should have been executed en masse.

"They haven't even the virtue of courage," said Fumichon. "I see no bravery in cowering behind a barricade!"

"Oh yes, do tell us about Dussardier!" said Monsieur Dambreuse, turning to Frédéric.

The worthy clerk was now a hero, like Sallesse, the Jeanson brothers, the Pelliquet woman, and the rest.

Frédéric needed no urging to tell the story of his friend's feat; it cast a kind of reflected glory on him.

This led, quite naturally, to a discussion of various courageous acts. According to the diplomat, it was not difficult to meet death face to face, as witness all the people who fought duels.

"We could ask the viscount about that," said Martinon.

The viscount blushed hotly.

The guests stared at him; and Louise, more surprised than anyone else, murmured:

"What does that mean?"

"He made a poor showing when he fought Frédéric," Arnoux replied in a low voice.

"Do you know anything about this, Mademoiselle?" Nonancourt asked at once, and he passed her answer on to Madame Dambreuse, who leaned forward a little and fixed her eyes on Frédéric.

Martinon did not wait for Cécile to question him. He told her that the incident had concerned an unmentionable person, and the girl drew back a little on her chair, as if to avoid any contact with such a libertine.

The conversation had started up again. Some first-class Bordeaux was going around the table, and the guests grew animated; Pellerin bore a grudge against the Revolution because of the Spanish Museum, which was now lost forever. This was what distressed him most, as a painter. At that word, Monsieur Roque broke in with a question:

"Are you not the author of a very remarkable painting?"

"Possibly! What one?"

"It represents a . . . well . . . a rather lightly clothed lady, holding a purse, with a peacock behind her."

Frédéric blushed in his turn. Pellerin pretended not to understand.

"But I'm sure it's your work! Your name is written at the bottom with an inscription on the frame stating that it belongs to Monsieur Moreau."

One day, while Monsieur Roque and his daughter had been waiting for Frédéric at his house, they had noticed the Maréchale's portrait. The old fellow had even taken it for "a gothic picture."

"No," said Pellerin churlishly; "it's the portrait of a woman."

Martinon added:

"Of a woman who's very much alive! Isn't that so, Cisy?"

"I know nothing about it!"

"I thought you knew her. But if it's a painful topic do please excuse me!"

Cisy lowered his eyes, proving by his embarrassment that he must have played some pitiable role in connection with the portrait. As for Frédéric, the model had to be his mistress. This was one of those convictions arrived at instantly and the faces around the table showed it clearly.

"How he lied to me!" said Madame Arnoux to herself.

"So that's why he left me!" thought Louise.

When they went out into the garden, Frédéric, feeling that these two stories could damage his reputation, reproached Martinon for bringing them up.

Mademoiselle Cécile's suitor laughed in his face:

"Oh, you've got it all wrong! They'll be useful to you! Go ahead!"

What could he mean? And what was the reason for his

most unusual display of goodwill? Without further discussion, he went off to the end of the garden, where the ladies were sitting. The men remained standing, with Pellerin holding forth in the middle of the group. The regime most congenial to the arts was an enlightened monarchy. The modern age disgusted him "if only because of the National Guards"; he lamented the passing of the Middle Ages and Louis XIV. Monsieur Roque congratulated him on his opinions, even going so far as to admit that they had erased all his prejudices against artists. But he moved away almost immediately afterwards, drawn by the sound of Fumichon's voice. Arnoux was trying to establish that there are two socialisms, one good and one bad. The industrialist could see no difference between them, he almost suffocated with rage at the word "property."

"It's a right inscribed in the laws of Nature. Children cling to their toys; all the nations agree with me, so do the beasts; the lion himself, if he could speak, would declare himself a landowner! I myself, gentlemen, began with a capital of fifteen thousand francs. For thirty years I got up regularly at four o'clock in the morning. I had to work like a demon to make my fortune. And now they tell me that I'm not the master, that my money is not mine, in fact that property is theft!"*

"But Proudhon . . ."

"Oh, don't bother me with your Proudhon! If he was here I believe I'd strangle him!"

And he would have strangled him. Partly as a result of the liqueurs, Fumichon was beside himself; and his apoplectic face seemed ready to explode like a shell.

"Hello, Arnoux," said Hussonnet, walking briskly across the lawn.

He had brought Monsieur the first page of a pamphlet entitled "The Hydra," for the bohemian was now the spokesman for a reactionary group, and the banker presented him as such to his guests.

Hussonnet entertained them, first by maintaining that the candlemakers had hired three hundred and eighty-four urchins to shout "Lights! Lights!"† every evening, then by making fun of the principles of 1789, the abolition of slavery, and the orators of the left; he even went so far as to do a skit, "The Wise Man on the Barricades,"

*A reference to Proudhon's famous saying: "Property is theft," from his *Qu'est-ce que la propriété* which was published in 1840.

†See note page 313.

perhaps out of a naïve jealousy of these bourgeois who had just finished a good dinner. The sally had only a middling success. Their faces grew longer.

Anyhow, this was no time for jokes; Nonancourt pointed this out, recalling the deaths of Monseigneur Affre and General Bréa. They were always being recalled; people used them as arguments. Monsieur Roque declared that the Archbishop's death had been "completely sublime." Fumichon awarded the palm to the soldier and, instead of simply deploring these two murders, they argued over which of them should arouse the greater indignation. Then a second parallel was drawn, this time between Lamoricière and Cavaignac, with Monsieur Dambreuse extolling Cavaignac and Nonancourt Lamoricière.* No one present, excepting Arnoux, had seen them in action; nevertheless they all pronounced an irrevocable judgment on their operations. Frédéric declined to join in, confessing that he had not taken part in the fighting. The diplomat and Monsieur Dambreuse nodded approval. For in fact, to have put down the revolt was to defend the Republic. The result, although good in itself, had strengthened the government. And now that they were rid of the vanquished, they hoped that the victors would go too.

They had hardly entered the garden when Madame Dambreuse took Cisy to one side and scolded him for his clumsiness; at the sight of Martinon she dismissed the nobleman, then asked her future nephew the reason for his jokes at the Viscount's expense.

"None at all."

"It's as if you were trying to cast Monsieur Moreau in a favorable light! Why did you do it?"

"No reason. Frédéric's a delightful fellow. I'm fond of him."

"So am I! I want to talk to him. Go and find him!"

After two or three banal remarks, she began by gently criticizing her other guests, a method of putting Frédéric into a higher category. He did not fail to disparage the other women a little, a subtle way of complimenting her. But she left him from time to time; she was "at home" that evening and ladies kept arriving; then she would return to her place, and the fortuitous arrangement of the chairs allowed them to talk without being overheard.

*Cavaignac was in command of the army during the fighting in June, 1848. Lamoricière had become Minister of War that year and played a part in suppressing the rebellion.

Turn by turn she was lively, serious, melancholy, and intelligent. She took little interest in the topics of the day; there was a whole class of less transitory sentiments. She complained of poets who misrepresented the truth, then looked up at the sky and asked him the name of a star.

Two or three Chinese lanterns had been hung in the trees; they swayed in the wind, and shafts of colored light played over her white dress. As usual, she was leaning back a little in her armchair, with a stool under her feet; the toe of one black satin shoe showed, and from time to time she would say something in a louder voice, or even laugh.

These flirtatious tricks made no impression on Martinon, who was busy with Cécile, but they struck the young Roque girl, who was talking to Madame Arnoux. She was the only woman there who did not seem haughty to Louise. She had come to sit beside her, and then, wanting to confide in someone, she said:

"Doesn't Frédéric Moreau talk well!"

"Do you know him?"

"Oh, very well! We're neighbors. He used to play with me when I was a little girl."

Madame Arnoux gave her a long look which meant: "You're not in love with him, I suppose?"

The girl's answering glance was one of untroubled assent.

"So you see him often?"

"Oh no! Only when he comes to stay with his mother. He hasn't been there for ten months! Although he did promise to come back sooner!"

"You mustn't put too much faith in men's promises, my dear."

"But he's never deceived me!"

"There are those he has!"

Louise shivered, thinking: "Could he possibly have promised her something as well?" and her face contracted with distrust and hatred.

Madame Arnoux was almost frightened of her; she wished she could take back her words. Then they both fell silent.

As Frédéric happened to be sitting on a folding chair opposite them, they both gazed at him, one discreetly, from under lowered lids, the other frankly, open-mouthed, so that Madame Dambreuse said to him:

"Do turn round so that she can see you!"

"Who do you mean?"

"Why, Monsieur Roque's daughter!"

And she teased him about the young country girl's lovelorn state. He denied it, trying to laugh it off:

"It's incredible! I ask you! An ugly creature like that!"

Still, he was immensely flattered. He remembered the other evening, when he had left the party with his heart full of humiliation, and drew a deep breath; he felt that he was in his true setting, almost on his own estate, as if everything there, including the Dambreuses' house, belonged to him. A semicircle of listening ladies gathered around him and, in order to shine, he pronounced himself in favor of the reestablishment of divorce, which should be made so easy that couples could split apart and come together again indefinitely, as often as they wanted. There were cries at this, and whispers; the sound of voices came in little spurts from the shadows at the foot of the vine-covered wall. It sounded like hens cackling gaily to each other, and Frédéric developed his theory with the self-confidence that springs from knowing one has scored a success. A servant brought a tray of ices into the arbor. The gentlemen came over. They were talking about the arrests.

Frédéric now took revenge on the viscount by persuading him that he might possibly be arrested as a Legitimist. Cisy objected that he had not left his room, but his adversary piled up all the odds against him; even Messieurs Dambreuse and de Grémonville were amused. They complimented Frédéric, while remarking that it was a pity he did not use his gifts for the defense of order, and their handshakes were cordial; from now on he could count on them. Finally, as everyone was leaving, the viscount bowed very low in front of Cécile:

"Mademoiselle, I have the honor of wishing you a very good night!"

She replied: "Good night!" in curt tones. But she smiled at Martinon.

So that he could continue his discussion with Arnoux, Old Roque suggested that he see him home "and your wife too," since they were going in the same direction. Louise and Frédéric walked in front. She had seized him by the arm and, as soon as she was a little way from the others, she exclaimed:

"At last! At last! How I've suffered all evening! How cruel these women are! What airs they give themselves!"

He tried to defend them.

"In the first place, you could have come and spoken

to me when you came in, when it's a year since you've been to Nogent!"

"It's not a year," said Frédéric, happy to take her up on this detail so as to avoid the others.

"All right! It seemed a long time to me, that's all! But, during that abominable dinner party, you acted as if you were ashamed of me! Oh, I understand, I'm not attractive like they are!"

"You're mistaken," said Frédéric.

"Truly? Swear to me you don't love any of them?"

Frédéric swore.

"And you love only me?"

"Of course!"

This assurance made her happy. She would have liked to lose her way in the streets, so that they could have walked together all night.

"I was so unhappy at home! They all talked of nothing but the barricades! I saw you falling on your back, covered with blood! Your mother was in bed with her rheumatism. She knew nothing about it. I had to keep quiet! I couldn't stand it any longer! So I brought Catherine and came ahead!"

And she described her departure, her whole journey, and the lie she had told her father.

"He's taking me back in two days. Come around tomorrow evening, as if we hadn't spoken, and take the opportunity to ask for my hand."

Never had Frédéric been further from marriage. Anyhow, Mademoiselle Roque seemed a rather ridiculous little thing to him. What a contrast between her and a woman like Madame Dambreuse! He was destined for quite a different future! Today he was sure of it; so this was not the moment to come to a decision of such importance on a sentimental impulse. Now was the time to be practical—and, moreover, he had seen Madame Arnoux again. But Louise's candor embarrassed him. He replied:

"Have you really thought this over?"

"What!" she cried, frozen with surprise and indignation. He said that to marry now would be madness.

"So you don't want me?"

"But you don't understand!"

And he launched into an immensely complicated speech, intended to persuade her that he was held back by important considerations, that he was up to his ears in business, even that his fortune was in danger (Louise cut him short with a blunt comment), and finally that

political conditions were against it. The most reasonable
course, therefore, was to be patient for a little. Things
would probably sort themselves out; at least he hoped
so; and, finding no further arguments, he pretended that
he had suddenly remembered he should have been at
Dussardier's two hours ago.

Then, after saying "good night" to the others, he
plunged into the Rue Hauteville, circled the Gymnase, re-
emerged onto the boulevard and mounted Rosanette's
four flights of stairs at a run.

Monsieur and Madame Arnoux left Roque and his
daughter at the corner of the Rue Saint-Denis. The Arnouxs
went home without exchanging a word, he exhausted by
so much talk, and she the prey of a deep lassitude;
she even leaned on his shoulder. He was the only man
who had displayed any real feeling during the evening.
She felt full of indulgence toward him. He, however,
still bore a slight grudge against Frédéric.

"Did you see his face when they were discussing the
portrait? Didn't I tell you that he was her lover? You
wouldn't believe me!"

"Oh yes, I was wrong!"

Arnoux, pleased by his victory, persisted:

"I'm even prepared to wager that when he left us
just now, he was going to see her! He's with her now,
believe me! He's spending the night there."

Madame Arnoux had drawn her hood low over her face.

"But you're trembling!"

"I'm cold," she replied.

As soon as her father was asleep, Louise went into
Catherine's room and, shaking her by the shoulder, hissed:

"Get up! . . . Quick! Quicker than that! And go and
find me a cab."

Catherine replied that there were none available at this
time of night.

"Will you take me there yourself then?"

"Where?"

"To Frédéric's house!"

"Impossible! Why?"

She wanted to talk to him. She couldn't wait. She
wanted to see him immediately.

"What are you thinking of? Turn up like that at
someone's house in the middle of the night! Anyhow,
he'll be asleep by now!"

"I'll wake him up!"

"But it's not proper for a young lady!"

"I'm not a young lady! I'm his wife! I love him! Come on, put on your shawl!"

Catherine thought it over, standing beside her bed. Finally she said:

"No! I won't do it!"

"Well stay then! I'm going!"

Louise slid off down the staircase like a snake. Catherine rushed after her and caught her on the sidewalk. Her protests were useless and she followed her mistress, fastening her dressing jacket as she went. It seemed to her to be an extremely long way. She complained of her old legs.

"After all, I haven't the same reasons for hurrying as you, not by a long shot!"

Then she became sentimental:

"Poor sweetheart! You've still only got your Katy, haven't you!"

From time to time her scruples would revive.

"Oh, this is a fine thing you're making me do! Suppose your father wakes up! Lordy, lordy! I just hope nothing awful happens!"

In front of the Théâtre de Variétés, they were stopped by a patrol of National Guards. Louise said at once that she and her maid were going to the Rue Rumfort to fetch a doctor. They were allowed to pass.

At the corner of the Madeleine, they encountered a second patrol and, as Louise was giving the same explanation, one of the citizens asked:

"Is it for the nine-month's sickness, doll?"

"Gougibaud!" cried the captain, "no dirty talk in the ranks! Proceed, ladies!"

In spite of his injunction the shafts of wit continued to fly.

"Have fun!"

"My respects to the doctor!"

"Watch out for the wolf!"

"They like a joke," observed Catherine loudly. "They're young!"

Finally they reached Frédéric's house. Louise gave the bell-pull several hearty tugs. The door opened a crack and the concierge answered her question with a "no!"

"But he must be in bed?"

"I've told you he isn't here! It must be nearly three months since he slept in his own bed!"

And the little square window of the lodge thudded back into place like a guillotine. They stood in the darkness under the gateway.

"Go away!"

The door opened again and they went out.

Louise was forced to sit down on a stone post; and with her head in her hands she wept profusely, with all her heart. Dawn was breaking, some carts went past.

Catherine got her home, supporting her, kissing her, giving her all kinds of good advice culled from her own experience. Lovers were not worth making oneself unhappy over. If this one failed her, she would find others!

Chapter Three

When Rosanette's enthusiasm for the Mobile Guards had subsided, she became more enchanting than ever, and Frédéric, without noticing it, fell into the habit of living at her apartment.

The best part of the day was the morning, on their terrace. Wearing a cambric jacket, with slippers on her bare feet, she flitted around him, cleaning out the cage where she kept her canaries, giving fresh water to her goldfish, and gardening with a fire shovel in the window-box from which nasturtiums climbed up a trellis against the wall. Then, with their elbows on the rail of their balcony, they watched the carriages and passersby together and warmed themselves in the sun while they made plans for the evening. He would go off for two hours at the most, after which they would visit some theater or other, sitting in a stage box, and Rosanette, a large bouquet in hand, listened to the orchestra, while Frédéric leaned down to whisper jovial or gallant remarks into her ear. On other evenings they would hire a barouche to take them to the Bois de Boulogne, drive around until it was late, the middle of the night; then come back by the Arc de Triomphe and the great avenue, savoring the night air, with the stars above them and before them, as far as they could see, all the lighted gas lamps forming a double string of luminous pearls.

Frédéric always had to wait for her when they were going out; she took a long time to tie the ribbons of her bonnet under her chin and she would smile at herself in her wardrobe mirror. Then, linking arms with him and forcing him to look at them together, she would say:

"How handsome we look like that, side by side! Oh, my poor darling, I shall eat you up!"

He was now her thing, her property. This gave her countenance a perpetual radiance; at the same time her manner seemed more languorous and her figure more rounded and, without being able to pinpoint what was different, Frédéric nevertheless felt that she had changed.

One day she told him, as if it was very important, that Arnoux had opened a draper's shop for a woman who used to work in his factory; he went there every evening, "had spent a great deal; only last week he had even given her a suite of rosewood furniture."

"How do you know about it?" asked Frédéric.

"Oh, I'm quite sure!"

Delphine, on her orders, had made inquiries. She must love Arnoux very much to be so concerned about him! He contented himself with asking:

"What's it got to do with you?"

Rosanette looked surprised at the question.

"But the dog owes me money! It's dreadful to see him keeping whores!"

Then, with an expression of triumphant hatred:

"What's more, she's making a complete fool of him! She has three other men. Well, good! Let her bleed him white! I'll be glad!"

Arnoux was indeed letting the Bordelaise exploit him with all the indulgence of an old man in love.

His factory was no longer operating; his affairs in general were in such a poor state that, to get them afloat again, he had first thought of establishing a music hall, where nothing but patriotic songs would be sung; with a subsidy from the government the place would have become at once a center for propaganda and a source of income. The change in leadership had made this scheme impossible. Now he was thinking of starting a large military hat-shop, but he lacked the necessary capital.

He was no better off in his private life. Madame Arnoux treated him less gently, was sometimes even a little harsh with him. Marthe always took her father's side. This increased the discord, and the household became intolerable. He often left it early in the morning, spent the day rambling about to tire himself out, and dined in some tavern in the country, lost in his own thoughts.

Frédéric's prolonged absence upset his normal routine. So one afternoon he came round to beg him to visit as he used to. Frédéric promised to do so.

He dared not return to Madame Arnoux's. He felt that he had betrayed her. But this behavior was cowardly. He could find no excuse for staying away. He would have to come round to it in the end so, one evening, he set off.

It was raining and he had just turned into the Passage Jouffroy when, in the light from the shop windows, a fat little man in a cap accosted him. Frédéric had no trouble recognizing Compain, the orator whose motion had caused so much laughter at the club. He was leaning on the arm of a man wearing the red cap of a Zouave, with a very long upper lip, a complexion as jaundiced as an orange, and a goatee on his chin, whose eyes as he gazed at Compain were dewy with admiration.

Compain was apparently proud of this devotion, for he said:

"Allow me to present this good fellow! He's a bootmaker of my acquaintance, a patriot! Shall we have a drink?"

When Frédéric declined, he at once started to thunder against Rateau's proposal* as a maneuver of the aristocrats. The only way to get rid of them was to start '93 all over again! Then he asked after Regimbart and a few others who were just as well known, like Masselin, Sanson, Lecornu, Maréchal, and a certain Deslauriers, who had been mixed up in the business of the carbines intercepted at Troyes.

All this came as news to Frédéric. Compain knew no more about it. He parted from Frédéric with the words:

"I'll see you soon, I imagine—you're in on it, aren't you?"

"On what?"

"The calf's head!"

"What calf's head?"

"Oh, you old fox!" said Compain, poking him in the stomach. And the two terrorists disappeared into a café.

Ten minutes later Frédéric's thoughts were no longer on Deslauriers. He was standing on the sidewalk before a house in the Rue Paradis and looking at the lamplight behind the curtains on the second floor.

Finally he climbed the stairs.

"Is Arnoux in?"

The maid replied:

"No, but come in just the same."

*Rateau, a deputy from Charente, had proposed the dissolution of the constituent assembly and the election of a legislative assembly. This proposition was adopted on January 29, 1849.

And, opening a door abruptly, she said:

"Madame, here is Monsieur Moreau!"

She stood up, as white as her collar. She was trembling:

"To what do I owe the honor of . . . such an unexpected visit?"

"Nothing! The pleasure of seeing old friends!"

And, as he sat down:

"How is Arnoux?"

"Very well! He's out."

"Oh, I understand. Still the same old habits! A little amusement in the evenings!"

"Why not? After a day spent doing arithmetic, the brain needs a rest!"

She even praised her husband as a hard worker. This irritated Frédéric and, pointing to a piece of black material with blue braid that lay on her knees, he said:

"What are you doing with that?"

"It's a jacket I'm altering for my daughter."

"By the way, I don't see her. Where is she?"

"At boarding school," replied Madame Arnoux.

Her eyes filled with tears; she held them back, plying her needle rapidly. To keep his poise he had taken up a copy of *L'Illustration* from the table beside her.

"These caricatures of Cham's are very funny, aren't they?"

"Yes."

Then they fell silent again.

A sudden gust of wind shook the window.

"What weather!" said Frédéric.

"Yes, it's really very good of you to have come in this horrible rain!"

"Oh, it doesn't worry me! I'm not one of those people it stops from keeping their appointments!"

"What appointment?" she asked innocently.

"Don't you remember?"

She trembled and bowed her head.

He put his hand gently on her arm.

"I can tell you that I suffered terribly!"

She replied, in a mournful voice:

"But I was terrified for my child!"

She told him about little Eugène's illness and all the anguish of that day.

"Thank you! Ah, thank you! My doubts are gone! I love you now as I always have!"

"No! That's not true!"

"Why not?"

She looked at him coldly:

"You're forgetting about the other woman! The one you take to the races! The one whose portrait is in your house! Your mistress!"

"Yes!" cried Frédéric. "I deny nothing. I'm a swine! Listen to me!" He had taken her as his mistress out of despair, as one commits suicide. Anyhow, he had made her very unhappy, to avenge his own shame on her. "It was agonizing! Don't you understand?"

Madame Arnoux turned her beautiful face toward him, holding out her hand, and they shut their eyes, absorbed in an infinite, sweet ecstasy. Then they sat close together, gazing into each other's faces.

"Did you really believe that I no longer loved you?" She replied in a low voice, full of tenderness:

"No, in spite of everything, I felt in the bottom of my heart that it was impossible and that one day the obstacle between us would disappear!"

"So did I! And I longed to see you again so much I nearly died of it!"

"Once," she continued, "in the Palais-Royal, I walked past you!"

"Really?"

And he told her how happy he had been to see her again at the Dambreuses.

"But how I loathed you when I left that evening!"

"Poor boy!"

"My life is so sad!"

"So is mine! . . . If it were only the sorrows, the worries, the humiliations, all that I endure as a wife and as a mother, I would not complain, since we must all die; but the terrible thing is my isolation, with no one . . ."

"But I am here!"

"Oh, yes!"

Her bosom swelled with a sob of tenderness. She opened her arms and they stood locked together in a long kiss.

The floor creaked. A woman stood beside them. It was Rosanette. Madame Arnoux had recognized her; she examined her, her wide-stretched eyes full of surprise and indignation. Finally Rosanette said:

"I've come to speak to Monsieur Arnoux about business."

"You can see he isn't here."

"Yes, that's true!" replied the Maréchale, "your maid was right! I beg your pardon!"

Then, turning to Frédéric:

"So this is where you are, darling!"

The use of this endearment in front of her made Madame Arnoux flush as if she had been slapped in the face.

"I repeat, my husband is not here!"

Then the Maréchale, who was gazing round the room, said calmly:

"Shall we go home? I've got a cab downstairs."

He pretended not to hear her.

"Come on, let's go!"

"Oh, yes! Since you've got the cab! Go! Go!" said Madame Arnoux.

They went out. She leaned over the banisters to see the last of them, and a shrill, heart-rending laugh came down to them from the top of the stairs. Frédéric pushed Rosanette into the cab, sat down opposite her, and did not utter a word during the entire journey.

He himself had brought on this hideous scene, whose consequences were so disastrous to him. He felt, at the same time, shame for his crushing humiliation and regret for his lost happiness; when he had at last been on the point of grasping it, it had gone forever out of reach! And it was her fault, this slut, this whore! He would have liked to strangle her; he was choking with rage. When they reached home he flung his hat down on a chair, tore off his cravat and said:

"Well, you've just done a beautiful job, haven't you?"

She stood proudly in front of him:

"Well, what of it? What's the harm?"

"What! You're spying on me aren't you?"

"Is it my fault? Why do you go off to amuse yourself with decent women?"

"That's got nothing to do with it! I won't have you insulting them."

"How did I insult her?"

He had no answer and, in a voice filled with loathing, said:

"But that other time, at the Champ de Mars . . ."

"What a bore you are, with your old girlfriends!"

"Bitch!"

He raised his fist.

"Don't kill me! I'm pregnant!"

Frédéric recoiled:

"You're lying!"

"Just look at me!"

She picked up a candle and, pointing to her face, said: "Do you know the symptoms?"

Her skin was unusually bloated and speckled with small yellow spots. Frédéric did not deny the evidence. He went over to the window and opened it, walked up and down the room a few times, and then slumped into an armchair.

This turn of events was a calamity, which to begin with would defer their separation and would upset all his plans besides. Moreover, the idea of being a father seemed to him grotesque. But why? If, instead of the Maréchale? . . . And his daydream became so absorbing that he had a kind of hallucination. He saw, on the rug in front of the fireplace, a little girl. She looked like Madame Arnoux and a little like him: brown-haired, white-skinned, with dark eyes, thick brows, and a pink ribbon in her curly hair. (Oh, how he would have loved her!) And he seemed to hear her voice: "Papa! Papa!"

Rosanette, who had just undressed, came up to him, saw a tear in the corner of his eye, and kissed him gravely on the forehead. He got up, saying:

"Well, we're not going to kill the brat!"

At this she broke into a flood of chatter. It would certainly be a boy! They would call him Frédéric. She must start getting clothes for him—and, seeing her so happy, he was filled with pity. Since he no longer felt any anger now, he asked her the reason for her actions earlier in the evening.

It was because that very day Mademoiselle Vatnaz had sent her a bill she had owed for a long time, and she had rushed round to Arnoux's house to get some money.

"I would have given it to you!" said Frédéric.

"It was simpler to collect what belongs to me from him and give her a thousand francs."

"I hope that's all that you owe her?"

"Certainly," she replied.

The next day, at nine in the evening (the time recommended by the porter), Frédéric went to call on Mademoiselle Vatnaz.

In the hall he bumped into piles of furniture. But, guided by the sound of voices and music, he opened a door and found himself in the middle of a "reception." A young lady in spectacles was playing the piano and Delmar stood in front of it, serious as a pontiff, declaiming some humanitarian verses on prostitution; his echoing voice rolled round the room, supported by sustained chords. Against the wall sat a row of women dressed, for the

most part, in dark colors, without collars or cuffs. Five
or six men, all intellectuals, were dotted about on chairs.
An old writer of fables, a wreck of a man, sat in an
armchair—and the acrid smell from the two lamps
mingled with the aroma of the chocolate which filled the
bowls on the card table.

Mademoiselle Vatnaz, with an Oriental scarf around her
waist, was standing on one side of the fireplace. Dussardier
stood at the other, opposite her; he seemed a little em-
barrased by his position. Besides, this artistic group in-
timidated him.

Had the Vatnaz made a final break with Delmar? No,
perhaps not. However, she seemed to keep a jealous eye
on the worthy clerk and, when Frédéric asked her for a
word in private, she signaled him to accompany them to
her room. When the thousand francs had been counted
out she demanded the interest as well.

"It's not worth bothering about!" said Dussardier.

"Keep your mouth shut!"

This show of cowardice in such a courageous man
pleased Frédéric for it seemed to justify his own. He
brought back the bill and never mentioned the scene at
Madame Arnoux's again. But from that moment on, all
the Maréchale's defects became apparent to him.

Her taste was incurably bad, her laziness beyond be-
lief. She was as ignorant as a savage, to the point of
considering Doctor Desrogis a celebrity, and she was
proud to invite him and his wife to her house because
they were "married people." She fussily ruled over the
life of Mademoiselle Irma, a pathetic little creature
with a tiny voice, whose protector, a "very gentlemanly"
former customs official, was good at card tricks; Rosanette
called him "ducky." Now could Frédéric bear the way
she repeated stupid phrases like: "Bunk!" "Go to the
dickens!" and "You never can tell!"; and she insisted on
dusting her knicknacks every morning with an old pair of
white gloves! But the way she behaved to her maid revolted him more than anything else—the woman's wages
were always overdue and she even lent money to her
mistress. On the day when they settled their accounts they
wrangled like two fishwives, then embraced as a sign of
reconciliation. Rosanette's company had lost its charm. It
was a relief to him when Madame Dambreuse's evening
parties started again.

She amused him, at least! She knew all the society
intrigues, the ambassadors' activities, the people who

worked for the fashion houses; and if she let fall a commonplace remark, it was couched in such banal terms that you could take it seriously or ironically. She was in her element in a group of twenty or so people who were talking together, forgetting nobody, eliciting the answers she wanted, avoiding those that might be dangerous! When she made them, the simplest remarks seemed confidences, the least of her smiles could start one dreaming, and her charm, like the exquisite perfume she usually wore, was complex and indefinable. In her company Frédéric always felt the pleasures of discovery and, yet, each time he saw her she showed the same serenity, like the shimmer of clear water. But why was she so cold toward her niece? Sometimes she even looked at her very strangely.

As soon as the question of marriage had been raised, she had protested to Monsieur Dambreuse on the grounds of the "dear child's health," and had taken her straight off to the spa at Balaruc. On their return new objections had arisen: the young man had no position, this grand passion did not seem very serious, nothing would be lost by waiting. Martinon had replied that he would wait. His conduct had been irreproachable. He extolled Frédéric. He did more; he told him how to please Madame Dambreuse, even hinting that he knew of the aunt's feeling through the niece.

As for Monsieur Dambreuse, far from showing signs of jealousy, he surrounded his young friend with kindness, consulted him about various things, and even concerned himself with his future, so that one day when Old Roque's name was mentioned he whispered to him slyly:

"You were wise there."

And Cécile, Miss John, the servants, the porter, everyone in the house was charming to him. He went there every evening, deserting Rosanette. Her future motherhood had made her graver, even a little sad, as if she were tormented by anxiety. To all his questions she replied:

"You're mistaken. I'm feeling fine!"

It was five notes she had signed in the old days. Not daring to tell Frédéric after he had paid the first, she had gone back to Arnoux, who had promised her in writing a third of his profits from a company that sold gas lighting to towns in the Languedoc (a marvelous outfit!) but asking her not to use the letter before the stockholders' meeting; the meeting kept being put off from week to week.

Meanwhile the Maréchale needed money. She would rather have died than ask Frédéric. She didn't want it from him. It would have spoiled their love. He certainly took care of the household expenses; but a little carriage he hired by the month, and other expenses which had become necessary since he saw so much of the Dambreuses, prevented him from doing more for his mistress. On two or three occasions, when he had come in unexpectedly, he thought he had seen masculine backs vanishing through doorways, and she often went out without saying where she was going. Frédéric did not attempt to dig any deeper. One of these days he would do something decisive. He dreamed of a different life, which would be pleasanter and nobler in every way. Such an ideal made him indulgent toward the Dambreuses' circle.

It was closely linked to the Rue de Poitiers.* There he met the great M. A., the illustrious B., the profound C., the eloquent Z., the tremendous Y., the elderly stars of the center left, the paladins of the right, the burgraves of the solid center, the eternal characters of the political comedy. He was astounded by their execrable language, their small-mindedness, their spite, their bad faith—all these men who had voted for the Constitution were doing their best to destroy it—and they were very busy, putting out manifestos, pamphlets, and biographies; Hussonnet's on Fumichon was a masterpiece. Nonancourt was in charge of propaganda in the countryside, Monsieur de Grémonville worked on the clergy, Martinon rallied the youth of the middle classes. Everyone had a task suitable to his talents, even Cisy himself. Now that his thoughts had turned to serious matters, he spent the entire day doing errands for the party in his cabriolet.

Like a barometer, Monsieur Dambreuse always showed the latest variation in the political line. Whenever Lamartine's name was mentioned he quoted the words of a laborer: "That's enough of the lyre now!"†

Cavaignac was nothing but a traitor in his eyes. The president,‡ whom he had admired for three months, was beginning to drop in his estimation (not having displayed

---

*The "Réunion of the Rue de Poitiers" was a Legitimist/Orléanist club, which was working for the restoration of the monarchy.

†When the rioters invaded the Chamber of Deputies on May 15, 1848, Lamartine attempted to calm them down and one of the mob shouted: "*Assez de lyre comme ça!*"

‡Louis-Napoléon Bonaparte, elected president December, 1848, replacing General Cavaignac.

the "necessary energy") and, as he always had to have some savior, his gratitude since the affair at the Conservatoire* had gone to Changarnier: "Changarnier, thank God . . . Let's hope that Changarnier . . . Oh, there's nothing to fear as long as Changarnier . . ."

Monsieur Thiers won most praise of all because of his anti-socialist book, in which he had shown himself a thinker as well as a writer. They laughed uproariously at Pierre Leroux, who quoted from the philosophies in the Chamber. They joked about Fourier's followers. They went to applaud the *Foire aux Idées*† and compared its authors to Aristophanes. Frédéric went along, like the others.

Political chatter and the good life were turning his morality flabby. Although he found these people mediocre, he was proud of knowing them and in his heart he longed for their esteem. A mistress like Madame Dambreuse would establish his position.

He started to take the necessary steps.

She would encounter him when she went for a walk, he always spent a few moments in her box at the theater and, knowing the hours she went to church, he would station himself behind a pillar in a melancholic pose. There was a continual flow of little notes concerning curios or concerts, the borrowing of books or magazines. Apart from his visit in the evening, he would sometimes pay another toward the end of the day; and his pleasure would grow by stages as he passed in turn through the main gateway, the courtyard, the hall, and the two drawing rooms. Finally he would arrive at her boudoir, which was as secret as the grave and as warm as an alcove, where one bumped into tufted furniture, surrounded by objects of every description: chiffonniers, screens, bowls and dishes made of lacquer, tortoise-shell, ivory, malachite, expensive trifles, constantly changing. There were also some simple things: three pebbles from Étretat for paperweights, a Frisian cap hanging from a Chinese screen, but all these objects contributed to a harmonious whole, one was even struck by a sense of grandeur which may have come from the high ceiling, the opulent door-curtains, and the long

---

*A riot on June 13, 1849, centered on the district around the Conservatory of Arts and Crafts and was put down by Changarnier, commander in chief of the army in Paris and of the National Guard.

†A political revue by Leuven and Brunswick which played at the Vaudeville from January to October, 1849.

silk fringes hanging down over the gilded legs of the stools.

She was nearly always sitting on a little sofa next to the flower-stand that filled the window recess. He would place himself on the edge of a large pouf with casters and pay her the aptest possible compliments, and she would watch him, smiling, her head tilted a little to one side.

He read poetry to her, putting his whole soul into the lines in an attempt to move her and to compel her admiration. She would stop him with a disparaging comment or some practical remark, and their conversation kept returning to the eternal subject of Love. They discussed what inspired it, if women felt it more keenly than men, how their own ideas about it differed. Frédéric tried to state his opinions while steering clear of both coarseness and insipidity. It became a kind of contest between them, sometimes agreeable, sometimes irksome.

When he was with her he did not feel the ravishment of his whole being that drew him to Madame Arnoux, nor the gay licentiousness that Rosanette had originally inspired in him. But he coveted her as something unusual and difficult to achieve because she was noble, because she was rich, because she was pious—imagining that she had delicate sentiments as rare as her laces, with holy medals against her skin and modesty in the midst of depravity.

He made use of his old love. He described, as if she had inspired them, all the sentiments that Madame Arnoux had once aroused in him, his languors, his apprehensions, his dreams. She received it all like someone accustomed to this sort of thing, without rejecting him formally but ceding nothing, and he had no more success in seducing her than Martinon had in getting married. To get rid of her niece's suitor, Madame Dambreuse accused him of having an eye on her money, and even begged her husband to test him. Monsieur Dambreuse accordingly told the young man that Cécile, being the orphaned daughter of poor parents, had neither expectations nor dowry.

Martinon, either disbelieving him, or feeling that he had gone too far to back out, or with that idiotic stubbornness which sometimes turns out to be an act of genius, replied that his own income of fifteen thousand livres annually would be enough to keep them. This unforeseen disinterestedness touched the banker's heart. He promised to get him a position as tax inspector and offered to put up his bond and, in May, 1850, Martinon married Mademoiselle Cécile. There was no ball. The young people left for Italy that same evening. Frédéric paid a call on Madame Dambreuse the following day. She seemed paler than usual and contradicted him sharply on two or three minor points. Anyhow, all men were egoists!

Yet some were capable of devotion, at least *he* was.

"Oh, nonsense! You're the same as the rest!"

Her eyelids were red; she was crying. Then, forcing a smile, she said:

"Forgive me! I'm behaving badly! It was just a sad thought I had."

He didn't understand her.

"But it doesn't matter. She's weaker than I realized," he thought.

She rang for a glass of water, drank a mouthful, sent it away, then complained that her servants were abominable. To amuse her he offered his services as a domestic, alleging that he was capable of serving at table, dusting, announcing visitors, in fact that he could be a valet or rather a footman, although they were now out of fashion. He would have liked to stand on the back of her carriage, wearing a hat with cock's feathers.

"And how majestically I would walk behind you, carrying a little dog!"

"How gay you are!" said Madame Dambreuse.

Wasn't it stupid, he replied, to take everything seriously? There was quite enough misery in the world without making more for oneself. Nothing was worth sorrowing over. Madame Dambreuse raised her eyebrows, in a gesture of vague approbation.

This similarity of feeling encouraged Frédéric to greater boldness. He had learned something from his earlier mistakes. He went on:

"Our grandfathers knew how to live better than we do. Why not follow our impulses?" After all, love was not such a dreadfully important thing in itself.

"But what you're saying is immoral!"

She had settled herself once more on the little sofa. He sat down on the edge, next to her feet.

"Can't you see that I'm lying? To please a woman we've got to parade either the frivolity of a clown, or epic passions! They laugh at us if we tell them simply that we love them! To me all these extravagances they enjoy are a profanation of real love, so that now it's come to be

impossible to speak of it, especially to women who are
. . . very intelligent."

She looked at him through her half-shut eyelids. He
lowered his voice and leaned toward her:

"Yes, you frighten me! Do I offend you? . . . Forgive
me! . . . I didn't mean to say all that! But it's not my
fault! You are so beautiful!"

Madame Dambreuse closed her eyes and he was surprised by the ease of his conquest. The great trees in the
garden had been rustling softly; now they were still. The
sky was streaked with long red bands of motionless clouds
and it seemed that the whole universe waited in suspense.
A confused memory of other evenings like this, with similar silences, came into his mind. Where could it have been?

He knelt, took her hand, and swore he would love her
forever. Then, as he was leaving, she beckoned him back
and whispered:

"Come back to dinner! We shall be alone!"

It seemed to Frédéric, as he went down the staircase,
that he had become a new man, that the scented air of
hothouses surrounded him, that he had finally entered the
superior world of patrician adultery and high intrigue. All
that he needed to occupy the top rank in it was a woman
like Madame Dambreuse. Probably avid for power and
action, and married to a mediocrity whom she had helped
enormously, she needed a strong man to guide her. Nothing was impossible now! He felt capable of riding two
hundred leagues or working sleeplessly, night after night,
without tiring; his heart was bursting with pride.

A man was walking along the sidewalk in front of him,
dressed in an old overcoat, his head bowed, and with
such a dejected air that Frédéric turned round to look at
him. The other raised his eyes. It was Deslauriers. He
hesitated. Frédéric threw his arms round him.

"What! My poor old friend! Is it really you?"

And he dragged him off to his house, asking him dozens
of questions at the same time.

Ledru-Rollin's ex-commissioner told him first of the
troubles he had suffered. He preached brotherhood to the
conservatives and respect for the law to the socialists, so
the former had tried to shoot him and the latter had
brought a rope to hang him with. After the June uprising he had been abruptly dismissed. He had thrown
himself into a conspiracy, the business of the weapons
seized at Troyes. He had been released for lack of evidence. After that, the action committee sent him to Lon-

don, where he had come to blows with his colleagues in the middle of a banquet. Back in Paris . . .

"Why didn't you come to see me?"

"You were always out! Your porter put on mysterious airs, so I didn't know what to think; and then I didn't want to turn up as a failure."

He had knocked on the door of democracy, offering to serve her with his pen, his tongue, his best efforts; everywhere he had been rejected; people mistrusted him; and he had sold off his watch, his library, and his linen.

"I'd be better off rotting on the pontoons at Belle-Isle with Sénécal."*

Frédéric, who was tying his cravat at that moment, did not seem terribly disturbed by this news.

"Oh, old Sénécal's been transported, has he?"

Deslauriers replied, with an envious glance round the room:

"Not everyone has your luck!"

"You'll have to excuse me," said Frédéric, without picking up the allusion, "but I'm dining out. They'll give you something to eat; order whatever you like! You can even have my bed."

In the face of this overwhelming cordiality, Deslauriers' bitterness disappeared.

"Your bed? But won't that . . . put you out?"

"Not at all. I have others!"

"Oh, very good," replied the lawyer, with a laugh. "Where are you dining, eh?"

"At Madame Dambreuse's."

"Is it . . . by any chance . . . could it be?"

"You're too curious," said Frédéric, with a smile that confirmed his conjecture.

Then, after glancing at the clock, he sat down again.

"Well, that's life. And you mustn't despair, my old champion of the people!"

"Mercy! Someone else can take that on!"

The lawyer detested the workers, for he had suffered at their hands in his province, a coal-mining district. Each pit had elected a provisional government which had given him orders.

"Anyhow, they behaved delightfully everywhere: at Lyons, at Lille, at Le Havre, at Paris! They acted just like the manufacturers who wanted to ban all imports— demanding that all English, German, Belgian, and Savoy

*The June rioters were now imprisoned at Belle-Isle.

workers be kicked out! And as for their intelligence, what good were their famous trade unions under the Restoration? They joined the National Guard in eighteen-thirty but didn't have sense enough to take control of it! And right after the rising in forty-eight, didn't the trade guilds reappear each with its own banner! They even asked for their own deputies, who would have spoken on their behalf alone! Just like the beet-root deputies, who only worry about beet-root! I've had enough of those characters, prostrating themselves successively before Robespierre's scaffold, the Emperor's boots, and Louis-Philippe's umbrella—rabble, eternally ready to serve anyone who will throw them a mouthful of bread! People are always condemning the venality of Talleyrand and Mirabeau, but the messenger downstairs would sell his country for fifty centimes if you promised him that he could henceforth charge three francs for each errand! Oh, what a failure it's been! We should have set the whole of Europe in flames!"

Frédéric replied:

"But the spark was missing! You were nothing but petty shopkeepers, and the best of you were armchair theorists! And the workers do have a right to complain: except for a million subtracted from the civil list, which you granted them with the basest flattery, you have given them nothing but words! The account book is still in the boss' hands; and the employee, even in a court of law, is still inferior to his master, since no one will take his word for anything. In short, the Republic seems to me to be out of date. Who knows? Maybe progress is only attainable through an aristocracy, or a single man? The initiative always comes from above! The people, whatever one may pretend, are immature!"

"You may be right," said Deslauriers.

According to Frédéric, the great mass of people wanted simply to be left in peace (he had profited from the conversations at the Dambreuses' house), and all the odds were in favor of the Conservatives. But the party needed new blood.

"If you offered yourself I am sure . . ."

He didn't finish. Deslauriers understood, passed his hands over his forehead, then suddenly said:

"But what about you? There's nothing to prevent you, is there? Why shouldn't you be a deputy?" There was a vacancy for a candidate in the Aube, as the result of a double election. Monsieur Dambreuse, who had been re-elected to the legislature, represented a different constituency. "Would you like me to do something about it?" He knew lots of tavern-keepers, teachers, doctors, lawyers' clerks, and their employers. "Anyhow, one can make the peasants believe anything at all!"

Frédéric felt his ambition rekindle.

Deslauriers added:

"You should certainly find me a job in Paris."

"Oh, that won't be hard, through Monsieur Dambreuse."

"Speaking of coal," went on the lawyer, "whatever became of his great company? That's the kind of job I need! And I would be useful to them without losing my independence."

Frédéric promised to take him to see the banker in the next three days.

His dinner alone with Madame Dambreuse was an exquisite experience. She sat opposite him, on the other side of the table, smiling over a basket of flowers, by the light of a hanging lamp; and, as the window was open, they could see the stars. They spoke seldom, probably because they didn't trust themselves, but as soon as the servants turned their backs they blew kisses to one another. He told her of his idea of running for the Assembly. She approved, and even offered to get Monsieur Dambreuse to work on his behalf.

That evening a few friends turned up to congratulate and commiserate with her. She must be so sad to have lost her niece? However, it was a good thing that the young couple had gone abroad now; later there would be children and other hindrances! But Italy did not live up to expectations. Still, they were at the age of illusions! And then everything seemed beautiful on a honeymoon! The last two to leave were Frédéric and Monsieur de Grémonville. The diplomat didn't want to go. At last, at twelve o'clock, he got up. Madame Dambreuse signaled Frédéric to leave with him, and thanked him for his obedience with a squeeze of her hand sweeter than all the rest.

The Maréchale gave a cry of joy on seeing him. She had been waiting for him since five o'clock. He excused himself by saying he had been involved in an undertaking essential to Deslauriers' interests. He wore a triumphant expression, a sort of halo, that dazzled Rosanette.

"It may be because of your evening clothes—they suit you so well—but I've never seen you look so handsome! How handsome you are!"

In an ecstasy of feeling, she swore inwardly that she

would never again give herself to another man, no matter what might happen, even if she should die of starvation!

And her beautiful, dewy eyes sparkled with such passion that Frédéric drew her onto his knees, saying to himself: "What a bastard I am!" glorying in his own perversity.

Chapter Four

When Deslauriers went to see him, Monsieur Dambreuse was thinking of reviving his great coal scheme. But the idea of merging all the different companies into a single entity was in bad odor; there was a hue and cry now over monopoly, as if you didn't need enormous capital for this kind of undertaking!

Deslauriers, who had made a point of reading Gobet's book and Monsieur Chappe's article in the *Journal des Mines*, knew the subject inside out. He proved that the law of 1810 gave the owner of a concession inalienable rights to the profits from it. Moreover, the enterprise could be given a democratic color: to forbid the merging of coal firms was an attack on the very principle of association.

Monsieur Dambreuse gave him some notes to work up into a memorandum. As for payment for his work, he made promises that were all the better for being somewhat vague.

Deslauriers went back to Frédéric's and told him about the meeting. What's more, he had seen Madame Dambreuse at the foot of the stairs as he went out.

"I certainly congratulate you there!"

Then they spoke of the election. Some plan would have to be devised.

Three days later, Deslauriers reappeared with a sheet of paper, destined for the newspaper, which turned out to be a friendly letter in which Monsieur Dambreuse gave his blessing to Frédéric's candidacy. Upheld by a conservative and extolled by a red, this should certainly succeed. How had the capitalist come to sign such a confection? The lawyer, on his own initiative and without the slightest embarrassment, had gone to show it to Madame Dam-

365

breuse, who had found it very good and had done the rest.

This proceeding took Frédéric by surprise. However, he approved of it; then, as Deslauriers would be dealing with Monsieur Roque, he told him about his situation with regard to Louise.

"Tell them anything you like; that I'm having business worries, that I'll sort things out; she's young enough to wait!"

Deslauriers left and Frédéric considered himself a man of decision. Besides, he had a feeling of gratification, generally, of deep satisfaction. His joy in possessing a rich woman was unspoilt by any contrast; his feelings harmonized with their setting. His whole life, nowadays, was filled with pleasures.

The greatest, perhaps, was to watch Madame Dambreuse in her salon, surrounded by a group of people. The seemliness of her manners made him think of other poses; while she conversed in chilly tones he remembered her stammered words of love; all the respect shown to her virtue delighted him as an indirect homage to himself, and he sometimes longed to cry:

"But I know her better than you do! She's mine!"

Their liaison was soon acknowledged and accepted. During that whole winter Madame Dambreuse took Frédéric into society.

He nearly always arrived before she did; and he would watch her come in, her arms bare, a fan in her hand, pearls in her hair. She would pause on the threshold, framed in the doorway, and there would be a moment of indecision as she narrowed her eyes to see if he were there. She took him home in her carriage; the rain whipped at the windows, the passersby scuttled past in the mud like shadows and, pressed closely together, they took it all in vaguely, with a calm disdain. On different pretexts he would spend a good hour more in her room.

It was mainly through boredom that Madame Dambreuse had yielded. But she was determined not to waste this final experience. She wanted a grand passion and set about loading him with adulation and caresses.

She sent him flowers; she made him a tapestry chair; she gave him a cigar case, an inkstand, dozens of little objects of everyday use, so that he could not perform the smallest action without being reminded of her. These attentions charmed him at first, but soon he took them for granted.

She would take a cab to one end of an alley, leave by

the other and, gliding along by the walls, with a double veil over her face, reach the corner where Frédéric was waiting to give her his arm and hurry her off to his house. His two servants would be out and the porter doing errands; she used to glance around, see there was nothing to fear, and sigh like an exile setting foot once more in his native land. Their luck made them bolder. Their meetings grew more frequent. One evening she even turned up unexpectedly in full evening dress. This sort of surprise might be dangerous; he scolded her for taking such a risk. Moreover, she was not attractive in her ball dress, whose low-cut bodice displayed too much of her skinny chest.

At that moment, he admitted what he had hitherto concealed from himself; the disillusionment of his senses. This did not prevent him from feigning great ardor, but to feel it he had to evoke the image of Rosanette or Madame Arnoux.

This atrophy of the heart left his head entirely free; and his ambition for a great position in society was stronger than ever. Since he had such a convenient stepping-stone, the least he could do was to make use of it.

One morning, toward the middle of January, Sénécal came into his study and, in response to his exclamation of surprise, explained that he was now Deslauriers' secretary. He had in fact brought Frédéric a letter. It contained good news, but nevertheless reproved him for his negligence. He must visit his constituency.

The future deputy said that he would set out in two days time.

Sénécal expressed no opinion of Frédéric's candidacy. He spoke of himself and the affairs of the nation.

Although the latter were in a lamentable condition, he was delighted, for this would lead to communism. In the first place, the administration was moving in that direction whether they liked it or not, since every day more and more things were being managed by the government. As for the rights of property, the Constitution of 1848, in spite of its weaknesses, had dealt with them unsparingly; in the name of the public good, the State could henceforth take over whatever it judged necessary to itself. Sénécal declared himself in favor of Authority; and Frédéric noticed in what he said an exaggeration of his own words to Deslauriers. The republican even railed against the inadequacy of the masses.

Defending the rights of a minority, "Robespierre

brought Louis XVI before the national convention and saved the people. The end justifies the means. Dictatorship is sometimes indispensable. Long live tyranny, provided that the tyrant does the right thing!"

They talked for a long time and, as he was leaving, Sénécal admitted (which may have been the object of his visit) that Deslauriers was growing very impatient at Monsieur Dambreuse's silence.

But Monsieur Dambreuse was ill. Frédéric, as a friend of the family, was allowed to see him every day.

General Changarnier's dismissal had greatly alarmed the capitalist.* That very evening a burning pain had started in his chest, accompanied by such difficulty in breathing that he was unable to lie down. The application of leeches brought immediate relief. His dry cough disappeared, his breathing became more and more regular and, eight days later, as he was drinking his broth, he remarked:

"Ah, I feel better now! But I nearly crossed the Great Divide!"

"Not without me!" cried Madame Dambreuse, implying that she would have been unable to survive him.

Instead of replying he bestowed on her and her lover a singular smile, compounded of indulgence, irony, and even a dash of amusement.

Frédéric wanted to leave for Nogent. Madame Dambreuse objected, and he alternately packed and unpacked his bags according to the changing course of the illness.

Suddenly, Monsieur Dambreuse started to spit blood profusely. The "princes of science" who were consulted could advise nothing new. His legs swelled and he grew weaker. He had several times expressed a desire to see Cécile who was at the other end of France with her husband; for he had taken up his post as a tax inspector a month before. He gave explicit directions that she was to be sent for. Madame Dambreuse wrote three letters, which she showed to him.

She would not trust even the nursing sister, and refused to leave him for an instant, going without sleep. The people who came to write their names in the book at the lodge inquired after her with admiration, and the passersby

---

*As commander of the National Guard, Changarnier had acquired a great reputation as an energetic suppressor of riots. Louis-Napoléon, whose policies he had opposed, relieved him of his command in January, 1851, in preparation for his *coup d'état* at the end of that year.

were filled with respect at the quantity of straw which had been laid in the street under the banker's windows.

At five o'clock on February 12th, an alarming hemorrhage from the lungs occurred. The attending physician gave them warning that he was in critical condition and someone rushed to fetch a priest.

While Monsieur Dambreuse was making his confession, his wife watched him with curiosity from a distance. Afterwards, the young doctor applied a blister-patch and waited.

The lamps, concealed behind the furniture, shed an uneven light over the room. From the foot of the bed, Frédéric and Madame Dambreuse kept watch over the dying man. The priest and doctor murmured together in a window recess, and the nun muttered prayers on her knees.

At last the death rattle was heard. The hands grew cold, the face began to pale. From time to time, he would suddenly take an enormous breath; these became rarer and rarer; he babbled two or three confused words, breathed a little sigh as he rolled up his eyes, and the head fell to one side on the pillow.

For a moment everyone remained motionless.

Madame Dambreuse approached and, without any sign of repugnance, with the simplicity of one who does her duty, closed his eyes.

Then she threw out her arms, twisting about as if in a spasm of controlled despair, and left the room leaning on the doctor and the nun. A quarter of an hour later, Frédéric went up to her bedroom.

There was an indefinable fragrance in the air, an emanation of all the delicate things that filled the room. A black dress was spread out in the middle of the bed, contrasting with the pink coverlet.

Madame Dambreuse was standing by the fireplace. Although he did not imagine that she was deeply grieved, he thought that she might be a little sad and, in a sympathetic voice, he said:

"Are you unhappy?"

"Me? No, not at all."

As she turned round she caught sight of the dress and examined it, then she told him to make himself at home:

"Smoke if you like! This is my house now!"

And she added, with a deep sigh:

"Oh, Blessed Mother, what a relief!"

Frédéric was astonished. He replied, kissing her hand:

"But we were left quite free!"

This allusion to the facility of their love affair seemed to wound Madame Dambreuse.

"Oh, you don't know what I did for him, nor the agony I've been through!"

"What do you mean?"

"Yes, of course! What security could I enjoy with his bastard always near me, a child he introduced into the house after we had been married for five years and who, if it hadn't been for me, would certainly have led him into some foolish action."

Then she explained her financial situation. They had married under the system of separation of property. Her own inheritance amounted to three hundred thousand francs. In their marriage contract, Monsieur Dambreuse had undertaken to leave her, should she survive him, an annual income of fifteen thousand francs and the ownership of the house. But shortly afterwards he had made a will leaving her his entire fortune; this she evaluated, as far as it could be judged at the moment, at more than three million francs.

Frédéric opened his eyes wide.

"That's worth taking some trouble over, isn't it? Anyhow, I helped amass it! I was defending my own property; Cécile would have deprived me of it, unjustly!"

"Why didn't she come to see her father?" asked Frédéric.

At this question, Madame Dambreuse considered him for a moment, then replied sharply:

"I can't imagine! No heart! Oh, I know all about her! She won't get a penny out of me!"

But she hadn't been any trouble, at any rate since her marriage.

"Oh, her marriage!" sneered Madame Dambreuse.

And she blamed herself for having been too kind to that jealous, selfish, hypocritical creature.

"All her father's defects!"

She spoke of him more and more disparagingly. He had been completely insincere, ruthless, and hard as stone, "a bad man, a bad man!"

Even the wisest of us make occasional mistakes. This outburst of hatred was one of Madame Dambreuse's. Sitting opposite her in an armchair, Frédéric pondered it, scandalized.

She came over and sat down gently on his knee.

"You're the only one who's really good. The only person I love!"

As she looked at him her heart softened, a nervous reaction brought tears to her eyes, and she murmured:

"Would you like to marry me?"

At first he couldn't believe his ears. The thought of so much money made him dizzy. She repeated in a louder voice:

"Would you like to marry me?"

At last he replied with a smile:

"Can you doubt it?"

Then he felt a twinge of shame and, as a kind of reparation to the dead man, he offered to keep the vigil over the body himself. But, as he was ashamed of this pious sentiment, he added in an offhand manner:

"It might be more in keeping with the proprieties."

"Yes, you may be right," she said, "because of the servants!"

The bed had been pulled right out of the alcove. The nun was at its foot and a priest was stationed at its head, a different man, tall and thin, with a fanatical, Spanish look about him. Three candles were burning on the bedside table, which had been covered with a white cloth.

Frédéric took a chair and gazed at the dead man. His face was as yellow as straw and there was a little bloody foam at the corners of his mouth. A silk handkerchief had been tied round his head and he was wearing a cardigan; a silver crucifix lay on his chest between his folded arms.

So his busy life was over! How many times had he gone from office to office on some errand, added up figures, dabbled in businesses, listened to reports. How much claptrap, smiling, cringing! For he had acclaimed Napoléon, the Cossacks, Louis XVIII, 1830, the workers, every regime in turn, so in love with Power that he would have paid to sell himself.

But he left behind him the estate of La Fortelle, three factories in Picardy, the forest of Crancé in the Yonne, a farm near Orléans, and quantities of valuable goods and chattels.

Frédéric added up his fortune again; all this was going to belong to him! He thought first of what "people would say," then of a present for his mother, of his future teams of carriage horses, of an old family coachman whom he would like to have as his porter. The livery would have to be changed, naturally. He would take the large drawing room as his study. By knocking down three walls it would be perfectly possible to create a picture gallery on the second floor. It might be feasible to build a Turkish bath in the basement. As for Monsieur Dambreuse's study, an unattractive room, what could they do with that?

These daydreams would be brutally interrupted by the priest blowing his nose or the nun poking the fire. But reality confirmed them; the corpse was still there. His eyelids had opened again and his eyes, though veiled in viscous shadows, had an enigmatic expression that Frédéric found intolerable. He seemed to read in them a judgment on himself; and he felt something that was almost remorse, for he had never been ill-treated by this man; on the contrary he . . . "Come on! He was an old rogue!" And he looked at him more closely, to fortify himself, mentally shouting:

"Well, what is it? I didn't kill you, did I?"

Meanwhile the priest read his breviary, the nun dozed, motionless, and the wicks of the three candles grew longer.

For two hours, the carts on their way in to the Halles passed with a hollow rumble. Then the windows turned white, a cab went past, followed by a herd of female donkeys trotting along the road; and the noise of hammering, the cries of street vendors, the bray of a trumpet, all were blending into the great voice of the awakening city.

Frédéric set off. First he went to the town hall to register the death; then, when the medical officer had given him a certificate, he went back to the town hall to notify them which cemetery the family had chosen and to make arrangements with the undertakers.

An assistant showed him a price-list and a drawing, the one giving all the different classes of funeral, the other showing complete details of all the trappings involved. Did they want a hearse with beading round the top or a hearse with plumes? Should the horses' manes be plaited? Should there be aigrettes for the attendants, initials or a coat of arms, funeral lamps, a man to carry the decorations? And how many carriages? Frédéric was lavish; Madame Dambreuse was insistent that nothing should be skimped.

Then he went to the church.

The curate in charge of funerals began by criticizing

the undertaker's arrangements; for instance, the man to carry the decorations was quite useless; much better spend the money on having a lot of candles. They agreed on a low mass with music. Frédéric signed the necessary agreements, making himself responsible for all the expenses.

He went to the Hôtel de Ville next, to purchase the plot of land for the grave. A plot six foot by three cost five hundred francs. Was the grant to be for fifty years or in perpetuity?

"Oh, in perpetuity!" said Frédéric.

He took the matter seriously and went to great trouble over it. A marble cutter was waiting in the courtyard of the Dambreuses' house to show him estimates and plans for Greek, Egyptian, and Moorish tombs; but the architect of the house had already talked it over with Madame Dambreuse; and the table in the hall was covered with all sorts of prospectuses about the cleaning of mattresses, the disinfection of rooms, and the various embalming processes.

After dinner, he went back to the tailor to arrange about mourning clothes for the servants; and then there was one last errand to accomplish: he had ordered beaver gloves while the proper thing was floss-silk.

When he arrived at ten o'clock the next morning, the large drawing room was filling up with people, nearly all of whom spoke in melancholy tones and said:

"To think it's only a month since I last saw him! Oh well, we all come to it in the end!"

"Yes, but let's try to put it off as long as possible!"

Then they would give a little titter of satisfaction and even start conversations having nothing whatever to do with the matter in hand. Finally the master of ceremonies, in a black coat, knee breeches, cloak, and weepers, his rapier by his side and his three-cornered hat under his arm, bowed to them and uttered the traditional words:

"Gentlemen, at your convenience."

They set off.

It was flower market day on the place de la Madeleine. The weather was clear and mild; and the breeze that shook the canvas stalls a little puffed out the edges of the immense black cloth hanging down over the portal. Monsieur Dambreuse's escutcheon, worked onto a velvet square, appeared on it three times. It was *sable, with arm or sinister, the clenched fist gauntleted argent*, with a count's coronet and the motto: *By every way*.

The bearers carried the heavy coffin to the top of the steps and they all went in.

The six chapels, the apse, and the chairs were hung with black. The catafalque at the bottom of the choir with its large candles formed a single focus of yellow light. At both corners, flames fed by alcohol were rising from candelabra.

The principal mourners took their places in the sanctuary, the others in the nave, and the service started.

With a few exceptions, the ignorance of all those present in matters of religion was so profound that the master of ceremonies had to signal to them from time to time to stand up, kneel, and sit down. The organ and the two double-basses alternated with the choir; during the intervals of silence, the priest could be heard mumbling away at the altar; then the music and the chanting started again.

A pale light came from the three cupolas, but through the open door flooded a horizontal stream of white radiance that lit up all the bared heads, while halfway up the building a belt of shadows was penetrated by the reflected light gleaming from the gold that decorated the ridges of the pendentives and the foliage on the capitals of the pillars.

Frédéric passed the time by listening to the *Dies irae;* he looked at the rest of the congregation and tried to see the paintings of the life of Mary Magdalene, but they were too high up. Luckily, Pellerin came to sit beside him and immediately began a long dissertation on the frescos. The bell tolled. They left the church.

The hearse, adorned with hanging draperies and tall bunches of feathers, took the road toward the Père-Lachaise cemetery. It was drawn by four black horses with plaited manes and plumes on their heads, enveloped to their hooves in long caparisons embroidered with silver. Their driver wore riding boots and a three-cornered hat with a long crepe ribbon. The cords were held by four men: one of the treasurers of the National Assembly, a member of the general council of the Aube, a delegate from the coal-mining company, and Fumichon, as a friend. The deceased's barouche and twelve carriages full of mourners followed. Behind them the congregation filled the center of the boulevard.

The passersby stopped to look at all this; women stood on chairs, holding their children in their arms; and people who were drinking in the cafés appeared at the windows, billiard cues in hand.

It was a long way and, as if they were at a banquet where one is at first reserved and later convivial, the general behavior soon became more relaxed. The only subject of conversation was the Assembly's refusal to grant an increased allowance to the President.* Monsieur Piscatory had been too harsh, Montalembert "magnificent, as usual," and Messieurs Chambolle, Pidoux, Creton, the whole committee in fact, would have done better, perhaps, to follow the advice of Messieurs Quentin-Bauchard and Dufour.

These conversations continued in the Rue de la Roquette, which was lined with shops selling nothing but chains of colored glass beads and round black plaques covered with designs and letters in gold—which made them look like grottos full of stalactites, or china shops. But when they reached the gate of the cemetery, everyone immediately fell silent.

The tombs rose up in the midst of the trees; broken columns, pyramids, temples, dolmens, obelisques, Etruscan vaults with bronze doors. Some of them had rustic seats and folding chairs, making a kind of funereal boudoir. Cobwebs hung like rags from the chains of the urns, and the bunches of satin ribbons and crucifixes were covered with dust. Everywhere, between the railings and on top of the tombstones, were wreaths of immortelles, candle-holders, vases of flowers, black disks embossed with gold lettering, and plaster statuettes. There were little boys and girls, or cherubim, suspended in midair by brass wires; several of them even had zinc roofs over their heads. Enormous ropes of black, white, and blue spun-glass hung in great snaking coils from the top of the steles to the foot of the gravestones. They glittered in the sunlight among the black wooden crosses—and the hearse made its way along the main paths, which were paved like city streets. Occasionally, the axles creaked. Women knelt, their dresses trailing on the grass, to speak softly to the dead. White wisps of smoke curled

---

*On February 10, 1851, the Legislative Assembly refused a request from the minister of finance for an additional 1,800,000 francs for the prince-president (Louis-Napoléon). Piscatory was one of the leaders of the opposition to Louis-Napoléon, and Chambolle, a deputy from the Vendée and a royalist, would be arrested on December 2, 1851, as a member of the opposition.

up from the green yews. Someone was burning dead flowers and other rubbish.

Monsieur Dambreuse's grave was near those of Manuel and Benjamin Constant. In this area the ground falls away in a steep slope. Below one can see green treetops, and beyond them the chimneys of the steam pumps, and then the whole great city.

Frédéric was able to admire the view during the funeral orations.

The first was on behalf of the Chamber of Deputies, the second on behalf of the general council of the Aube, the third on behalf of the Saone-et-Loire Coal Mining Company, the fourth on behalf of the agricultural society of the Yonne, and there was another on behalf of a philanthropic association. Finally, as people were on the point of leaving, an unknown man started to read a sixth oration, on behalf of the Amiens society of Antiquaries.

All the speakers took advantage of the occasion to denounce socialism, of which Monsieur Dambreuse had died a victim. It was the spectacle of anarchy and his own devotion to order which had shortened his life. They extolled his wisdom, his probity, his generosity, and even his silence as a representative of the people; for if he was not an orator he made up for it by those solid qualities that were infinitely preferable, and so forth, using all the necessary phrases: "Premature end—eternal regrets—that other land—farewell, or rather, 'till we meet again'!"

Earth and pebbles fell back into place; and that was the end of Monsieur Dambreuse as far as the world was concerned.

There was a little more talk of him as the congregation made their way out of the cemetery and they had no hesitation in saying what they really thought. Hussonnet, who would have to write an account of the funeral for the papers, even parodied all the orations—for old Dambreuse, after all, had been one of the most distinguished palm-greasers of the previous reign. Then the mourning coaches took the businessmen back to their offices, congratulating themselves that the ceremony had not taken too long.

Frédéric went home exhausted.

When he arrived at the Dambreuses the following morning, he was told that Madame was working downstairs, in the office. The boxes and drawers were standing open in disorder, account books had been thrown in every direction, a roll of papers labeled "Outstanding debts—no prospect of collection" lay on the floor; he nearly fell over it and bent down to pick it up. Madame Dambreuse, almost invisible, was buried in the big armchair.

"Oh, there you are. What's going on?"

She bounded to her feet.

"What's going on? I'm ruined, ruined! Do you understand?"

Monsieur Adolphe Langlois, the lawyer, had asked her to come to his office, where he had shown her a will made by her husband before their marriage. He had left everything to Cécile; and the other will could not be found. Frédéric turned very pale. Perhaps she had not looked properly?

"See for yourself!" said Madame Dambreuse, with a wave of her hand.

The two safes yawned open, staved in with a cleaver, and she had turned out the desk, rummaged in the cupboards and shaken the mats. Suddenly, with a sharp little cry, she rushed to a corner where she had just noticed a small box with a brass lock; she opened it, nothing!

"Oh, the wretch! After I looked after him with such devotion!"

And she burst into sobs.

"Could it be anywhere else?" asked Frédéric.

"No, it was there, in that safe. I saw it quite recently. It's been burned! I'm sure of it!"

One day, at the beginning of his illness, Monsieur Dambreuse had gone down to the study to sign some documents.

"That's when he must have done it!"

And she fell back onto a chair, annihilated. A bereaved mother beside an empty cradle could not have been more pitiable than Madame Dambreuse before the gaping strongboxes. In fact her grief, in spite of the baseness of its cause, seemed so profound that he attempted to console her, telling her that, after all, she was not in a state of destitution.

"It is destitution, since I can't offer you a great fortune!"

She had no more than thirty thousand francs a year, not counting the house, which might be worth eighteen or twenty thousand.

Although this was wealth to Frédéric, he still felt his disappointment. Farewell to his dreams and to the grand life that he would have led. Honor obliged him to marry Madame Dambreuse. He thought for a moment, then said tenderly:

"I shall still have you!"

She threw herself into his arms and he clasped her to his chest with an emotion that was mingled with some admiration for himself. Her tears at an end, Madame Dambreuse raised her face, radiant with happiness, and, as she took his hand she said:

"Ah, I never doubted you! I counted on you!"

This premature confidence in what he regarded as a generous action annoyed the young man.

After this she took him up to her room and they made plans. Frédéric must now concentrate on making his way in the world. She even gave him some excellent advice about his candidacy.

The first thing to do was to memorize two or three maxims of political economy. Then select a specialty, horse-breeding for example; write several articles on some subject of local interest; always have a few licenses for post offices and tobacco shops to distribute; and perform a hundred little favors for the constituents. Monsieur Dambreuse had been impeccable in this respect. For example once, when they were in the country, he had stopped his wagonload of friends at a cobbler's shop and bought a dozen pairs of shoes for his guests and some dreadful boots for himself—which he had been hero enough to wear for a fortnight. This anecdote cheered them up. She told others, with a revival of grace, youth, and wit.

She approved of his plan for an immediate trip to Nogent. They said farewell tenderly, and at the door she murmured once again:

"You do love me, don't you?"

"Forever!" he replied.

A messenger was waiting for him at home with a penciled note telling him that Rosanette was about to give birth. There had been so much going on during the last three days that he had forgotten all about her. She had taken a room in a nursing home at Chaillot.

Frédéric hailed a cab and set off.

At the corner of the Rue de Marbeuf he saw a sign with large letters: "Nursing and Maternity Home under the direction of Madame Alessandri, First-Class Midwife, Graduate of the Maternity Hospital, author of several works, etc." Then on the entrance in the middle of the block, which was a cross between a gateway and a door, there was a similar notice but without the word "Maternity": "Madame Alessandri's Nursing Home," and all her titles. Frédéric knocked.

A maid, who looked like a soubrette, ushered him into the drawing room furnished with a mahogany table, armchairs in garnet velvet, and a clock under a glass dome.

A moment later her mistress appeared. She was a tall, slender brunette of forty, with beautiful eyes and a society manner. She told him that the mother had been safely delivered and took him up to her room.

Rosanette gave an ineffable smile and, as if overwhelmed by waves of love that were choking her, said in a low voice:

"A boy, there, there!" pointing to a bassinet next to her bed.

He drew aside the curtains and saw, amid the sheets, something reddish-yellow, extremely wrinkled, which smelled unpleasant and mewed.

"Kiss him!"

To hide his repugnance he replied:

"But suppose I hurt him?"

"No! No!"

So he gave his son a reluctant kiss.

"How like you he is!"

And she threw her frail arms round his neck and clung to him with a surge of emotion greater than he had ever seen in her.

The recollection of Madame Dambreuse came back to him. He upbraided himself for his monstrous behavior in betraying this poor creature, who loved and suffered with all the candor of her nature. For several days he stayed with her until the evening.

She was happy in this discreet house, where even the shutters over the street windows were always closed. Her room, with its gay chintz hangings looked out onto a large garden and Madame Alessandri, whose sole defect was a habit of quoting famous doctors as though they were her intimate friends, surrounded her with special attentions. Her fellow patients, who were nearly all young ladies from the country, got very bored, having no visitors. Rosanette realized, as she proudly informed Frédéric, that she was an object of envy. But they had to talk softly, for the partitions were thin and everyone was always eavesdropping, in spite of the ceaseless noise from the pianos.*

He was finally on the point of leaving for Nogent when he received a letter from Deslauriers.

Two new candidates had entered the lists, the one a conservative and the other a red; a third, no matter who he was, would have no chance. It was Frédéric's own fault; he had let his opportunity slip; he should have come earlier and been more active. "You didn't even turn up at the agricultural show!" The lawyer reproached him with having no connections with the press. "If only you'd followed my advice in the old days! If only we had a paper of our own!" He made much of this point. Moreover, many people who would have voted for him out of a desire to oblige Monsieur Dambreuse would now abandon him. Deslauriers was one of these. Having no further expectations from the capitalist he was deserting his protégé.

Frédéric took his letter to Madame Dambreuse.

"You haven't been in Nogent, then?" she asked.

"Why?"

"Because I saw Deslauriers three days ago."

Hearing of her husband's death the lawyer had come to return the material on the coal mines and to offer his services as her business manager. It sounded odd to Frédéric; and what had his friend been up to in Nogent?

Madame Dambreuse wanted to know what he had been doing since they last met.

"I've been ill," he replied.

"You might at least have let me know."

"Oh, it wasn't worth it." Anyhow, he had had a mass of things to do, appointments, visits.

From then on he led a double life, invariably sleeping at the Maréchale's and spending his afternoons with Madame Dambreuse, so that he had barely an hour to himself in the middle of the day.

The child was in the country, at Andilly. They went to see him every week.

The nurse's house was on a hill above the village, with a little yard as dark as a well, littered with straw, with chickens pecking about, and a vegetable cart in the shed. Rosanette would begin by kissing the child frantically; then, in a sort of delirium, she would wander about,

*It is difficult to see what these pianos are doing in a nursing home. The text is obscure and probably defective.

attempt to milk the goat, eat coarse bread, sniff the smell from the dunghill, and suggest that she put a little of it into her handkerchief.

Then they would go for long walks; she would tramp round the nursery gardens, break off branches of lilac hanging over the walls, shout: "Gee-up, little donkey!" to the asses pulling light vans, and pause to peer through wrought-iron gates into beautiful gardens. On other days, the nurse would put the baby in the shade of a walnut tree and the two women would spend hours talking the most boring nonsense.

Beside them, Frédéric would contemplate the square fields of vines on the valley slopes, with here and there the tuft of a tree. The dusty paths looked like gray ribbons; the houses were white and red splashes amid the green; and occasionally the smoke of a locomotive drew a horizontal streak along the foot of the leafy hills, like a gigantic ostrich feather whose airy tip kept melting away.

Then his eyes would rest on his son again. He imagined him as a young man; he would make a companion of him but he might turn out to be stupid and he would certainly be unfortunate. His illegitimacy would always handicap him; it would have been better if he had never been born; and Frédéric would murmur: "Poor child!" his heart swelling with an incomprehensible sadness.

Often they missed the last train. Then Madame Dambreuse would scold him for his unpunctuality and he would have to invent some explanation.

He had to do the same thing for Rosanette. She could not understand what he was doing every evening and why, when she sent round to his house, he was never in! One day when he was home, they turned up almost simultaneously. He made the Maréchale leave and hid Madame Dambreuse, telling her that his mother was about to arrive.

Soon these lies came to amuse him: he would repeat to one of them the oath he had just sworn to the other, send them two similar bunches of flowers, write to them at the same time, and then compare them with one another—but a third woman was always in his mind. The impossibility of possessing her justified his acts of treachery, which heightened his pleasure by giving it variety; and the more he cheated either of them the more she would love him, as if each woman's love added fuel to the other's, as if by a kind of emulation each meant to make him forget the other.

"See what confidence I have in you!" Madame Dambreuse said to him one day, unfolding a note warning her that Monsieur Moreau and a certain Rose Bron were living together as husband and wife. "Is she the young lady of the racecourse, by any chance?"

"What nonsense!" he replied. "Let me see."

The letter, written in capitals, was unsigned. In the beginning Madame Dambreuse had tolerated this mistress, who served as a cloak for their adultery. But when her passion became stronger, she had demanded that Frédéric break with Rosanette, and he claimed that he had long since done so. When he had finished his protestations she replied, half-closing her eyes, which gleamed like stiletto points through a muslin veil:

"And what about the other one?"

"What other one?"

"The china-maker's wife!"

He shrugged his shoulders disdainfully, and she did not press the point.

But, a month later, as they were talking of honor and fidelity, and as Frédéric was vaunting his own (in an incidental way, as a precaution) she said:

"Yes, it's true that you've behaved honestly; you don't go there anymore."

Frédéric, thinking of the Maréchale, stammered:

"Where do you mean?"

"To Madame Arnoux's."

He begged her to tell him how she knew this. It was through her second dressmaker, Madame Regimbart.

So she had information on his life, while he knew nothing about hers!

He had found in her dressing room a miniature of a man with long moustaches; was this the one involved in some vague story of suicide he had once heard? But he had no means of learning more. What would be the use anyhow? Women's hearts are like those little pieces of furniture full of secret drawers within drawers; you take a lot of trouble, break your fingernails, and find a dried flower, a little dust, or nothing at all! And then he may have been afraid of learning too much.

She made him refuse invitations to parties where she could not accompany him, kept him near her, was frightened of losing him; yet in spite of this relation growing closer every day, great chasms would suddenly open between them over some insignificant matter—their judgment of a person, perhaps, or of a work of art.

She had a hard, correct way of playing the piano. Her spiritualism (for Madame Dambreuse believed in the transmigration of souls to the stars) did not prevent her from keeping a close eye on her cashbox. She was haughty with her servants, and the tatters of the poor left her dry-eyed. An artless egotism showed in her habitual turns of phrase: "What do I care? I'd be a fool to do that! What good does it do me?" and in a thousand tiny actions, which defied analysis but were somehow odious. She would have listened at doors; she must lie to her confessor. Out of a desire to dominate, she insisted that Frédéric accompany her to church on Sundays. He obeyed, and carried her missal.

The loss of her inheritance had changed her a great deal. These signs of grief, which were attributed to her loss of Monsieur Dambreuse, made her more interesting and, as before, she had many visitors. Since Frédéric's electoral disappointment she had set her sights on a legation in Germany for the two of them; so the first thing to be done was to conform to current trends.

Some wanted the Empire back, others the house of Orléans, others the Count de Chambord; but they all agreed on the urgency of decentralization. Several methods were proposed, among them the division of Paris into a collection of main streets in order to develop village units around them; the transfer of the seat of government to Versailles; the relocation of the university at Bourges; the suppression of the libraries, or turning everything over to the major generals—and country life was praised to the skies, illiterates being by nature the most sensible of men. Hatred flourished: hatred of primary school teachers and of wine merchants, of philosophy classes, history courses, novels, red vests, long beards, of all independence, of any manifestation of individuality, since the cardinal necessity was to "restore the principle of authority," which might be exercised in whatever name and from whatever source, provided it was Force, Authority! The Conservatives were now talking like Sénécal. Frédéric could no longer make head or tail of it; and when he went to Rosanette's he heard the same ideas expressed by the same men.

The courtesans' salons (whose importance dates from this period) offered a neutral terrain where the reactionaries of different parties met. Hussonnet, who spent his time running down the celebrities of the day (an excellent way to promote the restoration of order), inspired Rosanette with the desire to hold evenings like everyone else;

he would report them in the papers; and the first person he brought was Fumichon, who carried a certain weight. After him came Nonancourt, Monsieur de Grémonville, Monsieur de Larsillois the ex-prefect, and Cisy who was now an agronomist living in Brittany and more devout than ever.

Some of the Maréchale's former lovers came as well, among them the Baron de Comaing, the Count de Jumillac and a few others; their free and easy manners offended Frédéric.

To make clear his position as master of the household, he raised their style of living. They took on a groom, changed apartments, and bought new furniture. These expenditures had the advantage of making his prospective marriage seem less disproportionate to his own fortune. But at the same time they depleted it to a frightening extent—and Rosanette couldn't make out what was going on.

A bourgeoise at heart, she adored domestic life, a cosy, peaceful existence. However, she enjoyed having an "at home" day, referred to her fellow courtesans as "those women!" wanted to be a "society lady," and believed that she had managed it. She asked Frédéric not to smoke in the drawing room and tried to keep him from eating meat on abstinence days for the sake of appearances.

She was, in fact, betraying her role, for she became serious and even made a habit of displaying a little melancholy before going to bed, like cypress trees at a tavern door.

He discovered the reason: she, too, was dreaming of marriage! This exasperated Frédéric. For one thing, he remembered her appearance at Madame Arnoux's house, and then he still resented her long resistance to his courtship.

He was still interested in finding out who her lovers had been, though. She denied them all. A sort of jealousy took possession of him. He objected to gifts she had received, and was still receiving—and, as her character irritated him more and more, a harsh, bestial sensual urge would drive him into her arms, a momentary illusion that would dissolve into hatred.

Her words, her voice, her smile, everything about her became odious to him, especially the look in her eyes, that limpid, fatuous female gaze. At times he was so exasperated by her that he could have watched her die without feeling. But how could he be angry with her? She was so heartbreakingly sweet-natured.

Deslauriers reappeared and explained his stay in Nogent by saying that he had been negotiating for a lawyer's practice there. Frédéric was happy to see him again; he was someone special! He made him a third in their company.

The lawyer dined with them from time to time and, when there was a little disagreement, invariably took Rosanette's part, so that on one occasion Frédéric said: "Go on, sleep with her if it amuses you!" such was his longing for something to happen that would rid him of her.

Toward the middle of June she received a summons: a Maître Athanase Gautherot, bailiff, enjoined her to pay Mademoiselle Clémence Vatnaz the four thousand francs due to her, failing which he would come to seize her possessions the following day.

Of the four bills originally signed, only one had, in fact, been paid—any money that she had obtained since then having been put to other uses.

She rushed to the Arnoux's house. He was now living in the Faubourg Saint-Germain, and the porter did not know the address. She went round to see several friends, all of whom were out, and returned home in despair. She was unwilling to tell Frédéric about it for fear that this new problem might jeopardize her marriage.

The following day Maître Athanase Gautherot arrived, escorted by two acolytes; one was a pale, weasel-faced man, who seemed eaten up with envy, and the other, in detachable collar and trousers straining at their footstraps, had a black taffeta casing on one finger. They were both revoltingly dirty, with greasy collars and frock coats whose sleeves were too short.

Their employer, who was on the contrary a very good-looking man, began by apologizing for having come on such a painful mission, meanwhile looking round the apartment, "full of nice things, upon my word!" He added "apart from those we cannot seize" and, at a gesture, the two assistants disappeared.

Then his compliments increased. Was it possible that so . . . charming a person did not have some friend? A sale by court order was a real disaster! People never recovered from it. He tried to frighten her; then, seeing that she was upset, suddenly adopted a paternal tone. He was a man of the world, knew all sorts of ladies and, as he named them, examined the pictures on the walls. They were some old paintings from Arnoux's time, sketches by Sombaz, watercolors by Burieu, three landscapes by Dittmer. It was obvious Rosanette had no idea how much they were worth. Maître Gautherot turned to her:

"Look! To show you what a good-hearted fellow I am, let's strike a bargain: give me those Dittmers and I'll pay the lot. Agreed?"

At that moment Frédéric, whom Delphine had briefed in the hall and who had just seen the two assistants, burst roughly into the room, his hat still on his head. Maître Gautherot resumed his dignity and, as the door was still open, shouted:

"Come along, gentlemen, write this down! In the second room we have: one oak table with two extra leaves, two sideboards . . ."

Frédéric stopped him and asked if there were any way of preventing the seizure.

"Yes, of course! Who paid for the furniture?"

"I did."

"Then put in a claim for it. It will at least gain you a little time."

Maître Gautherot hastily finished his inventory, citing Mademoiselle Bron in his official report to the judge in chambers, and left.

Frédéric did not utter a word of reproach. He gazed at the muddy footprints the bailiff's assistants had left on the carpet, as if to himself:

"I'm going to have to find some money!"

"Oh, good God, what a fool I am!" exclaimed the Maréchale.

She rummaged in a drawer, took out a letter and hurried round to the office of the Languedoc Lighting Company to arrange for the transfer of her shares.

She returned an hour later. The shares had been sold to someone else! The clerk, after examining her paper, Arnoux's written promise, had told her:

"This document does not give you any claim on the shares. It is not recognized by the company."

In short, he had dismissed her without ceremony and she was furious; Frédéric must go round to see Arnoux at once and clear matters up.

But Arnoux might believe that he had really come to try and recover the fifteen thousand francs of his lost mortgage; and then the idea of asking money of a man who had been his mistress' lover seemed ignoble. He took a middle course, got Madame Regimbart's address at the Dambreuse house, sent a messenger to see her, to find out the name of the café which the Citizen now patronized.

It was a little bar on the Place de la Bastille, where he sat all day long in the back right-hand corner, no more active than if he had been part of the fixtures.

Having tried in succession coffee, grog, bishop, punch, mulled wine, and even a mixture of wine and water, he had returned to beer, and every half hour would let fall the word: "Bock!" having cut his conversation to the irreducible minimum. Frédéric asked him if he ever saw Arnoux:

"No!"

"Well, why not?"

"An idiot!"

Perhaps politics had come between them, and Frédéric thought it tactful to inquire after Compain.

"What a fool!" said Regimbart.

"Why do you say that?

"Him and his calf's head!"

"Oh, do tell me! What is this calf's head business?" Regimbart smiled pityingly.

"A lot of nonsense!"

After a long silence Frédéric went on:

"So he's moved?"

"Who?"

"Arnoux!"

"Yes, to the Rue de Fleurus!"

"What number?"

"Would I have anything to do with Jesuits?"

"What do you mean, Jesuits?"

Furious, the Citizen replied:

"That swine took money from a patriot I introduced him to and set up as a rosary dealer!"

"Impossible!"

"Go and see for yourself!"

It was the gospel truth; Arnoux, weakened by an illness, had turned to religion—anyway he "had always been devout at heart" and, with that combination of commercial guile and ingenuousness which had always characterized him, he had set out to save his soul and make his fortune at the same time by selling religious articles.

Frédéric had no trouble in finding his shop, which had a sign proclaiming: "*Gothic Arts, Inc.,*—Church Restora-

tion—Religious Ornaments—Polychrome Sculpture—
Three Kings' Incense, etc., etc."

In either corner of the window stood a wooden statue,
streaked with gold, cinnabar, and blue: one representing
Saint John the Baptist with his sheepskin, and the other
Sainte Geneviève, her apron full of roses and a distaff
under her arm. Then there were several groups in plaster:
a nun teaching a little girl, a mother kneeling beside a
crib, three school children at the communion rail. The
prettiest was a sort of chalet representing a nativity scene,
with the ass, the ox and the Infant Jesus lying on straw—
real straw. Ranged on the shelves were dozens of medals,
rosaries of all kinds, holy water stoups in the shape of
scallop shells, and portraits of notable ecclesiastics, prominent among whom were Monsignor Affre and the Holy
Father, both of them smiling.

Arnoux, behind his counter, was dozing with his head
on his chest. He had aged extraordinarily and even had a
crown of pink pimples around his temples, which
glowed in the sunlight reflected from the gold crosses.

The sight of this deterioration filled Frédéric with sadness. But out of loyalty to the Maréchale, he plucked up
his courage and moved forward. Madame Arnoux appeared at the back of the shop; he turned on his heel.

"I couldn't find him," he said on returning home.

And though he insisted that he would write immediately
to his notary in Le Havre, asking him to send the money,
Rosanette flew into a rage. There had never been anyone
so weak, so spineless; while she was enduring endless
privations, other people were living off the fat of the land.

Frédéric thought of poor Madame Arnoux, picturing
to himself the heartbreaking drabness of her home. He sat
down at the desk and, as Rosanette's shrill voice continued, he cried:

"Oh, for the love of God shut up!"

"Are you trying to stand up for them?"

"Well, why not?" he exclaimed; "what makes you so
implacable anyway?"

"Why don't you want them to pay up? It's because
you're afraid of hurting your old love. Admit it!"

He felt like hitting her with the clock; words failed
him. He said nothing. Rosanette, pacing up and down the
room, added:

"I'll slap a suit on your Arnoux. Oh, I don't need your
help!" and, pursing her lips, she added: "I'll get a lawyer."

Three days later Delphine ran in, crying:

"Madame, Madame, there's a man out there with a paste pot—he frightens me!"

Rosanette went to the kitchen and found a pockmarked thug with a paralyzed arm, three-quarters drunk and stammering.

This was Maître Gautherot's bill-sticker. The objection to the seizure had been disallowed and the sale was naturally going ahead.

First, the man demanded a drink for his trouble climbing the stairs, and then he asked for some theater tickets as a favor, for he had got it into his head that Madame was an actress. Then several minutes passed in incomprehensible winks; finally he offered, for forty sous, to tear off the corners of the bill he had already posted next to the street door. Rosanette was called by name on it, an unusually severe measure which showed how much La Vatnaz hated her.

She had been tender-hearted once, and had even written to consult Béranger about a love affair. But the harsh buffetting of life had embittered her for she had successively taught piano, run a boarding house, worked for fashion magazines, sublet apartments, and sold lace to the courtesans—where her connections permitted her to do favors for many people, Arnoux among them. Before that she had worked for a business firm.

There she had charge of the working-girls' wages; each of them had two account books, one permanently in Mademoiselle Vatnaz's hands. Out of kindness, Dussardier looked after the book belonging to a girl called Hortense Baslin; he was by the cashier's desk one day when Mademoiselle Vatnaz presented this girl's account, one thousand six hundred and eighty-two francs, which the cashier paid over to her. Now, the previous evening Dussardier had added up the Baslin girl's book and it had come to only one thousand and eighty-two. He asked her to let him have it back, on some pretext or other; and then, to cover up the theft, he told her he had lost it. The girl naïvely repeated his lie to Mademoiselle Vatnaz, and she, to put her mind at rest, mentioned the matter to the worthy clerk. He replied only: "I have burned it"; nothing more. She left the firm shortly afterwards, without believing in the destruction of the book and thinking that Dussardier still had it.

When she heard that he had been wounded, she hurried round to his apartment with the idea of getting it back. Then, finding nothing despite the most meticulous search, she had been gripped with respect, and soon with love, for this young man who was so honest, so gentle, so heroic, and so strong! Such a stroke of luck was more than she could have hoped at her age. She threw herself on him with the appetite of an ogress—and for his sake, she had abandoned literature, socialism, "consoling doctrines and generous utopias," the course of lectures she was giving on "The De-Subordination of Women," everything, even Delmar himself; finally she proposed to Dussardier that they should marry.

Even though she was his mistress he was not in the least in love with her. For one thing, he had not forgotten her theft. For another she was too rich. He refused. At this she burst into tears and told him her dream that they would one day open a dress shop together. She had the necessary initial capital, which would be increased by four thousand francs the following week; and she informed him of her proceedings against the Maréchale.

This saddened Dussardier because of his friendship for Frédéric. He remembered the cigar case offered to him in the police station, the evenings at the Quai Napoléon, the pleasant conversations they had had, the books he had been lent, the other's countless kindnesses. He begged the Vatnaz to desist.

She scoffed at his good nature, displaying an inexplicable hatred for Rosanette; even her desire to make a fortune was only so as to be able to crush her afterwards beneath the wheels of her carriage.

This abyss of wickedness frightened Dussardier and, as soon as he was sure of the date of the sale, he left. Early the next morning he called on Frédéric and said, with an embarrassed look:

"I owe you an apology."

"What on earth for?"

"You must think I'm an ungrateful wretch, since she's my . . ." he stammered. "Oh, I'll never speak to her again. I won't be her accomplice!" And, as Frédéric looked at him in great surprise: "They're going to auction your mistress' furniture in three days, aren't they?"

"Who told you so?"

"La Vatnaz herself! But I'm afraid of offending you . . ."

"My dear chap, that would be impossible!"

"Yes, that's true, you're so good!"

And he bashfully held out a cheap little leather wallet. It contained four thousand francs, his entire savings. "What! Oh no, no . . ."

"I knew I'd hurt your feelings," said Dussardier, his eyes full of tears.

Frédéric grasped his hand and the worthy fellow went on, in a mournful voice:

"Take it! Give me that pleasure! I'm so unhappy. Anyhow, everything's finished now, isn't it? When the Revolution began I thought everyone was going to be happy. Do you remember how fine it was? How free we felt? But now we're back in a worse state than ever."

And, fixing his eyes on the ground, he went on:

"Now they're killing our Republic, the way they killed the Roman one! And poor Venice, poor Poland, poor Hungary! Such crimes! First they cut down the Trees of Liberty, then they restricted the franchise, closed the clubs, reestablished censorship and handed the schools over to the priests, till they get around to setting up the Inquisition.* Well, why not? Some Conservatives would love to loose the Cossacks on us.† The newspapers are punished for arguing against the death penalty, Paris is bristling with bayonets, sixteen of the departments are in a state of seige, and they've rejected the idea of an amnesty again!"

He clutched his head in his hands; then, stretching out his arms as if in great distress, he said:

"If only people would try! If we all acted in good faith we'd be able to come to an understanding! But it's no good! The workers are no better than the bourgeois! At Elbeuf the other day they refused to help put out a fire. Some dogs even call Barbès an aristocrat! They've made the people a laughingstock by trying to nominate Nadaud, for the presidency! A mason! I ask you! And there's nothing to be done! It can't be stopped! Everyone is against us! —Look, I've never done anyone any harm and yet it's like a weight on my stomach. I'll go mad if it keeps up like this! I feel like getting myself killed.

*As early as January, 1851, in the course of a speech in the Assembly, Thiers pronounced the famous words: *"L'Empire est faite!"* Rome was handed back to the Pope by a French army in July, 1849, and in the same year Venice was reoccupied by the Austrians, Poland torn between the rival ambitions of Prussia and Austria, and the Hungarian revolt crushed. In 1850, Carlier, the chief of police, ordered the Trees of Liberty cut down. Later that year laws were passed effectively reducing the electorate by three million. Schoolmasters were placed under the supervision of the clergy, and the clubs and the freedom of the press were curbed.

‡†An allusion to the invasion and occupation of France in 1814–15.

I don't need my money, I tell you! You'll give it back to me, dammit! I'll make you a loan."

Forced by necessity, Frédéric ended by taking his four thousand francs. So they had no more worries from the Vatnaz side.

But Rosanette soon lost her case against Arnoux, and, out of stubbornness, was determined to appeal.

Deslauriers wore himself out trying to make her understand that Arnoux's pledge constituted neither a gift nor a legal transfer; she wouldn't even listen to him and declared the law was unjust; it was because she was a woman, men always stuck up for each other! In the end, however, she followed his advice.

He made himself so much at home in the household that he brought Sénécal round to dinner several times. This informality annoyed Frédéric, who lent him money and even had him fitted out by his own tailor. The lawyer gave his old coats to the socialist, whose means of livelihood were unknown.

However, he was anxious to help Rosanette. One day when she showed him twelve shares in the china-clay company (the business that had cost Arnoux a thirty-thousand-franc fine), Deslauriers said:

"This looks suspicious! Splendid!"

She could sue him for reimbursement of her claims. She would prove first that he was fully responsible for paying all the liabilities of the company, since he had declared personal debts as collective debts, and then that he had diverted several of the company's assets to his own use.

"All this makes him guilty of fraudulent bankruptcy under articles 586 and 587 of the commercial code, and we'll get him yet, my sweet, you can be sure of that!"

Rosanette threw her arms around his neck. He sent her round to see his former employer the next day; he was unable to take the case himself, as he had business in Nogent; Sénécal would write to him if there should be any emergency.

His negotiations for the purchase of a practice were a blind. He spent his time at Monsieur Roque's, where he had begun not only by singing their friend's praises but by imitating his mannerisms and speech as far as possible; this had won him Louise's confidence while he was gaining her father's by inveighing against Ledru-Rollin.

If Frédéric did not return, it was because he was moving in high society; and little by little Deslauriers told them that he loved someone, that he had a child, and that he was keeping a mistress.

Louise's despair was overwhelming and Madame Moreau's indignation was just as great. She saw her son whirling into the depths of a shadowy abyss; it was a blow to her religion of keeping up appearances and she felt personally disgraced. Then, suddenly, her attitude changed. When people asked after Frédéric, she would reply knowingly:

"He's doing well, very well."

She had heard of his approaching marriage with Madame Dambreuse.

The date had been fixed and he was already looking for some way of getting Rosanette to accept it.

Toward the middle of the autumn she won her case over the china-clay shares; Frédéric heard the news on his doorstep when he met Sénécal, who had just come from the trial.

Monsieur Arnoux had been found an accomplice in all the frauds, and the ex-schoolmaster seemed so pleased about it that Frédéric stopped him from coming in, assuring him that he would give Rosanette the message. He entered her room with a look of annoyance on his face and said:

"Well, you should be happy now!"

She took no notice but said:

"Look!"

And pointed to his child, who was lying in a crib in front of the fire. She had found him so ill when she visited the nurse that morning that she had brought him back to Paris with her.

All his limbs had become extraordinarily thin; and his lips were covered with white spots, which made the inside of his mouth look as though it were full of clots of milk.

"What did the doctor say?"

"Oh, the doctor! He says the journey has made whatever it is worse . . . I can't remember, some name ending in *itis* . . . anyhow that he has thrush. Have you heard of it?"

Frédéric was quick to reply: "Oh, of course," adding that it was nothing serious.

But that evening he was frightened by the child's feeble look and the spread of the blue-white patches that resembled mold, as if life had already abandoned the poor little body and left nothing but a piece of inanimate

matter on which vegetation was growing. The child's
hands were cold, he could no longer drink, and the
nurse, a new one the concierge had hired at random
from an agency, kept repeating:

"He looks very poorly, very poorly!"

Rosanette was up all night.

In the morning, she went to get Frédéric.

"Come and see. He isn't moving."

He was, in fact, dead. She picked him up, shook him,
hugged him to her, called him all his pet names, covered
him with kisses and sobs—then she turned wildly on
herself, tearing her hair and screaming—until she collapsed onto the edge of the divan, where she lay with
her mouth open, her eyes fixed and streaming with tears.
Then she lapsed into a state of torpor and the apartment
regained its calm. The furniture had been overturned.
Two or three towels lay about. It struck six. The night
light went out.

Looking at all this, Frédéric almost believed he was
dreaming. His heart contracted with anguish. It seemed
to him that this death was only a beginning and that
worse was soon to follow.

Suddenly Rosanette said tenderly:

"We'll preserve him, won't we?"

She wanted to have him embalmed. But there were
a great many arguments against it. The strongest, according to Frédéric, was that the process was impractical
for such a young child. A portrait would be better. She
agreed; he wrote a note to Pellerin and Delphine hurried
off with it.

Pellerin arrived promptly, anxious to efface by his
zeal any memories of his former conduct. At first he
said:

"Poor little angel! Good Lord, what a tragedy!"

But, little by little the artist in him gained the upper
hand and he declared that nothing could be done with
those dark eyes and that livid face; it was a real still-
life, he'd need all his talent, and he murmured:

"It's not going to be easy at all!"

"As long as it's a good likeness!" objected Rosanette.

"What do I care about the likeness! Down with realism!
It's the spirit we're after in painting! Leave me alone!
I'm going to try and work out how it should be done."

He reflected, his forehead in his left hand, his elbow
in his right; then, suddenly he said:

"Ah, I've got it! A pastel! With strong half-tones, laid

on almost flat, you can get a good relief effect, in the outlines."

He sent the maid to get his box; then, with one chair under his feet and another beside him, he began to sketch in the main contours, as calmly as if he were working from the round. He praised Correggio's little Saint Johns, Velasquez' pink Infanta, Reynolds' milky flesh-tints, the distinction of Lawrence's children, especially the long-haired child on Lady Gower's knee.

"Anyhow, what could be more charming than those brats! The pinnacle of the sublime (Raphael proved it with his Madonnas) is probably a mother with her child."

Choking, Rosanette left the room, and Pellerin at once said:

"Well, have you heard about Arnoux?"

"No—what?"

"Of course it was bound to end like that!"

"What are you talking about?"

"At this very moment he may be . . . Excuse me!"

And the artist got up to raise the head of the little corpse.

"You were saying . . . " insisted Frédéric.

And, closing one eye to take his measurements better, Pellerin replied:

"I was saying that our friend Arnoux may be locked up at this very moment!"

Then, in a satisfied voice:

"Take a look? How's that?"

"Yes, excellent! But what about Arnoux?"

Pellerin put down his crayon.

"As far as I can make out, he's being sued by a man called Mignot, a friend of Regimbart's. There's a real brain for you! What a numbskull! Do you know that one day . . . "

"But we weren't talking about Regimbart!"

"That's true. Well, yesterday evening Arnoux had to find twelve thousand francs—if not, he'd had it."

"Oh, it's probably an exaggeration," said Frédéric.

"Not in the least. It looked serious to me, very serious!"

Just then Rosanette reappeared, with red marks under her eyes, as brilliant as patches of rouge. She went over to the picture and looked at it. Pellerin signaled that he would keep quiet because of her, but Frédéric took no notice:

"Still, I can't believe . . . " he said.

"I tell you I saw him last night," said the artist,

396 *Gustave Flaubert*

"at seven o'clock, in the Rue Jacob. He even had his passport on him, as a precaution, and he was talking about shipping out at Le Havre with his whole tribe."

"What! With his wife?"

"I expect so. He's too much of a family man to live by himself."

"And you're certain of this!"

"Of course! Where do you think he could have laid his hands on twelve thousand francs?"

Frédéric paced up and down the room once or twice. He was breathing heavily and biting his lips; then he picked up his hat.

"Where are you going?" asked Rosanette.

He made no answer and disappeared.

Chapter Five

He had to find twelve thousand francs, or else he would never see Madame Arnoux again; and, even now, he still harbored some unconquerable hope. Was she not the substance of his heart, the very foundation of his life? For a few minutes he hesitated on the sidewalk, gnawed by anxiety yet glad to have escaped from the other woman's house.

Where could he get the money? Frédéric knew by experience how difficult it was to obtain on short notice, no matter what terms one offered. Only one person could help him—Madame Dambreuse. She always kept several bank notes in her desk. He went to her house and said boldly:

"Have you twelve thousand francs you could lend me?"

"Why?"

It was someone else's secret. She insisted upon knowing. He would not give way. Both of them were obstinate on the point. Finally she declared that she would give him nothing without knowing what it was for. Frédéric became very red in the face. A friend of his had committed a theft. The money must be returned that very day.

"What's his name? Come on! Tell me his name!"

"Dussardier!"

And he knelt beside her, supplicating her to say nothing about it.

"What do you take me for?" replied Madame Dambreuse. "Anyone would think you'd done it yourself. Stop all this theatrical behavior! Here you are, and much good may it do him!"

He hurried round to Arnoux's. The merchant was not in

his shop. But he was still living in the Rue Paradis, for he had two houses.

In the Rue Paradis the porter swore that Monsieur Arnoux had been absent since the previous evening; as for Madame, he wouldn't like to say. Frédéric shot up the stairs and glued his ear to the keyhole. At last the door opened. Madame had left with Monsieur. The maid did not know when they would be back; her wages had been paid and she was leaving herself.

Suddenly, Frédéric heard the creak of a door hinge.

"But is there someone there?"

"Oh no sir, it's the wind."

So he left. Still, there was something inexplicable about such a prompt disappearance.

Perhaps Regimbart, as Mignot's friend, might be able to throw some light on the matter? And Frédéric had himself driven to his home in the Rue de l'Empereur, Montmartre.

There was a little garden at the side of the house, fenced in with railings backed with sheetmetal. A flight of three steps set off the white façade, and passersby on the sidewalk could see into the two rooms on the ground floor, one of which was a sitting room, with dresses lying about on the furniture, and the other the workshop for Madame Regimbart's seamstresses.

The latter were all convinced that Monsieur had important business and grand connections; that he was someone quite extraordinary. When he walked down the corridor with his hat with its turned-up brim, his long, serious face and his green frock coat, they would interrupt their work to watch him. Nor did he ever fail to say something encouraging to them, a sententious compliment—and later, in their own homes, they would feel discontent because they had adopted him as the ideal.

None of them, however, loved him as much as Madame Regimbart, an intelligent little woman who supported him by her dressmaking.

As soon as Monsieur Moreau gave his name she hastenened to greet him, aware through the servants of his relations with Madame Dambreuse. Her husband would be back "at any moment" and, as he followed her, Frédéric admired the neatness of the house and the profusion of its oilcloth. Then he waited for a few minutes in a sort of study where the Citizen would retire to think.

He greeted Frédéric less crossly than usual and re-

counted the full story of Arnoux's troubles. The ex-
china-maker had wooed Mignot, a patriot who owned
a hundred shares in *le Siècle,* and persuaded him that in
the interest of democracy, it was imperative to change
the management and editorial policy of the paper. Then
on the pretext of arranging to put over that position at
the next shareholders' meeting, he had asked him for
fifty shares which he would hand out to reliable friends
who would support his motion; Mignot would have no
responsibility, would make no enemies and, once they
had succeeded, Arnoux would see to it that he was given
a good administrative position worth at least five or six
thousand francs a year. The shares had been handed
over. But Arnoux had immediately sold them and used
the money to go into partnership with a dealer in
religious articles. After this there had been complaints
from Mignot and lot of shilly-shallying from Arnoux;
finally the patriot had threatened to sue him for fraud
unless he returned the shares or the cash equivalent:
fifty thousand francs.

Frédéric's face fell.

"And that isn't all," said the Citizen. "Mignot, who's
a good fellow, lowered his demands to a quarter of the
original sum. Fresh promises from Arnoux, just more
humbug, of course. To cut a long story short, the morning of the day before yesterday Mignot summoned him
to hand over twelve thousand francs within twenty-four
hours, without prejudice to the rest of the debt."

"But I've got them!" said Frédéric.

The Citizen turned around slowly:

"You're joking!"

"No, they're here in my pocket. I was taking them
to him."

"You don't waste time, do you? I'll be damned!
Anyhow, it's too late; the complaint has been lodged
and Arnoux's gone."

"Alone?"

"No, with his wife. Someone saw them at the Le Havre
station."

Frédéric grew terribly pale. Madame Regimbart thought
he was about to faint. He controlled himself and even
had the strength to ask two or three questions about
the affair. Regimbart was depressed by the whole business;
it was damaging to the cause of democracy. Arnoux
had always been short of any sense of order and decency.

"A harebrained creature! He burned the candle at

both ends! It was the skirts that did him in. It's not him I'm sorry for, it's his poor wife!" For the Citizen admired virtuous women and had a high regard for Madame Arnoux. "She must have had a terrible time!"

Frédéric was grateful for his sympathy and shook hands effusively, as if Regimbart had done him some favor.

"Have you made all the arrangements?" asked Rosanette when she saw him again.

He replied that he had not had the heart, and had been walking the streets aimlessly to deaden his grief.

At eight o'clock they went into the dining room, but they sat opposite each other in silence, sighing deeply from time to time, and sent their plates back to the kitchen untouched. Frédéric drank some brandy. He felt completely exhausted, crushed, prostrate, no longer conscious of anything but an overpowering fatigue.

Rosanette went to fetch the portrait. Patches of red, yellow, green and indigo clashed violently and made it hideous, almost laughable.

Moreover the dead child himself was now unrecognizable. The violet tone of his lips emphasized the pallor of his skin, his nostrils were more pinched than ever, and his eyes sunk deeper into his head, which rested on a blue taffeta pillow strewn with the petals of camellias, autumn roses, and violets. This had been an idea of the maid's, and the two women had devoutly arranged him in this fashion. The mantelpiece had been covered by a lace cloth; on it stood vermeil candlesticks with bunches of blessed boxwood; aromatic pastilles were burning in the vases at either end and, together with the cradle, the whole thing formed a kind of altar of repose; Frédéric was reminded of his vigil over Monsieur Dambreuse.

About every quarter of an hour, Rosanette would open the curtains to contemplate her child. She saw him as he would have been in a few months' time, beginning to walk, then at school playing prisoner's base in the yard, then at twenty, a young man; and each of these images she created seemed to her yet another son lost, the intensity of her grief multiplying her motherhood.

Frédéric sat motionless in the other armchair, thinking of Madame Arnoux.

She was probably in a railway carriage, gazing through the window at the countryside flying past toward Paris; or perhaps she was on the deck of a steamship, as she had been the first time he saw her, but this one was sailing on indefinitely to countries from which she would never return. Then he imagined her in a bedroom at an inn with trunks on the floor, tattered wallpaper and a door rattling in the wind. And afterwards? What would become of her? A schoolteacher, a companion, perhaps a chambermaid? She was at the mercy of all the hazards of poverty. He was tortured by his ignorance of her fate. He should have prevented her flight, or pursued her. Was he not her true husband? And, at the thought that he would never see her again, that it was really over, that she was irrevocably lost, he felt as if his whole being were tearing apart and the tears that had been gathering since the morning overflowed.

Rosanette noticed.

"Oh, you're crying too! Do you feel sad?"

"Yes, yes, I do!"

He held her to his heart and they wept in each other's arms.

Madame Dambreuse was weeping too, lying face down on her bed, her head in her hands.

Olympe Regimbart had come that evening to fit her first colored dress; she had told her of Frédéric's visit and even that he had twelve thousand francs all ready to hand over to Monsieur Arnoux.

So the money, her own money, was intended to prevent the other woman's departure, to keep his mistress in Paris!

At first she was furious, and resolved to dismiss him like a lackey. But a long fit of tears calmed her. It would be better to conceal her knowledge and say nothing.

The next day, Frédéric brought back the twelve thousand francs.

She urged him to keep them, in case his friend should need them, and she questioned him closely about this gentleman. What could have led him to so abuse his employer's confidence? It must have been a woman! Women led men into all kinds of crimes.

Frédéric was disconcerted by this bantering tone. He felt great remorse at slandering Dussardier. But the thought that Madame Dambreuse could not possibly know the truth reassured him.

She was persistent, however; the following day she again inquired after his little chum and then after another friend, Deslauriers.

"Is he reliable and intelligent?"

Frédéric sang his praises.

"Ask him to come round to the house some morning: I want to ask his advice about some business."

She had found a bundle of papers among which were some bills of Arnoux's, properly protested, which had been signed by Madame Arnoux. It was on their account that Frédéric had once come to see Monsieur Dambreuse during his lunch; and although the banker had decided not to sue for the money, he had obtained a judgment from the commercial court condemning not only Arnoux but also his wife—who knew nothing about it, her husband not having thought fit to inform her.

Now there was a weapon! Madame Dambreuse had no doubt of it. But her own lawyer might advise her to drop the matter; she preferred to use someone obscure, and she had remembered the tall fellow with an impudent face who had offered her his services.

Frédéric innocently delivered her message.

The lawyer was delighted to be put in touch with such a great lady. He hurried to visit her.

She told him that her niece was to inherit the property, another reason to clear up these debts; she would hand the money over to the Martinons, thus heaping coals of fire on their heads.

Deslauriers realized that there was something mysterious about the whole affair. He thought it over, gazing at the bills. Madame Arnoux's name, in her own handwriting, brought her back before him, and he remembered how she had insulted him. Here was an opportunity for revenge; why not take advantage of it?

So he advised Madame Dambreuse to sell off all the bad debts of the estate at auction. They would have a cat's-paw buy them back and start proceedings against the debtors. He undertook to provide the agent.

Toward the end of November, as Frédéric walked down the street where Madame Arnoux had lived, he glanced up at her windows and saw a notice on the door saying in large letters:

"Sale of luxurious effects and furnishings, consisting of kitchen utensils, underclothing, table linen, chemises, laces, petticoats, knickers, French and Indian cashmeres, an Erard piano, two Renaissance oak chests, Venetian mirrors, Chinese and Japanese pottery."

"It's their furniture!" said Frédéric to himself, and the porter confirmed his suspicions.

The latter did not know who was having the stuff sold,

but he suggested that Maître Berthelmot, the auctioneer, might be able to give the gentleman some information.

This official at first refused to say which of the creditors had ordered the sale. Frédéric insisted on knowing. It was a certain Sénécal, a commercial agent, and Maître Berthelmot even carried his kindness so far as to lend the young man his own copy of the *Petites-Affiches*.

When he reached Rosanette's apartment, Frédéric threw the paper down, open, on the table.

"Go on, read it!"

"Well, what is it?" she asked, with such a placid air that he was revolted.

"That's right! Play innocent!"

"I don't understand."

"Are you the one who's having Madame Arnoux's things sold?"

She read the advertisement again:

"Where's her name?"

"Oh, it's her furniture all right! You know that better than I do!"

"What's it got to do with me?" said Rosanette, shrugging her shoulders.

"What's it got to do with you? You're getting your revenge, that's all! This is more of your persecution! Didn't you carry your insults to the point of going to her house? A common slut like you! And the loveliest, saintliest, best woman in the world! Why are you so determined to ruin her?"

"I tell you, you're making a mistake!"

"Nonsense! As if you hadn't put Sénécal up to it!"

"What a stupid idea!"

At this a wave of fury seized him:

"You're lying! You're lying, you miserable creature. You're jealous of her! You got a judgment against her husband! Sénécal's mixed up in your affairs before this! He loathes Arnoux; your two hatreds are a perfect match. I saw how delighted he was when you won your china clay case. Do you deny that?"

"I give you my word . . ."

"Oh, I know your word!"

And Frédéric reeled off a list of her lovers with their names and circumstantial details. Rosanette turned pale and drew back.

"That surprises you? You thought I was blind because I shut my eyes. I've had enough now! A man doesn't kill himself over the treachery of a woman like you. When it becomes too gross he simply leaves; it would be degrading to punish it!"

She wrung her hands.

"Dear God, what has changed you?"

"Nothing but you!"

"And all this for Madame Arnoux!" cried Rosanette, in tears.

He replied coldly:

"She is the only woman I have ever loved!"

At this insult her tears ceased:

"That shows your good taste! A middle-aged woman with a complexion like licorice, a thick waist, and eyes as big as caves, and just as empty! Since that's what you like, go and join her!"

"That's what I was waiting for! Thank you!"

Rosanette remained motionless, stupefied by this extraordinary behavior. She even let the door close behind him, then, with a bound, she followed him into the hall and threw her arms round him, exclaiming:

"But you're out of your mind! You're insane! It's absurd! I love you!" She entreated him: "In the name of our child!"

"Admit that you ordered the sale!" said Frédéric.

She again protested her innocence.

"You won't admit it?"

"No!"

"Then good-bye forever!"

"Listen to me!"

Frédéric turned round:

"If you knew me better you would realize that my decision is irrevocable!"

"Oh! Oh! You'll come back to me!"

"Never!"

And he slammed the door violently.

Rosanette wrote to Deslauriers that she needed him at once.

He arrived five days later, in the evening and, when she told him of the break, said:

"Is that all? What's so dreadful about that?"

At first she had imagined that he might be able to bring Frédéric back to her, but now all was lost. She had heard, through her porter, of his approaching marriage to Madame Dambreuse.

Deslauriers lectured her; he seemed curiously gay, full of jokes and, as it was very late, asked permission to spend the night in one of her armchairs. The following morning he set off once more for Nogent, telling her that there was no saying when they would see each other again; there might be a great change in his life in the near future.

Two hours after his return, the town was in a ferment. It was said that Monsieur Frédéric was going to marry Madame Dambreuse. Finally, the three Augert sisters, unable to bear it any longer, went round to see Madame Moreau, who proudly confirmed the news. Monsieur Roque was made quite ill by it and Louise shut herself in her room. A rumor even went round that she had gone mad.

Frédéric, meanwhile, was unable to hide his sorrow. Evidently to distract him Madame Dambreuse was more attentive than ever. Every afternoon she took him for a drive in her carriage; and one day, as they were crossing the Place de la Bourse, it occurred to her that it might be amusing to visit the auction galleries.

It was the first of December, the very day when Madame Arnoux's sale was to be held. He remembered the date and showed his reluctance, declaring the place was intolerably noisy and crowded. She just wanted to have a look. The brougham stopped. There was nothing to do but follow her.

The courtyard was littered with washstands without basins, the wooden frames of chairs, old baskets, shards of porcelain, empty bottles and mattresses. Vile-faced men in smocks or dirty frock coats, gray with dust, some with sacks over their shoulders, chatted in groups or shouted back and forth.

Frédéric again objected to going any further into the unpleasant setting.

"Oh, nonsense!"

And they mounted the stairs.

In the first room on the right, gentlemen with catalogues in their hands were examining pictures; in another a collection of Chinese weapons and armor was being sold; Madame Dambreuse decided to go downstairs. She looked at the numbers over the doors and led him to a room full of people at the far end of the corridor.

He instantly recognized the two sets of shelves from *L'Art Industriel,* her work table, and all her other furniture. They had been piled up at the far end of the room, with the tallest at the back, where they formed a broad slope reaching from the floor up to the windows; on the other sides of the room, curtains and carpets had been hung all along the walls. Below them were tiers of seats where old men sat dozing. On the left stood a kind of desk behind which the auctioneer, wearing a white cravat, was carelessly flourishing a little gavel. Next to him a young man was writing; and lower down stood a sturdy fellow, looking like a cross between a traveling salesman and a shady horse dealer, who shouted out descriptions of the sale lots. Three attendants carried them over to a table where the secondhand dealers were sitting. The crowd moved to and fro behind them.

When Frédéric came in, petticoats, scarves, handkerchiefs, and even chemises were being passed from hand to hand, turned inside out; sometimes they would be thrown from one end of the table to the other, a sudden flash of white through the air. Next they sold her dresses, then one of her hats whose broken feather dangled to one side, then her furs, then three pairs of boots; and the division of these relics in which he could vaguely descry the shape of her limbs, seemed to him an atrocity, as if he were watching crows tearing her body to pieces. The atmosphere of the room, laden with human breath, sickened him. Madame Dambreuse offered him her smelling salts; she said she was enjoying herself enormously.

The furniture from the bedroom was exhibited.

Maître Berthelmot would announce a price. The crier at once repeated it in a louder voice and the three attendants waited calmly for the tap of the hammer, then carried the object into the adjoining room. In this way there disappeared, one after the other, the big blue carpet sprinkled with camellias which her delicate feet had brushed as she came toward him; the little tapestry armchair in which he always sat opposite her when they were alone; the two fire screens whose ivory had been smoothed by the touch of her hands; and a velvet pincushion still bristling with pins. He felt as if fragments of his heart were being carried off; and the monotony of the same voices, the same gestures, numbed him with fatigue; he felt a deadly torpor, a sense of disintegration.

There was a rustling of silk in his ear; Rosanette touched his arm.

Frédéric himself had told her of the sale. Once her grief had passed, it occurred to her that she might find something worth buying. She had come to watch, wearing a white satin jacket with pearl buttons over a flounced dress, with tight gloves. Her expression was triumphant.

Frédéric paled with anger. She glanced at the woman beside him.

Madame Dambreuse had recognized her and, for a minute, they looked each other up and down, minutely searching for some defect or blemish—the one, perhaps, envying the other's youth, and the latter vexed by her rival's superb good taste and aristocratic simplicity.

Finally, Madame Dambreuse looked away, with a smile of unutterable insolence.

The crier had opend a piano—her piano! Still standing, he played a scale with his right hand, and started the bidding at twelve hundred francs, then came down to a thousand, to eight hundred, to seven hundred.

Madame Dambreuse playfully poked fun at the old wreck.

One of the assistants placed before the secondhand dealers a little casket with silver medallions, corners, and clasps, the one Frédéric had noticed the first time that he had been to dinner in the Rue de Choiseul. It had subsequently gone to Rosanette, then returned to Madame Arnoux; his eyes had often rested on it during their conversations; it was bound to his most cherished memories and his heart was melting with tenderness when Madame Dambreuse suddenly said:

"Well now, I think I'll buy that."

"But there's nothing unusual about it."

On the contrary, she thought it very pretty, and the crier extolled its delicate workmanship:

"A jewel of the Renaissance! Eight hundred francs, gentlemen! Almost entirely silver! With a little polish it'll shine up fine!"

And, as she pushed forward through the crowd, Frédéric commented:

"What an odd idea!"

"Does it annoy you?"

"No, but what could you use it for, a knickknack like that?"

"Who knows? For keeping love letters, perhaps!"

And she gave him a look that made the allusion crystal clear.

"Another reason for not robbing the dead of their secrets."

"I didn't think she was as dead as all that." She added loudly: "Eight hundred and eighty francs!"

"What you're doing is not right," murmured Frédéric. She laughed.

"But my dear woman, it's the first favor I've ever asked of you."

"You're not going to be a nice husband, you know?"

Someone had just made a higher bid; she raised her hand:

"Nine hundred francs!"

"Nine hundred francs!" repeated Maître Berthelmot.

"Nine hundred and ten . . . fifteen . . . twenty . . . thirty!" screeched the crier, running his eyes over the crowd with abrupt jerks of his head.

"Prove to me that my wife is a reasonable woman," said Frédéric.

He led her gently toward the door.

The auctioneer continued: "Come, come gentlemen, nine hundred and thirty! Is there a bidder at nine hundred and thirty?"

Madame Dambreuse had reached the doorway; she stopped and called in a loud voice:

"A thousand francs!"

A shiver passed through the crowd and there was a silence.

"A thousand francs, gentlemen, a thousand francs! There are no further bids? Going at a thousand francs! Going, going, gone!"

And the ivory gavel fell.

She passed her card forward and was handed the casket. She pushed it into her muff.

Frédéric felt a great chill pass through his heart.

Madame Dambreuse was still on his arm and she did not dare look him in the face until they had reached the street, where her carriage was waiting for them.

She scuttled into it like an escaping thief; then, when she had taken her seat, she turned to Frédéric. He had his hat in his hand.

"Aren't you getting in?"

"No, Madame!"

And with a cold bow, he shut the door and signaled the coachman to start.

At first he was elated by a feeling of joy and of independence regained. He was proud to have avenged Madame Arnoux by sacrificing a fortune to her; then his own act astonished him and he was stricken by a terrible dejection.

The next morning his servant told him the news. A state of siege had been declared, the Assembly dissolved, and some of the deputies sent to Mazas prison.* He was so preoccupied with his own affairs that those of the nation meant nothing to him.

He wrote to tradesmen to cancel various purchases in connection with his marriage, which now seemed to him a rather shabby piece of speculation; and he loathed Madame Dambreuse, because he had nearly committed a shameful act on her account. He had forgotten all about the Maréchale, and he no longer even worried about Madame Arnoux. He thought of himself and only himself —lost in the ruins of his dreams, sick, sorrowful and discouraged; and, despising the artificial setting where he had suffered so much, he longed for the freshness of grass, the tranquillity of the provinces, a sleepy life among unsophisticated people near the house where he was born. On Wednesday evening he finally went out.

There were many groups standing about on the boulevards. From time to time a patrol would disperse them, but they would gather again as soon as it had passed. People spoke freely and shouted jokes and insults at the soldiers but nothing more occurred.

"What! Isn't there going to be a fight?" inquired Frédéric of a worker.

The man, in the smock retorted:

"We're not such fools—why get ourselves killed for the sake of the rich! Let them work it out for themselves!"

And with a sidelong look at the proletarian, a gentleman growled:

"Socialist scum! Maybe this time we'll manage to exterminate them!"

Frédéric could make nothing of so much rancor and stupidity. It sharpened his disgust with Paris, and two days later he set out for Nogent by the first train.

Soon the houses disappeared and the countryside opened out. Alone in his carriage, his feet on the seat, he thought over the events of the last few days and of his whole past. The memory of Louise came back to him:

"There was a woman who loved me! I was wrong not to grasp at that happiness . . . Nonsense, I won't give it another thought!"

Then, five minutes later:

"Still, who knows? . . . Later . . . why not?"

His thoughts, like his eyes, were on distant horizons.

*This is Louis-Napoléon's *coup d'état,* which took place on the morning of December 2, 1851.

"She was naïve, a peasant, almost a savage, but she had a good heart!"

As they drew near to Nogent she became ever closer to him. When they crossed the meadows around Sourdun he seemed to see her under the poplars as in the old days, cutting rushes beside the pools. The train arrived and he got out.

Then he leaned over the bridge to see the island and the garden where they had walked together one sunny day—and the giddiness that came from travel and the fresh air combined with the weakness that still lingered after his recent agitation, to produce a sort of exaltation, so that he said to himself:

"She may be out for a walk; suppose I went to meet her!"

The bell of Saint-Laurent's was ringing and in the square in front of the church there was a crowd of poor people around a barouche, the only one in the neighborhood, which was used for weddings. Suddenly, amid a flood of bourgeois folk in white cravats, a bride and groom appeared in the doorway.

He thought he must be suffering a hallucination. But no! It was really she—Louise—in a white veil which fell from her red hair to her heels; and it was really he—Deslauriers—wearing a blue coat with silver embroidery, the uniform of a prefect. But why?

Frédéric hid behind the corner of a house to let the procession go by.

Ashamed, beaten, crushed, he retraced his steps to the railway and returned to Paris.

His cab-driver told him that the barricades were up from the Château-d'eau to the Gymnase, and went by way of the Faubourg Saint-Martin. At the corner of the Rue de Provence, Frédéric got out to walk to the boulevards on foot.

It was five o'clock; a light rain was falling. Middle-class townspeople were standing about on the sidewalk near the Opéra. The houses opposite were shut tight. There was no one at the windows. The whole breadth of the boulevard was filled with dragoons galloping at full speed, leaning over their horses' necks, their swords drawn. The plumes on their helmets and their great white cloaks billowing out behind them were silhouetted against the light of the street lamps, whose gas flames flickered in the wind that cut through the mist. The crowd watched them, silent and terrified.

Between the cavalry charges came squads of police, forcing the people back into the side streets.

But on the Tortoni steps stood a man—Dussardier—whose great size made him conspicuous from a distance, motionless as a caryatid.

One of the policemen marching in the front rank, his tricorne pulled down over his eyes, threatened him with his sword.

At this the other took a step forward and shouted:

"Long live the Republic!"

He fell on his back, his arms outstretched in the form of a cross.

A cry of horror rose from the crowd. The policeman turned to sweep them with his gaze and Frédéric, aghast, recognized Sénécal.

Chapter Six

He traveled.

He came to know the melancholy of the steamship, the cold awakening under canvas, the stupor induced by scenery and ruins, the bitterness of aborted friendships.

He returned.

He went about in society and knew other loves. But the ever-present memory of the first made them seem insipid; besides he had lost that vehemence of desire which is the very flower of feeling. His intellectual ambitions had diminished too. Years passed and he endured the idleness of his mind and his heart's inertia.

Toward the end of March, 1867, at twilight, as he was sitting alone in his study, a woman came in.

"Madame Arnoux!"

"Frédéric!"

She seized his hands, drew him gently to the window, and examined him, repeating to herself:

"It's he! It's really he!"

In the dim, evening light he could see nothing but her eyes beneath the black lace veil that covered her face.

When she had placed a small garnet velvet wallet on the mantelpiece she sat down. The two of them sat unable to speak, smiling at each other.

At length he asked her a multitude of questions about herself and her husband.

They lived in the depths of Brittany, to economize and pay their debts. Arnoux was ill most of the time, and looked like an old man. Her daughter was married and living in Bordeaux, and her son was garrisoned at Mostaganem. Then she raised her head:

"But I have seen you again! I am happy!"

He did not fail to tell her that he had hurried to their apartment as soon as he had heard of the disaster.

"I know!"

"How?"

She had seen him in the courtyard and had hidden from him.

"Why?"

Then, in a trembling voice, and with long pauses between her words, she replied:

"I was afraid! Yes . . . afraid of you . . . of myself!"

At this revelation he felt a pang of delight. His heart thudded wildly. She went on:

"Forgive me for not having come sooner." And, pointing to the little garnet wallet, which was covered with golden palms: "I embroidered it especially for you. It contains the sum for which the Belleville land was supposed to be the security."

Frédéric thanked her for the present, but chided her for taking so much trouble.

"No! That isn't the reason why I came! I wanted to visit you like this; then I shall go . . . back there."

And she told him about the place where she lived.

It was a low house, only one story high, with a garden filled with enormous box trees and a double avenue of chestnuts leading to the top of the hill, where there was a view of the sea.

"I go and sit there on a bench—I call it 'Frédéric's bench.'"

Then she gazed avidly at the furniture, the ornaments, the pictures, stamping them on her memory. The Maréchale's portrait was half hidden by a curtain. But the gold and white stood out amid the shadows and caught her attention.

"It seems to me that I know that woman?"

"You couldn't!" said Frédéric. "It's an old Italian painting."

She confessed she would like to stroll around the streets on his arm.

They went out.

From time to time the light from the shop windows would show him her pale profile; then the shadows closed around her again; and they moved through the carriages, the crowd, and the noise entirely absorbed in one another, hearing nothing, as if they were walking together in the country on a bed of dead leaves.

They talked about old times, the dinners in the days of

L'Art Industriel, Arnoux's eccentricities, his habit of tugging at the points of his detachable collar and smothering his moustache with pomade, about other things, deeper and more intimate. What rapture he had felt the first time he heard her sing! How beautiful she had looked, on her name-day, at Saint-Cloud! He reminded her of the little garden at Auteuil, of evenings at the theater, a meeting on the boulevard, old servants, her Negro woman-servant.

She was amazed at his memory. But then she said:

"Sometimes your words come back to me, like a distant echo, like the sound of a bell carried by the wind; and when I read the love passages in books it seems to me that you are with me."

"You have made me feel all the things that people think are exaggerated in those books," said Frédéric. "I understand Werther, and why he wasn't dismayed by Charlotte's bread and butter."

"My poor friend!"

She sighed and, after a long silence, said:

"Never mind, we have loved one another well."

"But never belonging to each other!"

"Perhaps it's better that way," she replied.

"No! Ah, no! How happy we should have been!"

"Yes, I can believe that, with a love like yours!"

And it must have been very strong to endure such a long separation.

Frédéric asked her how she had discovered his secret.

"It was one evening when you kissed my wrist, between the glove and the sleeve. I said to myself: 'But he loves me . . . He loves me.' But I was afraid of making sure. Your reserve was so charming that I delighted in it, as a continuous involuntary homage."

He had no regrets. His past sufferings had been repaid.

When they returned to the apartment, Madame Arnoux took off her hat. The lamp, standing on a console table, lit up her white hair. It was like a blow full in his chest.

To conceal his disillusionment he fell to his knees beside her and, taking her hands in his, spoke to her tenderly.

"Your person, your slightest movements, seemed to me to have an importance in the world that was more than human. My heart rose up like the dust at your footfall. You affected me like a moonlit summer night, when everything is perfume, gentle shadows, whiteness and infinity; and the delights of the flesh and the spirit were contained for me in your name—I would repeat it to myself, trying to kiss it on my lips. I could imagine nothing beyond it. It summoned up Madame Arnoux just as you were, with her two children, tender, serious, dazzlingly beautiful and so kind! That image effaced all the others. I didn't even waste a thought on them since I carried always, in my inmost heart, the music of your voice and the splendor of your eyes."

She accepted in ecstasy this adoration for the woman she no longer was. Frédéric, intoxicated by his own words, began to believe what he was saying. Her back to the light, Madame Arnoux stooped toward him. He felt the touch of her breath on his forehead and, through her clothes, a vague contact with her entire body. Their hands clasped. The point of her boot showed beneath her dress and, almost fainting, he murmured:

"The sight of your foot disturbs me!"

An impulse of modesty made her stand up. Then, motionless, and with the strange intonation of a sleep-walker, she said:

"At my age! Him! Frédéric! . . . No woman has ever been loved as I have been! No, no! What is the advantage of being young? Why should I care! I feel scorn for them, all the women who come here!"

"Oh, not many do!" he said, to please her.

Her face brightened, and she wanted to know if he would marry.

He swore that he never would.

"Are you sure? Why not?"

"Because of you," said Frédéric, clasping her in his arms.

She stayed there, leaning back, her mouth half open, her eyes turned upwards. Suddenly she pushed him away with a look of despair and, when he begged her to speak to him, said with a bowed head:

"I should have liked to make you happy."

Frédéric suspected that Madame Arnoux had come to offer herself to him, and once again he was seized by a furious, ravening lust, stronger than any he had known before. But he felt something inexpressible, a repulsion, and something like the dread of incest. Another fear held him back, that of feeling disgust later. Besides, what a problem it would be! And, impelled simultaneously by prudence and by the desire not to degrade his ideal, he turned on his heel and started to roll a cigarette.

She watched him, marveling.

"How chivalrous you are! There's no one like you, no one!"

Eleven o'clock struck.

"Already!" she said; "I shall go at quarter past."

She sat down again; but she was watching the clock and he continued to walk up and down, smoking. Neither of them could think of anything more to say. In every parting there comes a moment when the beloved is already gone from us.

Finally, when the minute hand showed that more than twenty-five minutes had passed, she slowly picked up her hat by the strings.

"Good-bye, my friend, my dear friend! I shall never see you again! This was my last act as a woman. My soul will never leave you. May all the blessings of heaven be upon you."

And she kissed him lightly on the forehead, like a mother.

But she seemed to be looking for something, and asked him for some scissors.

She undid her comb and all her white hair fell about her shoulders.

Roughly she cut off a long lock at the roots.

"Keep it! Good-bye!"

When she had gone out, Frédéric opened his window. Madame Arnoux, on the sidewalk, was hailing a passing cab. She got in. The carriage disappeared.

And that was all.

Chapter Seven

Toward the beginning of that winter, Frédéric and
Deslauriers were chatting beside the fire, reconciled yet
again by that fatality in their natures which always
drew them back together and renewed their friendship.

Frédéric gave a brief account of his quarrel with
Madame Dambreuse, who had subsequently married an
Englishman.

Deslauriers, without explaining how he had come to
marry Mademoiselle Roque, told how his wife, one fine
day, had run off with a singer. In an attempt to clear
himself of some of the ridicule which had followed,
he had ruined his chances in his post as prefect by an
excess of zeal for the government. He had been dismissed.
After that, he had been, successively, a director of
colonization in Algeria, secretary to a pasha, editor of
a paper, and an advertising agent, and had ended up
working in the legal department of an industrial organization.

As for Frédéric, having squandered two-thirds of his
fortune, he now lived like a small shopkeeper.

Then they discussed their old friends.

Martinon was now a senator.

Hussonnet held a high office that gave him control of
all the theaters and newspapers.

Cisy, deeply devout and the father of eight children,
lived in his ancestral mansion.

Pellerin, after dabbling in Fourierism, homeopathy,
spiritualism, gothic art, and humanitarian painting, had
become a photographer; and on all the walls of Paris
there were pictures of him wearing a black coat, with a
minute body and an enormous head.

"And your friend, Sénécal?" asked Frederic.

"Vanished! I have no idea where! And you, what about your great love, Madame Arnoux?"

"She must be in Rome with her son, who's a lieutenant in the cavalry."

"And her husband?"

"He died last year."

"Really?" said the lawyer.

Then, striking his forehead:

"Speaking of that, in a shop the other day I ran into that good soul the Maréchale, holding the hand of a little boy she had adopted. She's the widow of someone named Oudry and very fat, enormous. What a decline! Her waist used to be so slim in the old days!"

Deslauriers admitted frankly that he had taken advantage of her despair to find that out for himself.

"Anyhow, you gave me permission!"

This confession offset his silence about the attempt he had made to seduce Madame Arnoux. Frédéric would have forgiven him, since he had not succeeded.

Although this revelation vexed him a little, he pretended to be amused by it, and the thought of the Maréchale led to that of La Vatnaz.

Delsauriers had never met her, any more than many of the others who used to go to Arnoux's, but he remembered Regimbart perfectly.

"Is he still alive?"

"Hardly. Regularly every evening he drags himself along in front of the cafés, from the Rue de Grammont to the Rue Montmartre, feeble, bent double, empty, a ghost."

"And what about Compain?"

Frédéric gave a cry of delight and begged the ex-delegate of the provisional government to explain the mystery of the calf's head.

"It's an import from England. To parody the ceremony that the royalists used to hold on the thirtieth of January some of the independents founded an annual banquet where they ate calves' heads, drank red wine out of calves' skulls, and toasted the extermination of the Stuarts. After Thermidor, some of the terrorists organized a brotherhood along the same lines, which proves how fertile stupidity is!"

"Your political views seem to have moderated."

"Advancing age," said the lawyer.

And they summed up their lives.

They had both failed, the one who had dreamed of

love and the one who had dreamed of power. What was the reason?

"Perhaps it's because we didn't aim straight for the mark," suggested Frédéric.

"That may be true in your case. But my mistake, on the contrary, was being too rigid, without taking into account all those hundreds of secondary things which are the strongest of all in the end. I was too logical, and you were too sentimental."

Then they blamed chance, circumstances, the times they were born in.

Frédéric went on:

"This isn't how we expected to end up in the old days, at Sens, when you meant to write a critical history of philosophy and I a great medieval novel about Nogent. I had found the subject in Froissart: How Messire Brokars de Fénestranges and the Bishop of Troyes attacked Messire Eustache d'Ambrecicourt. Do you remember?"

And, as they exhumed their youth, they asked after every sentence:

"Do you remember?"

They could see the school courtyard, the chapel, the parlor, the gymnasium at the bottom of the staircase, the faces of the masters and pupils—Angelmarre, from Versaille, who used to cut himself trouser straps out of old boots; Monsieur Mirbal with his red whiskers; the two professors of geometric and artistic drawing, Varaud and Suriret, who were always quarreling; and the Pole, the compatriot of Copernicus, with his cardboard model of the planetary system, a traveling astrologer whose lesson had been paid for by a meal in the refectory—then a tremendous drunk they once had on an outing, the first pipes they had smoked, the prize ceremonies, the delights of the holidays.

It was during the holidays of 1837 that they had been to the house of "the Turk."

That was the nickname of a woman who was really called Zoraïde Turc; many people thought that she actually was a Moslem from Turkey, which added a touch of poetry to her establishment. It stood at the edge of the river, behind the ramparts. Even at midsummer there was shade round her house, which could be identified by a bowl of goldfish on the windowsill, next to a pot of mignonette. Young ladies in white wraps, with rouge on their cheeks, and long earrings, tapped on the windowpanes as one passed and, in the evening they sang softly in hoarse voices on the doorstep.

This den of perdition enjoyed an astounding reputation in the entire district. It was spoken of in euphemisms: "You know where I mean—a certain street—below the Bridges." It made the farmers' wives tremble for their husbands; the townswomen feared it for their maids because the sub-prefect's cook had been caught there; and, of course, it was the secret obsession of every adolescent.

One Sunday while everyone was at vespers, Frédéric and Deslauriers, having had their hair curled earlier in the day, picked some flowers in Madame Moreau's garden, then left by the gate into the fields and, after a long detour through the vineyards, came back by the Pêcherie and slipped into the Turk's house, still holding their fat bouquets.

Frédéric presented his like a lover to his fiancée. But the heat of the day, fear of the unknown, a kind of remorse, and even the pleasure of seeing at a single glance so many women at his disposal, affected him so strongly that he grew very pale and stood stock still without uttering a word. All the girls laughed, amused by his embarrassment; imagining that they were mocking him, he turned tail and fled and, as Frédéric had the money, Deslauriers was forced to follow him.

They were seen coming out. It caused a scandal which was still not forgotten three years later.

They told each other the story at length, each one supplementing the memory of the other, and, when they had finished:

"That was the best time we ever had!" said Frédéric.

"Yes, you may be right. That was our best time!" said Deslauriers.

AFTERWORD

The Sentimental Education was first published in the Paris of 1869, some thirteen years after the triumphant appearance there of *Madame Bovary;* and the later novel has remained ever since in the long, long shadow of the earlier one, waiting for full recognition. The reasons for this preference may seem cogent, at least to the average reader of novels. Thoroughly original in its conception and its language, *Madame Bovary* still rests on the ancient formula of sin and retribution and so moves steadily toward a decisive end: the suicide of Emma and the ruin of her family. Emma's adventures dominate the action; one's attention is the more acute for being fixed on a single line of development.

True, Emma is a wretched woman, and her character and culture are relentlessly dissected by the author. Yet she has the advantage for any reader of being violently real in her physical presence. Her lush irritated sensuality works on one's own sensuality, even to the moment when, agonizing on her deathbed, she "stretches out her neck" and "glues her lips" to the crucifix offered her by the priest. Emma dying is the same person as Emma living, the literal embodiment of unlimited *desire*. One might say that she has turned into the very stuff of her daydreams: the stuff of sex and body, of the money, jewels, marriages, draperies, and yards of dress goods she has coveted. And Emma's ghastly "materialization," so to speak, has a pathos about it. The impoverished *moeurs de province*, the phrase Flaubert uses for the book's subtitle, defeat her efforts to escape them. Confined to her dismal province, she feels permanently excluded from Paris, where all good things—sex, money, jewels, and the rest—presumably abound.

In *The Sentimental Education*, bountiful Paris is itself the scene of most of the drama. The characters with "life stories" are numerous and rather better endowed than Emma is with culture and experience. Nevertheless they come to ends which for the most part are not decisive ends at all; they just fade away into nothingness. The Paris of *The Sentimental Education* is "sick" in much the same secondary sense which that word has today. And during Flaubert's lifetime it was one thing to represent the provinces as "sick," quite another to represent as "sick" a great city, the capital of a great nation's culture as well as its government. On its first publication *The Sentimental Education* was dismissed by all but a few of Flaubert's contemporaries as ailing itself: it was called politically irresponsible, morally squalid, and an aesthetic failure. Until quite recently the book has been stuck with that reputation, so far as the large public was concerned, while *Madame Bovary* has continued to flourish.

Nothing in recent literary history is better known than the contagious fame won by *Madame Bovary*. Emma's appeal to readers was equaled by the appeal of the novel itself—its subject as well as the sophistications of its form and language—to young novelists in all the novel-producing countries. Flaubert's new, exacting realism was adapted to the life stories latent in other provinces, remote from France, where young men and women yearned for other capitals: Moscow, Madrid, New York, even Chicago. Deep within *Madame Bovary*, however, is a theme which only the greatest of Flaubert's progeny have laid hold of—insofar as it was not given by their own experience—and the theme becomes quite explicit in *The Sentimental Education;* though publicly neglected, the *Education* soon acquired an underground reputation, especially with writers. This theme was the existential one: the perception of a growing estrangement from "real experience" and the "lived life"—vague terms for elusive but powerful feelings—on the part of individuals living in whatever locale, provincial or metropolitan. This perception was at the heart of Flaubert's idea of modernity; he and Baudelaire were the first "modernists," not solely because of the innovations they brought to the art of writing but because each developed powerful conceptions of the nature of modernity itself.

The history of Flaubert's influence, as the author of both novels and of tales like *Un coeur simple,* is formidable. It has been a history, not of imitations—which don't matter—but of transformations, unpredictable, brilliant, self-perpetuating. Among the novelists strongly affected there was Henry James, especially in *The Bostonians,* and later there were Proust and Joyce (not to mention the several French writers who were Flaubert's immediate disciples). The least predictable episode in this history was the infusion of the Flaubertian spirit, together with the Baudelairean-*symboliste* spirit, into modernist *poetry,* chiefly the earlier poetry of Eliot and Pound. As Flaubert had fought for a prose that was as well written as poetry, so Pound fought for a poetry that was as well written as prose—meaning, in part, Flaubert's prose: its precise rhythms, its acutely particularized images. Both poets defied what, in Pound's words, "the age demanded," that is, the synthetic arts and morals of the age of modernity. Of the two poets, Eliot was the more susceptible to the existential theme. The theme was localized in his "Unreal City." Bored, restless, and afraid, the people of the Unreal City are subliminally anxious to hear the saving Word but can only hear the comforting commonplace: "Cousin Harriet, here is the *Boston Evening Transcript.*" Our knowledge of Eliot has helped us to identify and understand the function of commonplaces and banalities in *The Sentimental Education.* Madame Arnoux remarks to Frédéric: "Sometimes your words come back to me, like a distant echo, like the sound of a bell carried by the wind." Madame Arnoux talks like Eliot's too baffled, too articulate "lady of situations" in her several guises. The Flaubertian "tradition" has been a two-way thoroughfare.

Where Flaubert's influence is concerned, however, qualifications are called for. To his literary progeny Flaubert was assimilable only in part. He was a difficult father figure whose testament was full of discriminatory clauses that seemed to require contesting. Flaubert's pessimism was too unyielding, his work a triumph of artifice over art, his style a medium too solid to transmit the possible varieties of feeling implicit in his subjects. Henry James objected that Flaubert "had no faith in the power of the moral to offer a surface." This judgment was convincing if one agreed with James about how "the power of the moral" asserts itself upon the "surface," that is, in the necessarily aesthetic style and form of any good novel. For James "the moral" makes itself felt through a series of identifications between the best in the author and the best in his readers, with the characters acting as agents in the transaction: those of his characters, I mean, who at *their* best are capable of reaching states of consciousness about themselves and their situations, and then of acting decisively on the promptings of consciousness. Experience is the great teacher and the lesson is the primacy of mind, mind as awareness. In his own subtle fashion James was captivated by the *Bildungsroman* conception of literature. Flaubert was not. James' New World idealism was alien to Flaubert's conception of the average human potential in the age of modernity, itself a manifestation of the sovereignty of the average. *The Sentimental Education* is a negative *Bildungsroman*. With the characters, the education by experience doesn't "take." For readers, the novel is an *un*learning of indefensible sentiments and ideas.

Among Flaubert's other putative descendants, Eliot and Proust found different exits from the Flaubertian Limbo. For Eliot, the saving Word is really *there*, even if it comes to us garbled and attenuated, offering partial epiphanies and precarious conversions. For Proust transcendence is the peculiar privilege of the artist, a conclusion that gives his big-bodied novel, clamorous with suffering, a very small head.

Only Joyce among "moderns" surpassed Flaubert in greatness while possessing a similar vision of human limitation: both writers were Catholic Christians *manqués*. Joyce's Dublin, like Flaubert's Paris, is incurably stricken with paralysis (Mr. Victor Brombert astutely diagnoses the particular Parisian *mal* as a universal susceptibility to *prostitution*).* Dublin epiphanies range from the frankly false to the merely promising. The immanence of myth deflates reality. Molly Bloom is more Molly than earth mother. In Dublin nothing really happens, nothing transcendent. Dubliners simply reveal, for the reader's pitying or amused contemplation, the general lifeness-of-life: people are what they are, not in any past or future imagined by them, but in what they feel and do and imagine at any given moment or hour or day in their lives. For Joyce as for Flaubert, the "lived life" is a mere tautology. But there was at least one great difference between them. Flaubert's doctrine of "impersonality" in art was equally an item in Joyce's literary creed. But impersonality can be "cold" or "warm." Joyce's is warm in the profoundly, elusively, tempered way that the impersonality of Shakespeare and Cervantes is warm. Flaubert's is cold, with variations here and there. His relationship with his characters is, for the most part, incomplete, forming a void which the author's brilliant irony is seldom capable of displacing. But

The Novels and Tales of Gustave Flaubert.

if this is the most problematic element in his work, it is
not the whole story of his work. What Mark Van Doren
has written about Thomas Hardy, another stern ironist, is
true of Flaubert: "He is that most moving of men, the
kind that tries not to feel yet does." Flaubert does feel,
almost in spite of himself, when his subject is the betrayal
or exploitation of the helpless: Emma Bovary's husband;
the servant woman in *Un coeur simple;* and, in the
Education—among several others—Dussardier the worker, who is the captive and victim of his bourgeois friends.
The pity that comes easily to other writers is the more
moving in Flaubert because to him it comes hard.

A recent English, very English, critic condemned *The
Sentimental Education* as "an attack on human nature."
One admits the charge is true, while wondering what is so
great about human nature that it should be declared immune from attack. Flaubert's aloof, melancholic temperament caused some of the bleakness of his vision, as any
writer's negations or affirmations owe something to his
temperament. Yet the bleakness is also inherent in an Old
World skepticism, a pre-bourgeois *désabusement,* concerning human nature as manifested in society, the only form
in which human nature can be known. In Flaubert the
moralism of, say, Montaigne, Pascal, and La Roche-
foucauld (and of non-Frenchmen like Swift) survives, with
the newly bourgeoisified Paris rather than feudal Paris
as the object of his censure or derision. Calling attention
to a writer's traditions is an easy way of making him
respectable. Flaubert was the rare kind of writer, later
celebrated by Eliot in a famous essay, in whom a sense
of tradition interacts with great originality to produce the
work that is "new, really new."

Flaubert's immediate precedents for *The Sentimental
Education* were, it would seem, the comprehensive
eighteenth-century satires, among which *Candide* and
Gulliver's Travels were intimately known to him.

Like those earlier satires, *The Sentimental Education* is
an attack on the whole modern spectacle of human
bêtise, imbecility. Indeed, the *Education* has always been
taken too seriously or with the wrong kind of seriousness
by critics who are insufficiently tough-minded or are too
humorless to see that the book is essentially, if often
deceptively, comic. "Deceptively," because the comic effect is generally subdued to conform with the generally
dreary realities of bourgeois existence. If, however, the

method of the satires was comic fantasy touched here
and there with realism and pathos, Flaubert's method is
realism touched with the fantastic—many episodes of *The
Sentimental Education* being as outrageously funny as
anything in *Candide*. *Candide* was one of Flaubert's
"sacred books"; and the *Education* forms certain relation-
ships with *Candide* that are worth noting. Both narratives
move at a frantic pace, "cresting," like a flood, in a pair of
major phenomena, the Lisbon earthquake and the 1848
Revolution; in both narratives, too, the episodes are
strung along a continuous thread of romance: Candide's
enduring devotion to his much put-upon dream girl,
Cunégonde, and Frédéric Moreau's devotion to *his* much
put-upon Madame Arnoux, a rather mature dream girl.
While a playful irony attaches to Candide's affair, an
irony that is alternately light and corrosive informs Flaubert's account of Frédéric's affair. The two heroes are
essentially unalike. Candide is a thoroughgoing "innocent," whose continuing innocence is guaranteed by his
incorruptible goodwill. Frédéric is innocent only by virtue of the Romantic literary convention which tended to
attribute this quality to the young, so long, at least, as
they stayed young. (Flaubert's ironic subtitle to *The
Sentimental Education* is *l'Historie d'un jeune homme*.)
In his fine study of the novel,* Harry Levin calls the
mature Frédéric "a dilettante who has survived his innocence." I would only object that Frédéric's innocence,
and the goodwill it rests on, have been subject to corruption from the start. So Candide gets his reward, is at
last reunited with Cunégonde, and they are left cultivating
their garden; while Frédéric loses Madame Arnoux, the
possession of whom he has always blown hot and cold
about, and is left cultivating his memories. I mention
these parallels with *Candide* not to pronounce *The Sentimental Education* a classic by association but on the
contrary to affirm Flaubert's originality. In part, the
originality of the *Education* consists in Flaubert's bringing to bear a comic perspective, infinitely variable in its
intensity, on a mass of "real life" characters and stories
which normally were subject to serious, or occasionally
serio-comic, concern, especially in popular novels of the
time like Octave Feuillet's *Roman d'un jeune homme
pauvre*. In a larger sense, however, Flaubert's manner is
an adaptation of the traditionally French manner of work-

*The Gates of Horn: A Study of Five French Novelists.

ing within deliberately confined borders, the success of the performance depending, like the success of laboratory experiments, on just this principled selectivity. The Anglo-Saxon way is different, sometimes causing philistines of that community, even important philistines like D. H. Lawrence, to belittle the energy of French creation. Mr. V. S. Pritchett,* on the other hand, remarks: "We [English] tacitly refuse to abstract or isolate a subject or to work within severe limits . . . A native instinct warns him [the English writer] that he could learn more than is good for him. He could learn, for example, final fatalism and acceptance."

In *The Sentimental Education* it was Flaubert's feat, and one that followed from his comic aims, to have made an epic novel out of an accumulation of anecdotes. The novel is epic because the fates of numerous characters and of a major revolution are embraced in the action; it is anecdotal because each episode recounts—as I think anecdotes do by nature—the momentary defeat or the equivocal victory of someone in a particular situation. Each episode extracts from the situation a maximum of irony and then, having made its point with a precision consonant with its brevity, is caught up in the furious current of the enveloping narrative. By itself, anecdotal irony is self-contained, a blind alley. It is irony for irony's sake, such as is apt to inform the anecdotes that circulate in any group of acquaintances, real or fictional, getting from the reader or hearer only a laugh or amused sigh or a murmured "How typical of him!" Superior anecdotes make for superior gossip as distinct from mere tale-bearing. And the doings of the members of the circle—mostly career-bent intellectuals and their women—that centers on Frédéric Moreau in the *Education* make for superior gossip. However, the irony itself isn't, finally, of the blind alley kind, as the following episode should make clear.

For years Frédéric has been trying at intervals to seduce Madame Arnoux, the wife of his friend, the sportive art dealer Jacques Arnoux. Finally she consents to a rendezvous in a room Frédéric has rented and beautified for the occasion. But she doesn't show up. And after hours of frantic waiting and searching, Frédéric takes his whore to bed in the same room. Later she wakes up to find him weeping and asks why. "I'm too happy," he says, mean-

*Books in General, page 104.

ing the opposite. In itself the outcome of this little episode may deserve no more than a snort of recognition. "How typical of Frédéric!" But this primitive response doesn't stick. There's more to it.

The episode crawls with implications, not only amatory but domestic and political; and promptly caught up in the narrative stream, it goes to feed the rising flood of irony which will at last engulf the novel's entire scene, figuratively speaking. The whore, as I unjustly called her, is really a *lorette*, or kept woman, Rosanette Bron, and is at present the mistress of Jacques Arnoux. Rosanette is beautiful and weirdly charming, by turns affectionate and mean, supremely vulgar in her taste for lush boudoirs and Turkish parlors complete with hookahs, and no happier in her profession than Frédéric and his circle of fellow-intellectuals are in theirs, but a cut above them in her prodigious vitality. Madame Arnoux, for her part, has failed to keep the rendezvous because her young son having come down suddenly with a violent croup, she takes this as a judgment on her for her proposed betrayal of what she instinctively values most: husband, children, home; and for years to come she will rarely see the importunate Frédéric. Meanwhile, searching the streets for her, he hears a noise of rioting on the distant boulevards. "The pear is ripe," he has read in an excited note from his friend Deslauriers. Deslauriers is trying to involve Frédéric in the political struggle against the degenerate monarchy of Louis-Philippe, an involvement that Frédéric, busy with his love affairs, prefers to avoid. In short, his amatory mixup coincides with the outbreak of those disturbances which, extending from February through June, will be known to history as the Revolution of 1848.

As reported by Flaubert, the uprising generates its own irony and contributes to the epic, or mock-epic, character of the whole novel. It is not only the political "commitments" but even more the personal "motivations" of the participants that naturally fascinate the novelist, the participants including people of all political persuasions, not least the big industrialist, Dambreuse, who promptly declares himself a republican. And just as their motivations, better and worse, color the actions of people during the Revolution, so the actions are sometimes heroic, oftentimes fatuous and self-serving. Flaubert's account of the uprising is, again, episodic, his tone dispassionate. He doesn't want to make a monumental set-piece out of an event which will turn out to be, from his viewpoint in the novel, a tragic farce. So he touches in more or less detail on such episodes as the abdication and flight of Louis-Philippe; the eruption all across Paris of political meetings and street battles; the sacking of the Tuileries Palace by a mob; certain incidents connected with the gradual concentration of power in the middle classes and their military force, the National Guard; certain incidents connected with the corresponding loss of power by the working classes and *their* military arm, the Mobile Guards; the final defeat of the proles; the imprisonment of hundreds of them in vaults beneath the Tuileries facing the Seine where they are left to starve. In one instance, an imprisoned youth who screams too insistently for bread is shot to death by Old Roque, Frédéric's miserly home-town neighbor, who has hastened down to Paris to take his stand in the National Guard and who commits this decisive act in defense of private property (the memory of it sickens him a little, but not for long).

So the Revolution itself is caught in the embrace of Flaubert's irony. Just as the proletariat is—literally—put down by the republican middle classes, so those classes are presently put down—or bribed to surrender—by Louis-Napoléon when, in his coup of 1851, he converts the Second Republic into a Second Empire, with himself as Emperor. Flaubert soft-pedals this development, probably because Napoleon III was still in power and his censorship still in effect when Flaubert wrote the novel. But the implications of the coup are made clear. Louis-Napoléon has dreamed of playing the same role that his uncle, Napoleon the Great, played, when in 1799, he proclaimed the First Empire, with himself as Emperor, thus terminating the Great French Revolution of those years, and leaving France, with its burden of half-resolved problems, to a century of turmoil. Two years after the *Education* appeared, Napoleon III would be defeated by the Prussians and driven from France. Paris would again be the scene of an uprising, the Commune, which would again conclude with the slaughter of rebellious proles.

Flaubert's own politics, if any, were protean in the extreme. One might call them, paradoxically, a politics of noncommitment, except that he did now and then react impulsively, and stupidly, to events. He had been no more than a spectator of certain actions in '48, having been in Paris at the time more or less by chance. But his instinct for detecting the convulsions at work deep within the society was steady, profound, and, alas, prophetic. What James called, in a misguided attempt at reductive wit, Flaubert's "puerile dread of the grocer" was a dread of the entire acquisitive culture which corrupted, or threatened to corrupt, grocer, industrialist, and worker alike. Flaubert was far less knowledgeable about society than Balzac or Dickens were. Nevertheless, as concerns his visionary pessimism and its effects on his art, there was a point in his refusing to identify his fortunes with those of any existing or pre-existing social class, aristocratic, big bourgeois, little bourgeois, or proletarian. Having no faith in the power of the social—that is, of reformism or revolutionism—to offer a surface, he made what he could of his unimpeded, unqualified, bleakness of vision. He made, chiefly, *The Sentimental Education,* and the world has now caught up with the bleakness.

"The first time as tragedy, the second time as farce," Karl Marx wrote of the *coups d'état* of the two Napoleons, in words that have been often quoted ever since. Flaubert views the events of the years 1848-1851 in a similarly theatrical spirit, though with far less hopeful implications for the future of France and its working class than those entertained by Marx. In 1835, as a boy of fourteen, he had observed in a letter to a school friend that "our century is rich in bloody peripities." Such peripities as they affect the characters of the *Education* bring the harsh comedy of the novel to a climax. The tragic farce of the revolutionary years is a large-scale political manifestation of the farces, bitter or merely ludicrous, enacted by the characters in their individual lives.

The fiasco of 1848-51 hastens and intensifies all the processes at work in the novel. The temporal process is one of these; it pervades everything, and accordingly accelerates in the years following the Revolution. Yet there seem to be two kinds of Time at work in *The Sentimental Education,* and since the two interact in devious ways, neither is easy to define in itself. The first and more obvious may be identified with what we call "clock time." It consists of the hours, days, months and years—often specified by Flaubert—during which Frédéric and his circle pursue the objects of their various ambitions. The wretched painter Pellerin boasts that "art, science and love (those three faces of God)" are solely on view in Paris. And Paris, insofar as it is assumed to enjoy this exclusive privilege, represents the pure present, an eternity of *now*. Generally invisible to the characters, therefore, are the monuments of the city's past. In Flaubert's descriptive patches, they appear rarely: reminders of what Frédéric and company tend to ignore. Frédéric is first seen aboard the steamer bound for his home town of Nogent-sur-Seine. As the steamer pulls away from the quay and up the Seine, he gazes regretfully back at the city. "He gazed through the fog at the belfreys and buildings he could not identify," while glimpses of Nôtre-Dame and the Cité merge in his eyes with glimpses of riverside "shops, work-yards, and factories." Caught in the unlimited present, physical Paris is to the characters a faceless configuration of streets, shops, cafés, restaurants, and residences, among which they hustle, trying to meet or avoid meeting one another, and generally contesting for place and preferment like the counters on an immense checkerboard.

By contrast, the countryside is reserved for holidays and duty visits, and there Time's action is naturally decelerated, at least for the Parisians; sooner or later they must be off to the metropolis. It is the presence in the country of the Parisians and the Parisian idea that fills these rural scenes with the peculiar Flaubertian compound of yearning dreariness and elegiac charm. Here, as in *Madame Bovary,* some of his greatest passages are devoted to bringing out, through people's behavior, through the very look and feel and smell of trees, rivers, gardens, palaces and houses, this intermingling of past and present France, of artificial and natural time, of pastoral "poetry" and realistic "prose." No country scene in the novel is without its intrinsic serenity, no country scene fails to excite an intrinsic anxiety.

In the two chief country-based episodes, one in Frédéric's home town of Nogent, the other at Fontainebleau, love itself partakes of these contradictions, flowering on the serenity, withering with the anxiety. At Nogent as at Fontainebleau the presence of the past is complicated: in both places there are pasts within pasts. At Nogent Frédéric wanders with Louise Roque among waterside gardens strewn with the broken statues and ruined pavilions of a Directoire "folly." Louise is the neighbor girl, once an illegitimate waif, now a potential heiress, who has always adored Frédéric. Since he is at present low on funds and she will have money, it is now vaguely understood between them that he will propose marriage. Together they sit on the river bank and play in the sand like children, Louise remarking that the clouds are floating toward Paris. Her passion for Frédéric is awkwardly but violently physical; she envies the way fishes live: "It must be nice to glide in the water and feel oneself caressed all over." The two have reverted to their own pasts, but not for long. On the premises there is a big woodshed, and when Louise suggests they go inside it Frédéric is embarrassed and ignores the suggestion. She breaks into frank reproaches—the frankest and truest he ever gets from anyone—and the pastoral idyll limps to an end. The Parisianized Frédéric has refused to play his appointed role in the idyll. And Louise is left to ripen within the retarded medium of rural time—to ripen into a shrew.

The idyll motif recurs with variations in the later passage that describes the visit of several days that Frédéric and Rosanette pay to Fontainebleau hoping to get away from the turmoil of revolutionary Paris. Here too there is a monument to an earlier past within the perennial splendor of the great wooded park with its radiating carriage roads, it sunny clearings, deep glens, and outcroppings of ancient rock. The monument is the palace itself, heavy with grandiose mementos of Henry II and his mistress Diane de Poitiers. The palace excites in Frédéric "an indescribable feeling of retrospective lust." But Rosanette is bored and weary and can only say, "It brings back memories." In a way it does. But her memories concern herself—her past as an impoverished working-class girl in industrial Lyons, turned *lorette* at the age of fifteen. Her thoughts concern herself *and* Frédéric, whom she too adores, momentarily at least, dreaming of a lasting affair with him. ("One day she forgot herself and let slip her age: twenty-nine; she was growing old.") They daily explore the forest in a carriage, happy with each other, "their hearts swelling with the pride of a full life." Yet misgivings and embarrassments shadow their pastoral excursions. They recall other lovers—she, Arnoux in particular, he, Madame Arnoux. Each yearns discreetly for the lover who is absent. By turns the forest soothes them and disturbs them. The vistas into its dark interiors gloom at them; the rocks take on the shapes of wild beasts coming at them. One day Frédéric finds in a newspaper the name of Dussardier on a list of men wounded at the Paris barricades. Dussardier is a young man of heroic size and strength, the one authentic worker in Frédéric's circle. It is late June and the workers are making their last stand. Frédéric and the reluctant Rosanette leave for the city, Frédéric finally getting into Paris alone, past barriers and guard-posts manned by suspicious National Guardsmen, past wrecked barricades and shot-up houses, to the attic room in the house where the wounded Dussardier lies.

Meanwhile Flaubert's Paris, citadel of the pure present, is also subject to the workings, barely perceptible though they are, of natural time as distinct from artificial time. Natural time flows through the city with the river, drifts across its skies with the mists and clouds, manifests itself in the succession of day and night, in the changing seasons, in the winter wind that reddens Rosanette's cheeks, in the setting sun whose rays—in Frédéric's rather mercenary imagination—cover buildings with "plates of gold." If he is more susceptible than others are to these presences, it is, again, never for long. Pausing on bridges, he has exalted visions which, however (as Harry Levin points out), quickly resolve themselves into dreams of instant acquisition.

Parisian epiphanies, Parisian dreams. Yet it should be said that, whatever Flaubert himself thought of the city —and his pleasure in it was intermittent—he shapes the Paris of the *Education* to his own selective purposes in the novel. Those purposes have their bit of common truth *vis à vis* the real Paris. Surely Paris was, and is, a great city if there ever was one. It lends itself to satirization (in how many works besides the *Education!*) because its sillier inhabitants are tempted to believe that the city's greatness rubs off on themselves, causing them to feel unduly self-important. Pellerin's "three faces of God" slogan is the reduction to nonsense of this Parisophiliac madness. Pellerin himself, like so many of Frédéric's *copains,* suffers from this gratuitous sense of privilege. Haunted by the Idea of art, he never makes it as an artist in fact. The actual endowments of *les copains* are unequal to the expectations they have of themselves as Parisians or Parisianized provincials. They remain artists and intellectuals *manqués.* Flaubert knew that they were special types of the Parisian. Scattered through the pages of the *Education* are the names of actual, and variously distinguished, men of the period. Corresponding to Pellerin, there are Géricault and Delacroix; to the sometime littérateur Frédéric, Hugo, Chateaubriand, Lamartine; to the radical Sénécal, Prudhon, Barbès, Blanqui, Louis Blanc. The Paris that harbored such men has eluded Time in all senses, and lives on in an eternity of deserved fame. The high French culture of the period produced, of course, a second *siècle d'or*.

The varieties of time are merged into a single powerful force by the events of 1848-51. As the crisis deepens, Flaubert's characters undergo the same rapid changes of heart—from fear to exaltation to final disgust and fatigue —evidently experienced by the populace at large. Individual weaknesses come glaringly to light; everyone grows confused, demoralized, desperate. Even Dussardier is confused. The good if simple-minded prole has been beguiled, as many proles actually were, into fighting with the bourgeois National Guard during the June days. Now, his huge body stretched wounded on his bed, he begins to suspect that he has fought on the wrong side. He has killed a fellow-worker at the barricades. In 1851 Dussardier himself is shot to death by a policeman newly recruited to keep order in Louis-Napoléon's Second Empire. The policeman is Dussardier's old friend and mentor, Sénécal, once known as "the future Saint Just," long a strenuous advocate of socialist discipline, scientific logic, proletarian literature, and progress. Sénécal's motivation has been in excess of his socialist commitment. His real commitment is to power, even if exemplified in the lowly figure of the policeman with uniform and gun.

No other incident connected with the general decline is as lurid—and prophetic—as this one. Frédéric and the remaining *copains* merely prey on others, and on each other, in their abasement before the *new* God of three faces: sex, money, and power. Much that happens in the new situation is merely ludicrous. There is "the paper" and *its* change of heart. *Les copains* have long struggled to start and keep going the precious periodical without which no intellectual circle is complete. Their periodical has ended up as a gossip sheet. Frédéric's development is scarcely more interesting. He terminates his quest for greatness by trying, and failing, to marry money. Only one member of the group survives intact, preserved by the remarkable system he has imposed on his life. He is the stern republican, Regimbart, known as "the Citizen," and his system consists in his rushing around Paris each day in order to be present in the same cafés or restaurants at the precise hours scheduled for his presence at these establishments. Regimbart's regimen has constituted *his* career. Come revolutions or *coups d'état,* he remains the useful Parisian citizen, a sort of human clock, a walking landmark.

One tends to dwell with special delight on Regimbart and others of his type in the circle of *copains* that surrounds Frédéric Moreau. Frédéric, for reasons that I will go into later on, is not himself a compelling character, although he is the occasion for much anecdotal amusement. Nor are the habitués of that *other* Parisian scene, the Dambreuse salon, compelling either. The rich industrialist Dambreuse, a bourgeoisified nobleman, and his sleek fashionable wife, later widow, whom Frédéric woos for her money; their world of sumptuous parties, crooked deals, easy marital infidelities, illegitimate children, and contested wills is a pastiche of Balzac's world. Flaubert himself was an occasional frequenter of salons, including royal ones, and knew, for example, the illustrious Princess Mathilde, Louis-Napoléon's sister, whom Proust was to portray with wry conviction in his novel. But *in his imagination* Flaubert was not, as Proust was, a man of the world.

Regimbart and his type are not puppets. Regimbart, Sénécal, and Pellerin, for instance, are lively grotesques, literal embodiments of their obsessive ideas. Frozen in their characteristic attitudes, they suggest figures in Daumier, just as the milder people and their characteristic settings, the studio scenes, the rural scenes, suggest those of Courbet. There is, I believe, nothing quite like *les copains* elsewhere in literature, whether in the intellectual milieu of Dostoevsky's Petersburg or of Joyce's Dublin. Only in Paris, where the cultivation of arts and ideologies counts for so much in the *high* French culture, could such debased types of the artist and ideologue as Frédéric and company be found in such profusion.

No doubt the type of the intellectual *manqué* fascinated Flaubert, and for reasons that form part of the well-known Flaubert legend. Acknowledged master though he became at the age of 36, with his first publication, *Madame Bovary,* Flaubert had in him at all times a good deal of the perpetual amateur, the compulsive dreamer, the man of obsessive ideas. Born in 1821, he was admittedly, even proudly, a belated Romantic. Precociously literary from childhood, he was given to revering, as if they were holy relics, certain images of past beauty: old stones recalled from a visit he had made to the Acropolis, old paintings in oil or glass studied in cathedrals or museums, old books—*Candide, Don Quixote,* Rabelais—continually reread and pondered through the years; old professions like sainthood, monkhood and prostitution; old friendships and exalted moments. Familiar too as part of the legend is the detestation he nourished for the present, the age of "the grocer," as a corollary of his passion for the past. The present was given over to the worship of commodities, so much so that people, their possessions, their careers, their very dreams, and life itself as lived by them, belonged to the commodity realm. Divided souls like Flaubert's were of course common in the emergent industrial democracies of the mid-century, and the type has perpetuated itself into our own time. Far from despicable, the type has produced connoisseurs, collectors, critics, travelers, and, when the luck was good, fine writers, major and minor. Flaubert became a major figure in this tradition, partly by practicing in his literary work a unique form of the division of labor. He split his writings into historical fictions and fictions of contemporary life, while composing all of them with the same attention to style and form. To the world of his historical fictions (*Salammbô la Tentation de Saint Antoine, la Légend de saint Julien l'hospitalier, Hérodias*) he assigned the qualities he worshiped in the past: the heroism, idealism, romance, beauty, and so on; while to the novels of contemporary life (*Madame Bovary, l'Éducation sentimentale,*) he relegated, so to speak, his sense of the modern materialization of life. As he practiced it, the division of labor had its limitations. It was mechanical, it was invidious. Whether for this reason or another, the bulk of his work was small, in an age when novelists were prolific almost by definition.

The bulk of his *un*published work was considerable. He lived amid a clutter of dormant manuscripts, the constantly expanding archives of his restless creative spirit (many of these items have recently been exhumed and put into print). There were the notebooks; the first drafts; the more or less completed works which never saw print (among them an earlier version of *The Sentimental Education*); the assorted early projects that remained fragmentary; the plays that were unproducible or, if produced, as *le Candidat* was, were flops; the fairy tale briefly worked at in collaboration with friends; the *Dictionnaire des idées reçues,* a compilation of clichés to which he added items through the years and which was to have formed an appendix to *Bouvard et Pécuchet,* the great extravaganza of which he had completed the first part when, in 1880, he died. In addition, letters to friends poured from him in daily profusion; they now fill twelve indispensable volumes in the posthumously published *Cor-*

réspondance. The letters testify in dizzying detail to the quality of Flaubert's mind. His mind was more than chaotic: protean. It was by turns adult, juvenile, kind, cruel, masculine, feminine, myopic, prophetic, supremely fantastic, supremely intelligent. Given his genius, there were advantages in being, as Flaubert was, subject to epileptic seizures. He could produce extraordinary masterpieces and still live with his devastating knowledge of the precariousness of everything, one's genius included. To George Sand he confessed when he was quite old: "One doesn't shape one's destiny, one undergoes it. I was pusillanimous in my youth—I was afraid of life. One pays for everything." The condition of his existence was that he remain vulnerable, and for this too he ungrudgingly paid—to the extent, finally, of surrendering to his grasping niece whom he loved, and to her feckless husband who faced bankruptcy, much of the income on which his precious independence had rested, and then of looking about for jobs, as librarian or whatever, to support him in his old age. As the letters make clear, Flaubert himself was not the Flaubert of the invidious literary legend contrived by critics, whose praise for Flaubert's "technique" has been relative in intensity to their distaste for his unseemly habit of self-exposure, his *extremism,* in his novels as well as in his letters. The letters show that Flaubert was not the "confident master of his trade," "the technologist of fiction," that some critics have called him. His kind of realism, compounded of observation, research and certain specialties of style and construction, was no foolproof method. It was a looming *idea,* which he sought always to realize in different ways in his writings. Great innovator in fiction as he was, he recreated his innovations from work to work. Each work was a fresh start, preceded by anxious deliberation, accompanied in the actual writing by attacks of self-doubt, depression, panic, boredom, disgust. True, Flaubert's pride in his Idea and his finished work was great, and so was the almost Johnsonian authority he exercised over other writers of his time. Yet the pride and the authority rested on a consciousness, acute and pervasive, of possible failure. The great artist in Flaubert represented a continually renewed triumph over the artist *manqué* in him.

Flaubert's bond of sympathy with *les copains* and their women, when they have women, is therefore firm—firm in the degree that the sympathy is negative. Among them we find, perhaps, a couple of more or less "lovable rogues," if the traditional phrase really applies to Arnoux and Rosanette: one betrayed "saint" (Dussardier), and one woman (Madame Arnoux) who remains a veiled figure of presumptive goodness until, at the last, unveiling herself, she shows *slight* traces of being what was called in old novels about fallen women "damaged goods." But the fates of all, in particular of Frédéric, involved the broader problem of human freedom, a problem that is broached more explicitly, with more philosophic flair, in French literature than in most other literatures. French writers in the tradition of Montaigne and the rest generally raise the question in a negative manner. They harp on the data of human *un*freedom: the perverse impulse of people to enslave themselves to false ideas, ruinous passions, unwarranted pride. In this matter, again, Flaubert perpetuates a tradition by transforming it. His characters abase themselves before the very phenomena that are presumed to liberate them. There is the prevailing idea of progress itself. There are the comforts and luxuries, the printed books and periodicals, the lithographed art works ("the sublime for sixpence") provided by the new industrialism. Most ironically, there are the promises explicit in social revolutions ("No more kings! Do you understand? The whole world free!"). Enslavement to material affluence and vocational opportunity produces its own kind of moral failure. Frédéric, in whom this kind of failure is enlarged, as under a microscope, names it when in the final scene he casually remarks to Deslauriers that perhaps they had drifted from their course.

Drift! Flaubert did indeed have a faith in the power of the moral to offer a surface, and moral drifting is the word for it. But a man like Frédéric is incapable of fully recognizing the operation on himself of this universal force, which motivates our achievements while surviving them, prompts us to make commitments while eventually undermining them. A Frédéric is congenitally unable to reach those ideal states of consciousness which signify the power of the moral for Henry James. Drift is one of those elemental human phenomena, like hunger, of which James is perfectly aware but which he keeps in the background of life, for his own admirable purposes as a novelist. Drift occupies both the foreground and the background of *The Sentimental Education*.

Given this general concern with human freedom, French novelists are fairly consistent about the degree and kind of volition allowed to the characters in their fictional worlds. In general, Stendhal's is a world of the probable,

Zola's of the necessary, Flaubert's of the plausible. The "average sensual man" of common realism is largely of his making. But Flaubert brings to this humdrum domain the dashing energy of primary creation. His mastery of the *invention juste* more than equals his better known mastery of the *mot juste,* or precisely chosen word. Perhaps, as I said, his inventions owe something of their apposite brevity to the anecdote—the *ideal* anecdote which after making its ironic point goes on to waken in the reader amusing recognitions, poignant identifications. Ourselves may be Frédéric. Among our friends may be a Deslauriers, a Pellerin, a Sénécal, a Louise Roque, a Rosanette. Even so, Flaubert's invented actions have a remarkable way of being unpredictably predictable. He seems to be affirming the plausibility principle of realism, its capacity to liberate rather than to confine the imagination, by often stretching things to the verge of *im*plausibility. His intellectuals *manqués* and their women lend themselves readily to this kind of testing. In the men, the ambition to create is strong but the relevant concentration, patience, and intelligence required are nil. And it would seem to be the very extravagance of their exertions in this moral void that makes for much that is grotesque, fantastic, and ironic in the spectacle of their existence as mirrored in the *Education.*

By way of illustration, two highly developed scenes, first the masked ball and second Frédéric's last important encounter wtih Rosanette:

At Rosanette's ball, Frédéric and many of his acquaintances are present. Most of the guests come dressed as gypsies, Turks, angels, sphinxes—an assortment of standard disguises. Quite naturally, the party's mood changes from hour to hour, going from gay to raucous to boring. But as the dawn light comes through the windows, surprising everyone, the mood turns desperate. The entire scene—people, costumes, furniture—resolves itself into a tangle of debris, a riot of hysteria. "The Sphinx was drinking brandy, screaming with the full force of her lungs, and generally behaving like a lunatic. Suddenly her cheeks puffed out and, unable to keep back the blood choking her, she pressed her napkin to her lips, then threw it under the table." For Frédéric "it was as if he had caught a glimpse of worlds of misery and despair, a charcoal heater beside a trestle bed, and the corpses in the morgue dressed in leather aprons with cold water flowing from a tap onto their hair." The ball has become a *danse macabre*

(as in so many death-in-life party scenes in Proust, Mann,
Joyce). Yet the symbolism of Flaubert's scene is qualified
by the everyday realism of it. The remaining guests leave
to go about their business. Pellerin has a model waiting.
A woman has a rehearsal scheduled at the theater. "Hussonet, who was Paris correspondent for a provincial journal,
had to read fifty-three papers before lunch."

Symbolic invention also contends with plausibility in the
second of these exemplary scenes. Rosanette had originally
become Frédéric's mistress because, terrified by the first
uproar of the Revolution, she had thrown herself into his
arms and because he had at last summoned the brute
nerve to take advantage of such a situation. As a pro-
fessional, Rosanette has since had other lovers along
with Frédéric. But she still longs for money, sex, *and*
affection. Her vitality is more and more concentrated in
her hunger for some kind of lasting attachment. But with
whom among the several men in her life? Arnoux? Frédéric? The actor Delmar? She doesn't know, nor would
most of these men be available for a lasting affair, even if
she did know. Well, there *is* Frédéric, of whom she is
fond and whose vagueness of temperament makes him
seem available, especially since Madame Arnoux, his
dream girl, seems to him *un*available. Rosanette has a
child by Frédéric but the child, a boy, dies in early in-
fancy. Rosanette is frantic. "We'll preserve him, won't we?"
she asks Frédéric, and wants to have the skinny little
body embalmed and preserved indefinitely in her rooms.
Instead Frédéric suggests that Pellerin be asked to paint
the dead baby's portrait. Pellerin arrives promptly. No
commission is unacceptable to him so long as he can paint
the subject in his own manner—that is, as he says, in the
manner of Correggio's children. Or those of Velasquez or
Lawrence. Or of Raphael. "As long as it's a good likeness," Rosanette says. "What," Pellerin cries, "do I care
about the likeness? Down with realism! It's the spirit we're
after in painting! He decides to do the portrait in pastels.
The result when shown to Frédéric is a mess. Painted in
wildly clashing colors, his head resting "on a blue taffeta
pillow strewn with the petals of camellias, autumn roses,
and violets," the dead baby was now unrecognizable. But
the little corpse remains unburied for an unspecified time,
while Rosanette keeps gazing at it, seeing it as a young
child, a schoolboy, a youth of twenty. ". . . each of these
images she created seemed to her yet another son lost, the
intensity of her grief multiplying her motherhood." The

idea behind all this seems Balzacian or Dickensian in the extravagance of its pathos, but the passage remains pure Flaubert in its understated brevity. Another tragic farce has been played out, in miniature.

Frédéric Moreau is not one of Flaubert's triumphs of invention as applied to character. He is scarcely a character at all, and the fact that he is by intention the novel's unheroic hero, a prototype of the modern anti-hero, doesn't alone explain his dimness. Like Bloom and many lesser modern examples of the type, the anti-hero can be a character among the other characters in a novel, visibly occupying space as they do, making himself felt as they do by his physical presence, the sum of his distinctive modes of speech, gestures, movements, whatever. Apparently Frédéric was his author's alter ego, the sum of Flaubert's own refusals and malingerings; and one's alter ego is apt to be a shadowy creature by nature. Frédéric is all symptoms and no "surface." Flaubert knows him too well, sees through him with a clairvoyance that dissolves its object. The author's self-punishing hand is monotonously present in his hero's thoughts and actions.

The actions can be marvelous in themselves. For example, Frédéric decides to become a politician during the Revolution and so goes to make a speech at a noisy meeting where speakers are shouted down with slogans ("No more baccalauréat!" "Down with university degrees!" "Let us retain them . . . but let them be conferred by universal suffrage, by the people"). When Frédéric's turn to speak finally comes, the platform is seized by "a patriot from Barcelona," who harangues the audience in his native Spanish, a language nobody understands. Frédéric leaves the hall, disgusted with politics as a vocation.

Frédéric is Flaubert to the extent of having the same birthdate and background that Flaubert had: the provincial home town, the superior social status, the forceful widowed mother. Dim though he is, Frédéric has an essential part to play as the center of the innermost circle of characters. His symptoms, as distinct from his character, become interesting when he is seen in relation to the other members of the circle. Those who make it up are, besides Frédéric, Deslauriers, Arnoux, Madame Arnoux, and Rosanette. In the economy of the novel, these five are reserved for intimate inspection, at the point in their existences where social and emotional charges explosively meet. The five of them form a series of interlocking triangles, which are subject of course to frequent interference from the "out-siders": Madame Dambreuse, Delmar, the lurid, enig-matic career woman, Mademoiselle Vatnaz. What brings the five together, apart from their social ambitions, is an intricate configuration of emotional states: love and lust, love and marriage, love and friendship, love *in* friendship.

Primary, by reason of its unparalleled duration, is the friendship of Frédéric and Deslauriers, the poor, mis-treated, lonely, unloved and unlovely youth who becomes a lawyer by profession but will do anything that promises to relieve his desperate poverty and self-hatred. On Frédéric's part, the friendship is based on habit plus his need, from time to time, of Deslauriers' special kind of devo-tion. Deslauriers, however, really loves Frédéric, with a love that is definitely though discreetly shown to have a physical side to it. In his eyes Frédéric's good looks have something "feminine" about them. This impression ex-plains, or perhaps justifies for him, the warmth of their frequent embraces, which otherwise are just manly Latin hugs. It explains much else: Deslauriers' jealousy of Frédéric's friends; in one case his resentment of his own mis-tress, whom he cruelly denounces when she intrudes on the scene of one of their embraces; the fits of animosity that punctuate his relations with Frédéric; his conviction that Frédéric with his intermittent income owes him not only a living, so to speak, but a share in the hearts and beds of Frédéric's women, whom Deslauriers covets one after the other. In his milder way, Frédéric is subject to a similar tangle of feelings for the Arnoux, husband and wife. Fond of the rascally, philandering, amusing, good-natured Arnoux, a gourmet of life, an attenuated Fal-staff, Frédéric covets Arnoux's women: his wife and Rosa-nette, his mistress. The whole affair thrives on feelings which are, variously, filial, maternal, paternal, and sex-ual. Rosanette, on the other hand, is, as we have seen, given to bestowing her pent-up affections on whoever is available, including her dead infant, although Arnoux is her favorite. "I'm still fond of the old villain," she tells Frédéric at Fontainebleau.

Any mere initiate into the deeper psychology can see that Frédéric's instability, emotional and vocational, arises from his unconscious desire to remain a child, with a child's privilege of changing his mind and his allegiances at will; to the inevitable question, "What will you do when you grow up?" the child, like Frédéric, has at his bidding any number of answers. Frédéric is by turns "the French

Walter Scott," a painter, a politician, a man of the world. The friends and lovers who surround him make up a substitute family, complete with possible fathers, mothers, brothers, and one "kid sister" (Louise). His sexual desires for them are at once stimulated and constrained by the incestuous implications of the desires.

His prolonged, never consummated affair with Madame Arnoux must be understood in the light of these subconscious impulses. People have always tried to view the affair as a genuine sublimation. It is the Great Exception, the Saving Grace, in a novel that is otherwise totally disillusioning. One commentator, Anthony Goldsmith, the translator and editor of the Everyman's Library edition of the *Education*, sees the affair as a "pure romance," exempt from the evils of the World, the Flesh, and Time. To another, Victor Brombert, whose study of the novel is the most accomplished I know of, "Frédéric acquires nobility" from the affair. "For the sake of this 'image' [that of the unattainable Madame Arnoux] he has in the long run given up everything."

Such ideal interpretations rest partly on the established fact that Flaubert transferred to the Frédéric-Madame Arnoux affair many of his own memories of a boyhood infatuation, also never consummated, for a certain Madame Elisa Schlesinger, whose husband was, like Arnoux, feckless and faithless. Doubts have nevertheless been recently cast on the nature and the duration of Flaubert's love for Madame Schlesinger.* It is supposed that he loved her, as he did others—for example his sister, who died young, and a male friend who had also died young—in memory only, and his memory, as we have noted, was a wonderful storehouse of sacred things and moments. He actually saw Elisa rarely in later life, and probably saw her not at all after she and her husband moved to Germany, where she died at a great age, following a confinement of some thirteen years in a mental hospital. There she was visited by a friend of Flaubert's who reported that Elisa, thin and white-haired, was a lovely woman still.

To examine at all closely the passages in the *Education* that concern the Great Affair is to suspect that, in adapting the original relationship to his purposes in this novel, he gave it a searching look. In the *Education* there are, to be sure, charming scenes between Frédéric and Ma-

*See Benjamin F. Bart, *Flaubert*.

dame Arnoux. Troubled by the conflict between her fond-
ness for Frédéric and her attachment to her faithless husband, her children and her home, she is touching. Madame
Arnoux says little, and what she does voice are quite
conventional sentiments. Yet she means them, and her
speech is the more affecting because it is so unlike the
loud, self-serving, sloganeering speeches of *les copains*.
Frédéric's part in the affair is another matter. He alternately admires her from afar and tries to seduce her. His
doing this may be only "human," but does it make him
"noble"? On the contrary, one tends to agree with Madame Arnoux that her son's sudden illness is a kind of
judgment on her and on Frédéric, and that she is right to
avoid him.

Yet in the long run she *is* corrupted or half-corrupted,
though not entirely by him. Arnoux's ventures into "the
popularization of the arts" have gone from pretty bad to
atrocious, financially and artistically. Only a loan from
Frédéric has saved him from disgrace, and following this
episode the Arnoux family has disappeared into Brittany for some sixteen years. The Madame Arnoux who,
after this long separation, suddenly turns up alone one
evening in Frédéric's Paris apartment is much changed by
her sufferings, her isolation, and the sheer impact on her
of Time. The scene that follows between them has been
described as "heartbreaking." It is heartbreaking, chiefly,
in its falseness, in the sad failure of the two to rise to this
putatively great occasion. There are exchanges of remi-
niscence, professions of eternal love; all in the kind of
language that must have been taken for passionate in
popular novels like *le Roman d'un jeune homme pauvre*.
Frédéric is "intoxicated by his own words"; while Madame Arnoux, her former restraint gone, is all breathless
banalities. Telling him how she often broods by the sea,
she says: "I go and sit there on a bench—I call it 'Frédéric's bench.'" (It sounds no better in French.) Her sufferings and her age have made of Madame Arnoux a
sentimentalist. Frédéric, for all his rapture, lies to her
twice. She has brought him, in a velvet purse embroidered
by her own hand, the money owed to him by Arnoux. He
makes no move to refuse it. When she finally removes her
hat, and Frédéric discovers that her hair is white (like
Elisa's), he suspects that "she had come to offer herself
to him." He recoils from the suggestion for reasons
which, as Flaubert lists them, build up to a stunning anti-
climax. "He was seized by a furious, ravening lust, stronger

than any he had known before. But, he felt something inexpressible, a repulsion, and something like the dread of incest. Another fear held him back, that of feeling disgust later. Besides, what a problem it would be! And, impelled simultaneously by prudence and by the desire not to degrade his ideal, he turned on his heel and started to roll a cigarette." What can the poor woman do but exclaim, "How chivalrous you are!" and depart forever, after first cutting off a lock of her white hair to leave with him as a souvenir? Do his wildly mixed motives add up to chivalrousness or "nobility"? And how can Frédéric be said to have "given up everything for her image" when his entire existence has been a series of uncompleted moves on the checkerboard of life? The big scene is a fiasco.

One's skepticism about Frédéric and the Great Affair is confirmed by the final chapter, often called the "epilogue" of the *Education*. Frédéric, now in his forties, and Deslauriers have been reconciled after a long separation on *their* part and are alone together. Reliving their pasts, they hover between mild regrets, mild complacencies, and tentative self-reproaches. ("Perhaps it's because we didn't aim straight for the mark.") They end by recalling an incident from their boyhood. In his second chapter, Flaubert has sketched in the little incident very lightly, leaving it to the mature Frédéric and Deslauriers to clarify the importance which the incident has—for them. As boys in their teens at Nogent they had decided on Sunday to visit the town brothel. On arriving inside, Frédéric bearing a bouquet of flowers, they had been laughed at by the girls, and Frédéric, embarrassed, had fled the place, and because, as usual, Frédéric had the money, Deslauriers had fled too. Recounting the story in detail, the two men agree on its significance: "That was the best time we ever had."

That a long crowded narrative should conclude in this flippant manner has shocked many readers. Other long crowded novels end with real denouements, in which the complications of the plot are unraveled, the hero is reformed, and the ironic tensions are relaxed. For *this* long crowded novel, however, the epilogue is the perfect ending. The original brothel incident makes a miniature anecdote. That incident, as recalled and moralized by the middle-aged participants, is the apotheosis of the anecdotal form. It resolves nothing, leaves the hero unreformed, and perpetuates into the indefinite future the ironic tensions, the equivocations of drift, and the operations of the World, the Flesh, and Time.

—F. W. DUPEE

SIGNET CLASSICS by French Authors

SIGNET CLASSICS by British Authors